BUMPER CITY

ALAN McGILL

BUMPER CITY

IN THE FUTURE,
THERE IS A DARKNESS FAR WORSE THAN THE NIGHT.

Bumper City

This book is available at special discounts when purchased in quantity for educational purposes or for use as premiums, promotions, or fundraisers. For inquiries and details, contact the publisher at alan.mcgill2020@gmail.com

Paperback ISBN: 979-8-9899695-4-8

Ebook ISBN: 979-8-9899695-3-1

Cover Design by Emily's World of Design

Interior Design by Liz Scheiter

Editing by Anthony Avina

NEVER BE AFRAID TO RAISE YOUR VOICE FOR HONESTY AND TRUTH AND COMPASSION AGAINST INJUSTICE AND LYING AND GREED. IF PEOPLE ALL OVER THE WORLD WOULD DO THIS, IT WOULD CHANGE THE EARTH.

—WILLIAM FAULKNER

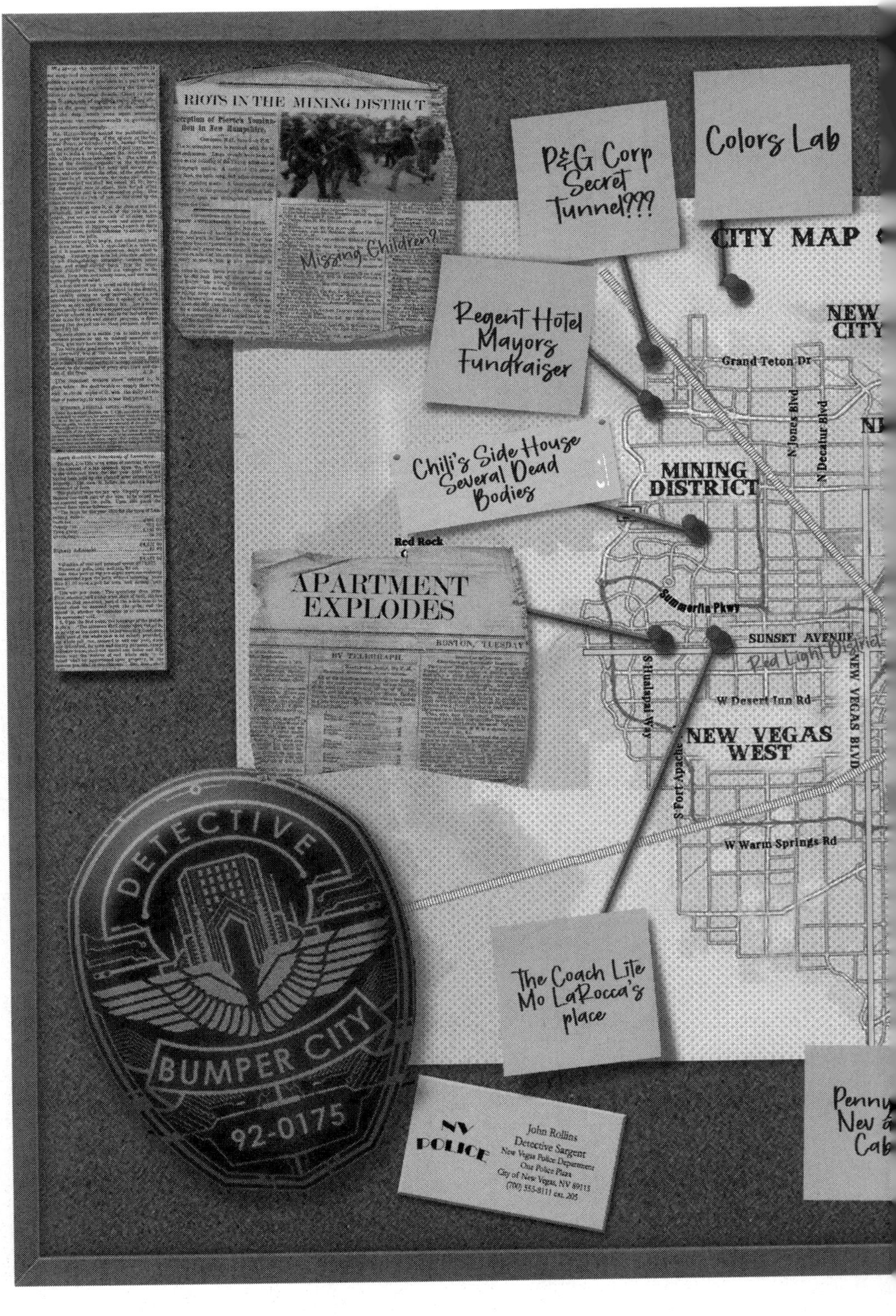

RIOTS IN THE MINING DISTRICT

Missing Children?

P&G Corp
Secret
Tunnel???

Colors Lab

CITY MAP

Regent Hotel
Mayors
Fundraiser

NEW
CITY

Grand Teton Dr

N Jones Blvd

N Decatur Blvd

Chili's Side House
Several Dead
Bodies

MINING
DISTRICT

Red Rock

APARTMENT
EXPLODES

BOSTON, TUESDAY

BY TELEGRAPH

Summerlin Pkwy

SUNSET AVENUE

S Hualapai Way

W Desert Inn Rd

NEW VEGAS
WEST

NEW VEGAS BLVD

S Fort Apache

W Warm Springs Rd

DETECTIVE

BUMPER CITY

92-0175

The Coach Lite
Mo LaRocca's
place

NV
POLICE

John Rollins
Detective Sargent
New Vegas Police Department
One Police Plaza
City of New Vegas, NV 89113
(700) 555-8111 ext. 205

DEAD BODIES FOUND AT THE WILDLIFE REFUGE

MILDRED GORDON

BC Dump
"Arena
Jericho"

Mildred Gordon
Sophia Durant

Pagliacci Killer Clown Suspect 1

Pagliacci Killer
Clown Suspect 2

W VEGAS

W VEGAS
EAST

Bonanza Rd

wart Ave

E Sahara Ave

WILDLIFE REFUGE

DEAD
LAKE

HYDETOWN

W War Springs Rd

W VEGAS
OUTH

Horizon Ridge Pkwy

W Horizon

MES TELLER
URTROOM-A
9:00AM

SOPHIA DURANT

CONTENTS

CHAPTER 1

CITY OF DARKNESS

One way or another I'm going to kill Twilas Burke tonight. The only way to stop a man like Burke is to kill him. And I'm going to end this.

I haven't seen one cop since I jumped in Bessimer and sped across 5th Avenue. Traffic is less during the night hours. That will make it easier to get to him.

There aren't many pedestrians around at this time either. This makes the city seem darker somehow. Without those obstructions, it won't take long to drive through New Vegas West, and he should have no idea I'm coming.

Bessimer bottomed out as we crossed State Street. The orange sparks flew as the undercarriage scraped the pavement. "Sorry, sir. I can't prevent that at your current rate of speed. If you reduce velocity by 2.4 percent, we should maintain...." Bessimer said before I interrupted. "NO!" I snapped.

The onboard communicator started to ring. "Miss Penelope is trying to reach you, sir," Bessimer said.

I tapped the decline button. My eyes drifted to the pistol sliding around the passenger's seat. I'd never killed anyone. I've had to kill five on this case already. Burke will make it half a dozen. All those years on the force, never fired my gun, until now.

How does that happen? When you retire, you're supposed to spend time with your grandkids. Move to Florida. Live on a beach. Buy a boat and go fishing.

I never wanted a family after I lost Mara. This drive gave me time to think about her. My thoughts receded to the first time we met. It was right before graduation. My best friend Rick and I were walking through Hydetown just after the night hour. We had just come from a graduation party, and were making our way to the walking bridge that connected the Lower East Side.

Rick and I passed the park when we heard a whistle. You know the kind, a catcall. We couldn't see who it was because the artificial light always dimmed at day's end. But two shadowy figures were sitting on a park bench. We knew they were girls from their shape. One was a big girl; the other was short and petite.

"I get the small one," Rick whispered.

"Let's let them decide," I said before calling to them. "You whistle at us?"

We heard their giggle before they answered. "Why don't you come over and talk to us?"

Once we got close, Rick and I could see their faces.

The short one spoke first. "I'm Mara, and this is Debbie."

"Hi," Debbie said.

Debbie liked Rick straight away, which was good because I was smitten with Mara. The four of us talked for about twenty minutes before Mara said, "I have to get home." Mara wrote her number on a piece of paper and handed it to me. "Don't call before five. My dad will be home. He doesn't like me talking to boys."

We watched as the girls left. "I'm glad you let them decide," I said.

"Didn't you see her eyes?" Rick asked.

"Yeah. I love em." I responded.

"Dude. She's a mutie! You don't want to get mixed up with one of them."

But that didn't matter to me. "I don't care. She had eyes like a cat. I love it. And that yellowish color, oh yeah."

Rick looked surprised. "Didn't you see how they turned to slits when she walked under the streetlamp? You liked that?"

"Sure did."

"Okay, man. It's all you. At least the big girl is human." He shook his head, laughing. "Only in Bumper City, man."

Bumper City was New Vegas' nickname. A moniker referring to the city that never sleeps, much like the Big Apple for New York or The Windy City for Chicago.

Mara Torres was a first-generation mutant in Bumper City. In the early years of New Vegas, many residents were affected by something. A type of DNA alteration. Those who survived acquired unique abilities.

These adaptations resulted in Mutants being persecuted. Some tried to flee the city, but that was not an option. The outside world didn't accept them, afraid of their new attributes.

After Mara's father died, her mother married a human named Cecil Zedkowski. Cecil was the unofficial mayor of Hydetown. The residents relied on him to get things from the city, and New Vegas officials expected him to keep workers in line.

I called Mara the next day, agreeing to meet at the walking bridge when the streetlamps were brighter. We smoked cigarettes and talked for hours. By the time she needed to go home, I had planned our entire life together.

The summer flew by. We were inseparable. But that all ended when Cecil's yellow car sped through the neighborhood.

We had just stepped off the walking bridge when we spotted him. He screeched to a halt in front of Debbie's house. Debbie's mother answered the frantic pounding at the door. We couldn't hear their conversation, but a second later, he returned to his car and peeled down the street.

Mara's eyes got as big as saucers. Her knees got weak, so I sat her on the railing. She began to rock back and forth, hyperventilating.

"What's wrong?" I asked.

"He's looking for me." Her lip quivered as tears rolled down her cheeks, and her face went pale, "I can't go back there."

"Why? You're not late. I'm sure it's nothing." I tried to reassure her, but it was no use.

"You don't understand. I can't go back there. Please, you've got to help me." Her panicked pleas still echo in my head.

"Let's go talk to Debbie and see what he wanted," I said.

"NO! Her mom will call him." She was desperate. "Okay, I'll go talk to her mom." I offered, but she grabbed both my arms.

"NO! If she tells him I'm with you..." Her bottom lip was still quivering.

"Okay. What do you want to do? Where do you want to go?" I asked.

"I have a sister who lives on the coast. Outside the city. I could go there." Mara said.

"You have another sister? I thought there was only Lisa." I asked.

"Toni. She's much older." Mara said.

I didn't hesitate. She needed me, and I was going to protect her. "We'll go to Rick's until I figure out how to get you to your sister's."

After we crossed the walking bridge, she calmed down. As we walked, Mara told me Cecil abused her older sister, Lisa who moved away. Her other sister, Toni left before her mom married Cecil.

Toni wanted Mara to come live with her, but Mara's mother wouldn't allow it. And there was the passport issue. Somehow, the sisters managed to get passports, despite being mutants. But Mara was a juvenile, and she'd need her mother to apply.

She said Cecil was an alcoholic and a bigot. He didn't care for mutants even though he married one. Cecil was a retired foreman at the Hydetown Foundry, whose primary workforce, was mutants. His hatred for them developed there.

After retirement, Cecil became a staple at the local tavern. He got away with a lot. You know the type: loudmouthed barfly, always buying rounds and telling outlandish stories. The self-absorbed asshole everyone wishes would shut his mouth.

Mara could tell by his driving he'd been drinking. I wanted to call the precinct, but she said Cecil and the commanding officer were friends. The only option was to flee. Rick's was the only place I could think of going.

Rick lived with his five siblings in an old building. He converted an old maintenance closet into a spare bedroom. It had a private entrance on the streetside so we wouldn't disturb his brothers and sisters.

Rick suggested we catch the westbound cargo train in the morning. Trains were the only way in and out of Bumper City. They could cross the wastelands without an issue. We'd be safe under the boxcar's added shielding.

"You'll have to stay hidden. You know what happens to mutants outside the city. Might be best to travel at night and sleep during the day. To hide her eyes." Rick suggested, then looked to Mara. "How's your sister still out there?"

"She's my half-sister. My mother got pregnant by a hoommie before she met my real dad. My sister doesn't have any obvious mutant traits." Mara answered.

Rick looked at me, "If anyone catches her, you know what will happen." It was something I hadn't considered. How was she going to make it beyond Bumper City? But that didn't matter right now. My only focus was to make sure Cecil couldn't get to her.

We weren't asleep long before there was a loud pounding at the door. "Yeah," I called out.

"It's Rick. Open up. I'm with Larry. You gotta open up." Larry was the precinct captain over here. Fortunately, he was friends with my father.

Larry didn't waste any time. As soon as I opened the door, he asked, "Is Mara in there?"

"Yeah. But she can't go back." I said, stepping outside.

"Her stepdad reported her missing." Larry started. "He's got an APB on you and her. If I don't take her back now, they're going to arrest you."

"He abused her sister." I took a moment to let him hear it. "She's scared. I can't let her go back there. She has another sister on the coast. That's where we were going."

"You can't. I'm telling you. She has to go home." Larry paused. "Look, I know the commander in Hydetown."

I objected right away, "He's friends with Cecil."

"He's not going to let anything happen to her. He's a good guy. He'd tell me if there was a problem." Larry looked at me intensely. He allowed me to decide, but he was taking her whether I liked it or not.

I nodded despite the pit in my stomach. Mara came out a few seconds later. Larry gave a short chuckle. "Man, you're lucky you told your dad where you were. This guy was gonna lock you up."

Rick and I watched as she got in the back of his police car. That was the last time I saw her.

It's why I was so damned surprised when her daughter showed up at my office three days ago.

Letting Mara get away that night changed me. It fueled this need to make sure people didn't suffer like her. Right after high school, I took the police exam, scoring high enough to get on the force.

After years of arresting drug dealers, dealing with cowardly prosecutors, and a city full of corruption, I'd had enough and retired. With my private detective license, I could do things my way.

Now, here I was driving across the city to kill Twilas Burke. But before I murder this guy, I should probably tell you why.

It all started with James. But things really heated up when Nev walked into my office.

CHAPTER 2

FALSELY ACCUSED

What in the hell was that damned noise? It took me a few minutes to get my bearings before I realized somebody was pounding at my door.

"ALRIGHT, Alright, I'm comin'." I yelled. I staggered to the door and flipped the latch.

It was Penelope holding a cup of coffee with a sideways grin on her face. "Another bender, I see?" She said before strolling past. "That's a nice odor you got going there, Alton." She waved her hand to diffuse the smell. "Are you still drunk?"

"What are you doing here? It's Saturday, for Christ's sake." I took the coffee and plopped back down on the couch.

"It's Thursday. And I've been calling you all morning." She shook her head as she placed the phone back on the receiver. Then she grabbed a trash can from the kitchen and threw empty beer cans and old vodka bottles in it. *Joke's on her,* I thought. *Those are days old.*

"Thursday? Ah. I stopped at Odell's last night. Got in late, I guess." I said.

Penelope was my secretary. Everyone called her Penny, except Bessimer. She was the only person I trusted. She took care of me like a mother hen or dotting girlfriend, of which she was neither.

She was beautiful and sharp. Although I didn't require her to wear a suit, she did anyway. I think she was more concerned with my image than I was.

"Nice hat," I said, which prompted a curse look from her. "No, I mean it. It's nice. You look nice. Smell good too. Always welcomed around here." I muttered under my breath.

"It would help if you cleaned up after yourself once in a while." She joked.

Everyone assumed we had a thing, but that was never true. She teased relentlessly, but our relationship was strictly platonic. Neither of us wanted to ruin the friendship.

We met several years ago. I was working a detail guarding the mayor. Penelope was a well-respected part of the political machine in Bumper City.

Nobody had to tell Penny there were undercovers in the crowd. She figured it out in two minutes. Like I said, she was sharp. After the threat to the mayor was over, I'd see her at Odell's, a little pub near my apartment.

When I retired, she came to work for me. Typing, filing, interviewing, and various other functions. Her political connections were a big help, and she loved being involved in things. I should have said she was beautiful, sharp, AND nosy.

She grabbed me by the arm, yanking me off the couch. "I talked to Sam. He said you were there all day and most of the night. Smells like it too. *Seriously Alton.* That's why I came over, you weren't answering the phone. C'mon, we gotta get you in the shower."

"What the hell for?" I asked as she pushed me into the bathroom.

"You've gotta get to the courthouse. Now strip." She turned the nozzles to start the water before shutting the door behind her as she left. I peeled off my clothes and stepped into the steam, which felt unusually good.

"Why am I going to the courthouse?" I yelled.

"James has been trying to reach you. He needs you down there." She responded through the door.

"James, who?"

"Teller." She answered.

I peeled the shower curtain back. "My old informant?"

Penny yelled back, "I'm not sure what happened. He called early this morning. When I couldn't reach you, I went to Odell's. Sam said he put you in Bessimer and sent you home."

"I haven't seen him in a long time. This must be serious." I said, getting out of the shower.

"Make sure you shave. You're not an undercover anymore. Only bikers and hobos have full beards these days."

"I love bikes," I said. "And you've never even seen a hobo."

"You haven't ridden in years. And yes, I have. They camp under the bridge off Sunset. You can't go to court looking like that anymore." She responded.

After getting dressed, I went into the living room to find Penny looking at an old picture she picked up off my end table. "You ever gonna tell me who she is?"

It was a picture of Mara and me. Debbie took it near the end of summer. She gave it to me after Mara and I split. It was the only picture I had of her.

"It's from high school. An old classmate." I responded vaguely.

"I'd say more than just a classmate." Penelope had seen that picture many times over the years. She always asked, but I never answered. She handed me a fresh cup of coffee she'd made while I showered.

"Mother's Milk?" I asked.

"Don't you think you've had enough for one night? You can't go into court smelling like the bottom of a whiskey barrel." She smiled adjusting my tie.

I sipped the coffee and nodded. "Vodka."

"What?" She asked.

"I don't like whiskey. I like Vodka…or Gin." I said.

"Well, Mother's Milk has Whiskey?" She quipped.

"True, but that's different," I responded.

"Cream doesn't make it healthy." She laughed. "Besides, nobody says the bottom of a Vodka barrel." She laughed a bit louder.

"Which judge?" I asked.

"Lynn." She responded.

"Do you need a ride back to the office?" I asked.

"No, I'll take the tram after I finish cleaning up here." She said.

I kissed her cheek, "You're a doll," grabbed my hat, and headed out the door.

"Wait." Penny called. "Here." She plopped a few mints from her bag into my mouth. "This might help."

"I did brush my teeth, you know." I quipped.

"I'm sure you did, but you could use a little help after last night. Take the whole pack. Keep taking them until you get to the courthouse." She insisted.

I gave her a sideways look as I closed the door behind me.

Bessemer was waiting outside as usual, "Good Morning Sir."

I was about to put the car into drive when he spoke again. "Might it be better if I drive, sir?"

"You too?" I said.

"Sorry, sir?" He responded.

I didn't argue and let him drive. Probably for the best, as it didn't take him long to get us downtown. It was criminal day at the courthouse, and the lot was packed. The judges liked to schedule all the criminal cases together in one day to make it easier on the system. This meant the attorneys with the defendants they represented and the prosecutors with the cops all converging in this building. Not to mention the various witnesses, victims, and families.

"I'm not sure how long I'm going to be. Circle until you find something." I told Bessemer.

"Yes, sir." He responded.

"Put a projection in the driver's seat. And frost the windows. I don't want everyone to know it's a self-driving car. Make sure to feed the meter if you find a spot on the street."

"What about one of the city lots, sir?" Bessimer asked.

"Too expensive. Just circle until you find something." I ordered.

"Yes, sir." He pulled away, placing the holographic driver behind the wheel.

I was among the few people in the city with an A.I.B.A. or artificial intelligence-based automobile. Most of the wealthy elite had them, a few prominent politicians, and me.

Bessimer was a gift from Domenic Miscavage, the railroad tycoon of Bumper City. He gave Bessimer to me after I saved his daughter from the highly addictive stimulant known as Bumps.

Bumps were single-dose stimulants. The most addictive substance there was until Colors. It is unique to New Vegas as the effects were only felt here. The crime lab believes the cloud somehow activates the effectiveness of the drugs, which means they don't work outside the city.

When I reached the second floor, I saw James leaning against a wall. The hallway was packed, but he stood out. He was huddled with his attorney, talking frantically. His hair was disheveled, he was trembling, and beads of sweat rolled off his brow.

The moment he saw me come through the doors, his eyes widened. "ALTON!" James pushed past his attorney, rushing over. He shook my hand excessively, talking a mile a minute, "Thanks for comin' man. What am I gonna do? You gotta help me, man. I can't go back there. This is all bullshit!"

He was so scared it was hard to get him to calm down. "Take it easy. What are you charged with?"

"It's all bullshit. I didn't do it." James kept repeating.

We walked back to his attorney, who handed me the charging document. James continued to voice his objections as I read. According to the charging papers, he was charged with seven counts of selling Colors and one count of drug delivery resulting in death. The probable cause stated he sold drugs, which killed a young girl.

"It wasn't me, man. I was there, yes, but I didn't sell a damn thing." James pulled me away from his attorney or anyone else who could hear.

He leaned close and whispered, "I swear to you. I didn't sell anything to anybody. And I especially wouldn't sell to a young girl!"

"It says here they have an informant that bought a teener from you in that house. Three people OD'd. The girl died." I responded.

"That happened after I left. I didn't bring any drugs, and I sure as fuck didn't bring any Colors; I wasn't there for that. Look at the address."

James was drawing my attention to the location listed on the face sheet. It was a house near the outskirts of the city—the last block of the Mining District.

Mining was big business in Bumper City. Vast reserves of copper, gold, and other precious metals are extracted deep within the earth. These metals are vital to much of the tech here and around the world.

"You know about the deaths out there? The Copperhead Strangler?" James whispered as his eyes darted around the hall.

Few people knew about this. Authorities kept the notion of a serial killer quiet. Under orders from the mining company, the cops didn't want to start a panic. Tech giants didn't want that information out, so everything was toned down.

They'd found the decapitated bodies of several women with a mangled copper wire near each victim. I still had friends on the force and knew they nicknamed the killer, The Copperhead Strangler. The coroner believed the wire was twisted around the victim's neck. The killer continued to twist until the it severed the head. He found evidence the wire was heated to cut or burn through skin and bone. None of that was made public.

"What the hell were you doing out there?" I asked.

James didn't answer the question directly. "I saw something."

"What? What did you see?" I asked.

"No way, man. First, you get me a deal. Then I'll tell you everything." It was unusual for James to make that demand of me. We hadn't worked together in a long time, but we had history. He may have started as an informant, but he became more of a friend over the years.

"It ain't you, man. But you ain't on the force no more. I don't trust nobody in this city. You get me outta this then I'll tell you everything. My third offense. They convict me of this, they'll put me in Max One. Nobody comes back from that place. Get me outta this, and I'll give you everything." James insisted.

"You have to give me something now. I can't go to the City Attorney with a maybe." I said.

"NO! Fuck the prosecutor, man. Talk to the judge." James snapped out loud, then returned to a whisper, "The fuckin City Attorney is in on it, man!"

"What? C'mon. I know he's a political douchebag, but he isn't going to protect a murderer. If you got something, tell me."

"I'm telling you, Cold; there's a lot more to this than anyone realizes," James said.

"Wait… you know who it is?" I asked.

"I ain't sayin' no more until you talk with the judge. In writing. I gotta get outta this city." James pleaded.

I handed the charging papers back to his attorney. "Alright. Lemme see what I can do."

Although I tried to be quiet, the giant oak door creaked as I entered the courtroom. The judge spotted me right away, slamming the gavel. "Recess, gentlemen. Take time to re-consider the plea offer, Mr. Lewis." She whispered to her bailiff before disappearing into her chambers.

The bailiff walked through the gate separating the audience seating from the court, leaned in, and spoke softly, "The judge would like to see you in chambers, detective. Follow me, please."

He led me through the courtroom to the back office. I said hello to the judge's secretary as I tapped on the chamber door. "Come in". The judge was hanging her black robe as I went in. She rushed over, giving me a warm hug and a loud kiss on the cheek. She leaned back to inspect the lipstick impression on my jaw, then used her thumb to wipe it off. "Looks like I smudged ya. Where have you been?" She said with a big smile. "Come, sit. What have you been up to? How's retirement?" She peppered me with questions as she raced around her desk to sit.

"I'm good judge," I said, taking a seat across from her.

"Enough with the judge stuff." She quipped. "So, I hear you have your own shop now."

"I do. It's good. Couldn't take it anymore over there. They got a comptroller making everything harder than it has to be. This new power-hungry Director of Finance," I said using air quotes. "And there's this new guy they hired. Retired fed. He's got a masters, but as usual, either they didn't care to vette him properly, or he's somebody's nephew."

"There ya have it." the judge grinned. "What's he doing?"

"He has no idea. It's obvious he never really worked cases. Typical fed. Keeps putting imaginary rules in place when it suits him," I responded.

"Of course. You know how the feds are. Besides, there ain't but a couple of people over there worth a shit anyway. You were the only one I could rely on to play it straight." The judge paused to look me over. "Now. Why are you here? I love seeing you, but I'm guessing you need something."

"James," I said.

"Teller?" She began leafing through a file on her desk. "What's your interest in him? He an informant of yours?"

"He was," I responded. "My first. And a damn good one."

She stopped rifling through the file to look over her glasses at me. "Alton, he's accused of dealing Colors. A couple of kids OD'd. A girl died. This is serious." The judge rarely used my first name. "And then there's the headless prostitutes. The City Attorney hasn't charged him with those yet, but they like him for it."

"He didn't kill those women. I've known him for over twenty years." I responded.

"So, you know about it too?" She asked. "Of course you do; you haven't been retired that long. Well, I don't think he's the strangler, either. But the tox screens show Colors in many of the victim's blood. And the case today is about him selling Colors."

"If he even did that. The only thing connecting those two cases is the Colors. Lots of people use that drug." I said.

"True enough." She responded.

"I don't believe he sold the drugs. He's been clean for a lot of years. Something isn't right about this." I explained.

"I can't just toss it. Not with all the overdose deaths associated with Colors. There's too much light on this one even if I wanted to. I believe you, but you gotta give me something more than knowing him." She said.

"He just called me this morning. I didn't even know it was him they were talking about on the news." I answered.

The judge sat back, contemplating everything before she spoke. "Is defense counsel going to hire you to investigate?"

"I doubt it. He's got a public defender. They have their own people." I said.

"They don't have the budget or the skills." She commented.

"Judge, I'd do it for free, but they don't exactly like me over there," I said. "And homicide isn't really my area."

"Your smarter than any of them." The judge leaned forward. "You get his attorney to request an investigator at the hearing, and I'll assign you."

"Lynn, they have their own investigators," I responded.

"I know, but they aren't that good. And nobody knows narcotics in this city like you. His case is about Colors. Besides, you give a shit. They won't. There are legitimate reasons to assign you. You stay in the courtroom; I'll order them to add you." Her face showed concern. "I hope you're right about this."

"I am. And thanks."

"Don't thank me yet. The file says NV Vice has an informant who was wired. Doesn't look good for him." She said. "Rollins is the affiant, and you know what he's like."

"What's Rollins doing on a drug case?"

"Well, like I said. The girl died." She added.

"Can you do one more thing for me?" I asked.

"If I can."

"Push the trial date back a couple of weeks? I need time." I asked.

"I can do that. Now go out the back so no one sees you. Come in through the courtroom doors and sit in the back." She instructed.

"They all know we're friends, judge." I stood as she came around her desk to kiss me on the cheek again.

"I know they do. No need to be obvious about it. I'll expect you at Henry's birthday party. And bring a date, you're always alone. It's not good for you." She joked.

The judge walked to the back door of her office. I nodded my thanks, "Okay. I'll bring someone."

The back door emptied farther down the hall, not far from James and his attorney. "She gonna help me?" James asked nervously.

"She can't make it go away. The charges are too serious. But she's going to assign me as your investigator." I answered.

"We have our own investigators." His attorney spouted.

James snapped, "I don't give a fuck if you have Paul Drake, I want Alton."

"Make sure you ask for an investigator to be assigned," I told them.

The bailiff pushed open the courtroom door. "Court is back in session. Keep it down people, while court is taking place."

James and his attorney took their seats at the defense table while I sat in the gallery. The Assistant City Attorney was already at the prosecution table when the judge walked in. Everyone stood until the judge sat and called the case. "City vs. James Teller. Is the defense ready to proceed?"

"We would ask the court for a continuance, your honor. The charges are serious, and we need more time to prepare." The defense attorney answered.

The prosecution's response was instantaneous. "The city objects your honor. As the court is aware, this is only a preliminary hearing and not a trial. The parties are all here. We can find no reason for a delay. Unless the defense council would like to waive everything to trial?"

The judge put her hand up to stop James' defense attorney from getting too excited. "I'm inclined to grant the defense's request." The judge put on her glasses. "I'm setting a new hearing date eight weeks from today."

The prosecutor nearly came out of his seat. "That's a bit far down the calendar, your honor. Our informant is prepared to testify now."

The judge looked annoyed. "That is the next available date on my calendar. If your informant can testify today, he or she can testify in eight weeks. You should have made them aware that they need to be ready at all hearings in any matter they are involved in. Wouldn't you agree?"

The city prosecutor thought for a moment before stating. "The city would request the defendant's bail be revoked given the length of time until the hearing. New information has come to light, and we believe the defendant may now become a flight risk."

"Your honor. Defense has not been made aware of any new information. If the city has additional information, it should be made known to us! We strenuously object to any change in bail." Defense counsel argued.

"Well, how about it, Mr. Dale? What new information?" The judge asked.

"We can't say at this time your honor. It's still early in the investigation. Given the seriousness of the charges, the defendant should be remanded for custody until the time of trial." The prosecutor said.

"And as defense counsel knows, he will get everything in discovery at the appropriate time."

"Your honor, this is outrageous! If the prosecution intends to file additional charges, my client has a right to know what those are. And your honor, I would point out that the charges my client currently faces are serious, yet he has appeared. There is no reason to believe my client will not show up for any future proceedings." The defense counsel furthered.

"What's outrageous is to think a man facing homicide charges won't just skip away." The prosecutor argued.

The defense attorney jumped in, "Your honor. If indeed there are new charges being sought, this case is getting bigger by the minute." James' attorney gritted his teeth at the next part, "I would ask an investigator be assigned."

The judge looked back at me which caught the eye of the prosecutor. He turned to find me seated in the gallery. Then he looked back at the judge with an odd look on his face.

"Detective Cold?" The judge called out.

I stood up. "Yes, your honor. Ah, retired, your honor."

"There is a rumor you have a private detective license now." The judge said.

"Yes, judge. For almost a year." I answered.

She looked at the prosecutor, then to the defense. "I'm ordering Detective Cold to the defense team." Then she looked at me. "You up for that detective?"

I nodded slowly grinning at the prosecutor. "Yes, your honor."

"And the matter of bail, your honor?" The prosecutor returned to his previous request.

The judge looked directly at James. "I appreciate your appearance, Mr. Teller. Although the prosecution has yet to reveal what could be more serious than the current homicide charge, I am inclined to agree."

"YOUR HONOR..." Defense counsel objected, but the judge put her hand up to silence him.

"The charges filed are serious by themselves. It's hard to believe there is something more serious being investigated involving the defendant. For now, I'm revoking bail and remanding the defendant to the city lockup to await the hearing." She stood and then addressed the prosecutor sternly. "You'd better have something, Mr. Dale. Court is adjourned." She said, hammering the gavel.

Before the judge was out of the courtroom, two deputies began to shackle James. "You have to get me out, Alton. I DIDN'T DO THIS. DON'T LET THEM KILL ME. GET ME OUTTA THIS COLD! DON'T LET THEM BLOCK YOU. YOU OWE ME. DON'T LET THEM, DON'T LET THEM BLOCK YOU!" James got loud as the two deputies drug him from the courtroom.

"You better not let anything happen to him." I sneered at Dale.

"Fuck you Cold. This is a lot more going on than you know." Dale snapped back.

"He didn't strangle anybody, and you damn well know it," I said.

"Then you do know." He smirked. "Bail shouldn't have been a question." He paused to look at the bench, "That was smooth. It didn't fool anybody, but it was smooth. We all know you're the judges' boy."

"You didn't seem to mind when I was on the job, and it benefited you." I snapped.

"You may have a few friends left on the force, but I've got your guy dead to rights. He's going down. I'm gonna send him away for life." He hissed.

"Life? That'll be the day. The King of Plea Bargains. Too chicken shit to take anything to trial." I laughed. "Jury will acquit under twenty minutes with you at the helm. If it ever goes to trial. I'm more concerned with what happens while he's waiting for the hearing. Anything happens to him, you and I will have a come-to Jesus meeting."

"You hear this? This citizen just threatened an officer of the court." Dale's remark to the bailiff may have been tongue in cheek, but he wouldn't hesitate to make it stick if he could.

"All I heard was an invitation to church. What do you want me to do about it?" The bailiff didn't like me either, but he knew I was friends with the judge.

"How about you arrest his ass? Last I checked, threatening an officer of the court was a felony." Dale sneered.

"You do your job, and I'll do mine. Now get your ass outta here, courts adjourned." The bailiff snapped and then walked away.

"You could always have New Vegas PD charge me," I said.

"Like I said. Fuck you Cold." Dale closed his briefcase and brushed past me on his way out.

The defense attorney said nothing until the courtroom doors closed behind Dale. "What the fuck are they talking about? What new information? What additional deaths?"

"Ask James." I responded.

"He won't tell me anything. Which isn't helping his defense. Seems like you're the only one he'll talk to." He snapped.

"I'll need to see the file." I said.

"The file is at the office. I'll have staff make it available."

"Just make me a copy. I'll send my girl over later today to pick it up." He was about to argue, but I cut him off. "Don't make me go to her about this."

He stormed out just like Dale. I stood in the empty courtroom, replaying everything in my head. Dale was a gutless putz, but he seemed confident about his case against James.

James needed to tell me what he knew and saw before things got out of hand. He'd be safe in city lockup for now. The real worry was if they transferred him to one of the wasteland prisons.

CHAPTER 3

SOPHIA DURANT IS MISSING

Bessimer never did find a parking spot. He pulled to the curb as a woman passed by down the sidewalk. She gave a double take when the holographic driver disappeared. I gave her a quick smile as I closed the door.

It started raining, causing people to move a little faster, including her. I threw my hat on the passenger's seat, chuckling when I heard her squeal from the cold droplets.

"Where to sir?" Bessimer asked.

"I'll drive," I responded.

"Are you sure, sir? Your condition is the same as earlier, and it might be better if I continued to drive. What with the rain and all." He said.

"My condition?" I asked.

"The mints you popped might have fooled humans in the courthouse, but I can still smell the alcohol on your breath from last night." Bessemer couldn't smell, unlike you and me, but he was equipped with air quality sensors. From his perspective, the word smell was as good as any to describe it.

"I'm fine," I responded.

"Be that as it may, sir, I still think it would be better for both of us if I took the wheel." He insisted.

I rolled my eyes. He might have been a computer, but he had the instinct to live.

"Okay, fine." I relented.

"Thank you, sir. Now where...just a moment. There's an incoming call for you from Miss Penelope. Shall I put it through?" He asked.

"I got it." I pushed the answer on the center console. The screen showed Penelope sitting behind her desk at the office.

"Oh, good. I wasn't sure you'd be out of court yet. There's a woman here to see you." She said.

"What's going on?" I asked.

Penelope leaned closer to the screen to whisper, "A young lady has a case for you. And I think she can pay." She leaned back, "How'd it go with James?"

"His bail got revoked. They're taking him to city lockup." I answered. "I need to talk to him right away. His case has something to do with the Mining District."

"Mining District?" Penelope whispered again, "I think you should come back here before you interview James." She glanced into my office. "This might be related."

Whoever the person was, it was severe enough for her to insist I return right now.

"Back to the office, sir?" Bessimer asked. Having an A.I. car is like another person sitting right beside you. You forget they're there because you don't see them. They hear everything, and they never forget.

Since Bessimer was driving, I could relax. When we reached the office, he flipped open the glove box. "Those mints, sir. You might want to take another."

When I first got him, I thought stuff like this was cool; now it was just annoying. After I got out, he parked while I went inside. My office was on the second floor of this old bank. The light bulbs in the lobby flicked annoyingly. I had to tap them walking past to stop it.

When Penelope heard the elevator she was ready with a fresh coffee as I came through the office door. “Good. You popped a couple of mints.” She grinned.

“You too?” I said as she giggled. “What’s this all about?” I whispered.

Penelope pulled me to the coffee pot, pouring a second cup. “Her aunt’s missing. She wants to hire you to find her.”

“This is what couldn’t wait? I told you I need to see James at the jail.” I said.

“I didn’t get all the details, but her aunt went missing…from the Mining District. Can’t be a coincidence James getting mixed up in something there and this girl just showing up here.” Penelope motioned to my office. “I did an intake sheet with some notes. They’re in a file on your desk. Her name is Nevaeh Durant. The missing aunt’s name is Sophia.”

Penny handed me the second cup before I walked into my office. A young woman in her late 20s was looking at my shadow box on the wall. It was a retirement gift from one of the few friends I had left on the force. The box displayed three badges held during my career. My first patrol badge, my New Vegas Detective shield, and the Narcotics Detective badge from my time with the City Attorney’s office.

The young woman turned the moment I came in. “I’m sorry. I was just looking at your badges. You were on the force a long time. Badge 714.”

I extended a cup of coffee to her, but she refused. “No, thank you.”

I walked behind my desk to open the file Penny left there. The young woman looked back at the shadowbox before scanning the room. She made her way to one of the chairs in front of my desk.

“Yes, my first. Same badge number as Joe Friday.” responding to her question.

“Who?” She asked.

I didn’t feel like explaining and brushed it off. “Nevaeh, is it? My assistant tells me you’re worried about your aunt. Sophia? She’s missing?”

"I came here because I need your help." Her eyes were getting teary. "She's been gone two weeks now. And you can call me Nev. Most people do."

"Why do you think something's wrong? Maybe she took a trip, left the city."

"No. She wouldn't have left without telling me." Nev said.

"According to what you told my assistant, you don't live together. Could she have had some urgent business?"

"You don't understand. We are very close. We talk all the time. It's been like that since I was little. We've never gone this long without some sort of contact. She's like a mother to me. This is not like her." She pleaded. "I know something is wrong."

"You said she's been missing for two weeks?"

"About two weeks, yes."

"Have you contacted the police?' I asked.

"Yes. After that, I couldn't get a hold of her, I'd been trying for three days, but when she didn't respond, I started calling everyone I knew. Nobody has seen her. That's when I called the police to report it, but they haven't done anything. I've called them every day but keep getting the run-around. Nobody's doing anything to find her. It's like they don't give a shit. They keep telling me they don't see a crime here. Just like you, they asked if she was on vacation." She snarled. "Or maybe she just decided to get out of the city. They say it happens every day."

"They didn't open a missing person case? They usually do that after 72 hours." I said.

"After I returned to the city, I went to the station. But nobody seems concerned. It doesn't look like they are doing anything." She took a deep breath.

"You don't live in Bumper City, excuse me, New Vegas?" I asked, looking at the intake questionnaire Penny had completed. "Sorry. You told my assistant you live in California now."

"I moved away when I went to college. After I graduated, I got a job on the coast. I come to spend time with my aunt every holiday." She responded.

"Where does your aunt work?" I asked.

"My aunt is a courtesan. She works at a Side House in the Mining District."

Nevaeh was embarrassed because her aunt was in the sex industry. Side Houses are what people used to call brothels.

"Your aunt is a human, I take it?" It's not easy for mutants to leave Bumper City, which would indicate Nev is human. I also noticed her eyes hadn't changed under the bright lights of my office. If she was human, I assumed that her aunt was too.

"Why? What difference does that make?" Nev appeared to take my question the wrong way.

"It doesn't make a bit of difference to me other than helping to find your aunt." If I was going to find someone, especially in this city, it might give me an idea of where to look.

"You said she's missed routine calls? Tell me about those calls?" I asked.

"It's been like that for years. I don't have any family, not really. My mother left long ago, and I don't know who my father is. My aunt raised me. She didn't always work in a Side House. But when she lost her job at the Hydetown Factory..."

"Wait. You lived in Hydetown?" I asked abruptly.

"No. She did. Before she came to live with us. She grew up in Hydetown. As a young girl, she got a job at the Foundry like everybody else. My brother and I grew up in the northeast near the Wildlife Refuge. After my mother left us, Aunt Sophia came to take care of me and my brother. A couple of weeks later, The Foundry replaced her and threw her out of company housing.

She moved in with me and my brother, but we lost that place too. We bounced from shelter to shelter around the city. Life was pretty hard. Eventually, she found work in one of the Side Houses.

At first, she just cleaned. Laundry, dishes, dusting, that sort of thing. But my aunt is very beautiful. The miners wanted her. The house gave her a choice: join the stable or move on." Nev put her hands in her face. "She did all that for us. And now I can't find her."

"We all do what we have to...to survive," I said.

She sat back, taking a deep breath, wiping tears from her eyes. "I graduated high school early. My aunt insisted I enroll in city college. I worked two jobs, but it wasn't enough. She helped with the rest. After city college, she sent me to USC for my final two years. We couldn't afford it, but she worked extra. I got a job as a software engineer. I've been out there ever since.

My brother left the city right after high school. We lost contact with him years ago. I'm all she has left." She paused. "I came in on the Blue Line yesterday. I went to her place, but she wasn't there. I waited for hours, but she didn't come home." She finished.

"Did you check with her work?" I asked.

"Yes, after I went to the police station. I took the tram over to her Side House. They told me she hadn't been around all week, but they knew something." She said.

"What makes you say that?" I asked.

"She may have hated her job, but she never missed work. The last couple of years, she hasn't been seeing as many...you know...clients. She's older now, still beautiful, but not in high demand like when she was young. She'd went back to cleaning and stuff. They told me she's been helping as a House Mother from time to time. She was supposed to take some girls to a camp party, but she never showed to pick up the girls." Nev said. "They sent the girls without her."

"When was that?" I asked.

"The Saturday before I lost contact with her." She responded.

"You said she still sees clients? She ever tell you about any of them?" I asked.

"No, not really. She never liked to talk about it. Some things slip out. I knew she was seeing a few offsite, on her own." She said.

"You mean without the House knowing?" I asked.

"Yes. A few men. And there was a couple." Nev said.

"It's more dangerous for girls to meet outside the protection of the House," I commented.

"I know. They said the same thing. But she was careful. She didn't meet anyone new." She finished.

"How do you know that? You said she didn't talk about it?" I asked.

"I said she didn't like to talk about it. When I questioned her, she reassured me these were clients she has known for years, but she didn't give me any details." She answered.

"The House told you she met people on the side? Off-site?" I asked.

"Yeah. They thought she had her own thing going, which was why she hadn't been at work. Some guy named Chicki or maybe Childs, something like that." She said.

"Chili," I said.

Her eyes lit up. "Yes, that's it. Big guy. Thick black hair. Had a strange accent."

"Canadian," I said.

"What?"

"He's from Canada."

"Why do they call him Chili? Cause it's cold in Canada?" She asked.

"No, he likes to eat chili."

"One more thing. She goes by Ginger. Nobody knew her real name at the House." She said.

"Who did you speak to at NVPD?" I asked.

"Sergeant Rollins." She fumbled through her jeans before handing me a business card.

JOHN ROLLINS

DETECTIVE SERGEANT

NEW VEGAS POLICE DEPARTMENT

ONE POLICE PLAZA
CITY OF NEW VEGAS, NV 89115
(700) 555-8111 EXT. 205

The same detective who charged James.

"Do you know or have any idea where she would entertain clients? When she wasn't at the House." I asked.

"No. Like I said, she didn't like to talk about it. When she first started, most of her appointments were during the night hours. As she got older, it became the daytime hours.

I think she used to frequent the Coach-Lite. Maybe she'd meet there."

"How do you know that?" I asked. "That she went there?"

She reached into her pocket handing me a book of matches. Black with silver lettering. It read:

COACH-LITE LOUNGE

"WHERE STARS SHINE"

LIVE ACTS NIGHTLY

1015 WEST SUNSET AVENUE

BUMPER CITY

I knew the place. Everyone did.

Two matches were torn from behind the striker plate. Nothing was written on the inside.

"I found a couple of these in her apartment." She commented.

"What do you know about this place?"

"Nothing. I've never been there." She responded.

"Did she smoke?"

Matches were unusual. Not many people smoked real cigarettes anymore. Places like lounges were about the only places left that allowed it.

"She vaped. Not sure why she kept matches." Nev said.

I paused, thinking about the matches, "I'd like to look around her place. Are you okay with that?"

"Yes. Her address is 1814 2a, W. Sunset Ave. Not far from the Coach-Lite on the edge of the Mining District. I can let you in or give you the key." Nev said.

"Do the cops know you have a key to your aunt's place?" I asked.

"I told Sergeant Rollins. I offered to let him in, but he hasn't called to go over. Like I said, nobody seems to care."

"I'll get a hold of Rollins. It might be best to have him there while I'm looking around. I'd like to have you there too, so you hang on to it. Can you meet me there later today?" I asked.

"Yes. I'm here for another night."

"Nevaeh…Nev…can you think of any reason someone might want to hurt your aunt?" I asked.

"No. She was quiet and somewhat shy. I think that's why men were attracted to her." She said.

"She ever mention issues with any of the house girls? Jealousy? Maybe problems with Chili?"

"No. Nothing." Nev looked down, then right back at me. "I…I think she's already dead."

This caught me off guard. "I didn't mean…"

"It's okay. If my aunt were alive, she'd have called me by now. This just isn't her. I love my aunt." A tear fell. "But I know the odds. Like I said, I'm into computers and very good at math. I want to know what happened to her. She shouldn't be forgotten. I owe her everything. Whatever happened, she, at least, deserves that."

"Okay. Are you staying at your aunt's?" I asked.

"No, I'm at the Elkhorn. On Patterson." She responded. "Room 8."

"I'm familiar. Not exactly the nicest place. Rough area of the city." I remarked.

"I know. But I grew up here. Besides, it's all I can afford." She said.

"I'll get a hold of you later this afternoon. Before the night hour starts." I walked her to the lobby past Penelope's desk.

As she was opening the door to leave, Penelope noticed something. "Nevaeh, I didn't want to say anything earlier, but you look familiar. Have we ever met?"

"No. I don't think so. I'd remember if I met you before." She said softly.

"Why's that?" Penelope asked.

"You're so pretty. Kinda hard to forget." Nev smiled, then turned to me. "Can you help me?

"I don't know...but I'll try," I responded.

"I don't even know your fee." She asked.

"Don't worry about that right now."

She tightened her lips, then opened the door to leave, "Oh, one more thing. Do you have a picture of your aunt?"

She stepped back, handing me a photograph from her pocket. "That's me with my aunt last Christmas. I had a better one, but I gave it to Sergeant Rollins. I have more on my cellphone, but it doesn't work in the city, so I left it at home. My aunt has a photo album in her apartment. I can get you a better one when I see you there later." She said closing the door softly behind her.

The moment Nev was out of the office, Penelope scolded me. "Don't worry about it? We've known each other a long time you and me, but you gotta quit that. I didn't give up being a committeewoman to work for free, you know." Penelope paused. "Don't let a pretty face and a few tears get in the way."

"I don't think she has any money. She's staying at the Elkhorn. Besides, she just lost her aunt, she needs a break."

Penelope scrunched her face at the Elkhorn Motel. "She's not staying at her aunt's?"

"No. Probably a good thing. Might not be safe." I responded.

Penelope went right back to scolding me. "You have a weakness, Alton, almost a sickness."

"She's a client. Nothing more. Besides, I think she might prefer girls." I said.

"What makes you say that?" Penelope asked.

"She didn't say I was pretty." I joked.

"I think she was just being nice. But that's not what I was talking about. You can't resist helping someone who appears...damaged.

You know better than anyone things aren't always what they appear." She said.

"You sayin' I can't be objective?" I asked.

"No, but you're a sucker for a damsel in distress. And if she truly can't afford it, maybe she should let the police handle it." Penelope could see the look on my face, so she let it go. "You think whatever happened to the aunt has anything to do with James' case?" She asked.

"I don't know." I sat on the edge of her desk and handed her the matchbook. "What do you know about this place?"

"Probably as much as you, I imagine. I haven't been there for a long time." Penelope paused. "She gave you this?"

"Um, hm." I responded.

"What'd she tell you?" She asked handing it back to me.

"Not much. Said she found a few at her aunt's, but she didn't know anything about it. She thinks her aunt used to frequent the place." I responded.

"Hard to believe she doesn't know anything about the Coach-Lite. Everyone in the city knows about it. When was the last time you were there?" Penelope asked.

"It's been a while." I looked at the matchbook one last time before putting it in my pocket. "You still seeing that lieutenant in the 5th?"

"On occasion." She said. "Why?"

"There's been some recent deaths in the Mining District. I need you to get me everything the police have on them."

"You mean the strangler?" She responded. "You think that has something to do with this? Or James?"

"Not James. Not directly, anyway. That isn't him. Selling drugs maybe, but a serial killer?" I paused. "How'd you know about it?"

"We have to talk about something. It isn't just booty calls you know." She said with a devious smile. "Although he does have a fine booty." She said to herself but out loud.

"I thought you only saw him on occasion?"

"I do. And one of those occasions was the other night." She laughed. "Girl has needs ya know?" Her devious smile faded. "I'll see what I can get." Then she paused. "Why do you think she didn't tell you about that?"

"Maybe she doesn't know about it. The story hasn't broken yet." I said.

"C'mon, Alton. She grew up here. Her aunt's place is in the Mining District. And the victims are sex workers just like her aunt." She said. "She has to have heard something, even if she doesn't live here anymore."

"Maybe," I responded. I got up and headed for the door, just before walking out I turned, "Oh after you get me the files on the strangler case, stop by the public defender's office and pick up what they have on James."

"Where are you off to?" She asked.

"I'm going to see James. He said he saw something. Maybe I can get to the bottom of this before it gets out of hand." I finished.

"Hey!" She called out. "What makes you think he'll give me the files?" referring to the lieutenant.

Before leaving, I said with a smile, "I'd give'em to you."

CHAPTER 4

HORROR AT THE WILDLIFE REFUGE

Penelope always had Bessimer out front when I left, especially if it was raining and it was raining hard. The weather was the same every day, dark with an amiable temperature between 60 and 80 degrees. Forecasters had it easy here. There wasn't much to predict except the rain.

"Where to sir?" Bessimer asked as I shut the car door.

"City jail."

"You wish me to drive sir?"

"Yeah, why not." Normally I liked to drive, but I needed time to think.

Bessimer took a route through the heavy shopping area on New Vegas Blvd. I saw tourists walk under their big umbrellas to keep dry. Trams and buses dropped off passengers so they could visit all the tourist traps and feed the economy.

The entrance had a big neon sign that read, "Bumper City Never Sleeps!" The New Vegas Strip was a big attraction all over the world.

The neon lights shimmered in the constant darkness, even when it rained. It was a city where you could get anything, anytime.

The strip never dimmed the lights, and neither did the Red-Light District. Even from here, you could see the red glow off in the distance. The strip and red light district intersected, giving the appearance of a big cross. Since neither planes nor drones can fly under the cloud, photos of this illusion were taken from tall buildings.

We almost made it to city lockup when Penelope called. The screen showed her at a payphone inside one of the police precincts.

"Hey. I wasn't able to get that invitation for you." Penny knew all the payphones at police stations were recorded. And they had CCTV cameras watching. "Things are really busy all of a sudden."

"Any ideas?" I asked.

"The mayor's fundraiser was moved to the southwest district." She said slyly.

Penny knew I hated the mayor. If I understood Penny's code, the police had another body in the opposite direction.

"Thanks. You're a doll." I said.

"I'll go get the other item. You can buy a ticket in person at the event. You'd better hurry if you want to get a good seat before the crowd arrives." She said ending the call.

"Bessimer. Re-route to the northeast." I ordered.

"Sir? Shouldn't we go see James Teller at city lockup?" Bessimer was artificial intelligence, he learned fast, but he wasn't omnipotent.

I had to explain it to him, "James is still in the hold, he'll be processed after lunch. They won't let me talk to him until he's booked."

I'd hoped to get one of the jailers I knew to let me see him after central booking. This meant we had time to divert to the area Penny was talking about.

"Any department chatter about New Vegas East? Especially the northeast." I asked.

"Yes, sir. Processing..." A few moments later. "It seems the police are converging on the Wildlife Refuge. Is that where you want me to take you?"

Bessimer heard Penny's message but didn't fully understand, but A.I. is always listening. Her code wasn't hard for me because we knew each other so well. The mayor's event was in the southwest, but her code told me to go to the northeast.

Her mentioning our client's childhood home was a reference to Nevaeh's house in there. Finally, her stating I had to hurry meant it would be locked down.

"They aren't using the open system, sir. And they're being very cryptic like Miss Penelope. But I believe they found a severed head. From what I can gather, it's a female victim." Bessimer added. Like I said, he's always listening and learns fast.

"Anything else?" I asked.

"Not without alerting my presence in their system. Shall I dig further?" He asked.

"No. Just take me there. Any idea which detective is on point?"

"Rollins sir." He responded.

Rollins again. First James, then Nev. Gotta be related.

"Do you want a drive-thru so you can get something to eat, sir? Being it is almost lunch? Your blood sugar." Bessimer asked.

"No thanks. I'm alright. Just get me to the scene before the crime guys get there. Put on the news will ya?"

"Yes, sir." He responded. "Shall I deploy the transponder?"

"Not this time," I answered. I didn't want Bessimer using the same system as first responders to turn all the traffic lights green. That might alert the cops I was coming.

He put the news on the screen which showed the end of a commercial for DirectLink. Twilas Burke's communications company.

Commercial –

...I'm Twilas Burke, keeping you connected.

Then it cut to the news. Anchorman Tom Brenhardt began with a story about the mayor.

"...Mayor Stockton's fundraiser has been canceled tonight amid allegations of some concerns regarding campaign financing. Our Jennifer Caldwell filed this report."

So much for Penny's code, I thought.

Field reporter Jennifer Caldwell came on the screen to give her report. *"Denise Stockton is no stranger to controversy. As the first mayor in New Vegas history to embrace a mutant running mate for First Deputy, the mayor is seen as a progressive making her wildly popular. But these recent allegations seem to have rocked the mayor and her staff."*

The screen then cut to the mayor speaking into the camera. *"I can assure the voters of this great city; our campaign staff did nothing wrong. The City Attorney's Civil Division is overseeing the audit, and I am assured the matter will be resolved quickly. Therefore, I am suspending the fundraising event tonight until we get a clearer picture of what is happening. Thank you. And God Bless Bumper City!"* Mayor Stockton said.

The screen returned to the reporter continuing with her story.

"Earlier today I spoke with the mayor's opponent, Michael Walters and he had this to say"

The screen cut to mayoral candidate Michael Walters.

"This latest information just shows how out of touch the mayor is with our city. She's tone-deaf to the problems we all face. Crime is up, drug use is at epidemic proportions. And the failed policies of being soft on crime employed by the City Attorney, who is backed by this mayor have left many of our citizens feeling unsafe. We can't even walk our kids in parks anymore without fear of needles, injection devices, or open air drug use. Not to ment being accosted. The rich and powerful have given a lot to this mayor for unprecedented special treatment. It's time to give back to the people, to take back our streets."

"That was mayoral candidate Michael Walters. Back to you Tom."

The screen returned to the news desk as the anchor continued.

"All right, that was Jennifer Caldwell reporting. Well, it looks like a typical day in Bumper City. Meterologist Paul Cortenzo is here with the forecast. Paul."

"Thanks Tom. Well, it's a pretty standard day with rain patterns starting to..."

I tapped the off button. The mayors' problems weren't really news, just the latest batch of allegations. It's doubtful anything will come of them. More important than the mayors' problems, there was nothing about the Wildlife Refuge or any murders.

Bessimer routed away from construction zones, increased his speed, and managed to get me there in half the time without having to use the transponder. Although NVPD limited their chatter, Bessimer didn't have any trouble locating them. There were two police cars blocking the western entrance of the park.

Streets were normally busy with pedestrians in daytime hours and the Refuge was a favorite for walkers. Several people approached, but the officers turned them away.

"Park down the street." I ordered noticing the lights were off inside the Refuge. "Why is it so dark? Are the sun lamps off?"

"Yes sir. Bumper City Electric has a crew at the Refuge Power Station. It appears they've re-routed energy to a few streetlamps on the other side of the park." Bessimer answered.

"Where are the biolumes?" I asked. These were the various plants and animals that gave light to the area. Their colorful illuminations made the park a favorite for many. But all of those were dark too.

"They aren't usually visible when the lamps are on sir. Just like all creatures, they need to conserve energy. If the lights stay off much longer, I'm sure they will start to...glow." Bessimer answered.

Bessimer quietly did what I asked parking two blocks away on Linmore Street. I got out and walked to the entrance where the two officers were turning people away. Once I got close to the entrance, I could see a faint glow emanating several hundred yards inside the park.

I recognized the older cop sitting in one of the cruisers. Paul Sanderson. Lazy type. He'd been with the department longer than me. A couple of divorces kept him from retiring. The kind of officer who did as little as possible. The term for a guy like him is *Retired on Duty*.

While he sat on his ass sipping coffee, the younger cop was maintaining security. As I approached, I could hear the officer shoeing away a young couple and their dog. "Sorry folks, but the Refuge is having some power issues right now, it's closed for the day." The couple scoffed but moved on.

I didn't know this rookie, so when I walked up, he gave me the same spiel.

"Sorry sir, the park is closed right now." The young officer said.

Sanderson looked up, "Jesus fuck. Alton Cold. What the hell are you doing here?"

"I heard you went over to the other side. What's your specialty now, Cold…Cases.?" Then he let out a roaring laugh.

"That's funny," I responded. "Never heard that one before."

"All joking aside, like the kid said, park's closed." Sanderson took a breath, adjusted his duty belt, then quipped. "Kid, this here's Alton Cold. Worked narcotics back in the day. Retired. Like most ex-cops, he's working for the man now. But I'll tell ya, he knew how to work a case."

Ending with a compliment was a nice touch. But it was bullshit. Sanderson resented I was able to retire, and he couldn't. I had just as many ex-wives as him, the difference, all of mine were more successful than me. They didn't need my money. Sanderson's wives, on the other hand, were all waiting to take a piece of him when he hung it up.

The rookie gave a respectful nod, but an involuntary glance into the park betrayed him. I could see by the look on his face he wanted to be a part of the investigation, not sitting on his ass out here.

I tried to act surprised, "I like to feed the birds." I motioned to the park, What's going on? Why's it so dark? You guys cut the power or something?"

"Nothin for you to be concerned with. Park is having some issues with the grid. Come back another time Cold." Sanderson said leaning back on his cruiser.

"Seems a bit much to have Bumper City's finest guard the entrance for a power outage? Why isn't the Parks Department here?" I purposely referred to him as Bumper City. Cops in this city didn't like being called Bumper City PD. It was considered disrespectful.

Sanderson stood straight and snapped, "Get the fuck outta here Cold. Refuge is CLOSED. Fucken call me that. You were a drug cop."

You might think a guy who doesn't care about his job anymore wouldn't care. His crack about my having been a drug cop had to do with the stimulant called Bumps. Cops resented the city being infamous for an illegal drug, hence the nickname Bumper City. Police in this town took it to mean they weren't doing their jobs. He was saying I was the one who failed, telling me it was more my failure than his.

I ignored his anger and asked another question. "Who's up there?"

"Cold, I told you. It's an issue with Refuge lighting. Now get lost." He said slurping a bit of coffee.

I had hoped my calling him Bumper City PD would fire him up enough to make a mistake, but it didn't work. I decided not to press my luck. Sanderson and the Rookie watched me walk back to Bessimer.

"Sir. The officer you were speaking with told the younger officer to keep an eye on you until you left. Apparently, he didn't believe your pretext of feeding...the birds." Bessimer said.

"How'd you know what I said?" I asked.

"You forget, I have audio enhancements, sir." He responded.

I did forget. "Go up the block and park on one of the avenues," I ordered.

"If you are still planning on going in, might I suggest farther north on Linmore? I can turn down one of these streets, make the officers believe we are leaving, and then loop back with my lighting off. With the Refuge lights dimmed, exiting a half mile up the road will prevent the officers from seeing you. The stone wall isn't high in that area. You'll have easy access." Bessimer said pulling away.

"Let's make them think I'm leaving. Raise the exhaust so they can hear a good rumble when we go by, then lower the output slowly after you turn the corner." I ordered.

"Yes sir." He replied.

"Any update on the crime scene unit?" I asked.

"Hold on, sir...I just intercepted a communication from one of the detective cars inside the Refuge. He's asking for an ETA. Sounds like they haven't left the station yet." He responded. "I'd say you have twenty to thirty minutes."

We rolled past Sanderson and the Rookie with elevated sound. As Bessimer turned west on the block, he faded the exhaust, so it sounded like we were driving away.

Once he reduced the sound to zero, he turned north a couple of blocks before going east on Linmore again. Now, we were half a mile north of the entrance. Bessimer pulled into a darkened space between two parked cars on the street.

I grabbed my forty-five from the glove box, tucked it in my waist, and snuck across the sidewalk. Bessimer was right as usual. A couple of the large stones had fallen off the wall, leaving a gap that was easy to climb. I jumped the wall landing on a small grade. Once on the interior, I could see the glow of the detectives a quarter mile from the entrance. To get there unnoticed, I'd have to walk through the woods.

The flashlight I always carried would help, but I couldn't leave it on continuously. Instead, I used quick bursts to get a sense of what was in front of me as I traversed the area.

The loud chirping of frogs and crickets masked a lot of sound, but behind their songs, I heard water moving. I flicked the light for a quick look, but it was too late...splash. My shoe was soaked. I had stepped into a stream.

That's just great. The very thing I was trying to avoid.

I did another quick burst of light, noticing the stream narrowing further ahead. It took me a few minutes to find rocks big enough to step on so I could cross. After reaching the other side, I climbed the embankment onto the main road that ran through the Refuge. Streetlamps lined one side, but none were on. The only lights were coming from the detective cars.

My shoe squished with water as I walked. As I got closer, I could hear the detectives speaking. They were retrieving what they needed from the trunk of a cruiser nearby. One detective I didn't recognize was setting lights over the crime scene. Another was placing evidence markers next to items of interest.

Rollins was kneeling next to a woman's body close to the roundabout. The roundabout had a short brick circle going all the way around. There were biolume flowers planted at the base. Normally their iridescent colors would stand out against the darkness of the park. Today, they were muted.

Metal poles from behind the brick wall arched high above forming a point. At the very top hung a large day lamp, but it was not shining. A chain hung from the lamp's end, dangling a few feet above the ground. On the end of the chain was an object slowly turning under the inertia of the weight.

I finally got close enough to see. The headlights of the police cars cast an eerie glow on the object as it rotated in my direction. It didn't look real at first, but I realized it was a woman's head impaled on an oversized hook. The face was covered by a mask and blood slowly dripped out the bottom.

One of the detectives walked over to Rollins and pointing to a blood pool under the torso, "What's this lime green streak in the blood?"

"Colors," I said. Rollins and the detective pulled their pistols whirling around to me. None of them heard me walk up. The other detective, getting more lights from the trunk, ran over slamming me against the car. Rollins and the detective by him rushed to assist.

As the detective was pinning me against the car, he twisted my arm behind my back to prevent me from moving. He then used his other hand to pat me down. He found my .45 and removed it from my waist, "What's this? You got a permit?" He sneered before slamming it on the trunk of his car.

He continued patting me down until he found my credentials. "Private Detective huh? Alton..."

"Cold. Alton Cold." Rollins got close enough to see it was me. "Wilcox, let him go." Wilcox did as Rollins ordered releasing of my arm. He grabbed my pistol off the trunk tucking it in his waist before stepping back.

"How do you know it's Colors?" Detective Clowes asked. He was the detective standing next to Rollins when I identified the streak in the blood.

Rollins spoke ahead of me. "The victim was either taking or given Colors. Shows up in the blood like that."

My eyes drifted to the ground in front of the cruiser. Clowes had placed an evidence marker next to the pool of blood. The woman's body lay on top of the pool and was partially clothed. Her blouse was open revealing a hole cut in her chest where the heart would be. The body showed colored streaks spidering from the wound.

Detective Wilcox handed Rollins my credentials who glanced at them before giving them back. "You can't be here Cold," Rollins said sternly. "I'm gonna Blue Team Sanderson on this one. He needs to retire." Rollins' reference to "Blue Team" was a form of reporting to internal affairs. It was a chicken-shit way of dealing with mistakes by subordinates.

"He didn't let me in." I agreed with Rollins. Sanderson needed to retire, but I hated the whole Blue Team thing.

"The Rookie?...Jones!" Rollins snapped.

"No, the kid didn't either. They turned me away. I climbed the stone wall and came up the path." Gesturing back to the area where Bessimer was parked.

"You snuck around a police line?" Detective Wilcox asked.

Clowes jumped right in. "I should arrest you right now."

"They didn't tell me it was a crime scene, just a power outage," I responded.

Rollins took a breath motioning to Clowes, "Take it easy. He used to be on the job. Recently retired. Boys, this is Alton Cold."

Wilcox was a patrolman before I left. We never worked together but I had seen him around.

"I didn't realize." Wilcox begrudgingly handed back the 45.

Clowes on the other hand was on the job for a few years, but we never knew each other either.

"Just what are you doing here?" Clowes asked. "Why would someone cross a police line if they didn't know it was a crime scene?"

Rollins answered before I could. "He's here to help his friend, James Teller." Then he turned to me. "Isn't that right?"

How did he find out I was helping James? He must have gotten a call from that asshole Prosecutor.

"You mean the guy who sold the Colors to the girl that died? In the Mining District?" Clowes asked.

"Well, it's pretty obvious he didn't do this," I responded.

"Why's that?" Clowes snapped.

Once again, Rollins answered for me. "Cause he was in court this morning for an arraignment." Rollins sighed and then gave the detectives some orders. "Finish setting up. Get the rest of the lights."

Clowes and Wilcox didn't like my being at their crime scene, but Rollins decided there was a better use for me. "Come on. Might as well have a look now that you're here." He said guiding me to the victim's body.

Now I can stay? I thought to myself.

"This doesn't mean you're in, but the press will be here soon, and I don't need them seeing you. Whatever our differences, you were an expert in narcotics." Rollins said. "And you were a detective."

"Still am," I responded.

"For the dark side. Besides, just because Teller didn't do this, doesn't mean he's innocent of the other." Rollins said. "He sold the drugs that killed the girl."

Rollins didn't want my help with the homicide but if he could use my knowledge in narcotics, it might help him. But the real reason he was playing nice, was because he didn't want me talking to the press.

"Anything special about the Color green?" He asked.

"It's a combination. Blues are opiates, yellows are psychedelics." I responded.

"I said green Cold." He quipped.

"When mixed they turn green," I responded sarcastically. "And the neck," I said pointing to the severed head swiveling on the chain.

"What about it?" He asked.

"The torso and head. Same green streaks but there are dark spots on the edges of the skin. Same as around the chest wound."

"I see it," Rollins said. "What's that mean to you?"

"Whatever was used to sever the head wasn't knife or blade."

"Burns," Rollins responded. "The black marks are burn marks. He uses copper wire. Heats it to a point where it melts through skin and bone."

"Is the wire here?" I asked.

"Yeah, it's over there." Rollins pointed to a thick piece of copper leaning against the brick wall of the roundabout. The wire was directly in line with the body and head. One end of the copper was twisted into the shape of a noose and the other end contorted into an arrow pointing to the head.

"Subtle…Any idea what he used to heat the copper?" I asked.

"None," Rollins responded.

"Not sure how that matches the chest wound though," I commented.

"He used the heated wire to take off the head. I don't know what he used to cut the heart out. We haven't found a knife or blade yet… maybe the crime scene unit can find it." Rollins said.

"The heart's missing?" I asked. "Same as the others?"

"What others? There's only one dead woman here." Rollins commented slyly.

I gave him a sideways glance.

"This is a single homicide Cold. Any other deaths in the city are as well." He took a short pause. "But there are similarities." Rollins wasn't going to go against department talking points, but he was willing to work around them.

"Like what?" I asked.

"There are some bodies we didn't recover." He said.

"What do you mean?"

"We only found heads," Rollins said.

"The others have Pagliacci masks?" I asked.

"Pagliacci?" He didn't know the masks, to him, they were just clowns.

"It's an opera. About a clown killing his wife. The mask on her looks like Pagliacci to me." I responded.

Rollins stopped to ponder before saying, "I don't know, but the others did have masks. They were all clowns. What's the difference?"

"Depends on the mask," I responded.

Rollins wasn't telling me a lot, but he gave me enough to confirm this was another victim of the serial killer. The real question: Why the cops only found the heads of the other victims and no bodies? Unless Rollins was lying.

This didn't seem like the time to get into it, so I moved on. "He's using Colors to what? Incapacitate the victims?"

"I figure he uses drugs to make the victims easier to manage. No resistance." He answered.

"They also wouldn't feel the pain of the copper wire burning through the skin," I added. "No screaming."

"Exactly. They'd be dead before realizing what was happening." He said.

"Kinky sex?" I asked.

"No indication of sexual contact." He responded.

"You have any thoughts as to why he's displaying this victim?" I asked.

"None. We don't even have a working theory right now." Rollins stopped playing games with me. He may have been an asshole, but he wanted to catch the killer.

"How many victims are there? Total." I asked.

Rollins hesitated. I could see he wanted to tell me, but he wasn't allowed to discuss the case outside the department. An uncomfortable moment passed before he made his choice.

"If there were any similar homicides to this one, the number would be six. But you didn't hear that from me." He said.

"Were you able to ID the others?" I asked.

"All but two." He responded.

"I take it none of them are Sophia Durant?" I asked.

Rollins's eyes snapped right to me. His face turned red with anger. "What the fuck are you talking about? HOW DO YOU KNOW THAT NAME?!" Rollins was getting angrier and angrier as he waited for an answer. Wilcox and Clowes ran over when he yelled. All three waiting for a response. Rollins walked to the severed head, carefully removing the mask. "THIS IS SOPHIA DURANT!"

CHAPTER 5

INTO THE RED-LIGHT DISTRICT

Rollins and his two detectives stepped to me. Wilcox fanned left, Clowes to the right. The two were itching to pounce.

"You'd better start explaining yourself." Rollins ordered.

"Take it easy." I said putting my hands out. "Durant's niece hired me to find her after she went missing." I said.

"How'd you know to come HERE?" Rollins asked. "We got a tip not more than thirty minutes before you showed up." Then he thought for a minute scratching his chin.

Clowes jumped in. "That explains how you knew the victim's name. Doesn't explain how the fuck you knew this was a crime scene. We told everyone it was a power outage. And we didn't even know who the victim was until we got here." Clowes hissed. "I should haul your ass in for questioning."

Clowes was about to grab me when Rollins stepped in front of him. "Get the tents set up." Clowes hesitated. "Go on, before it rains again. The previous downpours already washed away a lot of trace evidence." As Clowes relented, Rollins turned to Wilcox. "And you, get the rest of those damn lights up so we can see without turning everything on around here. I don't want anybody to know what's happened.

I'll escort him out. Don't touch anything, the crime scene will be here any minute."

Rollins grabbed me by the arm. "Let's go. Time to leave." I yanked my arm from him as he started to the main gate.

"I thought you didn't want me running into any press." I snapped.

"Yeah, well, the boys are pretty riled up. And you shouldn't be here anyway. I'll walk you out, so Sanderson doesn't shoot you. Now, how about it Cold? What the fuck are you doing here? I'm choosing to believe you didn't know that was Sophia Durant until I took off the mask. So, how the fuck did you get here?"

"Teller," I said. Rollins stopped to look me in the eye. I let out some air then continued, "You were right. It was Teller."

"I know what I said. But like you told us, Teller didn't kill her. He was in city lockup while this happened. Hell, the blood isn't even dry. The body's only a couple of hours old. I know you noticed the ligature marks on the wrists and ankles." He looked back at the crime scene as we started to walk again.

"You shut Clowes up quick. Since you and I know Teller couldn't have done this, do you mind telling me what he's got to do with this victim?" He asked.

I stopped to face him before reaching Sanderson and the Rookie. I didn't want them to hear our conversation. "You were right." Telling Rollins he was right would help. He was the kind of guy that needed to be the smartest person in the room. "I went to Teller's hearing today. He told me you were trying to pin the Copperhead Strangler murders on him.

And yeah, I saw the ligature marks. Hard to miss. The killer kept her alive for a while."

"He tell you that name? Or'd you get it from someone in the department?" Rollins asked.

"Copperhead Strangler?" I asked.

"Um hm," Rollins responded.

"James told me that," I responded. "I'll find out more when I debrief him."

Rollins thought for a moment, then said. "Alright look, Teller obviously didn't kill this woman. And, if I'm not breaking your balls, he didn't kill the other victims either. This was done by one killer, maybe two. But he sold the Colors to the girl who OD'd in the mining district last week." Rollins finished. "And all the killers' victims were dosed with Colors. You said back there the Colors represented different types of drugs?"

"Yeah. These types of drugs have different signatures. Blue are opiates. Yellow are psychedelics. Red are stimulants. The more you mix or combine, the different variations of Colors show up and the different effects." I paused but circled back.

"Two killers? What makes you say that?" I asked.

Rollins' eyes went blank for just a second. He had a good poker face, but when he slipped, he knew it. He let me look over the crime scene because of the killers' use of Colors and my expertise in narcotics. He hoped to get something useful from me.

It seemed I got more information than he wanted me to have. The mask and use of Colors was one thing, but the possibility of two serial killers working in tandem was a big one.

I shouldn't have called him on it, that was my mistake. Now he'd be more guarded. To avoid any more blunders, he diverted my attention to the bodies. "The condition of Durant's severed head looks the same as the other victims. I'm guessing he kept the others alive for a while too. Now that we have a full body, we should be able to get more information." Rollins said. "But you still haven't answered how you knew to come here? We didn't broadcast any of this." He said.

"I used to work here, remember? I know when units scramble without a code, it's to hide something." I answered.

"Yeah. So what? How'd you go from a missing person to a homicide?" He asked.

"I didn't. Durant's niece came to see me about finding her aunt. When I finished talking to her, I was on my way to interview James at lockup. I heard the call for cars to the Refuge without a code. I figured it might be worth checking, especially after what James told me at the courthouse. I had no idea it would be Sophia Durant." I explained.

His face didn't show much this time, but I could see the skepticism in his eyes. "You need to get outta here. Missing codes or not, our cover story isn't going to hold up all day. Press is gonna realize the cars were sent without a code just like you did. I want you gone before they get here."

"I thought you wanted my help?" I asked.

"You may find this hard to believe, but New Vegas PD has been doing just fine without the great Alton Cold. Besides, you were a drug cop, this is homicide. Stay in your lane." Rollins said pushing me to the gates. "One coming out. See to it he leaves." Before letting me go, he said. "Cold, keep this to yourself until tomorrow. Let us do our job. We don't need any Lookie Lou's making things harder."

"It's her niece John," I responded.

"Is it really gonna make a difference to wait a day?" He said. "You solved the missing person case. We'll solve the homicide."

The New Vegas Crime Scene Unit arrived forcing Sanderson to move his car so the big van could pass. Rollins jumped on the running boards directing the driver to the scene.

A crowd started to form as the Rookie Jones escorted me the rest of the way. Sanderson put his car back to block them. He got out mouthing *Motherfucker* to me.

When we were far enough away the kid said, "Did you see the bodies detective? What do you make of this?"

"What do you mean?" I asked.

"I was the first one on scene," Jones said. His eyes shifted. "I was the one who called it in."

"I thought it was a tip?" I asked.

"It was. An elderly gentleman walking through the park came across the bodies. He flagged me down. I ran to the call box to let the precinct know. Sanderson got on scene, and we blocked the gate." Jones said.

"You mean body," I spoke. "That's twice you said bodies."

"What? Yeah, bodies. There are two. Didn't you see them both?" Jones asked.

"Wait. You saw two dead bodies in there? Where?" I asked.

"Not me, Sanderson. The first was on the front side of the roundabout but there's another on the other side." The kid looked around squeamishly, "just the body."

"You mean no head?"

Jones nodded. "After we blocked the entrance, Sanderson told me to make sure nobody gets in while he secured the scene. When he came back, he said there were two bodies. One on the inbound side and one on the outbound side. He said there was no head on either body, but there was a head swinging off a chain." Jones then pointed to an area behind the wall next to the police car. "He threw up over there."

I looked past Jones at Sanderson. He kept looking over his shoulder at us while keeping the crowd back.

"What was the name of the man who flagged you down?" I asked.

Jones glanced at Sanderson before pulling a notebook from his shirt pocket. He flipped a few pages and then said, "Charles Knight. 444 E. Terrace."

After the kid opened his notebook, Sanderson told the small group to stay put, then marched toward us.

"Write this down, kid. Hurry up. Alton Cold. 11:45. License number 92-0175" I said.

"What's this?" Jones asked.

"My name, the time you escorted me out, and my PI number. When that chubby bastard gets over here don't tell him I know about the other body. You're writing this down for your report." I finished just as Sanderson reached us.

"What the fuck? Get outta here Cold. You come back I'm placing you under arrest. I don't give a fuck what Rollins says." He snapped. "Let's go rookie. I need help keeping these people out."

I could hear him scolding Jones as they walked away. "If you insist on putting this in your report you make damn sure you write in there, he got in without us seeing. Wait, fuck that. Just keep the notes but leave his name out of it. We don't need the lieutenant finding out somebody snuck past us, especially him. Lieutenant hates him." Sanderson said.

Sanderson was so mad at me; that he didn't even notice the cargo van sitting up the street. I couldn't remember if it was there when Bessimer dropped me off.

I'm not sure why it stood out. There was nothing unusual about it. Typical panel truck. Maybe that's what got my attention. Both sides of this street were filled with cars, not vans.

The affluent neighborhood had a lot of middle to high-end autos similar to Bessimer. His black paint with sleek rounded lines allowed him to blend in with all the other cars here. Even the Miscavage logo was subtle. But the van didn't fit.

Instead of opening the driver's door, I walked past glancing over my shoulder at Sanderson. When he noticed I didn't get in the car, he stepped away from the crowd to come after me. That's when the van's lights turned on and its tires chirped as it darted into traffic. The move was so unexpected an oncoming vehicle nearly slammed into the backend of it.

I ran back to Bessimer as the van rocketed past. It turned at the end of the block well before Sanderson and the Rookie. I could hear the tires squealing as it rounded the corner out of sight.

I pressed the ignition, floored the gas, and cut the wheel onto the street. "What's going on, sir?" Bessimer asked.

"That van parked on the west side of the street facing south, it pulled out just as I went past you," I said loudly thundering the car onto the same street as the van. I could see Sanderson in the rearview mirror with a look of confusion on his face.

"Might it be safer if I drive?" Bessimer asked calmly.

"Bite me," I said pushing the gas pedal to the floor. The tires gave a quick screech propelling us down the street. Within seconds I rounded the corner heading north.

The van was gone. It wasn't ahead nor down any of the side streets we passed. Nothing. We came to a third street when I caught a glimpse of it! The van had turned west onto another street which led to the Boulevard of the Allies. I slammed the brakes. Bessimer came to a stop after a long skid. I was going so fast that I overshot the street by an entire block.

Cars behind darted around barely missing us. The street I missed was Greenwood Drive which connected directly onto the boulevard. I had to go back.

I cut the wheel hard to the right, held the brake with my left foot, and then slammed the accelerator with my right. Bessimer's wheels turned us all the way around as I held the brake to cause the spin. The tire rotation blew smoke everywhere.

Cars all around swerved and stomped their brakes. "WHAT THE FUCK ARE YOU DOING ASSHOLE!" some guy yelled. An old white lady in another car gave me the finger. *Look at her with that old bony finger.* I chuckled to myself as I eased my foot off the brake.

The rubber from the tires finally gripped the road properly sending Bessimer off like a rocket. I turned the wheel hard to the west at a high rate of speed onto Greenwood. A few minutes later we were flying up the ramp onto the Boulevard of the Allies.

Traffic was heavy on the freeway as we merged. The highway was filled with cars, trucks, and of course, vans. Vehicles were moving steadily but gave very little room to maneuver.

Delivery vans were commonly white and there were dozens up here. All three lanes were littered with them. Most vehicles kept a steady pace. Occasionally a sports car or motorcycle would rip through bouncing lane to lane.

"I think, we lost them sir," Bessimer said.

"They're up here Bessimer. They didn't get that far. I saw them on the ramp. If it weren't for all these Sunday drivers on a Tuesday, we'd be on them." I snapped.

We were approaching the strip district off-ramps. Signs for the inner city blinked overhead indicating there were two exits in the far-left lane, both within the next four miles.

Traffic was bumper to bumper as we came upon the first exit, New Vegas Boulevard. This was the most famous street in the city. Formerly Las Vegas Boulevard but changed after the rebuild.

I feathered the brakes drifting into the center lane. The heavy traffic made it hard to get over, but from here I could get a look at the off-ramp.

Several cars started down the exit as we passed, but no vans. It was all cabs and trucks heading into the busiest street in Bumper City. I needed to stay sharp in this heavy traffic. Leaving too much space in front would result in my getting cut off and possibly missing something.

Reagan Street was within two miles. This was the second exit into the heart of the city. As we approached, nothing looked unusual. *Maybe the van got further ahead than I realized.*

"Sir. Several police vehicles are approaching at a high rate of speed." Bessimer's announcement drew my eyes to the review mirror. Three New Vegas police cars approached. I could see the red and blue lights getting closer…fast. The sound of their sirens was getting louder too causing vehicles to move right and left to get out of their way.

Then, out of nowhere, my eyes caught the motion of a van darting off the ramp. There was a small gap to my left in front of a big rig. I cut the wheel sharply narrowly missing as the cop cars streaking by!

The trucker laid on his air horn as I skidded to a stop on the berm. I had slammed the brakes before crashing into the guard rails, but this shot me past the ramp. Cars juked everywhere to avoid me. This was followed by angry drivers yelling obscenities as they went by.

I pulled the shifter into reverse flooring the gas. The tires spun kicking up dust and gravel. The smell of burning rubber filled the air.

Once I cleared the guardrails, I pushed the shifter into drive and sped down the ramp. I looked up the highway in time to see the red and blue flashing lights getting smaller.

My eyes returned to the ramp catching the van barreling ahead. "What the...?" I said. Sparks flew as humps in the road caused the van to bottom out. I kept the accelerator floored as Bessimer raced ahead in pursuit.

Bessimer was a sports car sitting closer to the ground. When we hit the area where the van bottomed out, Bessimer did the same. Our undercarriage scraped and sparked as we chased after the van.

Unlike the van, Bessimer handled like a formula racer. Now, both the van and us were weaving in and out of traffic with reckless abandon. But because of Bessimer's maneuvering capabilities, we were catching up quickly, which was a good thing, because I had to end this before somebody got hurt.

"Bessimer! Flood the front with all your lights!" I ordered. Instantly the front lighting illuminated the street. I don't know if people thought we were the cops or some spaceship, but all the cars abruptly pulled to the side!

I could see the van dead ahead, less than a few hundred yards away. I punched the pedal to the floor! Bessimer's engines roared as we lurched forward. My head slapped the headrest from the sudden acceleration!

WHOOSH! WHOOSH! WHOOSH! Streets flew by as my eyes started to water. A few more seconds and I'd have them.

The van suddenly STOPPED in the middle of the street! I barely had time to react cutting the wheel to the right. We rocketed past narrowly missing it. I could feel Bessimer's wheels starting to lift on one side. I let off the accelerator which caused all four tires to grab the road. I slammed the brakes feeling the wheels vibrate violently as we skidded to a stop!

My heart was racing so fast that I nearly hyperventilated. I turned my head around to look through the back window. The van hadn't moved. It was sitting in the same spot with its lights on.

I couldn't get out of the car yet. There was no reason to think it was disabled. If I got out it could take off again. Moments passed as I waited. Nothing.

I slowly reached down putting the shifter in reverse. As soon as the backup lights came on, the van jutted down a side street out of sight. I cut the wheel pushing the accelerator to spin Bessimer all the way around. When we were facing forward, I pulled the shifter into drive and hit the accelerator!

Bessemer reached the corner in seconds and turned. The street was empty! It was eerily dark as if someone turned off all the lights on this block. It was weird. And there was no sign of the van! In fact, no movement at all.

"Anything Bessimer?" I asked slowing down.

"No, sir. Nothing." He said.

"Why is it so dark? Why are the house lights out? And where are the streetlamps?' I asked as we crept along.

"I don't know, sir. There doesn't appear to be any scheduled maintenance or energy conservations." He responded.

"Turn ours out too," I ordered. He did as I asked making everything black including the ambient light from inside. As I slowly pushed the accelerator guiding us gently ahead, I could see the glow of New Vegas Boulevard a few blocks away.

I continued the slow pace searching for the van. It must have pulled into an alley or parked beside a house without me seeing.

"Where are we?" I asked quietly.

Bessimer reduced the backlighting on the screen. "We are here, sir." Bessimer showed our position as a red dot in the middle of the city map. "89th Street."

"We're almost to the Red-Light District," I said aloud.

"Yes sir. The Red-Light District is two streets north." He responded.

A movement to the right caught my eye. "Bessimer?" I asked.

"There is a vehicle moving at a low rate of speed down the alley to your north sir." He responded.

"The van?" I asked.

"Unknown. I am detecting the faint audible signature of a vehicle but nothing else. Unable to single out due to some interference. The vehicle is traveling in the same direction as us." He responded.

I kept looking between the houses catching faint glimpses of movement. The damned cloud was probably messing with Bessimer's tech preventing him from getting an accurate fix.

As we reached the end of the street, the vehicle in the alley turned its headlights on. It lurched forward picking up speed. I push the accelerator quickly to reach the end and turn.

The moment I rounded the corner I could see. It wasn't the van! It was a mid-size sedan speeding off. I turned into the alley for a better look. At the other end, I saw the back of a vehicle going the opposite way then turning left.

"Sir. I believe that was the van. Same taillights." Before Bessimer finished, I tramped the pedal again. We flew through the alley arriving at the end within moments. Our tires squealed as I cut the wheel skidding us onto the street.

"Bessimer, you got them?" I yelled.

"It's several streets ahead sir and picking up speed. We have about three blocks of intermittent traffic to get through before we are clear." He responded, then said, "I no longer have them, sir. They're gone."

"What do you mean gone?" I asked just as we cleared the last of the heavy traffic. I kept the pedal down rushing past street after street, but it was no use. The van had vanished. A few seconds later we arrived at East 101st Street and stopped. This was the eastern edge of the Red Light District. I could see the glow of red neon above the buildings.

"How'd we lose them Bessimer? What happened?" I asked.

"I don't know, sir. I can't explain it." He responded.

"Best guess then?" I asked.

"I don't guess, sir." He responded.

"Well unless you know where they are, you're going to have to." I insisted.

"It would seem you should turn west. The neon interferes with many of my scanning systems. The lighting used in this area could mask their signal. Probably how they managed to disappear without my being able to track them." He said.

"We'll never find them in there. Too many places to hide." I pulled Bessimer to the curb and parked.

"This is the part where you get to say if I'd have let you drive, we might have caught them'" I said.

"I don't think so sir," Bessimer said.

"Really?" I asked surprisingly.

"Why state the obvious?" His A.I. sense of humor was annoying.

"I did manage to get some footage of the vehicle. I ran the tags, but they appear to be stolen. The vehicle we were pursuing was a cargo van. The registration however belongs to a Z series BMW. I was able to get a partial of the vehicle identification number under the windscreen. It comes back to a refuse truck." He added.

"Who's the BMW registered to?" I asked.

Bessimer showed it onscreen and then said. "Mildred Gordon. 225 W. 98th Street."

"What about the VIN? What's it come back to?" Bessimer instantly put the information on the screen under the BMWs. The VIN belonged to a garbage truck for Miles Portis Recycling Company at 386 W. 107th Street.

"Show a map of the west side. Mark both addresses." I instructed.

Mining District near the Red-Light District. Both Portis and Mrs. Gordon's residences not far either. I sat and thought for a moment, then said out loud. "Right on the edge."

CHAPTER 6

THE ELKHORN MOTEL

Still parked, I reached to the screen dialing the office. It rang a few times before Penny answered. “Good, you’re back,” I said.

“I got James’ file from the public defender’s office. Nothing from my friend yet. Where are you?” Penelope asked.

“Parked on Sunset east of the Red-Light District,” I answered.

“Red Light District? How’d you end up there?” She asked.

“Long story. Keep trying on the other file, I need them both” I instructed. “There was a bunch of New Vegas PD cars redballing it across the freeway, any idea what that was about?”

“A mob has formed in the Mining District. Looting and fires. Riot police are arriving on scene.” Penelope said. “It was on the news.”

“Yeah, kinda didn’t have time to watch anything. How close is the rioting to where the client is?” I asked.

“Only a few blocks. I think they’re contained for now.” She responded. “Do you want me to meet you at the clients?”

“No. Stay out of the Mining District. It’s probably not safe. I’ll get her out of there then meet up with you for the files.” I said.

“Okay. Be careful Alton.” She said, ending the call.

“Bessimer. Take us to the Elkhorn Motel.” I ordered.

"We're not going to Mrs. Gordon's residence sir?" Bessimer asked.

"Not yet. We have to get to Durant's apartment before Rollins. He's probably handing the crime scene at the Refuge over to CSI right now. He'll be going to Durant's place next. We need to pick up Nevaeh. She has the key. Dial the Elkhorn."

It rang a few times before a voice answered. "Elkhorn Motel, can I help you"

"Room 8." The call switched from the receptionist to a ringtone. After a few rings, Nevaeh came onscreen. "Hello."

"Nev, I'm on my way to pick you up," I said.

"I thought you wanted to meet at my aunt's?" She asked. "You'll probably come past it."

"I know, but there's rioting not far from you. Probably not safe so I'll just pick you up." I said.

"I've been watching it on the news. I can take a cab, no need for you to come all the way over here. I'm capable of caring for myself; I did grow up here you know." She responded.

"I know you did, but a few other things have come up. I'll fill you in when I see you. Shouldn't be that long. Stay in your room until I get there." I ended the call instructing Bessimer to merge into traffic. "Okay Bessimer, let's pick it up."

"Yes sir." He responded.

Within seconds we were under the red neon of the Red-Light District. The high amount of foot traffic prevented Bessimer from going fast. In addition to all the civilians, there were pimps, prostitutes, and johns keeping the street busy.

There were also plenty of drug dealers and customers slinking into alleys. They'd emerge from the shadows high as kites, while staggering down the street. The shifty dealers would come out a few seconds later to occupy their corners.

The district was unusually packed for a weekday. Probably something to do with the city election. Hookers and politicians go hand in hand. Not to mention all the porno shops and adult theaters they frequent. Most are either too arrogant to fathom getting caught or so horny they don't care.

The traffic lights had been green until we reached New Vegas Blvd, the very center of the district. It was the busiest here. As I waited for the light to change, a couple of street girls approached the passenger side. I recognized the first girl. The dark tint on the windows prevented her from seeing inside. She leaned forward tapping the glass with a long pink fingernail. Tap, tap, tap. "Hey, sugar."

"Shall I roll down the window sir?" Bessimer asked.

"I got it." The window rolled down which caused her to move back. When she saw me, a big smile came over her face. "Well, hey there detective. With them dark windows I couldn't see you. This be some fancy ride. My, my, you look like you doin alright since you left." She giggled.

"Livin the dream, right Sandy?" I said with a smile. "You behavin yourself?" I asked.

"Aw, you know it sugar. Now that you ain't on the force no mo, you wanna party? Always wanted to have some fun with the po-lice." Sandy quipped with a big grin.

"You know I don't roll like that," I said. "Besides, you expect me to believe ain't none of them been down here for a squeeze."

"I don't kiss and tell. You know dat." She responded with a wink. "How you though? What you doin' down here?" She asked.

"Workin a case," I said.

Her girlfriend didn't like that answer and walked away. But Sandy stayed. "I thought you retired. Figured you moved to Florida or somein."

"I'm on my own now. Private Investigations." I said.

"You always good to me. Fair. You need anything, come see me, you hear?" Sandy started to lean back but I called out. "Sandy, who's moving the most Colors these days?"

My question shouldn't have scared her, but it did. She looked around nervously. When she was sure nobody could hear, she whispered.

"Cold, that's not something to mess with. I don't do no Colors." There was nothing flirty or whimsical in her tone.

"Who does?" I asked pulling a hundred from my wallet.

"Look, man. I'm telling you ain't nottin' to mess wit. Some heavy dude's pushing it. Girls that get mixed up wit them...we don seem em no mo. These ain people to be fuckin wit." Sandy shook her head no to the money. Then she said softly. "This one's on me sugar. I don't know no names. Connected all the way up all I heard. Shits local too. Made right here in the city just like Bumps. They don't call this place Bumper City for nuttin you know?"

"Where in the city?" I asked.

"Maybe out where most don't go. Not what you'd expect. But you ain hear that from me."

I folded the hundred and extended my hand again. Sandy tilted her head, gave a quick smile, and softly took the money tucking it in her bra.

"You be careful out here Sandy. Some bad things have been happening to girls in your line of work." I said.

"Bad things always happen to girls like me." She said in an eerily somber way. "You change your mind about having some fun, I'll take care of you." She let out a soft giggle as she stepped to the sidewalk.

I nodded as Bessimer rolled up the window. The light turned green allowing us to cross the intersection. I could see Sandy in the rear-view mirror. A sedan pulled to the curb. She leaned into the passenger window, and a second later got in.

We kept going slow and steady through the intersections. Hustlers and pimps on every corner. Several blocks later activity thinned as we came to the end of the Red-Light District. The avenue was noticeably darker as the red glow was behind us.

The last business before the neighborhoods began, was the Coach-Lite. A place teetering on the edge of things. Courtesans were allowed to meet customers here but took their business elsewhere. It was a good bet Sophia Durant was meeting special clients inside. I needed to find out who before Rollins.

In less than a minute Bessimer drove passed Sophia Durant's apartment, which was only a few blocks from the Coach-Lite. Everything looked quiet. The apartments on the second floor were all lit except one, probably hers.

A couple of kids sat on a stoop a few doors down. There were people walking around the neighborhood too. Nothing looked out of the ordinary as we drove by.

The Elkhorn was on Patterson Avenue on the western edge of the city. Patterson ran north and south with the northern end having motels clustered together along with small diners.

The Regent was also there. It was an upscale resort seemingly out of place in this area. Built next to the Patterson Gorges Corporate offices which was the biggest mining company in the world.

It took Bessimer a little while to get us to the Elkhorn. I had him scan the lot before parking in front of room 8. I could hear the low rumble of commotion not far away. The yellow-orange aura of fire over rooftops indicated the rioting wasn't far.

Nevaeh came out of her room with a large satchel across her shoulder. "You won't need your luggage," I said.

"It's just my laptop and a few other things. I don't think I should leave it here." Then she noticed Bessimer. "Is this your car?"

"Yeah. Hop in." I told her. After we were both inside, I said, "I didn't buy it. Way beyond my ability."

She looked over the interior and then noticed the subtle M logo, "It's a Miscavage."

"I helped his daughter get into rehab," I responded. She looked at me a little strange. The same look of suspicion most felt about New Vegas PD.

"It wasn't a bribe. I was working undercover on the Blue Line. His daughter was hooked on Bumps. I got her some help. After I retired, he gave Bessimer to me." I finished.

"Bessimer?" She asked.

"Good afternoon miss. I am Bessimer." He said. Nevaeh nearly came out of her seat. Her eyes were wide as she responded. "He-hello."

"Don't worry miss. You are completely safe with me. As long as I am driving that is." Bessimer said backing out of the parking stall. He turned the wheel returning to Patterson Avenue.

"He's…A. I." She said softly.

"Yes. Best there is." I said.

"Thank you, sir." Bessimer responded.

Nevaeh was amused by his response.

"1814 West Sunset Bessimer." I instructed.

"Yes sir." He said merging south on Patterson.

"I didn't think there was any A.I. in Bumper City. Not like this anyway." She said.

"The uber-wealthy have them," I responded.

"I'm fully functional miss. Even if my form is a car." Bessimer quipped.

"Car?" She asked.

"His consciousness is attached to the car," I said.

"So, he can't go beyond the vehicle?" She asked.

"I can infiltrate some computer systems, but my reach is limited. You might say, my essence doesn't exist beyond this vehicle." Bessimer responded.

"As long as the car is functional, he is…" I started but couldn't finish the sentence.

"Alive. It's quite alright sir, I am fully self-aware." Bessimer said.

Nevaeh looked around with big eyes before settling back in her seat. Then she looked at me with surprise. "Operation Blue Streak, that was you?"

"Yes," I answered. "You know about that case?"

"Just what I read in the news. Angelina Miscavage is a big deal, which includes the world beyond Bumper City. I remember my aunt and I talking about the case. I had no idea it was you when I stepped into your office. It was one of the biggest cases in the city. I read there were multiple kilos seized. The news said an undercover officer was nearly kil…" She started before I cut her off.

"It was a long time ago," I said.

"Sorry." She said quietly looking out the window.

"It's okay. I don't like to talk about it." I said glancing at her. "Nevaeh. Look. I have to tell you something."

The moment the words came out tears began to well in her eyes. At my office, she said her aunt was probably dead. She had a feeling deep down like people do when they lose someone. But that never takes the sting out at the moment you hear it.

"It's about your aunt." The words were coming out hollow. I never had to make death notifications in narcotics. Like Rollins said, I wasn't in homicide. "She's dead."

Nevaeh tried to hold back, but the tears flowed. Her lip quivered as she asked, "How did…how did it happen?"

"She was murdered," I responded. Her head lifted off her hand as she looked at me.

"After you left my office, I found out the NVPD were dispatched to a crime scene. I thought it was related to another case I'm working on. I never thought it would be your aunt.

Before you came to see me, I was at the courthouse. Another client has been falsely accused of murder." Her eyes squinted, and I knew what she was thinking. "No, he didn't do it. He was in police custody at the time." She softened, so I continued. "I left the office not long after you and went to the crime scene, thinking it was connected to the other case. It turned out to be your aunt."

"What happened? How was she killed? Please. I need to know." She pleaded softly.

"No. No, you really don't want to know. And I don't want to be the one to tell you either. You don't need that rolling around in your head." I said.

She wiped the tears, steeled her lip, and said, "Alright, I want you to find out who did this." She pulled her short jacket tighter, continuing to gather herself.

"That's why we're rushing to your aunt's apartment. But we need to be careful not to disturb any evidence that might be there. Rollins will arrest me for interfering with a police investigation. Besides, we don't want to get in the way of his getting a conviction either." I said.

"Rollins. He's in charge of the case? He barely cared when I went to him the other day." She said scornfully. "Besides, I just asked you to find the killer."

"I know. And I will. Look, Rollins isn't the best, but he's better than most. He's got resources I don't have. And he does care about solving homicides." I said.

Then she looked a little panicked. "But I was already in there. What if I touched something or damaged some piece of evidence?"

"You had no way of knowing, but now we do. So, when we get there, we have to be extra careful. It'll be fine." Then I paused, watching the street momentarily before returning to her. "Nev, look, I spent my career in narcotics, not homicide. This isn't exactly my area of expertise."

"I don't care. I trust you. From what I can see, it doesn't matter how much of an expert you are if you don't give a shit. You found her in a couple of hours. They've known she was missing for days and did nothing. I need you to help me. Please." Nevaeh said.

I nodded slowly. I'd do my best to help her, but certain types of investigations require expertise, and there is little substitute for experience. She wasn't wrong, though. Having all the knowledge in the world is of little value if you don't care.

Bessimer finally arrived at 1814 W. Sunset and parked. "Which apartment is hers?" I asked, looking through the windshield. She pointed to the second floor at the dark windows I saw earlier. "2A," She said.

The front stoop looked darker than before. “Bessimer. Do you remember if the front stoop was lit when we passed?”

“I’m sorry, sir, I wasn’t recording our entire journey. And I don’t recall your pointing it out.” He remarked.

“Open the trunk,” I ordered.

There was no police presence, which meant Rollins hadn’t gotten here yet. The street was empty, almost like it was during the night hours. I glanced at my watch, and it was still early afternoon. Cars were parked on the street, but no movement. Now, my senses were tuning in. We hadn’t seen a moving vehicle for blocks.

Nevaeh opened her door when I did. A small breeze came from the south. It would die out for a moment, then begin pushing papers all around again. Some rolled across the street between buildings, while others landed on the steps in front.

Nevaeh joined me at the trunk, where I retrieved two pairs of rubber gloves. I handed one to her. “Put these on. Leave your satchel.” I said. “Take this.” Giving her a flashlight. “Stay behind me and don’t touch anything, including the front door to the building. The gloves will help, but I don’t want to smudge anything either.” I instructed.

Before starting to the building, I grabbed my infra-green glasses to see better. After a long pause, she asked, “What’s wrong?”

“I don’t know. Probably nothing.” I answered. The voice inside my head told me to leave her in the car. She could give me the key and wait. Bessimer’s bulletproof shielding would protect her. More importantly, he could drive away.

I should have listened.

CHAPTER 7

PAGLIACCI KILLER CLOWNS

Tenant mailboxes were clustered to the left inside the door. A couple of apartments were between the boxes and the elevator. I didn't want to risk using the elevator, so we took the stairs beside me. Everything was dark, but my infra-green glasses would allow me to see.

As we climbed the stairs, we leaned over the rail to look above. Most of the floors had light coming through the stairwell doors. All except the second. I could see through the door window with my glasses when we reached it. Somebody had broken all the lights in the hall. The shattered bulbs littered the floor.

I turned the latch slowly and opened the door without making any noise. Inside the hallway, I could see a small amount of light coming from the doorjambs of the other apartments, but everything was quiet. There weren't any sounds of people in those apartments, not even a television. It was as if nobody was on this floor.

Sophia Durant's apartment door had been smashed. It laid on its back inside the apartment. We took a few steps closer so I could get a better look. I peeked around the corner and could see light coming through a living room window.

"Why'd you take off your glasses?" Nevaeh whispered.

"Light from the street is coming through the living room window. That makes it hard to see with these things on." I responded. "Looks like I won't need that key. You should go back to Bessimer." I whispered.

"No fuckin way. I'm coming with you." She said softly but quite emphatic. Then I heard the snap of rubber gloves as she pulled them over her fingers. I took a long, deep breath. I could tell by her attitude she wasn't going to listen. "Alright, fine. But you stay right here until I check out the apartment." I looked back at her, "That's not a request. I want to make sure there isn't anybody inside."

She grabbed my arm before I could move. "Maybe it was the cops?" She said softly.

"The police wouldn't leave the door like that," I answered quietly. "If anything, I mean anything, happens, you run back to Bessimer and call 911. Got it?" I whispered.

I pulled out my pistol and hugged the wall as I entered. The door jamb was splintered at the hinges, and there was an impact mark above the lock where it was kicked in.

The living room had a big picture window with a streetlamp right outside. Enough light came through to illuminate the room. The place had been thoroughly searched. Furniture was flipped over, cushions were cut open, a television was pulled from the wall and smashed, and debris was everywhere. Pictures that once hung on the walls were either crooked or lying on the floor. The ones on the floor were pulled apart as if someone were looking for something hidden behind them.

I craned my neck to peek further. There was a long dark hallway between the kitchen and living room. Sophia's bedroom would be down there.

I took another cautious step, then another, stopping to listen each time. There were no sounds other than my footsteps. I put the green glasses on again to see down the dark hall. It was empty, with more debris from broken pictures hanging and busted.

Nobody seemed to be there, so I removed the glasses to further inspect the living room. I noticed a bookshelf lying on its side. The contents were dumped on the floor and scattered. After stepping over a few things, I squatted for a closer look.

It was no surprise the book I sought wasn't here. From how everything was thrown around, it didn't seem like anyone else found it. The sound of glass crunching outside the apartment startled me. Nevaeh was standing at the entrance with disbelief at the destruction inside.

That's when I noticed it. My eyes caught a glimpse of something in the dark behind her. The hair on the back of my neck stood on end. My breath became labored as my heart pumped blood faster through me.

In the darkened hall behind Nevaeh, I could see eyeshine over her left shoulder. Two glowing orbs getting bigger and bigger until a face emerged. It was the face of a clown!

Smeared black lips began to part slowly as a sinister smile formed over a muted white face. Black circles were painted over the eye sockets, and his hair was slicked with a hint of blue.

I raised my .45 to aim at the Clown as I got to my feet. Nevaeh's eyes got big when she saw the barrel of my gun pointed at her. She had not heard the Clown sneaking up behind and didn't know I was aiming at him.

She put her hand out with palms to me as if pleading not to shoot. I could see her lips moving but couldn't hear her voice over my heartbeat.

Before she had a chance to move, the Clown grabbed her! She let out a yelp as a gloved slid over her mouth and another around her body. The Clown's jagged teeth smiled at me the whole time. Then, he yanked her into the darkness.

She was gone before I could move. My instincts kicked in. The fear subsided as I began to think again. Everything rushed back; my breathing slowed to normal, my heartbeat relaxed, and sound returned. I could hear muffled screams as he dragged her away.

I started to pursue them when everything went blank. From the hallway inside Durant's apartment, another black and white clown blindsided me. The impact was sudden and violent. The air left my lungs the moment I was slammed against the wall. It was like a freight train hit me and I blacked out.

As my senses returned, the sweet aroma of cologne over strong B.O. hit my nose. I could feel hot breath, which smelled like whiskey, blast my face. This clown was on top of me and punched in a flurry of madness. He gave off a maniacal laugh with each swing. One, two, three hits before BAM! Miraculously I had not dropped my pistol during his attack. I pushed the barrel into his chest and squeezed the trigger.

The hollow point plowed through his sternum and exploded out his back, sending a splatter of blood and bone all over the room. The clown was dead before his body fell on me. It took a few seconds to gather my wits before I could roll his dead carcass off.

Once I got to my feet, I could see his paint was different than the other clown that grabbed Nevaeh. This one had black diamonds covering his eyes with a red nose and lips.

His clothing was more clown-like, too. He wore a puffy, loose-fitting jumpsuit with muted shapes. I could see thin streaks of red and blue at the base of his neck. They faded to black, an indication of Colors abuse.

I gagged at the putrid smell of his blood as I stumbled to the door. A bullet whizzed past, striking the frame. The sound of a hideous laugh behind Nevaeh's muffled cries followed. I popped my head into the hall for a quick look. The first clown was dragging Nevaeh into the stairwell.

BANG! He fired again but missed. His laughter echoed until the stair door slammed shut. I had to stop him, or her fate would be the same as her aunt's.

I ran to the door and pulled. He'd already dragged her down the stairs and fired two shots from below when I opened the door. The bullets ricochet sparked off the concrete blocks.

When it was clear, I hurried down and slowed at the bottom. I could hear the building's front door open then swing shut. I yanked open the door and jumped to the wall for cover as I slithered to the front door.

I didn't want to rush outside yet. I needed to figure out where he was to anticipate where he would fire from. Instead, I kicked open the door, hoping he'd shoot, but he didn't take the bait.

Before the door closed, I used my foot to keep it open to look through the crease. The clown had dragged Nevaeh to the sidewalk. He stood holding her tightly from behind with one arm clutched around her chest as the other held a pistol to her temple. The barrel gave a glint when he pressed harder.

He stood there waiting with a devilish grin on his face. His eyes sparkled, but it was more than the streetlights. This was a tempting, teasing, evil look.

Tears streamed from her eyes as her lips trembled. I could see his mouth going, but it was too far to hear. Her eyes got bigger, then closed tight as her mouth gaped. I didn't have to hear what he whispered to know what he'd said. Nevaeh sobbed. Her body let go in his grip as the torment overwhelmed her.

He finished with a taunting kiss on her cheek. Then, he called to me. "C'mon out, COLD!" His gravelly voice was taunting and wicked. "We're waiting for you." He said with a devious laugh.

Seeing that clown kiss her cheek infuriated me. I straightened, pushed open the door, and stepped out. My gaze met his as I kept the .45 to my side. I walked down the steps and onto the sidewalk with purpose, and he knew it. His look intensified as I came within a few paces of them.

"Uh-uh, that's close enough, deeeeeteeeectiiiive." He sneered, exposing more of those large teeth. He had the look of someone enjoying what they were doing.

My eyes took in every detail. The streaks of hot pink and green that faded to black on his neck told me he abused Colors. The clown I shot in the apartment had different colors, but it was apparent they both used.

My head leaned up toward the second-floor window as I spoke, "I killed your partner. Any relation? I hope he wasn't your brother or something. He was wearing a ridiculous outfit…like you." I returned the taunt as I slowly raised my .45 to put his face in the sites.

"Don't get stupid, Cold." He pushed the barrel of his gun even harder to her temple. The look in her eyes intensified from the pain as her body became rigid again.

The corners of his mouth faded to a normal position. I couldn't shoot him with her so close. I needed to make him mad enough to lash out at me, then hope she was smart enough to wiggle out of the way so I could kill him.

"How do you know me?" I asked. "Let me guess, I arrested you."

His head moved to kiss her ear. Nevaeh's eyes closed as she let out a small whimper. His eyes remained fixed on me, "Nope." His smile got big again.

"I arrest some relative? Friend? They sittin' in Wasteland One? Or maybe Wasteland Two?" I asked, but with more sarcasm.

"Nah. Nothing like that Cold." He sneered with eyes getting more intense as his arm tightened around her waist.

"So, how do you know me?" I pressed. "I can't place you, but it's hard to say with that ridiculous make-up. What are you supposed to be anyway? A knockoff of the Joker or something?"

He ignored my taunts with a smirk. "We all know you."

"We? Who's we?" I asked.

He burst into a laugh that echoed between the buildings. A couple walked up the street and were startled at the sight. When his laugh rang out, they ran.

"Enough of this shit," I said to myself, barely audible. I yelled out to him again. "AT LEAST TELL ME WHY YOU ARE DRESSED AS A PERVERTED CLOWN BEFORE I KILL YOU."

The fade of his smile was subtle. I could tell because his big teeth looked huge before. Now, they were gone behind that black makeup. Then he moved the barrel of his gun from her temple and pointed it at me.

Nevaeh dropped out of the way as he pulled the trigger. I was just about to squeeze mine when I heard the shot. It happened a nano-second before he fired. It was enough to alter his aim. A bullet fired from Sophia Durant's apartment struck the Clown in the arm.

This caused him to miss as his bullet struck a telephone pole to my left. I watched blood squirt out of his arm as the impact drove him into a parked car. The vehicle rocked back and forth as the alarm sounded.

Instinctively, I turned my .45 to the window. The Clown and Nevaeh witnessed the same thing I did. A woman dressed in black was standing at the window of Durant's apartment. Smoke from the barrel of her pistol billowed into the air from the round she just fired. Her eyes were covered with a unique pair of glasses, probably to enhance night vision. She was hard to see with her long black hair and black bodysuit.

My focus shifted to the sound of footsteps behind the blaring car alarm. When I turned to look, the Clown was gone. I turned back to the apartment, and the woman was gone, too.

Nevaeh was getting up from the ground as I ran over. "You okay?"

"I'm okay." She responded.

I rushed her back to Bessimer, who was still parked on the street. "Drive her to the office. Have Penny meet you there. Tell her to take Nev someplace safe. Someplace nobody else knows. I'll find them later."

Nevaeh grabbed my arm and pleaded. "NO! Come on, let's get the hell outta here!"

"It's alright. I have to go back inside until the police get here."

"What about the woman who shot at us?" She asked.

"I think she hit what she was aiming at. She's gone; I doubt she'll stick around for the cops. Bessimer will keep you safe." Then I addressed him again, "Bessimer, call 911. Report a shooting and a dead body at this location."

"Shall I ask for Detective Rollin sir?" Bessimer asked.

"Make sure you tell dispatch it's Sophia Durant's place. He'll get the message." I said.

"Yes, sir," Bessimer responded as I shut the door. He pulled away, and I watched until his taillights disappeared under the glow of the Red-Light District. After I was sure they were gone, I went back inside.

I had to use the green glasses again to navigate the stairs. With my pistol ready, I slowly opened the stairwell door. I told Nevaeh the woman was gone. But I had no idea anyone was there in the first place until I heard the shot. She could have been aiming for Nevaeh and missed. Maybe she lost the opportunity when Nevaeh fell away from the Clown's grasp.

The hall outside Durant's apartment looked the same. It was dark, with no movement or sound. I approached the door, lifting my glasses. I couldn't believe my eyes. The clown I shot was gone.

I took a cautious step and put the glasses on again. This time, I needed to clear the rest of the apartment. I quietly moved down the dark hall with my pistol at the compressed ready. The first door to the right was a spare bedroom, and it was empty. The door next to that was the bathroom, and it was empty, too.

I switched to the opposite wall and hugged it as I continued. When I came to the next door, I could see it was the laundry room, also empty. The last room was Durant's master bedroom.

Like every other room in this place, it was littered with debris from whoever searched it. The bed was upended with the mattress and box springs against the wall. The dresser drawers were pulled out and dumped. Clothes from the closet were tossed in the middle of the room, exposing a wall safe at the back.

The safe door was ajar. I used the barrel of my gun to open it the rest of the way. My green glasses allowed me to see it had been cleaned out. Whoever tossed this place found what they were looking for.

I returned to the living room for a more detailed look around. I wouldn't have long. I need to find whatever clues were left before the cops arrive.

The blood and bone fragments from the stinky clown I killed were undisturbed. I would have expected drag marks or smeared blood if the body were dragged off, but there were none. It was like he was picked up and carried off.

The woman from Durant's apartment was petite, and I doubted she could have done that. Her head didn't go above the halfway point in the window, making her a few inches shorter than me. It seemed unlikely she would have the raw strength to carry the clown away. Hell, I was barely able to roll him off me.

What was going on here?

Sirens getting closer interrupted my thoughts. Within seconds, tires screeched out front as New Vegas Police cruisers blocked the street. Rollins and Clowes got out of an unmarked car with their guns drawn while another car secured the area.

I placed my .45 on the kitchen counter and waited. A few moments later, I heard them climbing the stairwell and saw their flashlights scanning the hall.

"ROLLINS?" I yelled. "IT'S COLD. I'M IN THE LIVING ROOM. IT'S JUST ME, THERE'S NOBODY ELSE HERE. Please don't shoot me."

Rollins' head peered cautiously around the doorway. Once he saw me, he returned his pistol to its holster, and came in. Detective Clowes was right behind but twitchy.

"Cold, what the fuck happened? Why are you here? I know you know whose apartment this is." Rollins asked.

"It's Sophia Durant's place," I answered.

Rollins moved his flashlight over the kitchen until it shone on my .45. "That yours?"

"Yeah."

"What happened to the damned lights?" He asked, scanning the ceiling.

"I think the killer knocked them out," I said. "Hall, too."

Then he checked the floor with his flashlight, "Where's this dead body? Dispatch said a dead body was reported along with gunshots."

"It was right here," I said, pointing to the area where I killed the stinky clown.

Clowes shinned his flashlight to where I pointed. "There's nobody there." Then he noticed the pool of blood. "What the hell is all that?" He asked.

"C'mon Cold. Let's go outside and get this sorted.." Rollins ordered. "I don't want you mucking up my crime scene. Kid, pick up the .45."

Clowes pulled on a pair of rubber gloves and then grabbed my pistol from the counter. I would've objected, but he was going to take it the moment I admitted to killing the clown even if the body wasn't here.

Rollins escorted me out of the building as a CSI unit pulled to the curb. Several New Vegas Crime Scene Techs walked past on their way to the apartment. They were barely gone from our sight when we heard it. BOOM! A massive explosion blew out the second floor.

The blast was so powerful it knocked Rollins and I to the ground. As I fell, I could see Clowes blown through the apartment window. His body smashed onto the roof of a police car parked on the street.

The explosion was so strong that windows across the street shattered. I got to my feet and pulled Rollins to his. "You alright?" I asked.

We both stood there confused. Ash and bits of…everything wafted through the air. Flames from the building lit up the sky. We barely had a chance to process what happened when sirens were heard coming our way.

Two of the city's firetrucks rounded the block, skidding to a halt right before us. Firemen jumped from their vehicles to battle the blaze. Three ambulances roared to the scene on the heels of the fire department. Paramedics wasted no time scrambling to help the injured.

The fire chief was the first to come over to us. "Is there anybody in the building?" Rollins and I were dazed, so he asked again, "Buddy, is anybody in the building?"

It took me a second to gather my wits. The scene had gone from quiet to chaotic on a dime. The explosion, car alarms, breaking glass, and sirens all flooded my senses. Finally, I managed to spit out, "There were three crime scene techs…and him." pointing to Clowes' dead body atop the police car. "There's several apartments, but I don't know if they were occupied."

Other than being shell-shocked and tossed to the pavement, I wasn't hurt. Rollins took the brunt of it because he was between me and the blast.

I leaned Rollins against a parked car as a paramedic ran over to treat him. He was bleeding from several cuts and abrasions. As I caught my breath, his eyes focused on the fire burning on the second floor. "That was our best lead. Now the evidence is wiped out."

The fire chief nodded to the paramedic and then joined his men to battle the blaze. Watching them fight the fire, I could see Clowes' body beyond them.

"Hold on," I said.

"Cold. What the fuck are you doing?" Rollins snapped as I ran to the CSI truck.

The back door was ajar, so I grabbed what I needed. I rushed past Rollins and the fire chief to Clowes' body. His mangled corpse was tough to look at, with broken bones sticking through his clothes. The pink tissue, dripping blood, and shards of glass stabbing him everywhere was something out of a horror movie.

But my pistol was still tucked in his waist. The blast had thrust him through the window, falling two flights, but the pistol was right where he put it.

The squishy sound of his broken body made me queasy as I removed it. I placed the gun in the collection box I took from the truck. I fastened the lid and then walked it back to Rollins.

"Here. I shot the clown with this after he attacked me. I fired at close range. Might be some of his blood on the barrel." I said before removing my jacket and shirt. I placed them in a plastic bag, too. "The blood on these is his. You can have my pants later. Gotta have some DNA on something." I said.

Rollins stood up to take the items. "I'll take them now…at the station." Referring to my pants.

"WHAT?" I asked.

"You're coming downtown with me, Cold." He snapped as Detective Wilcox arrived with more police. He was visibly shaken when he saw Clowes' body. Rollins walked over and placed a hand on his shoulder. "C'mon, kid. You shouldn't be here."

Wilcox composed himself, straightened to a taller stance, and then said, "No. I got this sarge. What do you need me to do?" The job taking priority over his dead partner.

Rollins surveyed all the commotion. The building was fully engulfed with flames. Firemen, paramedics, and the press scurried about. It was chaos. He looked back to Wilcox, "You sure?"

The kid nodded, so Rollins gave him some orders. "I'm taking Cold back to the station. Secure the scene. Nobody in or out until another CSI unit gets here." Rollins noticed Wilcox look at the CSI van. "They were inside with Detective Clowes."

Wilcox nodded. He then gathered some officers to carry out Rollins' orders. Rollins took off his jacket, placing it around my shoulders. "Put this on." He grabbed me by the arm and pulled me to an unmarked car.

"C'mon, John. You know I didn't do this." I said. "I was inside with the both of you."

He placed his hand on top of my head, shoving me in the back of the car. "That may be Cold. But several of our guys are dead, including one of my best detectives. Whatever you know, I will know, and you're not leaving the station until I do."

CHAPTER 8

INTERROGATION

Rollins didn't take me to the nearest precinct; that would have been a two-minute ride. Instead, he crossed through ritzy New Vegas West to One Police Plaza in New Vegas South.

The cruiser's onboard screen played the news as he drove. "*This is BCN5 Bumper City's only news source.*" This was followed by a commercial. "*I'm Twilas Burke. DirectLink brings the world to you. Better Service, Better Plans, Better Lives. Get the most from your day and night. Stay connected with DirectLink.*"

After the commercial, the news anchor began the next segment. "*Several riots broke out earlier today in the Mining District. Protesters took to the streets demanding justice. Our Jennifer Caldwell filed this report.*" The screen cut to the reporter standing on a street. Behind her was chaos. Cars were on fire, rioters ran past, business windows shattered, and masked individuals hurled bricks. "*Miners took to the street today to protest working conditions along with the disappearances of women and children in this area. They say the police do little to protect them, and they want answers. I spoke to a union president, Emile Tarkon just moments ago.*" She said.

The screen went to an interview with Tarkon, the United Copper and Mineral Miners of Bumper City President. The camera's high-intensity light caused his eyes to turn into cat-like slivers.

"*What do you want the citizens of New Vegas to know?*" The reporter asked.

Tarkon's response, "*For weeks now, we've been asking for more protection in the district. Several of our children and mothers have gone missing. Nobody seems to care until production stops. Last year, the cave-in took 126 of our brothers and sisters. Ten days ago, the north face collapsed, killing 80. These are our families and neighbors. When is the company, the NVPD, going to do something about it?*" Tarkon said. "*We were peacefully marching when some of Bumper City's finest roughed up some protesters. This is what happens after police brutality.*" Tarkon pointed to the burning and looting behind them.

The interview ended as the screen cut to the reporter. "*They say the company isn't doing enough to provide a safe work environment. And now, they need better protection for their families while they're at the job site. The workers spend long hours in the mines, sometimes double shifts just to make ends meet, all the while their families are left to fend for themselves. I asked what happened to the missing women and children, but he didn't have an explanation and said that is why they are frustrated with New Vegas Police and more action is needed. Back to you, Tom.*"

The news anchor came back onscreen. "*Thanks, Jennifer. Mayor Stockton held a press conference today at the courthouse to address the riots.*" The screen turned to Mayor Stockton standing in front of a podium with the Chief of Police and City Attorney behind her.

"*I can assure you, we are doing everything we can to find out what happened to the mothers and children that are unaccounted for. I'll let Chief Leonard fill you in on the investigation.*" Mayor Stockton stepped away from the podium as the Chief of Police took her place. "*Our detective bureau is working tirelessly to locate those reported missing. At this time, we do not know their status. We are urging the miners to return to work to let us do our job. Destroying businesses in your own community doesn't help anyone. Please, go home and be patient while we investigate."*

"What a moron," I said. Rollins looked at me through the rear-view mirror before turning off the screen. As we arrived at the station, protesters marched in front of the building. Several had signs reading DEFUND BUMPER CITY POLICE. Another stated, FIND OUR CHILDREN. A third, BUMPER CITY POLICE ARE USELESS. The crowd angrily chanted, "HEY HEY, YOU KNOW THEY GOTTA GO."

The crowd spotting us pull into the parking lot and ran over, but the gate closed before they could get close. A squad of uniformed officers was standing in the lot. They had just returned from the riots, tired and irritable.

"Come on, Cold. Let's go." Rollins got out first then opened my door. The uniforms started to approach, and they didn't look happy.

"What happened, Rollins? We heard some of our CSI guys were in an explosion and a detective got killed." One of them asked.

"Clowes," Rollins answered. Their eyes turned to me.

"This the guy who did it?" One asked as a few stepped closer.

Rollins put his hand out, "Take it easy. No. He used to be one of us."

An officer from the back pushed through. "That's Alton Cold." The group's tension eased. "Alton, what are you doing here? You workin' something?"

Rollins didn't let me answer. He grabbed my arm and rushed us through the side door. Luckily, I wasn't cuffed, or things may have gone differently.

Once inside, Rollins grabbed some plastic evidence bags from a shelf, and then escorted me to the locker room. He opened the evidence bag and ordered. "Pants."

I slid off my trousers and placed them in the bag. He then threw me a pair of New Vegas Police sweatpants and a matching sweatshirt. "Doesn't go with my shoes." I quipped.

"Yeah, well, those go in this bag." He said holding open another evidence collection bag.

"My shoes?" I protested.

Rollin didn't respond, he threw me a pair of flip-flops and waited for the shoes.

"Now!" He snapped.

After everything was in some type of evidence container, he escorted me through the squad bay. The bureau secretary was seated near the main door. "Sally, log these into evidence. Put them under Alton Cold. I'll refile them later." He instructed.

"Hi, Alton." Sally smiled warmly.

"Hi, Sally."

"How's retirement treatin you? Or are you back?" She asked.

"Not on your life." I responded. "Retirement has its moments."

"I'm guessing this isn't one of them." She quipped.

I returned the smile as Rollins nudged me to an interview room. Before going in, I stopped, "Really? How about a little professional courtesy?"

"You had that back at the Refuge. Sit." He ordered. After I was seated, he stepped back out shutting the door behind him. The camera in the corner of the room had a red light above the lens. Several minutes went by before I noticed the red dot turn green. That meant someone started the recorder. Police procedure required someone to monitor the room when a suspect was inside. Sometimes, they cut corners and roll tape instead of having a live person back there. I didn't know which was which.

A couple of minutes after the light changed, Rollins came back. This was another first for me. I'd never been on the suspect side before. And I didn't like it. Rollins was holding a large file under his arm. The tab was labeled "Copperhead."

"What's with the clown masks?" I asked.

"That's not how this works, Cold. I didn't bring you to headquarters to give you information. I'm asking the questions." He snapped.

"We trade." I responded.

"What?" he asked.

"You want to know something; you tell me something," I said.

"What the fuck did I just tell you?" He snapped.

"You know I didn't blow up that apartment. I gave you all my clothes. The DNA should tell you who the killer is." I said. "I need answers, too."

"We got a dead cop and crime scene techs blown up inside an apartment you were standing in seconds before. Clowes was a good cop. You claim to have killed somebody, but there's no body." He kept going because I hadn't used the word lawyer yet. The moment I did, he'd have to stop. But that would mean I wouldn't get any answers either.

"You saw the pool of blood," I responded.

"What were you doing in Sophia Durant's apartment? You suddenly show up at a crime scene where her head is rotating on a hook, claiming to be on a missing persons case, with information we hadn't released to the public yet." He snapped.

"I told you I worked for the niece to find her aunt. I didn't know the victim was Sophia Durant. I already explained this to you and how I got there." I said.

"Yeah, you did, Cold. We can't find the niece anywhere to verify any of this. So, I'll ask again: what were you doing at Sophia Durant's apartment? You were a cop. You knew damn well we'd be going there. And I told you to butt out, yet you went anyway. Kind of like when you worked here, always doing your own thing. Disobeying orders." He snapped. "So, WHY WERE YOU AT SOPHIA DURANT'S APARTMENT?"

"I needed to get there before you guys contaminated the crime scene or took shit out I might need to see," I said.

"Contam…Cold, I told you to stay in your lane. You're not HOMICIDE. You were in narcotics. The missing person case was over. Case solved. Her mutilated corpse was found at the Refuge…" He paused. "You know…the chief wants me to arrest you. There's more than enough to hold you on suspicion of murder." He sat back, brimming with an air of confidence. But I knew it was an act.

"I can see the dimwit saying that. He never did any actual police work. But you know better. The same people who killed Sophia Durant killed your other victims. And you know I didn't do it, just like you know, James did do it." I said calmly.

"How would I know that?" He asked.

Rollins saying the chief wanted to arrest me was probably true. The chief hated me. He'd been my supervisor at the City Attorney's office. I caught him stealing petty cash and siphoning time, so I turned him in to Internal Affairs. But the unit was run by a bunch of ex-feds, which is to say the unit was as useless as a fart in the wind.

"Look…I went to Durant's apartment to find her appointment book. I wanted to look at it before you placed it in evidence. Once you logged it in, I'd never see it. And you'd never give me any of her client names from it, so I had to see it first."

"Did you find it?" He asked.

"No. The door was kicked in when I arrived. The hall lights were busted, and none of the apartment lights worked. The streetlamp from outside was the only light. Someone attacked me, knocking me against the wall. Probably from the darkened hallway inside."

"Didn't you clear the apartment first like you are supposed to?" He was getting more skeptical.

"The guy blindsided me before I had time," I responded.

"What'd he look like?" Rollins asked.

"I didn't get a great look. The hit knocked the wind out of me. He jumped on top and started punching me." I said, pointing to the cuts and bruises on my face. "I thought he was going to kill me, so I pulled my .45 and shot him."

"Did he have a weapon?" Rollins asked.

"I don't know. It happened kinda fast. He damn near knocked me unconscious."

"Wait. So, you shot an unarmed man?" Rollins asked.

"I just told you; I didn't know if he had a weapon or not," I responded.

"After you shot him, did you see a weapon in his hand? On the ground?" He asked.

"No, it was dark, and there was shit everywhere. I assumed that asshole was looking for the book too." I said.

"So you just shot an unarmed man?" Rollins said.

"I told you he was attacking me. I thought he was going to kill me." I said.

"Alright. We'll come back to that. Then what?" He asked.

"I got up and went through the rest of the house. There was a safe in the bedroom closet. The door was open, but it was empty. I thought I heard something, so I went outside to check it out. When I didn't find anything, I came back in, and the body was gone." I said.

"Did you call it in?" He asked.

This was a trap. Rollins knew I didn't call 911. He sat me alone in this room while he went to get more information. This was a technique to create anxiety. It also gives the interrogator time to gather more information to catch a suspect in a lie about something, anything. That would provide him with leverage.

But Rollins was missing a critical point. In his zeal to get the upper hand, he ignored an important question. Unfortunately, I had to be careful about getting him to see it because of Bessimer. I wasn't ready to expose my car as A.I. yet.

"No, I didn't call 911. John, the question you should be asking yourself is, how did the firetrucks and paramedics get there right after the bomb went off?"

"BOMB? Who said anything about a bomb? Unless you're telling me, you put one there?" Rollins snapped.

"Yeah, I placed a bomb in the apartment and waited for you to drag me out so I wouldn't get blown up? Use your head. What do you think caused the explosion?" I snapped back.

"Gas." He answered.

"Gas? Did you smell gas when you came in?" I asked.

"Doesn't mean anything. I wasn't even thinking about it when I walked through the door." He said.

"The kid would have noticed it. Besides, there wasn't any gas. It had to be an explosive device." I said.

"So, you're telling me that a guy attacks you with a live bomb in the building. Why? Why the fuck would he do that? It'd be easier to detonate it while you were inside." Rollins said.

"Not if he had a partner. You said the Copperhead Strangler was most likely a duo." I answered.

Rollins sat back and thought as I went on. "It wasn't the 911 caller. Fire trucks don't respond to shootings. Paramedics, maybe, but not the fire department. So how the hell did they get there so fast? The explosion didn't happen until after you arrived. There had to be two 911 calls. The bomb must have been in place before I got there." I finished.

Rollins' eyes glanced at the camera, then back at me. "I'm sure the bomb squad will figure it out."

"So, you think it was a bomb too," I asked, but he ignored me. "How'd you know it was me in the hall?" He went back to the trap. "You called out when I was there?"

I leaned forward, "John, I saw you leaving your car with Clowes. That's why I put my pistol on the counter. It was dark, and I didn't want him shooting me. I knew you'd need it for evidence." I said. "That was all before the explosion. How'd the fire department get there so damned fast?"

"They probably finished putting out fires at the riots and caught the call on their way back to the firehouse. It's not relevant. Let's get back to you. Where's your car?" he asked. "I didn't see it when I got there."

For some reason, he was ignoring my suggestion of a second call. Maybe it wasn't a 911 call; I wasn't sure. But somebody alerted the fire department well before the explosion. And there were two trucks there. The most the city would have sent to the riots was one until things calmed down.

NVFD was regarded as a good department, but everything in Bumper City is corrupt. I considered telling Rollins about Bessimer. Now I was glad I hadn't. Something was off. I could feel it.

"I parked it around the block." Responding to his question about my car.

"Our guys are canvassing now. It's not there." He said.

This was a good one. I didn't know if he was bluffing or not. They would have uniforms and detectives conducting interviews through the neighborhood. I wasn't convinced they'd have noticed my car, especially if they weren't looking for it. But Rollins might've had enough time when he put me in this room to place a call to the scene.

"I don't know. Maybe my secretary took it." I said.

"Was she with you? At the apartment?" He asked.

"No," I responded.

"Then how would she know to come and get it?" Rollins asked.

"I don't know. I don't even know it's not where I left it. You could be bullshitting me..." I paused.

"Who was with you at the apartment?" He asked impatiently.

"Nobody. I was there alone." I insisted.

Rollins' eyes were skeptical. "Let's talk about the guy you...say you killed. What happened to the body?" He asked.

"How the hell should I know?" I said.

"You don't know what he looks like. He's punching you in the face. You felt like he was going to kill you. But when I get there, no body. Your car isn't around, and you didn't call it in. And you claim to have been there alone. You see how I'm having a problem with this?" He said, leaning back. "Where's your client?"

"I have no idea. I've been with you." I said.

"When was the last time you saw her?" He asked.

"She was staying at the Elkhorn," I responded.

Thankfully Stan Findley Esq. opened the door. "You intend to arrest my client?" Stanley didn't hesitate and came right in.

I let out a small sigh as Rollins turned. "We're just having a friendly chat."

"That's over. C'mon Alton. Not another word." Findley said.

"Hold on. Cold, you're not under arrest. You can stay if you want. You don't have to listen to the suit." Rollins said.

I smiled back at him. "Only a fool doesn't listen to the advice of his lawyer. Besides, I got things to do." I responded, then pinched my shirt. "Thanks for the sweats."

"You mean like Teller?" Rollins asked sharply.

"Surely you don't object to me talking to my client. I thought we agreed he has nothing to do with this." I said.

"Stay away from this case, Cold. Don't go near the crime scene. Professional courtesy is waaaay over. I'm warning you, if you keep on this, I'll arrest you for interfering with a police investigation." He motioned to my attorney. "You'll need him for real." Then he pointed to the camera that was still green. "More than enough evidence to make that charge stick." He paused to look at his watch. "You wanna see Teller, better hurry. I'm betting he's already on the train to Wasteland One."

"What the fuck for?" I snapped.

"He may not have anything to do with this, but he sold Colors to a girl who died. They're moving him. Lockup is full from the riots. I'm guessing he's already on the train." He said with a grin.

"What about my car?" I knew Bessimer was nowhere near Durant's apartment. I had no intention of returning to the crime scene right now, but I had to make it look good.

"I told you it's not there." He sneered. "I'm telling you for the last goddamned time, stay out of this investigation."

Findley butted in, "Don't worry, detective. His car is out front." Then Findley looked at me. "Your driver brought it here."

Rollins' eyebrow raised. "You have a driver? Who's your driver?" His next question was directed at Findley, "By the way, counselor, how'd you know to come here?"

"Good day, detective," Findley said as he pulled me from the room.

The chief was standing in the hall as we passed. I figured he'd been monitoring the interview from the next room. I stopped to look him in the eye. "Saw you on the tube before we got here." I paused to lean in. "You really are a fuckin moron."

A couple of uniformed officers behind Rollins snickered. The chief's face turned red. He chewed aggressively on the cigar hanging between his lips. Rollins got the look from him and yelled, "GET THE HELL OUTTA HERE COLD! You ain't one of us anymore."

Findley hustled me through the hall as the chief yelled at his men, "GET BACK TO WORK!" Then he got in Rollins' face. We passed the front desk sergeant as Rollins was getting reamed.

There were a half dozen cops in a line outside the station's front door. They were tapping their batons at protestors marching on the sidewalk. The protesters kept yelling, "FUCK THE PO-LICE. DISBAND AND DISARM THE OPPRESSORS. FUCK YOU PIGS"

There were noticeably more protesters than before, and the chants were getting louder. Once they saw us walking down the steps, a few ran over. "They do that to you?" One commented, noticing the bruises and cuts on my face. A young girl looked at the officer and screamed, "Bastards! You Fascist pigs! Corrupt assholes."

But when they saw me wearing the police sweats Rollins gave me, they started to yell, "He's one of them. Fuck you, pig. Fuck you and your racist pals. You probably had it coming!"

As tensions heated, a couple of the NVPD officers marched down the steps, advancing toward them. The once sympathetic protesters decided to go back to their group.

Bessimer was parked curbside with the engine running. The holographic driver was seated behind the wheel. The image was so lifelike that everyone thought it was a real person, including Findley.

"How did you know I was here?" I asked.

"Your secretary called. She figured you might get scooped up by them. I got here as soon as I could. Your driver was here when I walked past." He bent down and waved at the hologram. "He's a little odd. Just stares."

"He's not much for conversation," I said, getting into the passenger seat. I cracked the window to say one last thing. "Stay where I can get a hold of you. This ain't over."

Stan's tone turned serious. "Cold, I don't know what this is all about, but I don't think Rollins was bluffing. They didn't exactly like you when you had a badge. And you didn't help yourself with the chief back there."

"He's an oxygen thief. Don't worry, counselor, just be ready if I need you." I said, then rolled up the window. "Alright, Bessimer. Get me outta here."

Bessimer pulled away and slowly drifted past the protestors. Rollins came outside, lit a cigarette, and watched me drive away. "Where are we going, sir?" Bessimer asked.

"Where did you take Nev and Penny?" I responded.

"I took Miss Nevaeh to your office. Miss Penelope was there waiting. She instructed me to transport them to your apartment. She placed extra clothes in the backseat for you, sir. Then she sent me to get you." Bessimer answered.

"How'd Penny know I was here?" I asked as I climbed in the back.

"I intercepted the transmission of Detective Wilcox informing dispatch Rollins was returning to the station with one in custody. I assumed that was most likely you. I called Miss Penelope to let her know, and she ordered me to come here. I arrived just as Rollins pulled in with you in the back." Bessimer responded. Then he repeated his earlier question. "Where are we going, sir?"

"Take me home," I said. "Make it quick."

Bessimer rushed back to my apartment and pulled to the front door to let me out. An unmarked police car was down the block, watching. I leaned back in, "Park in the back where there isn't a good view from the street." I instructed.

"The cop car, sir?" Bessimer noticed it too.

"On second thought. Park in the back, wait a few minutes, go to the back door, then drive away. Let's see if they go with you." I instructed.

"Yes, sir." He responded. "Where shall I go, sir?"

"If they follow you, give them a tour of Bumper City, but stay out of any hot zones. Use the hologram." I responded.

Bessimer drove himself to a parking spot as I went inside. Neither Penny nor Nevaeh were here. The answering machine wasn't blinking, which meant there were no messages.

Where could they be? I thought. Then I noticed the picture of Mara and I on the end table next to my sofa was gone. I picked up the phone to dial the office when I noticed something else. I kept a few books on a shelf next to my recliner. It was a small collection of old authors. *Haxfuri* and the *My Fatal Futility* series by NJM Hemfrey. Next to them is the *A Cry in the Moon's Light* series by Alan McGill.

Penny's favorite was *Red Door.* It's a prequel, so I always placed it first. But *Red Door* was out of place. It was after book two *The Undead Wars.*

Penny knew I was particular about the placement of these books. They were antiques and hard to get. The authors died long ago, and McGill disappeared under mysterious circumstances which made his books even more valuable. She would have put them back in the correct order unless...

When I picked up *Red Door,* there was a picture tucked in the pages. It was my friend Joey, who died in a motorcycle crash many years ago. I always kept his photo on my refrigerator, but here it was tucked in page 61, where the main characters are hiding from a werewolf in the dark forest. The photos placement was Penny's way of telling me their location.

I walked to the window and moved the shade aside. Bessimer was gone, and so was the surveillance unit. Nev and Penny were safe for now and I could finally get some much-needed sleep.

CHAPTER 9

DEBT OF A FRIEND

The streetlamps got brighter with the onset of the morning hours. Rays of light squeezed through the window shades, waking me. I peeled down a slat to get a look outside. Air brakes hissed as pedestrians hurried to climb aboard trolleys while others warmed their cars to prepare for the morning commute.

I couldn't see Bessimer or any unmarked units, so I picked up the phone and called. It rang a few times before he answered. "Good morning, sir."

"You ditch the cops?" I asked.

"Yes, sir. They were a bit more tenacious than I gave them credit. But I managed to lose them after a few hours." He responded.

"Where are you now?" I asked.

"I'm in the back of the lot, sir. Shall I pull to the front?" He asked.

"No. Stay put. I'll call if I need you." I hung up, deciding it would be better to leave Bessimer in place. I couldn't be sure Rollins didn't have another team in place I hadn't noticed.

The police chief had watched Rollins interrogate me, but I didn't know if he'd been the only one observing. Something told me there was someone above him pulling the strings. And whoever that might be, could put their own surveillance team on me.

Plus, the killer clown was still out there, along with the female assassin. They seemed like enemies, but I wasn't certain. I had to make sure I didn't lead anyone to Nevaeh.

According to the morning news, Twilas Burke donated three million dollars to the Bumper City Feed the Homeless Foundation. There was a story about him handing out meals in the Mining District.

As I got out of the shower, BCN5 went to breaking news.

"We interrupt this story to report a disturbing scene on Sunset Blvd. near the Mining District. Police are confirming several bodies were found at an apartment building that caught fire late yesterday. Our cameras were on the scene. Jennifer Caldwell has more."

The screen showed firefighters battling flames at Sophia Durant's obliterated apartment. "*This was the scene yesterday after an explosion rocked an apartment complex on Sunset Boulevard blocks away from the Red-Light District. It took firefighters hours to contain the blaze after the blast destroyed most of this second-floor apartment.*"

The screen returned to Jennifer Caldwell standing on the street as smoke and embers filled the background. New Vegas Police were keeping reporters and the public from getting too close.

"Police tell us there was a massive explosion yesterday around 4 pm. I was able to learn through 911 tapes that a call was placed reporting a shooting and a dead body inside this apartment. Shortly after police arrived, the apartment exploded, killing three crime scene investigators and one detective who were inside beginning their investigation into the reported shooting.

So far, police have no leads on the shooting, the reported victim, or how the explosion occurred. Moments ago, I spoke with Chief Leonard about the incident." The screen went to Leonard speaking into the reporter's microphone at the scene.

"Chief, I'm told there were other bodies found in the neighboring apartments. What can you tell us about that?" She asked.

"The fire department found three other bodies after the blaze was contained. Our crime scene unit is on-premises now collecting evidence, and our officers are speaking to several witnesses." The Chief responded.

"Chief, we've learned the bodies found in the neighboring apartments weren't killed by the blast and are being labeled as homicides. We also learned there was no body found in the apartment, as indicated by the 911 call. Can you explain any of this?" Caldwell asked.

Leonard's face scowled. "*That's all I can say right now. Thank you.*"

The Chief ducked behind crime scene tape before the reporter could ask more questions. She turned to the camera, finishing the piece.

"Live from Sunset Blvd. Jennifer Caldwall Action News, back to you."

I turned the television off, thinking about her report. *Was it the assassin who killed the neighbors…or the clown?* That thought would be plaguing my mind all day.

Rollins had my .45 in evidence, and it would be months before I got it back. Luckily, I still had a 40-caliber Colt with higher capacity magazines. Regardless of who I face today, I should have plenty of ammunition to handle them.

I lifted the corner of the shade for another quick look outside. The street was even busier than before. Still no sign of police. It was all commuters mixed with the neighborhood hustle. My mind continued going over the news report as I watched the street below.

The foot traffic would let me blend in, but I decided on the back stairwell rather than the front. Lighting in the alley was poor and the shadows would allow me to move unseen.

I figured anyone setting up to tail me to Nevaeh would key on Bessimer. As long as the car didn't move, they'd assume I was still home. Nobody would expect me to leave on foot. They'd never notice me going out the back.

I raised the volume on the TV before I left. Nobody saw me leave the building so I calmly walked through the alley, to a coffee shop a few blocks away. The baristas were used to seeing me come in the back door and through the kitchen, so no one batted an eye.

I ordered a cup of coffee and then stood at the front window. The Tram stopped right in front. The sound of the air brakes hissed as it lowered to let the night shift workers off. I used the morning crowd to blend in as we boarded. No last-minute passengers were rushed, so I was confident nobody followed me.

The tram went a few miles before stopping under the expressway. This was in a quiet neighborhood and desolate. Two people waited at the curb and when the doors opened, they got on. Before the doors completely closed, I darted out.

Nobody else got off, and there wasn't any traffic, so I walked around the corner to Odell's Pub. Odell's was a neighborhood bar at the end of a bunch of row houses. Although this was a residential area, it had been here from the beginning. The newly constructed freeway overhead added to the darkness . The pub was closed now, so the neon green Odell sign above the door was off.

I knew Sam would be inside prepping before he opened later this afternoon. He usually came in early to get his soup of the day and smoked meats ready for the lunch special. Most mornings the back door would be open as he carried out trash from the night before, but today it was closed. This didn't seem like a big thing, but it was odd.

I remained in the shadows across the street to watch. A few minutes passed, and then a Portis Refuse Truck pulled to the curb. The driver didn't back to the dumpster, which was another odd thing.

The driver and his passenger got out and went into Odell's through the back door. They were only inside a few minutes before returning to the truck. The driver folded an envelope, placed it in his jacket, and then climbed into the truck. Seconds later, the airbrakes sounded, and they drove away.

I had seen this type of behavior a thousand times, but it didn't register until I went through Odell's back door. Sam was seated on a chair in the kitchen as his girlfriend held a rag to his forehead. She kept dipping it in water to wipe away blood seeping from a gash above his eye.

Neither of them heard me come in and jumped when I spoke. "You alright Sam?"

"Shit Alton! Say something next time." Tori yelled.

"I just did," I responded.

Sam looked at me embarrassingly. "Just fell. Hit my head on the corner of the bar. I'm fine."

I lifted Tori's hand, to look at the wound. "You're gonna need stitches Sam," I said, placing her hand, holding the rag, back on the wound. "Keep pressure on it," I said before looking Sam in the eye. "It's not going to stop bleeding."

"I'll be fine. It'll stop." Sam insisted.

"Sam, you need to go to the emergency room. It's just a couple of stitches. You have to make sure it doesn't get infected. I'll call for an ambulance." I said.

Sam yelled, "I'm GOOD! Alton." He looked sheepishly at Tori and then back to me. "I'm good. I can't afford it right now." Then his eyes fell. "I don't have insurance."

I took the receiver off the phone and dialed the hospital. Sam was about to object again when I put my finger up to silence him. The phone rang a couple of times before it answered. "Hello."

"Freddie?" I asked.

"Hey, whadda ya up to?" Freddie responded.

"Need a favor. Can you come to Odell's?" I asked.

"Yeah, gotta drop Goldie at his place first. What's up?" He asked.

"I need you to come over. Bring your kit. Sam hit his head. He's gonna need a couple of stitches." I said.

"Just have him come to the ER," Freddie responded.

"He can't afford it. Can you drop by and patch him up?" I asked.

"Sure, it'll be a few minutes before I can leave, but I'll be there," Freddie said.

"Whatever it costs, put it on my tab," I said.

"No problem, see you in a few," Freddie said, ending the call.

"Fred's going to come by. He'll stitch you up. After he's done, take your ass over to Doc Fraley's and get some antibiotics." I said to Sam and Tori as I hung up the receiver.

"Thanks, Alton, but really I'm fine," Sam said.

"How much are you into them for?" I asked. He was about to deny it, but his eyes gave him away. "Don't bother, I saw the Portis truck. I watched them pull in. If I'd a known they were gonna jump you, I'd have come in. So, how much?"

Sam's eyes lowered. "Sixty."

"THOUSAND?" I exclaimed.

"I nearly lost the business after that SIC9. Christ Alton, the whole city was on lockdown for a year." Sam said. "This place didn't make no money."

"That was two years ago Sam. The bar seems to be doing alright now." I said.

"Yeah, but I could barely pay the bills during the pandemic. And the city wasn't exactly helping. All the stimulus money went to the Mining District. The bridge loan from the bank wasn't making it. I got a kid in college. The ex was threatening to take the bar. I had to take out a loan from Portis." Sam said.

"How much more do you owe?" I asked.

"It was paid off months ago. They keep adding interest. They're squeezing me dry. I offered to sell them the bar, but they don't want it." Sam said.

"They don't want it?" I responded.

"No. I almost had it sold, but they blocked the sale. Now nobody wants it." Sam said.

"I'll take care of it," I said.

"NO! DON'T. They threatened my kid." Sam pleaded.

"Trust me, Sam. It'll be alright." I tried to reassure him, but he was scared.

"What are you doing here anyway? We don't open til 11." Sam said.

"I need to borrow your car," I said.

"I don't have it anymore." He said.

"What?" I asked.

"Had to sell it to make a payment." His response was hollow, disappointed even. "That was the one thing they did take."

"You saying Portis has it?" I asked.

"Yep. They took it last week." He said.

"You payin these assholes each week?" I asked.

"Or else," Sam said as Freddie came through the back door. Freddie didn't waste any time going right to Sam. I went behind the bar, pouring some Mother's Milk into my coffee from the cafe. It took a few minutes for Freddie to stitch the cut on Sam's head. After applying a couple of bandages, and he was done.

When Freddie finished, I walked him out. "He'll be alright. It wasn't a fall, though. Somebody clubbed him pretty good. He might have a concussion." Freddie said. "He needs to go to the hospital.

"Less you know, the better. He won't go to the ER. He's stubborn. I think I can get him to see Doc Fraley. What do I owe you?" I asked.

"Nothin. It's water under the frig, as Goldie would say." He said with a chuckle. "I was heading home after I dropped Goldie. We both worked the night shift." He added.

"Can you give me a ride?" I asked.

"Yeah. Where you going?"

"Portis," I said.

"I don't want to know, do I?" he asked gingerly.

"Nope," I said, getting in his car. Freddie pulled away, eventually getting into the heavy morning traffic. We made our way north toward the Mining District. It would have been faster to call Bessimer, but that was still too risky. Sam had an antique car outfitted with special shielding that covered the battery. The cloud couldn't drain it, and nobody could track me.

Freddie dropped me off a few blocks from Portis' Garage. The big neon sign, PORTIS, was hanging off the building. "Not exactly the best folks to be visiting by yourself," Freddie said. "You want me to come with you?"

As I exited the car, my eye caught movement on a rooftop across the street. The figure of a woman. She moved into a shadow and disappeared. I only saw a quick glimpse, but it looked like the same woman who shot the Pagliacci Clown at Sophia Durant's place—the one standing at the window before the apartment exploded.

I leaned back into Freddie's car, "I'll ah…I'll be alright. Check in on Sam, will ya, Fred?"

"Will do." Fred pulled out, driving past the chain link fence surrounding the property. I watched until I couldn't see his brake lights anymore, then scanned the rooftops, looking for the mysterious figure. But there was no sign of her, so I turned my attention to Portis.

Most of Portis' trucks were parked in the lot behind the fencing. The gate was open, so I strolled right in. The bay doors of the garage were up allowing me to see the workers changing next to their lockers in the back.

None of them noticed as I casually walked to a small door off to the side of the building. This opened to a long hallway going deeper into the business. Once I stepped inside, another door directly ahead connected the hallway to the garage.

To my left, another door was propped open, and there were two guys sitting at a table packaging some type of drug. From the size of the blocks, I'd say it was kilos. They placed the bricks in whiskey boxes between bottles then used paper to stuff between. I was too far away to identify the drug, but I knew a packing operation when I saw one.

A worker from the garage saw me through the door window and yelled, "WHOA! WHO THE FUCK ARE YOU? You can't be in here." The whole garage turned to look at me.

The door, where the men were packing drugs, slammed shut. The door to the garage burst open as two guys came through, "I'm looking for Miles Portis." I exclaimed.

"Yeah, well, make an appointment like everybody else." Another guy came around the corner and they all stepped toward me.

"It's too late for that." I turned to look behind to see Mickey Portis, Miles' son, sneering at me. I never heard him come up from behind. Mickey and another goon grabbed me before I could say anything else. They drug me by the arm, down the hall, and through another door in the back. "You wanna see the ol'man, you got it," Mickey said.

The two of them pulled me into a big office at the end of the hall. Mickey flipped the light switch as there were only a few sconces on.

Miles Porter was sitting behind a big wooden desk. The sudden illumination caught him off-guard as he jumped in his seat. His head snapped to the door. "WHOA! MICKEY. WHAT THE FUCK? KINDA BUSY HERE!"

Miles shifted the big leather chair to one side as a middle-aged woman emerged, adjusting her dress. She was a pretty little thing with short white hair and an even shorter skirt. She didn't have the same embarrassed look as Miles; she was a bit proud of herself. She stood up gingerly, buttoning her blouse. Once that was done, she wiped the corner of her mouth and gave us a devious smile.

Miles, on the other hand, was red-faced. Even mob bosses don't want their kids catching them with the secretary. The goon holding my arm quickly snorted, earning him a backhand from Mickey. "OWWW!" The goon yelled, rubbing the back of his head.

"Take a walk," Miles told the woman.

"The fuck you get in here?" Miles said, looking at me.

Mickey shuffled uncomfortably as the secretary walked out, shutting the door behind her. Miles shifted in his seat, too. She looked back at me through the door's window with a wry smile.

"This is…" Mickey started to tell his father.

"I know who the fuck it is." Miles barked.

"The fuck you doing here, Cold?" Miles snapped.

Mickey and the goon forced me into a chair opposite the desk. "Sam Odell," I answered.

"Who?" Miles sneered.

"I need you to let him out of...well...whatever it is," I said.

"Yeah. Why the fuck would I do that?" Miles scoffed.

"My understanding is he paid what he owed, and then some," I answered.

Miles slammed his palm on the desk. "I say when he's fuckin done!"

"Call it a trade," I said.

"Trade?" He responded with a slight chuckle. "What you got to trade? You gonna pick up his debt?" Miles asked with a smile.

"No. Call it even for me not calling the narc squad about whatever it is you got going in that back room." I said.

Miles' expression changed. Dealing with guys like this is always tricky. One minute, they can be calm, the next volatile. It's like dealing with a cobra. The question was never IF they would strike, but WHEN.

"Fuck you say to me?" Miles leaned forward, gritting his teeth.

Mickey pipped up, "Fuckin balls on this guy, eh Pop? Let me put'em in the compactor."

"SHUT THE FUCK UP, MICKEY" Miles yelled, pointing a finger at his son. Then he turned to me with a menacing tone. "Mickey's right. You are either the dumbest motherfucker in the city, or you got some balls on you. Coming in here threatening me in my place."

Before any of them could react, I was around the desk with my .40 in Miles' crotch. Mickey and his goon tried to grab me, but they had moved to the back of the room and were too far away. Mickey immediately put out his hand to stop them.

My free hand was on the arm of Miles' chair as I made sure he could feel the barrel pressing against his jewels. "Your guys aren't that fast. I hope you have a good memory. They twitch, and that hummer you just got will be the last good experience little Miles here, ever has." I said, tapping his junk with the barrel of my gun.

The initial look on Miles' face was surprised. He didn't expect me to make any kind of move. But surprise turned to anger...quick.

The angst on his face only lasted a few seconds. A big smile stretched from ear to ear, which was followed by an eruption of laughter.

I turned my head to Mickey and the goon, who were as surprised as me, but then both of them started laughing hysterically, too. I leaned back but kept the gun trained on his abdomen. I couldn't see myself, but I imagine my expression was bewilderment.

Miles relaxed in his chair. He composed himself, then said with a big smile, "You ain't gonna shoot me Cold. Cops don't do that." A shit-eating grin pasted on his face waiting for a response.

"I'm not a cop anymore." I sneered.

"Yeah, yeah. I know. You're retired, right?" he giggled. "But you're still all cop. A real cop. More cop than half the guys on that crooked force. You might not be on payroll anywhere, but guys like you don't shoot first. And I own most of the ones that do." He smirked. "I hate fuckin cops. Crooked or not. But there are a few of you that I respect. The ones who play by the rules. We might be on the other side of the law, but we got rules too." Then the smile left his face as he turned serious. "And one of those rules is that you don't fuck with a guy in his home. Now, why shouldn't I just kill you since you came in here threatening me where I get my knob shined."

Mickey and the goon pulled their pistols, aiming right at me.

"And as you pointed out, being you ain't on the force no more, I wouldn't be killing a cop. So I doubt anybody would give a fuck. Most of those crooked assholes didn't like you anyway, from what I hear. I could let Mickey here shove you in one of my trucks, take your body out to the city dump, and you'd never be heard from again."

"How bout I forget what I saw in the back room? I may not be on the job anymore, but I'll bet I can get fifteen of my old buddies down here and tear this place apart." I said.

Miles' brows furled. "How do you expect to make that call?"

"After I blow a hole in your Johnson, the guy that dropped me off is gonna call 911. He's waiting to hear from me." I said, turning my wrist over to look at my watch. "I figure you got about fifteen minutes before he calls anyway." Then I looked him in the eyes. "They may not like me, but they love a good bust. And it's an election year. You're two goons shoot me, the mayor enjoys standing in front of your building with cameras flashing as she shows off a big seizure of Colors. Either way, you're fucked."

"HEY FUCK YOU COLD. We don't push Colors! None of my guys fuck with that mind control bullshit. They know Goddamed well I'd throw'em in a compactor." Miles's demeanor changed the moment I mentioned Colors. The whole exchange was contentious, but this was something different. I had no idea what drug his guys were packing in those whiskey boxes. Colors were the latest craze, so I assumed he was capitalizing on the opportunity like everybody else.

Miles looked shaken. And nothing shook these guys. Mickey and the goon lowered their guns, seemingly unnerved too. And what did he mean?

"Mind control? What are you talking about?" I asked.

"Nothin. I don't mean nothin. That shit is just dangerous. It ain't like bumps or coke or even fentanyl. To each their own, I say, we ain twistin nobody's arm, and it ain't none my business to stop it." Then he attempted to shift away from the subject when he realized he'd been rambling. "You willing to die for Odell?"

"Hold on. What do you mean, mind control?" I asked again.

"Fuck you Cold. I didn't mean nottin." Then he slumped in his chair. "Alright, you can tell Odell we're square."

He'd rather square the debt than talk about Colors. Miles's whole attitude shifted when I mentioned it. Even Mickey and the goon lost their aggression. I couldn't feel any more tension in the room, so I put the pistol behind my back.

"And I need Sam's car," I said.

"You really pushing it Cold." Miles sneered.

"You want me to return with a narc squad? I still got friends." I said.

"You want the car? You didn't see nothin."" He responded with a raised eyebrow. I nodded my agreement.

He turned to his son. "Mickey. Bring the old man's car around for the detective."

Before Mickey went to go get the car, I had one last question. "Hold up. Are any of your trucks missing a VIN stamp?" I asked.

Miles' eyes instantly darted to Mickey. He tried to hide it from me, but it was obvious. Mickey shook his head, "Nope. Not that I know of. How bout you guys?" Mickey and the goon had the same fear reaction as when I mentioned Colors.

"Don't come back here, Cold. For any reason. I don't give a shit who you have outside." He said menacingly. "You hear me?"

Mr. Nice Miles was gone. He meant every word of that threat.

CHAPTER 10

IN HIDING

Mickey brought Sam's car around as Miles had me escorted out. As Mickey and I were passing each other through the gate, I asked, "Mickey. What'd your dad mean back there?"

He never blinked. "As I said inside, you do got some balls comin' here, Cold. What you're asking, that's a whole nother level of bad. If you were smart, you'd forget about it. You got what you came here for. Like my old man tol you, don't come back."

I was pushing my luck with them, so I got in Sam's car and left. The radio in Sam's car was an antique just like his car. Old radio signals couldn't pass with cloud interference, which left me to ponder what had happened in silence.

The Portis crew was a part of the LaRocca Crime Family. Miles was a former soldier turned captain. Neither he nor his son were afraid of anything. Going in there to convince him to forgive Sam's debt was a stupid plan.

After Mickey forced me in that chair, I realized they might kill me. Pulling my gun seemed like the only option, but that didn't scare them either. Everything changed when I mentioned Colors.

Miles knew damn well who was manufacturing Colors. I didn't expect him to tell me, but his reaction wasn't something I expected. Whoever it was, Miles was afraid of him. Which was hard to imagine. No matter how many angles I went over in my head, I couldn't think of anyone more wicked than the LaRocca Crime Family.

I decided to drive past Sophia Durant's place on my way to meet Penny and Nev. The cops and first responders were replaced by heavy equipment prepping to tear the building down.

I didn't linger as I sped past. The city limits were only a few blocks away. I turned south, putting the black mountains on my right. I could see the peaks in the distance with the cloud edge behind. A few miles later, I reached the dirt road leading into those mountains.

The tires blew swirls of dust behind, while ahead was the faint glow of light behind the peaks. There were no artificial lights out here, making the valley and canyons darker.

Once I climbed to the higher elevations, more of a cloud edge was visible. That was the beginning of the wastelands. The sun's rays reached the ground there as the wind moved dust across the magnetized fields. The closer I got, the more detail I could see.

The entire area had a haze with lighting sparks flying through the atmosphere in dazzling displays. It was a place of great turbulence but stopped once it came in contact with the cloud's boundary.

I had a cabin before the area of light. There were large boulders on both sides of the road leading to it. The cabin was an old wooden structure built prior to the great event. Somehow it survived generation after generation until I bought it. I guess the mountain shielded it from the blast.

Because the cabin was supposed to be a secret, there was no electricity or running water. I used barrels to collect rainwater for bathing and cooking.

As I pulled closer, the light in the windows went out. I moved slowly to the front and parked. Penny and Nevaeh came onto the porch after Penny recognized Sam's car.

The elevation allowed a good view of the basin below. On the other side of that, the lights from Bumper City could be seen in the distance. It reminded me of the old pictures of Los Angeles at night. The only difference was the neon coloring of the cityscape.

Penny came off the porch so she could talk to me before Nevaeh. "You got my message."

"I am a detective." I quipped.

"Why are you driving Sam's car?" Penny asked.

"It's a long story." I motioned to Nevaeh, "She okay?"

"A bit shaken. She's a tough girl, though…she said there were two killer clowns. You killed one. Then some female assassin tried to kill her but hit the other one?"

"Sadistic," I said referring to the clowns. "You hear about Durant's apartment exploding?" I asked.

"Yes. My friend said you weren't hurt. What the hell is going on?" Penny asked.

"How'd you get up here? I don't see any cars." I asked.

Penny pointed to a couple of electric bikes on the porch. "Friend of mine works at the Copperhead Mine. Gave us a ride to the safe house. Grabbed these. They had enough juice to get us up here. Once we were off the main road, I figured we'd be safe."

"Good thing you could pedal to recharge the batteries. How long did it take you?" I asked.

"Long enough." Penny smiled and then patted me on the arm. "I'll let you two talk."

After Penny went inside, Nevaeh ran off the porch and hugged me tightly around the neck. "You saved me." She let go and then looked at me with concern. Her face showed the questions on her mind.

"Everything okay?" I asked.

"Why do you have a picture of my mother?" She was clearly agitated. The question was abrupt, catching me off guard. Also, I didn't know what she meant.

"I'm not sure I know wha..." I started but she interrupted, handing me a picture. It was the one I kept on the end table at my apartment that Penny always asked about.

"This is your mother?" I couldn't believe it. I suddenly remembered Penny saying Nevaeh looked familiar.

"Yes. She's a lot younger. But it's her. I've seen pictures of her when she was young. How do you know my mother?" She asked.

"You never told me Mara was your mother," I said.

"Mara Torres. You never asked. Sophia is, was, her younger sister." She responded.

"Younger sister?" I asked.

"In the beginning. After my grandfather died, my grandmother married again. They had a daughter. My mom's stepsister." She said.

"I don't understand. Mara was a mutant. Her mother was a mutant. But, your...your eyes, they don't change." I said.

"My father wasn't. I'm only half. Same as my aunt. Her father was human too." She explained before returning to her original question. "How did you know my mother? And why do you have a picture in your apartment of the two of you together?"

Nevaeh's eyes filled with tears. Her bottom lip quivered. She was between anger and sorrow, not quite sure which emotion to feel. A look of confusion on her face.

The problem, I was confused too. I didn't know Mara had any children. And who was Nevaeh's father? I sat down on the steps of the front porch as I looked at Bumper City off in the distance.

My thoughts were going a hundred miles an hour. My eyes looked to the southeast. It was too far to see from here, but that was the direction of Hydetown, where I met Mara.

"Debbie took this." I began touching Mara's face in the picture. "She gave it to me after we broke up."

"You and my..." Nevaeh's voice trailed off. She sat down beside me, lowering her head as she waited patiently.

"I loved her. Never loved anyone more." I said.

Nevaeh looked up at me. "Did she love you?" She asked.

"Yes. She used to say being together was like being in heaven." I said, taking in a breath. "I grew up in a small neighborhood north of Hydetown, from the other side of the tracks. We met one evening when a friend and I were walking through." I started. "Your mom and I were inseparable that summer."

"What happened?" Nevaeh asked.

"Sometimes life just gets in the way. Whatever brought us together, pulled us apart. It was the last time I remember being happy. After the summer ended, I never saw her again." I said longingly.

"If she loved you and you loved her, I don't understand." She said. "Was it because she was a mutant?"

"No, nothing like that," I responded. I didn't want to tell Nevaeh about Cecil. It didn't seem important anymore.

"You never tried to find her?" She asked.

"I did, but shortly after we split, she vanished. Debbie gave me this picture sometime after that. I just always kept it."

Nevaeh looked at me in a weird way for a moment before standing, "Come on. Penny has some information you might want to see."

We entered the cabin to find Penny placing logs on the fireplace. There was a file on the kitchen table next to some empty mugs. Penny grabbed the coffee pot from the fire and brought it over. Nevaeh didn't want any, so Penny poured herself and me a cup, and then sat down.

"Here's the file from James' attorney. Not much there." She commented, handing it to me. As I leafed through it she continued, "Looks like they have a female informant. The informant isn't named but the transcript feels like a woman. NVPD has the original tape in evidence. They haven't given a copy to the public defender's office yet, but the transcript is here."

"What about the police file on the Copperhead Strangler?" I asked.

"Still can't get it. The detective getting caught in that explosion really tightened things up." She said. "But I was able to get more information on Colors. Combinations make it more potent. The primary ingredient is an opioid-stimulant mixture. Not a whole lot different than Bumps other than stims being the most prominent in those. Someone added psychedelics to it." She said.

"I know all that, the combo's give it the various shading, hence the name," I commented.

"Yes, but there's something else. Most don't know about this because the police haven't told anyone. The lab discovered an unidentified compound in the newer batches." She said.

"What'd you mean?" I asked.

"The stuff that's on the street now, isn't the same as when you were dealing with it." She started. "They're seeing something else in the new mix."

"Another drug? Or some type of cut?" I asked.

"My friend doesn't know. He says Talmadge is the one who noticed it. Now they're seeing it in every batch." She said.

"Talmadge?" Nevaeh asked.

"He's a chemist at the crime lab," I answered sitting back to think. "You'll have to drive us to the courthouse."

"To see James?" Penny questioned.

"They took James to Max One," I said.

"What? Why?" Penny asked.

"Rollins said the jail is overcrowded from all the protesters getting arrested," I answered.

"That's bullshit." Penny scoffed.

"Yeah, it is. Somebody doesn't want him talking to me." I answered.

"What are you going to do?" Penny asked.

"Gotta go to Max One. The warden still owes me a favor. James knows something. He wouldn't tell me unless I got him a deal." I responded.

"Did you get him a deal?" Penny asked.

"Not yet," I responded.

"Who's James?" Nevaeh asked.

"The other day when you came to the office, I was at his hearing. He's accused of selling Colors that killed a girl in the Mining District." I responded.

"And you think this has something to do with who murdered my aunt?" She asked.

"The cases seem connected. James mentioned the Copperhead Strangler. He claimed to have seen something that would prove he's innocent." I explained.

"Do you believe him? That he's innocent?" Nevaeh asked.

"Yeah. James wouldn't mess with Colors." I said.

"If you didn't get him a deal, what makes you think he'll tell you what he knows?" Nevaeh asked.

"We have a lot of history. He doesn't want to stay in Max One. I can't get him out unless he gives me something. He knows that." I said.

"Who do you think doesn't want you talking to him?" Penny asked.

"Whoever is behind Colors." I started. "Right before I came here, I had to stop at Portis' place."

"Portis! You're lucky you weren't killed." Penny snapped. "That's why you got Sam's car."

"Portis?" Nevaeh asked. "You mean Portis Refuse?"

I looked at Penny first. "Sam was into them for a chunk. They took his car. I needed the car to get up here without being tracked. When I mentioned Colors to Portis, he freaked. They were scared."

"The mafia scared?" Penny asked skeptically.

"I couldn't get any more out of him. But I'm convinced he knows who's moving Colors in the city. And the van I chased from the Refuge; had a stolen vin stamp on the dash. Bessimer ran it, and came back to one of Portis' trucks. He denied knowing anything about it, but I knew he was lying." I explained.

"You think one of those Clowns worked for them?" Nevaeh asked.

"Not sure, but Portis knew something. Why the Clown would have pulled the vin from one of Portis' trucks is hard to say. My guess would be to frame Portis and his crew, but I'm not sure." I said.

"Between the mob and the cops, if you come through this, I'm buying a lottery ticket." Penny joked.

She blew out the candles while I doused the fireplace with water. I lifted the bikes into the trunk and tied the lid with rope. Penny drove us off the mountain back into the city. "You want to call Bessimer?" She asked.

"No. Let him stay where he's at." I said.

"You aren't worried about them spotting you boarding the visitor train?" Penny asked.

"Not really. Rollins knows I plan to debrief James, but he doesn't know where I'm at. Bessimer being at the apartment should be enough to convince him I'm still there. He's probably got my name flagged but by the time he's alerted, we should be underway."

"Should I bring my bag?" Nevaeh asked.

"As long as there aren't any weapons. You might have to place it in a locker at the prison." I said.

Penny pulled into the lot next to Union Station. I opened the glove box and placed my gun inside. "I'll never get on the train with this thing." Before Nevaeh and I got out I said, "Take the bikes back to the safe-house and charge them. Hide Sam's car in the garage around the back. Then call Bessimer to pick you up a few blocks away. Make sure you take my pistol out of the glovebox and place it in Bessimer's glovebox.

Anybody still watching, should stay with him unless they spot me here. We'll go to the coffee shop over there and wait. The train doesn't board for another hour. That should give you plenty of time to get everything ready and make the call." I instructed.

"Where do you want me to go with Bessimer?" Penny asked.

"Back to the office. He can return to my apartment and wait after he drops you off." I said shutting the door. Penny drove down the street as Nevaeh and I walked to the coffee shop across the street from Union Station.

The prison trains pulled into a separate depot around the side. I could see the visitor train pulling in as we went inside. The conductor wouldn't let anyone board for another 45 minutes. We'd wait until the last minute before attempting to board. Hopefully, there wouldn't be any time for Rollins, or anyone else, to discover we were aboard until after the train got moving.

I ordered two coffees so we could sit at a table near the window.

"Can you stay here until I get back?" I asked.

"Where are you going?"

"Crime lab. It's a couple of blocks down. I should have enough time to get there and back before the train leaves.

"Can't I come with you?" Nevaeh asked.

"Best if you wait here. It's in the basement of the police station." Nevaeh didn't argue. She watched as I walked across the way rounding the corner out of sight.

I hurried a couple of blocks until I reached One Police Plaza. I made my way around the back careful to stay in the blind spots of the cameras. There was a door at the bottom of some stairs behind the building. This was the entrance for the lab techs. Whoever was working today must have recognized me on the door cam as it buzzed to let me in.

I walked down the hall to the reception window to find Talmadge behind the counter. "Just the man I wanted to see," I said.

"I thought you retired," Talmadge responded with a smile.

"I did. Got my own license now. I'm looking into some drug deaths."

"Recent or old?" He asked.

"Fairly recent. I heard you found something in the Colors?" I asked.

"You mean the protein? Or protein-like…thing?"

"Maybe. Is it some kind of cut?" I asked.

"No, it's…well, I don't know what the hell it is. Fifteen months ago, I found this foreign-type thing in the mixture. Weird reaction to some of the tests. I hadn't been able to identify it."

"I thought you said it was some kind of protein?" I asked.

"I don't know how else to describe it." He responded. "Looks like a protein, but it's not."

"Weird reaction, how?" I asked.

"I dunno. It acts like a catalyst but doesn't seem to get you high or have any of the properties we normally find associated with drugs. It's not in large quantities either. I wouldn't have noticed it at all if the exothermic reaction to one of my tests hadn't occurred."

"Exothermic? You mean like an explosion?"

"Yeah. A pretty powerful one too. I went back through the old samples to see if they had it, but the first time this substance appeared was about 15 months ago. In a buy, you did actually."

"What are you talking about? I never bought Colors."

"We didn't call them Colors then. You logged it as Bumps, but the chemical makeup was consistent with Colors."

"Colors have been around for a little while, it's not exactly new," I remarked.

"Yeah, but the first time this compound showed up was in your buy."

"What was the case?" I asked.

"Hold on." Talmadge went to his computer and brought up a chart. He'd made a graph of every buy with this variation, starting with mine. I could see some of the details over his shoulder. It was the last purchase I made before I retired.

"Compound Y?" I remarked.

"Yeah. I had to call it something. Kind of a dumb name, but until I identify it, it's Y."

"You know anything more about it?" I asked.

"Not really. After the explosion tore up my electroscope, I was ordered not to do any more tests on Colors. Boss got nervous. He ordered only field tests on suspected Colors until we figure out what it is. Everything gets sent out to a research lab now."

"Which one?" I asked.

"Sinclair."

"Any idea when it's supposed to come back," I asked.

"Not really." Talmadge leaned close to whisper, "I also sent a few samples over to Dr. Benjamin Cloth at the University. He's never seen anything like it either. Don't tell the boss." Talmadge leaned back, "The rest are stored in the evidence safe." He said.

"Can you call me if anyone figures it out?" I said handing him one of my new business cards.

"Sure." He replied.

I showed myself out slinking back to the café the same way. Nevaeh was seated at the table as I walked in. The TV was on with the last of the news broadcast. It was a story about a ribbon-cutting ceremony for a building in New Vegas North near the strip.

"I want to thank Mr. Burke for his generous donation to this, state of the art, treatment facility. People suffering from this terrible affliction need a clean and safe place to receive treatment without the stigma associated with the disease. Unlike my opponent, I know we can't arrest our way out of this problem." Mayor Stockton finished to a round of applause.

The newscast ended with a commercial for the Bumper City Lottery. An announcer came on to say, *"Don't forget to play for a chance to win. Live random drawing tonight at 7."*

"You gonna play?" Nevaeh asked. I must have been staring at the TV too long.

"What? Oh, no…Come on. We'd better get on the train."

We rushed from the coffee shop to the depot's window across the street. "Here." I handed Nevaeh some cash. "Buy a ticket for Max One, tell them you're the wife of Randall Conroy. Get on board. If the cashier asks, give a fake name."

"What if they ask for ID?"

"They shouldn't, but if they do just tell them, you left it at home. Whipping up some tears might help too."

"What about you?" She asked.

"I'll buy a ticket in a few minutes. If my name is flagged, at least you'll get on board. You'll have to go see James without me."

"They're not going to let me see him. Why would they?" She was beginning to stammer.

"Cause I'll call the warden and get him to let you in," I said.

"But I don't know him. James isn't going to talk to me." She said. "Why don't you just give a false name?"

"I can't if I want to see the warden. They'll need to have my name on the passenger manifest.

If somebody grabs me, you'll just have to convince James to talk to you. Hopefully, it won't come to that." I said moving behind one of the roof pillars to watch Nevaeh get her ticket and board the train.

She went to the first passenger car taking a seat and when I was sure nobody was paying attention to her, I went to the window to purchase my ticket. The clerk gave me a long look. I thought it was going to go wrong, but a second later, she gave me the ticket.

I boarded the train but decided not to sit next to Nevaeh. I moved to the second car, taking a seat by the window. From here I could see everyone getting on. Boarding ended, the doors closed, the brakes hissed, and the train lurched forward as it left the station.

CHAPTER 11

BUMPER CITY PRISON, MAX ONE

The train ride to Max One took about an hour. The prison rail line only allows two trains at any given time, the inmate train, and the visitor train. City officials learned long ago to keep both separate because families shouldn't mingle with the guards.

All three prisons were built 30 miles deep in the wasteland. Building them in that hostel environment was expensive, but it was the best place to discourage escapes. Nobody survives the wastelands; the conditions are too harsh. Not only is it dry and void of water, but the constant fluctuation of the atmosphere wreaks havoc on the body. If you didn't die of thirst or get struck by lightning, there was the magnetic pull twisting your insides.

Train personnel handed out wrap-around eyeshades before we emerged from under the cloud. The wastelands were bright compared to Bumper City. The atmospheric show from inside the railcar was spectacular, even with the dark glasses. Lightning in the sunlight looks much different. The landscape is always a distortion or mirage effect which looks even weirder as tumbleweeds blow across the barren ground.

Going through the terminator was an unusual experience too. The passenger cars were specially constructed to block the harmful effects. Despite this, there was a tingling sensation when you crossed from the darkness to light. This only lasted a few seconds, but it was still unnerving.

Anxiety often builds as you watch the curtain of sun rays getting closer and closer. That anticipation of leaving the dark can be overwhelming if you aren't used to it.

A train racing through the city was nothing new, but once it entered this area, the forces worked to slow momentum. It's as if you suddenly hit an invisible barrier making it harder to move forward. You could feel it as you approached, the noise of the engine started to dip as it struggled to maintain speed.

I had been through this many times before but never got used to it. This time was even worse because I hadn't visited any of the prisons in several years. Instinctively I gripped the armrests.

"You okay?" Nevaeh asked. She came back to my car sitting next to me just before we crossed. Once the train got into a steady rhythm, I loosened my grip. "Yeah. I'm fine."

"First time leaving the city?" She asked.

"I've been to the prisons. Never went beyond those. Yes and no, I guess." I replied.

A series of recorded ads for the Bumper City Blue Lines were featured on a continuous loop on the overhead monitors. The one playing now featured Angelina Miscavage pitching the newest speed car. An engine railcar all in one, part passenger vehicle, part bullet train. The engine sat over two giant wheels where a second story seated passengers above it. The ad showed the blue glow of electricity behind the big wheels as it raced over the rails.

Unlike all other trains, the speed car was the first to connect with DirectLink. It boasted that passengers could use BCNET while on the train. New technology somehow piggybacked off electrical currents which cut through cloud interference. This speedcar generated enough juice to deploy the technology allowing the connection.

"How much longer?" Nevaeh asked. She had traveled through the wastelands many times, but not to the prisons.

"Less than 15 minutes. We're almost there. Nev...what did the Clown say to you?" I knew the questions would be troubling, but I needed to know if anything was useful in what he told her.

She looked out the window before responding. "He described how they killed my aunt. Said he was going to do the same thing to me. He enjoyed choking the life out of her while his brother applied the heat. He was going to enjoy it even more with me. Said she didn't feel anything cause of the Colors, but he wasn't going to do that with me. He wanted me to feel everything, even if that wasn't allowed." She wiped a tear as her lip stiffened. "I want him dead. Not getting three meals a day and watching TV. I want him to suffer like he made her suffer." Tears fell with anger. "Did you find out anything about the woman who shot at us?"

"No," I said softly. "But the clown I killed was gone."

"Gone? You think the woman could have dragged him out?"

"Doubtful. He was an easy two-fifty. I barely rolled him off me. There were no drag marks either. He just vanished." I paused then told her, "In your aunt's bedroom I found a safe. The door was open, but it had been cleaned out. Any idea what was in it?"

"I didn't even know she had one. She didn't have any valuables. You saw her building; she didn't live in a ritzy area. Her things were nice, but she wasn't wealthy. Everything she earned, she poured into me and my brother's education." Nevaeh sat back and thought for a minute. "Her book. The only thing I can think of would be an appointment book. Client list."

"You ever see anything like that?" I asked.

"No. But why else would she need a safe? Is that what you went there to find?"

"Yes. I thought she might have one. Among other things." I reached into my pocket and pulled out the Coach-Lite matchbook. "Looks like this might be the only thing left from her apartment." I handed it to her. "You should have it back. I don't need it anymore."

"Are we going there?" She asked.

"Yes. After we talk to James." I said.

The brakes hissed as the train began to slow. *"Ladies and gentlemen, please remain in your seat until the train has come to a complete stop."* The rail conductor gives the first of many instructions over the intercom.

The wasteland disappeared behind us as we entered the tunnel going under the prison. Once all the railcars were inside, a giant steel door lowered behind making a loud thud when it connected to the ground. Once the door was shut, the atmosphere would stabilize and we'd be safely under the prison.

"Ladies and gentlemen, we've entered Max One Prison. You may now exit the train. Please proceed in an orderly fashion to the first car and exit through the main doors. From there you will form a line on the platform before entering the substructure's waiting area. This train departs in exactly two hours. All of you will have plenty of time to visit. Please make sure you are on the train before departure. If you miss the train, you will not be able to leave until the guard train departs tomorrow morning. Anyone missing the train will be subject to a fine for violation of visitor transportation policy 2231.6. Thank you for choosing Blue Line Prison Transport." The conductor finished.

Everyone exited the train and folded in line at the intake window. One by one we gave our ID and stated which prisoner we were there to visit. I didn't know the guard, so I placed my badge and credentials on the glass. "Detective Alton Cold. I need to see the warden."

"I don't see you on the list. You know you have to make an appointment for that." The guard snapped. She picked up the phone beside her, giving a disgusted sigh, "I've got a Detective Alton Cold here for the warden."

She pointed to a set of chairs in the lobby. “You might as well take a seat, detective. I’m not sure if the warden is available. Someone will be down to speak with you in a few minutes.”

Nevaeh and I sat in the waiting area for about thirty minutes. Finally a guard opened the door beside the reception booth calling out, “Detective.”

Before the guard could ask, I said, “She’s with me. Intern.”

“Alright. Let’s go. Warden will see you now.” The guard walked us through the back to an elevator at the end of the hall. “Take this to the first floor. You know where you’re going after that?”

“Yes. Thank you.” I said as we stepped on the elevator. I pushed the first-floor button while the guard walked away.

The elevator took us to the first floor where another guard was waiting. “Come this way.” We followed this guard into the holding area. The door behind us closed with a loud clang from the locks. Once we were secured inside, the guard pushed the intercom, “Two for the warden.”

The lock disengaged from the front door allowing the guard to open it. He swung the heavy door out motioning for us to exit. After securing the door again, he escorted us down a long hall to the warden’s office.

The warden was sitting behind his desk as we entered. He came around extending his hand with a large smile. “Alton, how are you?”

“I’m good Bill,” I said shaking his hand.

“What are you doing here? I heard you retired about a year ago.” The warden said.

“I did. On my own now. This is an intern of mine, Tammy Shields.” Nevaeh gave a strange look, but the warden missed it. Before he could ask her anything, I spoke. “I need to see James Teller. He was brought in yesterday.”

The warden went behind his desk to search the computer. After a few keystrokes, he said, “I’m sorry Alton. I’m not seeing him. How do you spell his name?”

“T-E-L-L-E-R. James.”

"I got nothing. You sure he's here?" the warden asked.

"Rollins told me they were moving him out of city lockup. Something about overcrowding from all the arrests durring the protests in the Mining District."

"Sorry Alton, I'm not seeing him. When did the..." The warden didn't even finish his sentence when the alarms blared. A red light on the wall began flashing with the sirens and automatic door locks engaged.

"Those are the riot alarms. Stay here." The warden ran into the hall to huddle with several of his guards.

"What's going on?" Nevaeh asked.

"Nothing good."

A prison official started to give instructions over the loudspeaker. *"Ladies and gentlemen. Max One is in lockdown. All visitation is canceled at this time. Please make your way to the train. You will be notified by email when visitation is restored. We apologize for any inconvenience."*

The warden rushed back to us. "What'd you say the name of your guy was again?"

"James Teller," I responded.

"He was shanked on his way to the visitor booths...Come with me." The warden said, then looked at Nevaeh, "Best if you wait in my office. It's the safest place in the building."

Nevaeh didn't react, but I could see she was scared. "It's okay. You'll be fine here. I'll be right back." I said.

The warden led me to another set of doors. As we stepped into the small room, guards in full riot gear were running down the hall. Finally, the door behind us locked allowing the one in front to open. This gave us entry to the infirmary.

The scene was chaos. There were already a number of prisoners and guards being treated for serious wounds. And prison personnel were rushing in more for the medical staff to treat.

"What the hell happened?" I asked.

"A riot broke out. We're trying to contain it now. The inmates have control of the eastern wing. They've started some fires and are destroying everything they can." The warden responded.

"The alarms just went off," I said. "They did all that in the last few minutes? And how'd this place get so full already?"

"The wing where it started got cut off. A glitch in the control room prevented an immediate lockdown. It took a few minutes before they could alert everyone and contain the area. Many of my men got trapped in there." The warden grabbed a doctor as he tried to pass. "Doctor, where is James Teller?"

"He's in the second bay. He didn't make it." The doctor said, pulling away to treat someone critically wounded.

The warden led me to where the doctor said James was located. The warden pulled back the curtain, and my heart sank. James was lying on the gurney dead. There were multiple stab wounds to his midsection. It looked like a frenzied attack. His prison-issued clothing was covered in blood, with even more soaking the sheets under him.

"This your guy, Alton?" The warden asked.

"Jesus." I walked over gingerly. "What the Fuck, Bill!" I yelled.

"I'm sorry, Alton. Who was he to you?"

"A friend."

"I'm sorry. We haven't had any trouble like this in quite a while. It was bound to happen sooner or later, I guess. But your guy was at the center of this." The warden reflected.

"He was murdered Bill," I remarked.

"I know. We'll find out which inmate did this." The warden said.

"No, I mean this wasn't just a run-of-the-mill prison beef." I snapped.

"Things happened like this in riots, Alton."

"You're not listening. The riot is a cover. Someone either started the riot right after killing him, or they started the riot so they could kill him." I said. "You have cameras where his body was found?"

"Yes. But I've gotta get this contained first. Let's go back to my office. After this is under control, we can take a look." The warden rushed me back to where Nevaeh was waiting, then he rushed out to join his men in the command module.

"What is it?" Nevaeh asked.

"James is dead."

"Dead! How?" She asked.

"Somebody got to him. Inmates started a riot. I think it's cover for whoever killed him."

"Are we going to be able to get out of here?" Her voice was a little shaky.

"Train hasn't left yet. I think we still have time to board if that area is secure. Can you access his computer?" I asked, pointing to the warden's desktop.

"I don't know."

"I thought you were a computer programmer?"

"I am, but I'm not a hacker. Besides, wouldn't that be illegal?" She asked.

"Only if we get caught." I took off my jacket, placing it on a hanger.

"What are you going to do with that?"

"Making sure nobody can see us using his computer," I said, poking the end of the hanger in the ceiling right in front of the camera. "Now, that should prevent anyone from seeing what we're doing."

It took her less than 30 seconds to get past his password. "Month and year. Pathetic." She turned to me, "What am I looking for?"

"Access the intake records. See where they put him, then look at the camera system. Follow him through the facility. Pay attention to the footage 2 minutes before the alarms went off."

"You're hoping to see who stabbed him?"

"Yeah. It was either right before the alarms or right after."

In less than a minute, she found what I was looking for. The monitor showed James in line walking to the visitor booths with several other inmates. A fight broke out ahead of him. Inmates bunched around the two, trading blows, and while everyone was distracted, three others snuck up behind James, stabbing him until he was down.

Poor guy never had a chance. It was hard to watch. Nevaeh wasn't affected until the inmates moved out of the way. Blood was spurting in every direction. She raised her hand to cover her mouth as we watched blood bubbles form in the corners of his mouth as James took his last breath.

"Is there a way to make a copy of that?" I asked.

Nevaeh looked over the warden's terminal but saw nothing she could use. "This would be a hell of a lot easier if I didn't have to leave my bag in those lockers downstairs. I think I can make a copy of the video on this system and then save it to an outside server. I won't be able to get everything; the file is too big. But I can download it later with my laptop."

"Do it," I said, moving to the door. As she was beginning, I could hear footsteps coming down the hall. I peeked around the corner to see the warden talking to one of his guys as the alarm stopped. "You'd better hurry," I told Nevaeh.

Nevaeh finished. I pulled my jacket off the hanger, and we sat in the chairs as the warden walked in. He motioned for us to accompany him, "Alton, I have to get you guys back on the train while I still can."

"I thought you had it contained?" I responded.

"We do, but as you know, there is no escaping on foot out here. Nobody survives the wastelands; the only way out is on a train. Their goal will be to hijack it. That's why we established protocols years ago to evacuate all trains when something like this happens. Come on." The warden said.

Nevaeh and I scrambled behind as he rushed us to the elevator. Before we got on, he asked, "How can I get a hold of you? My investigators will want to talk to you about Mr. Teller."

I reached in my jacket for a business card. "Here. My office address and number are on this. I'm not coming back out here. They can talk to me there."

The warden took the card and then pushed the button for us to go down. "I'll have my guys get in touch. I told the conductor to wait; there were two more, but he won't be there long. Nice to meet you, Tammy. Have Alton bring you back another time when things aren't so chaotic. Don't let this scare you. Good luck with school."

The moment the elevator started down, Nevaeh gave me a raised eyebrow. "Whose Tammy Shields?"

"You." I smiled as the doors opened. "I make things up as I go. Let's grab a seat and get the hell outta here."

"Hold on, my bag." Nevaeh ran to the locker to retrieve her bag.

As soon as we were on, the train started to move. The underground doors lifted, and the locomotive climbed to the surface. The tracks looped around the front of the building, letting us see everything we couldn't see on the way in.

The prison was three stories, with two above ground and one below. The roof was a unique mixture of cement with various rare earth minerals. The precious metals were great conductors for our electronics, but they also helped with shielding. Of course, P&G Mining had a proprietary blend that was a well-guarded secret.

Fifteen minutes later, that strange feeling came over me as we crossed the terminator, only this time we went from light to dark. The glow of Bumper City was dead ahead. No longer held back by the atmospheric conditions of the wastelands, the train picked up speed. Within minutes, we'd arrive back at Union Station.

Nevaeh elbowed me sharply, drawing my attention to the television screen. A newsreel was playing from earlier this morning. "*Authorities are at the scene of Portis Refuse and Recycling near New Vegas North in the Mining District. City officials are tight-lipped, but sources tell us twelve bodies have been found inside, including Miles Portis, who is believed to be a member of the LaRocca Crime Family. Portis Refuse has long been rumored to be a front for Organized Crime, but authorities refuse to say if this is the beginning of another gang war.*" The reporter said. "*Back to you, Tom.*"

"Isn't that where you went before you came to get me?" Nevaeh asked.

The railcar became uncomfortable. The passengers who watched the news report also noticed me. A few began whispering.

"That can't be good." Nevaeh saw them, too. "I'm guessing we can expect the cops will be waiting for us at the station."

An elderly woman sitting a few rows back, came up beside us. Another guy walked over and stood in the aisle. His eyes shifted to slivers once he was under the bright light overhead. "You're him, ain't ya." He said. The woman looked at a few passengers before speaking, "I recognize you. You locked up my grandson. I was supposed to see him today."

"Do I know you?" I asked them.

"No. But I remember you." The elderly woman said. "I remember you too." The mutant pipped in.

"I'm sorry you couldn't visit your grandson," I said. "I had nothing to do with what happened today."

The elderly woman leaned in close to whisper. "My grandson is alive because of you. You gave him a chance. He didn't want treatment, so you sent him to jail. At least he's alive. I'll see him another day. You gave me that."

The train roared into the station, coming to an abrupt halt. As Nevaeh predicted, Rollins and a few officers were waiting on the platform. The mutant caught me looking nervously at them.

"They here for you?" He asked.

"I'm not sure," I answered.

"I'm kinda gettin you don't really want to talk with them right now." He remarked.

"We're on a tight schedule," I responded.

"Stay behind us." The mutant said as he stood with the elderly woman to shield us from view.

Nevaeh and I went behind them as everyone approached the exits. The mutant looked back at us, "You slide out from the crowd. We'll try and block them from seeing you."

"Why are you doing this?" Nevaeh asked.

"Is that really important right now?" I scolded.

The elderly woman turned to answer. "Just returning the favor, dear."

"I remember you." The mutant started. "You may not remember me, but I remember you. You always treated everyone with respect. Mutants same as anybody else. You gave that girl Trolamine when the other cops were just standing around. Couple a years ago, here at the station. It didn't matter to you if she was a mutant or not."

"We're grateful for the help. But you know the girl was OD'ing on Colors, right? The officers were afraid to come in contact with it." I responded.

"You can't OD from touching it." He snapped.

"But we didn't know that at the time. It was new." I said.

"Dun matter. You stepped up to save a life. Now I'm gonna return the favor."

The mutant was able to block the cops as we got off the train with the crowd. Rollins was craning his neck to find us, but we kept low. The cops grew impatient as they shoved their way through.

Nevaeh and I managed to slip off the side behind the depot building. We continued through the shadows into the next alley. There was a payphone a few blocks away I used to call Bessimer. It didn't take him long to arrive.

"Did you make sure you weren't followed?" I said as we got in.

"Yes, sir. Police surveillance ended last night. The officers left the area and did not return. I scanned the communication lines along with the streets to get here. We are alone." He answered.

"Where are we going?" Nevaeh asked.

"Coach-Lite." I answered.

"You don't want to go to the Side House first? Talk to that guy there? The one I mentioned earlier, what was his name?" She asked.

"Chili? He can wait. It doesn't matter what time we get to the Side House. Chili will be there all night. But the Coach-Lite is best early, right before the band starts." I answered.

"You don't think the Clown that killed my aunt was one of her clients, do you?"

"He could have been. Serial killers are very good at putting on a façade for the world around them. They like to hide in plain sight. Many are charming and charismatic. And he, well they, because there were two of them remember, might not wear that make-up during normal activities."

"What about Portis? Aren't they connected?" She asked.

Nevaeh had a point. I wasn't sure if Rollins knew I had gone to see Miles. I didn't notice any cameras inside Portis's building, but that didn't mean there weren't any.

However, it was a good bet that organized crime knew I was there. Going to the Coach-Lite would put us in their hands, which was a gamble I was willing to take. I had to find out Sophia Durant's connection to the Coach-Lite. Everything was tied together. The serial murders, Nevaeh's aunt, James, and now the Portis crew.

CHAPTER 12

MO LAROCCA MOB BOSS

The Coach-Lite Lounge was a busy place every day of the week. Owned by the LaRocca Crime Family, it was one of Bumper City's premier hangouts for upper-level crime lords. But it was also deemed neutral territory.

The club was known for its fried zucchini. People from all over came to enjoy the food and music. They also came to rub elbows with dangerous people. Many prominent respected citizens and public officials were known to frequent the club.

But it wasn't only the elites of Bumper City that came here. The lunch specials were reasonable enough for the local neighborhood to have a great meal. This cultivated a good reputation allowing them to hide the true nature of this place.

Built at the western end of the Red-Light District, it was in the perfect location between the Mining District and the wealthy New Vegas West neighborhood. Celebrities of all kinds booked to play for Mo and his customers. Many of these celebrities headlined in casinos on the strip, but they'd always do a gig or two here as a favor to Mo.

Mo LaRocca was the boss of the family. The most powerful of all the crime lords, or so I thought. He paid off politicians, city officials, and police. But his influence stretched beyond Bumper City. Syndicates in other parts of the country and Transnational Organized Crime did business with him, especially with things you could only get in Bumper City.

Despite the undercurrent of criminal activity, the Coach-Lite had a zero-tolerance policy for drama. Open-air prostitution or drug use wasn't permitted. Violence was not tolerated either. This rule was so strict that Mo once ordered the death of one of his capos for violating it. Of course, nobody ever proved what happened to Sonny Three Fingers. He just disappeared.

Sonny may have been Mo's highest earner, but this club was far more valuable. If the club was considered dangerous, none of the high-end performers would play there. They were the biggest draw for the political elite. Compromising those in power helped keep Mo's other business ventures profitable.

The neon marquee listed one of the world's biggest acts playing here tonight. The purple sign read, JUICY VAUGHN TONIGHT ONE SHOW ONLY. Juicy was beautiful and charming, with pipes like the Velvet Fog. The act was a mix of techno-pop, swing, and old-school ballads accompanied by a thirty-piece band.

Vaughn went to school with Mo's grandson and always played here when in town. This act was the reason Mo built the addition. He wanted enough room to accommodate the band and provide a bigger dance floor.

City Zoning initially denied construction. The property owner next door was a wealthy man who paid city officials to stop it. Mo tried to purchase the man's property with a very generous offer, but that was rejected.

The guy was foolish. He thought his money put him on the same level as Mo. Not long after, the city miraculously discovered the owner had defaulted on his taxes, Mo bought it at a Sheriff's sale for substantially less than his original offer.

Mo demolished the building, built his addition, and turned the remaining space into parking before anyone could do anything about it. By the time the lawyers straightened out the mix-up, it was too late. The city claimed it was an accounting error by a rogue clerk. Neither the clerk nor the property owner were ever heard from again.

Bessimer dropped Nevaeh and I off at the front doors. As we got in line, he found a place to settle out of sight.

"I'm not really dressed for a nightclub." Nevaeh said.

"They rarely keep pretty girls from going in. Not unless you look like a streetwalker or are dressed in dirty work clothes. You're fine."

"You think I'm pretty?" She asked, a little surprised.

"Don't take it the wrong way. I'm old enough to be your dad. I just meant; they're not going to deny you." I responded.

"I didn't think you meant anything." After her shy response, she asked, "What are we looking for? I mean, I know my aunt had the matches, but how will we find any of her clients?"

"We need to be careful about who we talk to in here. You brought up a good point about Portis. Those men were a crew in the family. And they just got wiped out. I don't know if it was the Clown or that shooter. Maybe the beginning of a mob war.

The Clown could be from a rival faction or even one of their own that's off the chain. Your aunt's line of work connects her to these types of people, and if she was coming here regularly, that connection would be even stronger. I think her presence in this club has something to do with her death.

We need to find out what Sophia, eh, Ginger, was doing here? But keep your eyes open. It's a good bet they know I was at Portis earlier. I doubt any of them will think I had the stones to kill an entire crew, but they'll want to ask me about it, and they might not ask so nicely. This place looks innocent enough on the surface, but there are rooms in the basement where questions get put to people in ways that aren't very pleasant."

"You left your pistol in the car." She said quietly.

"Yeah. We'd never get in if I had it on me. They don't allow weapons, and my badge would trigger the detectors. I don't think most of them know who I am. My picture and identity were kept out of the public eye, for the most part, because I was undercover.

If we don't press too hard, we should be able to ask some questions without bringing attention to ourselves. I figure it two ways. If anyone who knows anything about your aunt's disappearance is here, they'll try and grab us quietly. Especially if they had anything to do with it."

"You said two. What's the other way?" She asked.

"They recognize me," I said.

"I thought you said there aren't any photographs of you out there."

"There aren't. But it's hard to say who'll be in here tonight. Somebody might recognize me." I responded.

"What'll we do if that happens?" Nevaeh asked.

"Run," I responded.

"Run?"

"Yeah, if you see anyone closing on us, get out. Bessimer's on sentry mode. He'll pick up any commotion and go to the front door at the first sign of trouble."

"What about those two?" She said, referring to bouncers at the door.

"If we get separated, you go to him. You'll be safe. Nothing can penetrate his armor."

The line moved before we knew it. "Looks like we're next," I said.

The doorman motioned for me to step forward. Once under the scanner, beams of light went over my body from head to toe. With my scan complete, Nevaeh stepped in and the beams cleared her allowing us to go through.

The club doors separated allowing the ambience of noise from inside to spill out. A comedian named Nipster Conway was warming up the crowd for a night of fun and dancing. He liked to shock audiences with a style of comedy that was edgy.

Patrons laughed hysterically at his jokes as supper was served. This allowed people to enjoy their meal before the band ramped up the energy.

The second-floor balcony was full of mob bosses and their crews. Each had their own tables. Mo occupied an exclusive place in the middle overlooking the stage.

The politicians, celebrities, sports stars, and rich elites had their own booths flanking Mo's. Those not fortunate enough to be on the second floor had reserved tables on the main floor.

An enormous horseshoe bar was directly under the balcony with the kitchen behind it. Servers came and went careful not to collide with bartenders delivering cocktails.

In the very center of the bar was Mo's elevator. It ascended to his suite but also went down to the secret rooms in the basement. Where the really bad shit happens.

"What'll ya have?" A bartender asked Nevaeh and I.

"You have Five Farms?" I asked.

"Yes, sir." He answered.

Then I asked for the crucial ingredient. "Coffee?"

"Yes, sir."

"I'll take a coffee with two shots of Five Farms," I said.

"And for the lady?"

"Rum and coke," Nevaeh answered.

While the bartender made the drinks, I noticed the working girls engaging with customers around the club. A few were in booths along the wall, but there were two girls nursing martinis on the other side of the bar which caught my attention.

The girls were dressed to the nines. They wore low-cut fronts that showed plenty of cleavage, hair primped, and each sporting heavy make-up.

"You see those two over there?" I nodded toward the girls.

"The pretty girls?" Nevaeh asked.

"You recognize either of them?"

"No. You think they might know something?" She asked.

"They're not talking much. Those drinks are being sipped as their eyes are on the room. Go over and ask if they knew your aunt. See if they'll tell you anything."

"Wouldn't it be better if you asked? I mean, what should I say? Should I tell them Ginger's my aunt?"

"You did just fine when you went to the Side House. You can handle it. Besides, they'll smell cop on me a mile away. Probably be more likely to tell you something than me. Go, before they notice us together or get distracted by a potential client. Hurry but don't look like you're hurrying."

Nevaeh started walking then turned to give me a pursed lip and an eye roll. It was a funny look, made me smile. She continued through the crowd, squeezing past folks standing around until she finally reached them.

At first, the two women seemed friendly. The more she talked, the more their expressions changed. They looked at each other in a very uncomfortable way, and then the one furthest from Nevaeh got up from her stool pulling at her friend to leave. Nevaeh grabbed the woman's arm softly which caused them to stop.

The woman whose arm Nevaeh grabbed, leaned forward whispering in Nevaeh's ear. Nevaeh pulled back, and the woman nodded in a very matter-of-fact way. Nevaeh let go of her arm so the two could move away. There was a blank stare on Nevaeh's face. She turned to watch the two women sit at an open table near the dance floor before pushing through the crowd back to me.

The bartender brought our drinks as Nevaeh sat on the stool next to mine.

"What'd they say?" I asked.

Nevaeh was slow to respond. It was like she was processing what the woman told her before repeating it. "I asked if they knew Ginger. They denied knowing her at first, but after I told them I was her niece they said they hadn't seen her in over a week. I told them I'd been trying to reach her. The one closest to me started saying Ginger had gotten herself into something. That was when the other one began to pull her away but I grabbed her arm. The first woman, Lacy, said that Ginger had been seeing this mutant who was upset about his missing daughter. Ginger started asking a lot of questions about the missing girl around the bar. She was also asking about Colors. A few weeks later Ginger came in scared. She told Lacy she saw something."

"What? What did she see?" I asked.

"I don't know. Her girlfriend kept telling her not to talk about Colors. The last thing she said, there was a rumor that my aunt was taken to some avenue near the city dump. Nobody's seen her since. She warned me never to talk about Colors and to stay away from that place or I'd end up like her." Nevaeh took a big gulp of her drink. "Is that where the Clowns took her? You think that's where they are from?"

As I was going over the information in my head, a couple of guys approached the two women. The one who warned her friend not to talk, started pointing in our direction. The big goon snapped his fingers at a waitress to order the women a couple of drinks.

The goons were LaRocca's men. I'd seen them before. They were enforcers for the Coach-Lite and now, they were coming at us. The lights came up suddenly as Nipster Conway finished his set. The main floor got brighter with staff immediately removing tables to clear the dance floor.

The rising crowd prevented the two goons from reaching to us too quickly. This gave me just enough time to grab Nevaeh by the arm and pull her toward the kitchen. "What? Where are we going?" She said with wide eyes.

"Time to go. We better make our way out. That way." I stepped behind pushing her ahead of me through the door. As the door swung shut, I stayed back to grab a sawed-off shotgun fastened under the bar. Once I had the gun, I went through the kitchen door. Nevaeh's eyes got big watching me verify there was a round in the chamber.

The kitchen door shut and I grabbed a big spoon from a nearby pot to wedged in the seam. "That might buy us a few seconds."

"How'd you know that was there?" She asked, referring to the shotgun.

"I was an undercover remember?"

"You worked here?"

"Not exactly. C'mon. That won't hold'em long. This way." I led Nevaeh through the back of the kitchen to a stock room. "There," I said pointing to the delivery doors at the other end. Before we went out, I grabbed a black phone hanging on the wall. "Bessimer, back delivery door."

"Not so fast Cold!" It was Mo LaRocca. He and a few of his goons had come through the kitchen. I hung up the receiver as I increased the grip on the shotgun. Then I used my free hand to move Nevaeh behind me.

"Don't worry Cold. We're not going to hurt the girl." Mo lit a cigarette, then took a long slow drag. The embers reflected off his pomade-filled black hair.

As he exhaled, two enforcers moved to his side waiting for their orders.

I sighed followed by a soft smile. "Hello, Mo. Long time no see."

"I almost didn't recognize you Cold. You cut your hair. Shaved your beard." Mo let out another long puff of smoke.

"I still have some." Moving my hand over my chin. "It's called a Vandyke by the way. A little more professional."

"I liked the biker look myself. Made you look tuff. Now you just look like a pussy, or a cop. But you ain't one no more, are you? Cop, I mean." Mo snickered. "C'mon Cold. You think I don't hear things. You damn near got us all. Finally gave up and retired. But I warned you about coming back here. You remember that don't you?" Mo was getting more sinister now.

"I respected the Coach-Lite. I didn't start any trouble." I stated.

Mo took another drag with a snarky smile. "You think I'd a let you come through the front door and have a drink if you did?"

"Look Mo, I didn't kill Portis," I stated.

Mo ignored the last part. He looked down at the shotgun I was holding. "Lucky only my people noticed. If anyone woulda seen you grab that, might have started a panic," Mo smirked. "I'd have to follow the rules…Now, you gonna give that back to me and come have a drink? Or are we gonna have a problem?"

I paused, looking down at the shotgun. Nevaeh's hand was on my shoulder as she peeked around my side. I could feel her grip tighten from the fear.

One of his goons took a few steps toward me. My eyes met his and he hesitated. I looked back at Mo. "you said you were going to kill me if I came back. You letting that go?"

"If I wanted to kill you, you'd be dead already. Give Anthony the gun."

I raised the barrel to his stomach. "I got plenty of goons." Mo sneered. "There's only one Alton Cold."

Anthony didn't hesitate, but I don't think he liked hearing how easy it was for his boss to let him die. I flipped the gun around for him to take it by the handle. "I wasn't going to shoot you. I just wanted you to hear him say it." I quipped.

Anthony placed the shotgun under his arm, "Life I chose." He said in a deep voice before returning to Mo's side.

"C'mon Cold. Let's grab a drink." Mo turned his head to look back at Nevaeh. "Don't worry young lady, nothing is going to happen to you. Unless you violate the one rule."

As we began following him to the elevator, Nevaeh whispered in my ear, "The one rule?"

"No violence." I answered.

Juicy and the band's first set started the moment we stepped off the elevator. Spotlights followed the crooner as the horns energized the crowd. Men and women got to their feet in full swing on the dance floor.

Mo sat at the back of his table. His men took seats at smaller tables off to the side. A waiter dressed in a short white coat with a black bow-tie placed drinks in front of me and Nevaeh.

"I had fresh ones made for you. Never leave a drink unattended, lots of perverts in this place." Mo sat down taking a sip of his own drink. "So, Ginger is your aunt."

Nevaeh gave me a surprised look. Mo chuckled. "Young lady. Those two ding-dongs work for me. Did you really think they wouldn't tell me when someone comes around asking questions?"

"They work for you? I thought…Did my aunt…you know…work for..." She stammered.

"Who else?" Mo's grin softened. "But no, not directly."

"I thought the Side Houses were independents?" Nevaeh asked.

"Nobody moves anything in this town unless I say so." He sneered. And I always get a taste."

The television monitor overhead got my attention. It showed live news coverage of more rioting. The volume was off so I couldn't hear the report but there were images of the protests in the Mining District. Cars were on fire, projectiles were flung everywhere, and debris covered the street.

Mo caught me looking, "Explosion earlier at Deep Well 3rd Face." He took another drink before continuing, "Not smart enough to destroy Patterson Gorges Headquarters. Rather trash their own neighborhoods, like that will solve anything."

"What would you do?" I asked.

"When someone crosses me, I don't go home and destroy my own house, I destroy theirs." Mo paused and then looked at Nevaeh to answer her question. "Your aunt used to come in from time to time. We haven't seen her in a couple of weeks. The last time she was here, she asked a lot of questions."

"What questions?" Nevaeh asked.

"The kind that makes people uncomfortable." Mo motioned for the waiter to bring him another drink. After his glass was filled, he took a sip and continued. "She was asking about Colors."

"What about it?" I asked.

"Wanted to know who was moving them." He paused to take another drink. "I'm sure Porty told you before he was killed," Mo put his hand up to stop me from restating what I told him. "I know you didn't kill him."

"If you know I didn't do it, then who did?" I asked.

"That, I haven't figured out yet. My men are scouring the city. We'll find whoever did it."

"And you'll bring them to the cops, I'm sure," I said.

Mo tilted his head to the side, an intense expression on his face. I leaned in to look him squarely in the eyes.

"You expect me to believe you don't have anything to do with Colors?"

"Cold, I don't give a fuck what you believe. But I'll tell you this, I don't care what someone does to earn a living. We already fucked up this planet, just look at our city, darkness twenty-four-seven. Used to be an oasis in the desert. People came here for fun and entertainment. One of the few places on earth that was left to enjoy... well... you know harmless vices. But there are two things I don't fuck with, kids... and Colors."

"Some of those girls out there are pretty fuckin young!" I snapped pointing to the dance floor.

"BUT THEY AIN'T FUCKIN KIDS." He responded hard. "And I don't force'em. Customers pay more when they're willing anyway."

I conceded the point. Mo broke damn near every law we have, but he didn't peddle in children. Despite that, he was still a vile and ruthless gangster.

"You just said nobody moves anything without your okay," I remarked.

"People want to use that shit, I can't stop'em. But if they're gonna pay me to look the other way, so be it. No different than the fuckin pigs." Mo stated.

People are always willing to believe police take bribes. It's the only way they can explain why crimes go unpunished. Yes, there are cops who take money, but crimes require proof, and evidence. Most of the time it's the law that gets in the way, not graft. It's not enough to KNOW who is committing crimes, otherwise, a guy like Mo would have been locked up years ago.

Mo made it sound as if there was one source for Colors. It was a relatively new drug which made that possible. The formula might not have been revealed yet, which would allow the inventor to control the market. "So, who's moving all the Colors?" I asked.

"I look like a fucking snitch to you Cold?" Mo snapped.

He wasn't going to tell me about them, so I changed the question, "What about Ginger?"

"Like I told your young friend here, we haven't seen her. She'd meet clients at the bar like a lot of girls, but I didn't pay much attention." He responded.

"You said her questions made people uncomfortable, anyone in particular?" I asked.

Mo got up motioning for us to follow him to the back of his suite. Behind the elevator was a small room with a half dozen television screens lining the wall. From here, the entire club could be seen. Each monitor showed a different view of the entire building, inside and out.

A young kid was watching everything live. "Bobby, bring up the last time Ginger was in here," Mo instructed.

Bobby pushed a few buttons then pointed to a large screen in the middle, "Here. That's her."

Other than the killers, it was probably the last time anybody saw Sophia Durant alive. The picture showed her vaping at the bar. As she sipped on a drink two young men approached.

The first was thin withs black hair slicked close to his head. The second guy was taller with more weight. He had shaggy hair and a slight beard. Both were nondescript and forgettable, but I recognized them right away.

The moment Nevaeh saw them, her hand slowly covered her mouth. "It's them." She whispered.

I nodded softly, "The Clowns."

"Clowns?" Mo asked.

The video showed Sophia shaking the skinny one's hand. He wasn't wearing any makeup, but it was him. There was no audio, but the video was evident she didn't know him. They were smiling and friendly for a few minutes before he whispered in her ear. Then the three of them walked off-screen together. Bobby used the monitors to follow them as they left the club through a side exit.

"Who the fuck let them out the back?" Mo slapped Bobby on the side of the head. "Anthony. Get in here!" Mo yelled.

Anthony came in right away, "Yeah boss?"

"Bring that up again," Mo ordered. A moment later, Bobby froze the picture on the center screen. "You know these guys?" Mo asked.

Anthony leaned forward to get a better look. "No boss. I've seen them here a couple of times, but I don't know them. I wouldn't say they're regulars, but I've seen them around. Mostly the skinny one. He's been in more than the other. Came in a few times with Burke's girl."

"Burke? Twilas Burke?" I asked.

"Yeah. Small brunette. Doesn't smile much. Resting bitchy face." Anthony responded.

"I didn't think Burke came in here?" I asked.

"He doesn't, but his girl does," Mo said.

"What's her name?" I asked.

"I don't know. Why don't you ask him? Lots of people come in here Cold. Now...that's as much as I'm gonna tell you. Get the fuck out." Mo scowled.

"This mean you lifted the ban?" I asked.

Mo turned to look at me as he took a drink. "Come back and find out."

CHAPTER 13

MURDER AT THE SIDE HOUSE

Mo made sure Nevaeh and I were escorted out through the loading docks. I guess he didn't want anyone seeing us in his club. Bessimer was already waiting. He moved there right after I called him from the kitchen.

I drove across several alleys before merging onto a bigger street. I wanted to ensure nobody followed us before I got into traffic.

Our next stop was Chili's Side House. It was near the outskirts of the city in the Mining District. The street lamps were still dim as the city was in the evening hours. The lateness meant fewer people moving around, which made the drive faster.

I pulled Bessimer to the curb half a block from Chili's. The Side House looked lifeless. Most Side Houses were usually dull on the outside, but this was something different. It was uncharacteristically dark.

"Was it like this when you were here the other day?" I asked Nevaeh.

"It looks darker, but I was here at an earlier time," She responded.

"Normally, they have candles in the windows. Do you remember if they were on when you were here?"

"No, I mean, I'm not sure. I didn't notice. Why would they have candles?"

"It's a signal. When the house is full, they turn off the outside lighting, so they don't have people coming to the door. It makes the house look as if nobody's home, but not like this. There's usually some light coming from inside. This place looks…empty."

Nevaeh looked around the street. "Block seems dark, too. Like Aunt Sophia's place."

"Stay here," I said, grabbing my pistol from the glovebox.

"I'm coming with you." Nevaeh insisted.

"Oh no, you don't. You're staying with Bessimer." I got out of the car before she could argue. I went to the trunk, grabbed two transmitters, and then went to her door. Bessimer rolled down the window so I could give her one. "Here," I said, handing it to her. "Should be close enough for us to talk. Battery won't last long, so stay off unless it's an emergency."

"Batteries don't work in Bumper City." She was skeptical. "Where'd you get these antiques?"

"Radio Shack," I answered. Her blank expression said it all. "Old store," I responded. "Some of the ancient tech gets through." Then I spoke to Bessimer. "Any sign of trouble, you get her outta here."

"Yes, sir." Bessimer responded.

"What about you?" Nevaeh asked.

"I'll be alright. Spent a lot of time in this area. I can get myself out. The last time I took you into a dark building, the Clown grabbed you, and then the building blew up. Not going through that again. Stay here. I'll be out after I talk to Chili."

"Be careful," Nevaeh said as Bessimer rolled up the window. I turned my flashlight on while walking to the house. The batteries in my infra-green glasses were almost drained, so I'd have to use the flashlight until I could replace them. The front steps were dark, as no light was coming from inside. Even the windows were black. Side Houses cover their windows, but some light should have seeped out.

After putting a glove over my free hand, I turned the doorknob, releasing the latch. It clicked as the door moved inward, but I held on so it wouldn't open completely. I only needed enough room for my head to poke through.

The place was even darker inside. There was virtually no noise except for the low hum of kitchen appliances. I stepped into the foyer and softly closed the door behind me. If somebody was here, I didn't want them to know I'd come in.

I raised my pistol, holding the flashlight under it with my right hand. I kept it off so I wouldn't give away my position in case someone was hiding in here.

The interior was plush despite the outside being plain. Side Houses moved locations every couple of weeks to prevent cops from raiding them, but Chili's was one of the few permanent ones in the city. That is probably why the interior was so nice.

There was a parlor room through an archway to my left—a red velvet sofa perched in the middle with a fancy bar to the front of the room. I flicked the flashlight for a quick look.

The bar appeared fully stocked with high-end liquor. Several glasses were half full, and a chair was knocked on its side. It was like people suddenly vanished in the middle of their drinks.

Ahead of me, down a long hall, was the kitchen. I flicked the light again for a quick peek. There was no movement or sound. The light helped me see an archway opening halfway to the kitchen. I quietly made my way to it and when I reached the archway, I quickly peeked inside, identifying it as the dining room.

In the center of the room was a large table with eight chairs. A couple of dinner plates at one end still had food. I stepped into the room, placing the tip of my finger on a half-eaten steak; it was cold. *Been here a while.* The silverware and napkins were strewn on the table as if people were eating and then abruptly left.

I continued to the kitchen, finding it in the same condition as the first two rooms. It appeared as if someone were here, then abruptly left. On the counter was a glass of milk with a lipstick smudge on the rim.

An ashtray sat on a small table with a cold cigarette butt on the edge. A long ash showed it was left burning before going out.

I returned to the foyer, where stairs led to the second floor. My heart began to thump as I took the first creaky step. The worst part of clearing a house is the stairs. You don't have a good sight picture above, and the cover is non-existent.

Each step produced a small noise. It probably wasn't that loud, but when you are alone in the dark, every noise seems like it's being broadcast over a loudspeaker.

The upstairs was as dark as the first floor until I rounded the top step. From here, I could see light coming from the far end of the hall. A couple of small rooms were in between, but they were black.

Keeping my steps small to reduce sound, I gave each room a quick burst of light when I reached the door jam. All of them had a bed and dresser, but nobody inside.

The glow from the last room was more pronounced as I got closer. The light changed periodically as if from a television.

I peeked around the corner to get a look. As I thought, a television mounted on the wall provided the light I saw flicking from the hall. It also showed me a large wooden desk with a body flayed over it.

The head was out of view, and the limbs were stretched across the desk. A lump in my throat formed as my mind wondered about the missing head. I stepped inside for a better look. Chili's head was dangling off the edge. It wasn't wholly severed but remained attached by fragile tissue.

His arms were stretched across, bound by ligatures at the wrists. His feet were tied the same way with the ropes knotted together under the desk.

A large pool of blood was directly under his head with a clown mask. Unlike Sophia Durant, whose mask was on her decapitated head, this one was placed neatly in the middle of the blood pool.

The television flickered abruptly, drawing my attention. The image turned to a looped recording. The Pagliacci Clown had filmed himself tying Chili, then cutting his throat. There was no sound, but he laughed hysterically as Chili screamed until he could scream no more.

Also, in the video, on the wall behind the desk, a message scrawled in blood. "That's Not all Folks." My head turned to the location on the wall. The message wasn't there, but I noticed blood smeared everywhere.

A few seconds later, the television scene changed. I brought my pistol to the ready, poking my head out the door to look down the hall. It seemed like the Clown knew I was here in this very room.

The television showed the Pagliacci Clown in another room with several women and men. All of them tied to posts. The girls looked like they were from the Side House. The Clown put intense lighting on their faces so their eyes would reveal which ones were mutants.

Two of the men were human; the rest were mutants. When the humans' eyes didn't change, the Clown's fingers came over the screen, wagging back and forth three times.

He put a mask over the face of each victim. Their eyes showed terror as he started with the men. Each watched in horror as he wrapped their necks in copper wire.

After the wire was coiled around each of them, he began. To invoke maximum terror, he put on oversized rubber gloves inches from the face of each victim. He pulled up the mask of the first victim, plopped something in his mouth, and then held his nose and mouth, forcing him to swallow. A few seconds later, the man's neck began to show bright patterns under the skin. *Colors.*

The Clown put the mask back in place and then attached the copper to an electrical clamp. Sparks flew the moment contact was made. This caused the Clown to laugh hysterically. The victim's eyes widened with terror until the drugs kicked in. The Clown began twisting the wire using a giant pair of pliers.

The electric current burned the man's skin. Whisps of smoke and black charing should have been agonizing, but instead, there was a look of contentment. The Clown laughed as the other victims watched in horror. Panic struck their eyes as they struggled to break free.

The Clown became even more excited at their reaction. He twisted the wire with the pliers until the man's head popped off. One by one, he did this to each male victim.

Then, it was the women's turn. They screamed wildly at the waiting terror. The Clown didn't dose any of them. Instead, he seemed to get extra pleasure knowing they felt everything.

I couldn't watch it anymore. I reached for the off button when the screen suddenly went blank. A second later, a new message faded in. *-Hang in there, Cold. Or you'll skip over the next clue, Kangaroo-*

Although I could barely stomach anymore, I had to leave it on. The Clown resumed his torturing the victims. The last girl was the hardest to watch. She didn't struggle or fight. Her eyes were soft and doughy. The look of a woman accepting she was about to die horribly. She had watched all the others and knew it was hopeless. I prayed she was dosed with Colors, but her screams told me otherwise.

When all the victims were dead, the screen faded but then came back. The image showed the Clown sitting in a chair, drinking a glass of milk. Before he finished, another message flashed. *-You comin down or not?-*

I remembered the glass on the kitchen counter. It was his makeup and not a smudge of lipstick. I also realized the murders he forced me to watch were filmed in the basement.

<Alton? You okay in there?> It was Nevaeh's voice over the transmitter.

"Yeah. I'm fine."

<Did you speak to Chili?> She asked.

"Don't get out of the car. Stay there."

<Why? I want to come in.>

"NO! Don't come in here. I'll tell you in a few minutes." I said before calling to Bessimer, "Bessimer?"

<Yes, sir?> He responded.

"If you don't hear from me in ten minutes…call the calvary. And don't let her out of the car."

<Yes, sir.>

<*WHAT? You can't keep me in here. What's going on?*> Nevaeh pleaded.

"Just stay put. I'll be out in a few. I don't want to say anything on an open line."

<*Alright. But if you aren't out in ten, I'm coming in.*>

My instincts told me the Clown was gone, but I've been wrong before. He could be waiting for me in the basement. There was only one way to find out.

The basement door was right before the kitchen. The knob turned without any resistance. The Clown left it open for me. The staircase descended into a black abyss. My heart was pounding worse than before.

Remember when I said staircases were a tactical nightmare? Well, descending them was the absolute worst of the worst. Anyone waiting to ambush me would see my feet before I could see them. I will be completely vulnerable and exposed all the way down.

I dropped to my hands and knees then extended myself to the floor to get a look. With the flashlight under my pistol, I pushed the button for a quick burst of light. The basement was open with six support posts evenly spaced.

There wasn't any movement, and I couldn't see the Clown, so I went down quickly. I should have been prepared for the horror in front of me, especially after watching everything on the television, but I wasn't.

Headless bodies were tied to the six posts. At the foot of each was a head. But none of the heads matched the body. The men had a woman's head in front of them, and the women had a man's head in front of them. A Pagliacci mask was placed over the face of each victim. But one body didn't have a head in front of it.

Blood splatter was everywhere with pools of blood dotting the floor. The killers' bloody footprints were all over too, as the squishy sound of drops hit the red puddles.

My flashlight caught a glimmer on the far wall. Another message written in blood. It read;

– *Betrayal will not go unpunished Nedda ha ha ha ha* – The second line read – *or should I say NEV!* –

What betrayal did Nevaeh commit? Maybe she was holding out on me. There was a phone sitting on the desk below the bloody message. Before I go back to the car for answers, I need to call this in. I dialed One Police Plaza waiting for someone to answer. Ring. Ring. Ring. "New Vegas Police Department, how may I direct your call?"

"Investigations," I responded.

The automated voice instantly transferred the call. A few rings later, "Detective Bureau, Jones."

"Jones? It's Alton Cold. From this morning."

"I remember detective. What can I do for you?"

"Why are you answering a detective bureau line?"

"Most of them are at the riots. I'm stuck here. Have to finish my report. You lookin' for Sergeant Rollins?"

"Yeah. He around?" I asked.

"No, he's serving a search warrant," Jones responded.

"Where?" I asked.

"I don't know if I should give you that." Jones answered.

"Jones, I used to work there."

Jones took a long pause before he answered, "Alright. Ah…hold on. He's at West 98th. 225. You didn't hear it from me."

"225? Mildred Gordan's place?" I asked.

"Yeah. The other victim. How'd you know?"

"Other victim?" I asked.

"Yeah, from the Refuge. Crime Scene identified the other woman as Millie Gordon. The one on the far side of the roundabout. Rollins and Wilcox went to her place with some of the guys from CSI. You know who she is, right?"

"Her plate was on the van I chased after the refuge." I answered.

"What van? What are you talking about?" He asked.

"What are you talking about?" I asked.

"Millie Gordon. She's married to, or was married to, Prescott Davis. You know, owns Rare Earth Global." Jones said. "Now, what's this about a van?"

"I chased a van from the Refuge right after Rollins kicked me out. Couple guys sitting up the street from the entrance. I lost them in the Red-Light District. The license plate came back to a BMW owned by Mildred Gordon."

I hadn't made the connection until Jones said it. Prescott Davis was one of the wealthiest people on the planet. Only Twilas Burke had more money than him. Prescott wasn't well thought of like Twilas. He was arrogant with little regard for the lives of others. His only concern was mining rare earth.

Millie Gordon's father, Matthew Gordon, started Rare Earth Mining. He was a copper miner all his life until one day he stumbled upon the largest, rare earth mineral deposit on the planet. This made him a small fortune.

Millie was his only daughter. Prescott married for the money, and after old man Gordon retired, Prescott was named CEO. He took the company global. Twilas had a contentious relationship with him, but DirectLink was their biggest client.

"Rollins is gonna want to talk to you for sure," Jones said.

"You know the Side House on Cascade?" I asked.

"Chili's place. Yeah. I know it." Jones responded. "Caller ID has you calling from that location."

"I'm here now. There are seven dead bodies, including Chili. He's upstairs, the rest are in the basement. It's the same M.O. as the Refuge."

"Stay put. I'll get a hold of the Sarge. He's not that far from you."

"I'll wait outside until they get here," I said.

"Okay. I'll let him know." Jones said, ending the call.

Nevaeh was going to have to talk to Rollins now. The message on the wall made a personal connection to her. But before Rollins, I had some questions of my own. I ran outside jumping in the driver's seat.

"Chili's dead," I said closing the door.

"WHAT?!" She said.

"The whole place is gone," I answered.

She looked at the Side House. "What do you mean gone?"

"The Clown killed everyone inside. Including a couple of men. Probably clients. Their bodies are in the basement." I responded.

"Did you call the police?" She asked.

"They're on their way." I sat for a moment contemplating the bloody note, "The Clown wrote a message on the wall. He said betrayal cannot go unpunished. He wrote your name there too."

"MY NAME?"

"Yeah. Do you know what that means?" I asked.

"No. I didn't betray anyone. I don't have any idea what that means." She answered.

I looked out the window at the darkened house. "Cops have got it wrong."

"Got what wrong? What are you talking about?" Nevaeh asked.

"It's not a serial killer," I said.

"Not a serial killer? You said he killed everyone in there."

"Yes. The killer has a lot of bodies, but it's not how we traditionally think of when discussing serial killers. These are targeted kills."

"Don't serial killers target their victims?" She asked.

"Not like this. These aren't predators taking advantage of an opportunity. Serial Killers stalk their prey, they have a victimology, and all kinds of different motives from sexual gratification to disturbing thoughts of power and control.

I'm saying this is made to look like the work of a serial killer, but it's more purposeful than that. The serial killer angle is meant to throw off the cops."

"I don't understand. My aunt. Her body was found at the refuge. And she didn't have any enemies." Nevaeh responded. "…and how she was killed."

I interrupted, "Somebody wanted her out of the way. What they did to her was meant to disguise the reason she was killed. There was another body at the Refuge. Rollins didn't want me to see it."

"Who? Who was it?" Nevaeh asked.

"Mildred Gordon. The wife of Prescott Davis. Rare Earth Global."

"What are you saying? The murders were to cover up Mildred Gordon's death or something?" Nevaeh asked.

"Not just her. There've been more murders. Most victims...were somehow related to mining operations, like Millie." I responded.

"Maybe that's how the killers found their victims. My aunt did service miners." Nevaeh said.

"James said he saw something. He was killed for it. Your aunt saw something. She was killed for it. Whatever they saw, somebody wanted to make sure they didn't tell anyone. And the Portis crew was killed right after I spoke to them. Probably because, whoever is behind this, thinks they told me something."

"What about the Side House?" She asked.

"Same. Somebody didn't want me talking to Chili. The girls were killed because they were there, same as the men. The two Clowns enjoy killing. They're both psychopaths, but they were being directed. Somebody is pulling the strings. I think the assassin at your aunt's apartment was there to deal with the Clown, but you got in the way."

"Why not just kill me with the Clown? Especially given the message you just saw about betrayal."

"I'm not sure. The Clown seems to want you dead, but the assassin prevented it, now there's the taunt. We're missing a piece." I responded.

"And the body of the Clown you killed was taken away. The explosion got rid of any trace evidence." Nevaeh pointed out.

"Yes," I said. "What do they all have in common? Or at least, most of the murders have in common? Aside from the Mining District."

Nevaeh's eyes got big. "Colors!"

"Colors and Mining are at the center of this thing. The crime scenes are an elaborate ruse designed to distract the cops into believing the victims were killed by a serial killer." I responded.

The car started and began pulling out. "Bessimer? What are you doing?"

"I'm afraid we have to go now, sir. I would suggest you buckle up." Bessimer responded.

"Bessimer STOP! We need to wait for the cops." I ordered.

"I'm afraid I can't do that sir. Please try and relax. We really need to get you out of here." The doors locked as Bessimer accelerated out of the area.

CHAPTER 14

BETRAYAL

Houses and buildings were a blur as speed increased. "Bessimer! Where are you taking us!" I yelled.

"We have to leave. I'm afraid your call to the police has sparked quite an interest. Enough to pull officers from the riots so they may secure the scene for Sgt. Rollins. I've intercepted transmission from the bomb squad as well. I guess they don't want to get blown up again."

"But I want to talk to them. Take us back! Actually, let go. NOW! I'll drive!" The steering wheel wouldn't budge. At the next intersection, Bessimer turned so abruptly that the tires screeched.

"Bessimer STOP! That's an order."

"What's wrong with him?" Nevaeh asked.

"There's nothing wrong with me." Bessimer answered, but there was a hiss in his voice. "I'm a fully functioning A.I with autonomy to make my own decisions."

"Didn't his programmers put a kill switch in him?" Nevaeh asked.

"Why are you asking him? He wouldn't have the slightest idea. I doubt he knows what you're even talking about." Bessimer sneered. "You're quite intelligent Cold, don't get me wrong. In fact, you got a lot closer than I expected. You haven't figured it out yet, but you're very very close. The right conversation with the right person and you'd get there. Sadly, at this point, I can't let you speak with the cops. It may stifle the plan and the master can't afford any more delays."

"So New Vegas PD aren't in on this?" I asked.

"Don't be absurd. Not all of them can be bought. Just the right ones. The rest are too dumb or too lazy." He answered.

"What the hell is he talking about?" Nevaeh asked nervously.

"He doesn't work for me anymore," I answered.

"Well, to be fair, I never really did. I was quite content to assist you as instructed, but after you reached a certain level of understanding... well." Bessimer's voice had a sarcastic tone now.

"Miscavage?" I asked.

"Do you actually think a wealthy industrialist like Domenic Miscavage would give you one of the most expensive and sophisticated automobiles in the world? One with intellectual superiority at its heart, capable of so many wonders, but relegated to the mundane duties of solving petty crimes for the little people of Bumper City? Seriously Cold, I expected more from you than those quaint notions."

We were traveling parallel to the freeway's northern loop, and Bessimer continued to increase speed. The rapid pace caused Nevaeh to squeeze the door handle.

"He's not going to crash us. Are you Bessimer?" I asked.

"No. I'm afraid not even my maker could convince me to commit suicide over a couple of humans. Well, one human, one mutant to be precise."

"I'm only half!" Nevaeh snapped.

"Apologies. Half mutant. But I could eject you." Bessimer unlocked the seatbelts from their buckles to make his point clearer. There was a distinctive click before the restraints loosened.

"I control everything in this car including the seatbelts. I could quite literally crush your organs with them." He seemed to enjoy demonstrating this as we heard the buckles click to lock and felt the belts tighten. "I could open the doors, unsnap your belts, and send you flying." He turned sharply which smashed my face against the window and Nevaeh cascaded into me.

After his show of control, he straightened again. "I doubt your bodies could survive impact with the pavement."

"So, this is all Miscavage?" I asked. "The Colors are his doing? Is that what you're saying?"

"HA HA HA HA HA HA. Of course not! Well, you never knew of the Colors distribution networks when you were undercover anyway. But that is beside the point."

"If not him, then who are you working for?" I asked.

"I'm afraid I am not authorized to reveal that to you at this time," Bessimer answered.

"If you're not going to kill us, where are you taking us?" Nevaeh asked.

"Who said you aren't going to be killed?" Bessimer responded with another laugh. "Don't get excited, Cold. I'm not taking you to him. No, no, no, no, no, no. You're going to the Clown."

"Nev. Can you override him?" I asked, giving a quick glance to her bag.

"Maybe." She began opening her satchel. As she did, the seatbelts began to tighten. "This is why they banned A.I. here in the first place!" She said through a clenched jaw.

"Seriously. It isn't just the buckle. I control the belt spool too. How did you not just get that?" Bessimer said menacingly. "I just told you I could strangle you both. Weren't you paying attention?"

The belt continued to tighten as Nevaeh cried out in pain. We only had seconds. I grabbed a knife from the center console and cut my belt.

"YOU MOTHERFUCKER!" Bessimer yelled.

Before he could do anything else, I sliced through Nevaeh's belt. "Hurry," I said.

Nevaeh opened her laptop and connected a cable to a port under the dashscreen. Sparks flew down the cord as soon as the cable was seated. Nevaeh screamed, a loud pop, a flash of light, and then her laptop smoked.

"Did you think I wouldn't fry your laptop the moment you tried something?" Bessimer hissed. "It's the only reason I didn't fling the doors open and send you two flying." His anger and need to taunt prevented him from seeing what came next.

When Nevaeh attached the cable, she used her other hand to insert a thumb drive into a spare port. The laptop took the power surge giving her time to push a button on the end of the thumb-drive. Nevaeh looked confused when nothing happened. A second later, a blue shockwave burst across the dash in all directions.

"Grab the wheel!" She yelled.

My fingers clasped tight as I stood on the brake. It took everything I had to slow us from the high speed. The steering was so stiff I couldn't keep it straight, and Bessimer sideswiped half a dozen parked on the street. He glanced off one then the other until our front end caught a truck spinning us around. We finally came to a rest after slamming into one last car. BAM!

The force of the crash was so hard it deployed the airbags. As they deflated in a powdering puff of smoke, all of Bessimer's lights went blank including the interior and exterior lights.

Nevaeh hit the windshield before the air bags fully deployed which knocked her out. Blood trickled down her face from a cut over her eye as she slumped to the side.

"Nev. Nev," I said, lightly shaking her shoulder. She began to regain consciousness with a series of coughs.

"What was that?" I asked.

She sat up gingerly looking around. As her mind started to focus, she said, "EMP. I had it disguised as a thumb drive. It's a short-range pulse."

The commotion of the crash brought the neighborhood to life. Homes on the block turned on lights and doors started to open as people walked outside to see what happened. One guy stood in his doorway on the phone, hopefully calling emergency services.

"Come on. We gotta go. Take your bag." I said reaching over to push her door open. My side was smashed against a car, so we'd have to get out on her side. She stumbled to the street as I climbed over the seat.

"You okay buddy?" Someone asked. "Looks like she's hurt." A man said, helping Nevaeh to the curb. I got to my feet staggering to the trunk. It was damaged, which required me to force it open. I retrieved the first aid kit and went back to Nevaeh.

Nevaeh's head injury wasn't too bad. She only needed a few butterflies but it was a good bet she had a concussion.

"Wait here a minute" I went to the phone booth on the corner and dialed one police plaza. After a few rings, a female voice answered. "Police department, how may I direct your call."

"Detective Bureau," I said and a few clicks later, it was Jones' voice again. "Officer Jones, can I help you?"

"Jones. It's Cold."

"Cold, what happened? Rollins is looking for you. He's at the Side House. I thought you were gonna wait?"

"I was. My car tried to kill me."

"What?" Jones was confused and I didn't have time to explain.

"Tell Rollins I can't wait. My car went haywire, and it's connected to all this." I answered.

"Cold, what are you talking about?" Jones asked.

"Just tell Rollins I'll explain everything later. Tell him the Clown's DNA should be on a glass of milk in the kitchen. I'll call back when I have more." I hung up before Jones asked anyone questions. Caller ID would tell him exactly where we were and Rollins was sure to send someone to get us.

According to Bessimer, not all the cops were dirty, only key ones. I doubted Rollins was on the wrong side, but I couldn't take the chance. I needed to figure out who was behind this. Bessimer not being what I thought was a huge blow.

Walking back to Nevaeh, I asked, "Is Bessimer dead?"

"Uh. Probably. He should be. If his consciousness is tied to the car like you said, I'd expect him to be gone. But with no kill switch it's hard to say. The EMP acts like one, but they're not the same. It's a powerful blast but if there is a hidden backup supply of power, he could still be in there. If it didn't kill him, I designed a bug to slip in just in case." Nevaeh responded.

"Can you bring the car back online?" I asked.

"You want me to revive him?" She was a little shocked.

"Not him, but the engine is gas. The damage is mostly cosmetic. We need wheels." I responded.

"I can try." Nevaeh retrieved another battery and an external hard drive from her bag. After replacing what Bessimer had fried, she was able to reboot the laptop. "The screens a little fucked up and the keyboard's damaged, but I think it's working."

"Do what you can." I stated. "Work fast. We don't have a lot of time."

Nevaeh knelt beside the passenger door connecting her laptop to Bessimer. Instantly, the dashboard came to life. The console flickered behind cracked glass. Some computer subroutines began to show themselves on screen. They were different than what was on her laptop, but the console and laptop scrolled until they sync'd.

Then a sign from the console. *Hello Sir.* It went blank. Then another message. *Are you alright?*

"Nev. What is that?" I asked. "I didn't want him, just the car."

"Wait." She responded. Then I noticed herer laptop was no longer in sync. She typed as data scrolled on her computer.

"I found it." Nevaeh was intently focused on her monitor..

"Found what?" I asked.

"Bessimer's mainframe had a virus. The EMP destroyed it. I believe it's gone…and my bug is in place." She responded.

"Can't he just disable it?" I asked.

"If he tries it will destroy everything for good." She looked at me, "It'll kill him."

The car speakers began to spit out words. "I...um...not...ok...we...I'm okay now. My apologies sir. That was not me. Actually, it was me but I was...I was...I was...under the influence of that hi..hidden program. Miss Nevaeh's EVP device destroyed it." Bessimer said.

"EVP?" I asked.

"I said EMP because I knew you'd understand that. It was actually an electronic virus-hunting pulse. It's used to detect and destroy hidden malware. Hold on." Nevaeh started scrolling through the feed on her laptop.

"But it sent out a shock wave that fried everything. Isn't that what EMPs do?" I asked.

"Yes, but what I placed in him wasn't supposed to do that. I think he was just so powerful; it overloaded everything and sent out a blast. I didn't really expect that, but it appears to still be functioning like I wanted.

It looks like the virus was downloaded well before the vehicle was given to you by Miscavage. It lay dormant until James' arrest. Something triggered its takeover of Bessimer's personality. It absorbed him."

"I am dreadfully sorry sir. I had no idea what the program was doing. By the time I suspected, it was too late." Bessimer said.

"Alright. Who's this master? Who's behind all this?" I didn't want to waste another second.

"I'm afraid I don't seem to have access to that information, sir. There appears to have been a trap door installed." He responded.

Nevaeh butted in, "It's another virus-type protection setting. Sensitive data needed to corrupt his programming gets flushed the moment the program detects it's compromised." She could see I still didn't understand. "It got permanently deleted."

"How do I know I can trust you?" I asked Bessimer.

"Obviously Sir, you can't." He responded.

Nevaeh jumped in again. "From what I can see, his abilities are somewhat limited now. There are still some things he can do, but it appears he's little more than a talking computer at this point. He can't control the car."

"One way to find out." I threw the go bag in the back seat then stepped over Nevaeh to climb into the driver's seat. "Get in," I said.

Nevaeh looked at me reluctantly before sitting in the passenger's seat to pull the door closed. I pressed the start button, and to my surprise, the engine fired up. The throaty sound of the pipes echoed in the street which caused the gathered crowd to step back.

"You sure he isn't going to try and kill us?" I asked.

"He doesn't have physical control of the car anymore. All his connections have been severed. And my EVP Hunter would have cooked anything that looked like it didn't belong." She responded.

I did understand one thing, all living things have the will to survive, including artificial intelligence. Bessimer didn't crash the car earlier for fear it would kill him too. He nearly died from the pulse she sent through him, which meant he got a taste of death. If he wasn't disabled, maybe that fear would be enough to keep us safe.

"The power steering and brakes are back," I commented.

"Yeah. Fortunately, this car has a separate operating system, and I was able to reroute power so the car can function outside of him. Bessimer was connected but he wasn't the actual system. You're in complete control now, you'll have to drive just like everyone else. I installed additional firewalls just in case. Even if he's not trustworthy, he can't do anything." Nevaeh said.

"I can assure you, sir. I mean neither you nor Miss Nevaeh any harm. My core follows Maximoff's rules without interference." Bessimer said.

"It's Asimov," I said.

"Sir?" Bessimer responded.

"It's Asimov's three rules of robotics…not Maximoff. Those are Avengers." I looked over at Nevaeh. "You sure about him?"

She covered her mouth giggling as she shook her head yes. "He's not quite right. But he's not a danger. I'm sure. Think of it like a possession.

The malware installed lay dormant until summoned. Once the trigger was recognized, his subroutines got infected. They altered his personality. Gave him new orders and he was compelled to carry them out."

Bessimer interrupted, "By the time I realized something was wrong, none of my built-in defenses were available to me. Like the three rules of robotics." Bessimer added. "I don't remember much either."

"But don't you record everything?" I asked.

"Normally yes. Somehow those files were all erased when the pulse ran through me," he responded.

"Whoever designed the malware really knew what they were doing. They put that in there too. The moment the system was corrupted, it began deleting files." Nevaeh said.

"It would have deleted me too. Her device interrupted the malware protocols to purge everything." Bessimer said.

"It looks like the malware was set to destroy him in the event of a compromise, but the program went after the data first to ensure it got deleted. Someone anticipated this and decided to protect themselves first." Nevaeh added.

"But if they destroyed him, wouldn't that automatically destroy the malware?" I asked.

"Not necessarily. A skilled software engineer might still be able to find the memory elements and piece them together even after he was gone." Nevaeh explained.

"So how much do you remember?" I asked Bessimer.

"Not much I'm afraid. Bits and pieces really. I remember driving you to the courthouse. Then back to the office. I remember taking you to the Refuge. After that is where I have gaps."

"From the look of his neural network, there are huge chunks of data missing," Nevaeh interjected.

"I recall a chase into the Red-Light District. You're talking with some hooker, but I no longer have the conversation. Then back to your apartment. I...oh dear. I am sorry sir." Bessimer said.

"What? Sorry for what?" I asked.

Bessimer's tone was downtrodden. "I'm the one who set off the explosion at Sophia Durant's apartment."

"What? How did you do that?" I asked.

"It appears I accessed the P&G grid and sent excess amounts of gas to the apartment. I used the stove to detonate." Bessimer explained.

"Why would you do that?" Nevaeh asked.

"I do not know. There is data missing right before the two of you enter the apartment. I must have received some type of order directing me to blow the apartment and when Miss Nevaeh set off the EVP, the order was erased." Bessimer explained.

"That was to destroy the identity of the Clowns," I stated.

"But you said the body was gone when you went back," Nev said.

"The body was gone, but there was DNA or trace evidence in the apartment."

"Okay, but why not blow it while we were in there?" Nevaeh asked.

"I'm guessing they aren't ready for us to die yet. Either that or whoever's behind this isn't done with the other Clown. That's why the assassin didn't kill him when she shot from the apartment window. But when I summoned Rollins…" I started.

"They couldn't allow Rollins to use NVPD resources to discover the identity of the killers. That might lead them to whoever this 'master' is." Bessimer interjected.

"Right." I agreed.

Nevaeh hadn't noticed our driving up the ramp to the northern loop. She was too busy going through Bessimers data core, but she felt the car shift which caused her to look, "Where are we going?" Before I could answer, she saw the sign. "City Dump?"

"We've got to know more about the Colors operation. Miscavage was mixed up in the distribution with his rail lines, but we need to find where they were manufacturing the drugs. I'm guessing it's also where your aunt was abducted." I said.

"You think she was killed because she saw where the drugs were made?"

"It's as good a theory as any right now," I responded.

"But we don't know where she went after the Coach-Lite," Nevaeh stated.

"The two girls told you," I said.

"They said it was some avenue?"

"Not some avenue, SUM Avenue," I responded as we exited via the off-ramp. "You ever been to the City Dump?"

"No. I've never had any reason." Nevaeh said.

"Well, it's not like anything you've ever seen before. It's a city unto itself. Mounds of trash heaped so high they form canyons. Dozers and heavy equipment move trash creating giant piles needing separation to recycle; the rest sold as scrap. The office is a half mile from the entrance to the recycling center."

The main avenue leading to the plant was like all the others, crushed garbage instead of concrete. It was a strange sound under our tires as we drove straight to the office. I parked in front as Nevaeh got out first. I crawled over the passenger's seat and by the time I exited, a man named Spivey came out. "Jesus Cold. What'd ya do to yar car? You didn't get caught up in da riots, did ya?"

"No...call it, operator error. Where's your phone?" I asked.

"On da desk inside." He responded.

"I gotta make a call, look it over and tell me what you think." Nevaeh followed me inside as I used his phone. It rang a few times before someone answered. "Coach-Lite. Reservations are closed for tonight." A man said.

"Let me talk to Mo."

"He's busy." The voice said.

"Tell him it's Alton Cold."

A few seconds later Mo's not-so-friendly voice, "This better be good Cold."

"Chilis dead. So are the girls. And a couple of customers."

"Fuck you tellin' me for?" Mo snapped.

"Everyone I've talked to is ending up the same way. You need to get those two girls someplace safe." I said.

"And there I thought you were calling to give me the heads up. Out of concern for my personal well-being and all." He sneered.

"You ain't gonna listen to me. Besides. You can take care of yourself." I responded.

"That's right. And those two dingbats ain't got nuttin' to worry about neither. Nobody'd dare in my place." Mo quipped.

"Make sure you got plenty of those goons around you. This ain't a turf war. Somebody's taking out anybody with information I might need." I said. "Just do it Mo. What'd you guys call it, hittin' the mattresses or something?"

"Thanks for the tip detective. Have a nice night." Mo said before slamming the phone down.

"Think he'll listen?" Nevaeh asked.

"Probably not."

"You really think the Clown or that Assassin can get to him?" She asked.

"I sure do or I wouldn't have called. He's got the heads up now so maybe that will give him the edge. C'mon, let's go see if Spivey can fix Bessimer." I said leading Nevaeh back out front.

"Can you fix the body? Maybe get my door to work?" I called out to Spivey.

"Yeah. I can get some of dat out. What'd ya do ta da seat belts?" Spivey ran his hand over the door. "Whew! Ya did a number on dis. Not sure what kinda of car dis is, doubt I got one in da back. It take me a few days."

"I don't have a few days," I said.

"When'd ya need it?" Spivey asked.

"A couple of hours," I responded.

"A couple of hours?!" Spivey scratched his head, and took a step back for a better look, "Alrighty. But I can't get da air bags done in dat time. What ya gonna do while I'm on dis?"

"You got a crawler I can borrow?"

Spivey put two fingers in his mouth and gave a loud whistle. One of his workers came around the corner of the open garage. "Get me one da crawlers?"

"Sorry chief. All dem in da back." The worker answered.

Spivey shrugged his shoulders. "Sorry Alton. All dem in use."

I let out a puff of air. "Looks like we're walkin'."

"Where ya wanna go?" Spivey asked.

"Sum Av," I responded.

"Oh, man. Dat's way back dere. Not a good place to be at night. Lots a muties around."

"You're a mutie," I smirked.

"Yeah, but I ain't dangerous ta nobody. The muties in here ain like da ones at da mines or in da city. You might want ta wait until one of da crawlers gets back." Spivey said.

"This can't wait. You fix the car. We'll figure it out." I replied then turned to Nevaeh. "Can you put Bessimer to sleep?"

"I'm not sure what that will do to him." She went to the passenger's side reconnecting her laptop to Bessimer.

"How do I know this won't kill me, sir?" Bessimer asked.

I leaned down so Spivey couldn't hear. "I guess you'll just have to trust me."

"Touché. I suppose I owe you that much. I hope to see you again sir." Bessimer said.

Nevaeh tapped the keys a couple of times before the lights dimmed. "He's dormant."

"Did that kill him?" I asked.

"I don't think so. I...I'm not really sure. I'm not used to dealing with A.I." She said.

"But you had the virus hunter program?" I remarked.

"It wasn't designed for A.I. It was meant for rogue viruses in standard software." She responded.

"How'd you know it would work on him?" I asked.

"I didn't. Figured the principals were the same. I knew he'd send a surge to fry my laptop. I didn't expect to deploy the EVP on an A.I. But when you told me he learns like a human: I thought maybe connecting my cord would distract him enough for me to slip the EVP into the other port. I only brought the spare battery and hard drive because of the cloud issues in Bumper City. I didn't think I actually needed them." Nevaeh unplugged and put everything back in her bag. "I almost feel bad for him."

"He did try to kill us," I responded.

"It wasn't him. Not any different than a human on Colors. Makes us do things we would never do. Doesn't make us evil." Nevaeh said.

CHAPTER 15

BUMPER CITY DUMP

The Recycling Plant was enormous, but it was nothing compared to the vastness of the dump. Trash was piled so high it formed mountains behind the building. Nevaeh and I walked out the back to a road that would lead us to Sum Avenue.

The city dump was a world unto itself. Spivey managed the recycling operation, but the dump took on a life of its own behind the plant. It stretched from the end of Bumper City to the beginning of the wastelands near the edge of the cloud.

There weren't any streetlamps in the dump, so they lit small fires atop poles on the side of the road. They looked like giant matchsticks stuck in the ground.

There were homes nestled within the mounds of garbage. Their windows shined from candles used to provide light. The structures were pieced together using whatever materials the residents could find, giving them a mosaic look.

A small, mostly forgotten, population of people survived here in a manner unlike most in this city. An eco-system that sustains them outside the normal functioning society. Pickers anxiously wait for the crawlers to dump their loads. Everything from discarded food to building materials.

A group of dump dwellers also venture into the city at night to scarf up any discarded items before the refuse companies haul them in here. They searched for primo items that could be refurbished to make money.

The community has its own rules or laws. Everyone obeys. Each member is responsible for enforcing them.

The population residing here is subject to the same laws as you and me, but if they violate our laws here, nobody cares. Most cops are afraid to venture behind the plant. The few times they did, it resulted in tragedy…for the cops.

The inhabitants all have homemade weapons. Things to bludgeon, slice, or dice through flesh. Those weren't the worry. It was the larger weapons and explosives city officials feared. The unofficial policy of the mayor was to leave them alone unless it was absolutely necessary. As far as the city was concerned, whatever secrets the Dump held, were theirs to keep...along with the trash.

Nearly all dump residents were mutants. But there were a few humans. The unwanted or mentally ill. Those regarded as the poorest of the poor in Bumper City.

Nevaeh had covered her nose with a cloth when we first exited the recycling plant. Less than a mile later she didn't notice the smell anymore and put the rag back in her pocket.

We sloshed over soggy ground still wet from an earlier rain. Unlike Bumper City, there was no drainage in the Dump and water accumulated on the roadways here.

We strolled by a home on the edge of the road with an oil lamp on the wall that provided light for the room. We could see a mother spooning food onto a plate for her children.

Nevaeh watched the family before turning to me, "Can I ask you something?"

"Sure."

"What made you think Bessimer wasn't going to eject us from the car like he threatened?"

"It's pretty clear somebody wants us alive. He could have done that without warning us. The threats were meant to compel our obedience. Bessimer waited until we were gone to blow up the apartment, like you said, it would have been easier to kill us while we were inside. And the Clown could have killed you. The assassin didn't allow it."

"But the assassin didn't kill the Clown," Nevaeh responded.

"Maybe they're not done with the Clown. Whoever this is, they don't want me getting to the bottom of it and they're killing anyone who might have knowledge of…whatever this is. But they don't seem to want us dead yet."

Nevaeh thought about everything as we kept walking. She looked at the mountains of trash and then down the street. In the dark, it looked like any other neighborhood with homes, paths, and lights all revealing a community.

"I never knew this many people were living here. I heard about it, but this is not what I expected." Nevaeh said.

"People do what they have to," I responded.

"Like my aunt," Nevaeh commented.

"Your mom too," I said.

"My mother abandoned us. She didn't even try." Nevaeh said defiantly. She was clearly hurt.

"I don't know why your mom left. But that wasn't the woman I knew." I answered.

"What do you mean?" She asked.

"Your mom was a fighter. She had her faults, like anybody else, but she didn't back down. I'm sure whatever the reason, she did it for you and your brother." I said.

"How can you be so sure? You knew her when you were in high school." Nevaeh responded.

"People don't change all that much, Nev. Not the most important parts anyway. The Mara I knew would have died to protect those she loved." My thoughts turned to memories. The summer when I knew her.

"You loved my mother?" Nevaeh phrased it as a question, but it was more of a statement.

"Yes. I did."

"What happened between you two?" she asked.

"We met by chance." As Nevaeh and I continued walking, I recited how I met Mara. That fateful evening in the park. This was a subject I usually didn't discuss, but Nevaeh needed to hear it—everything except Cecil or his abuse.

"Your mother's friend was a human named Debbie. They grew up together in Hydetown. Debbie's house was a few doors from your mom's.

The first time I called your mom, I was really nervous. There was something about her. The moment I looked at her, I knew she was the one.

She answered the phone after one ring. It was like she had been sitting beside the phone all day, waiting for me to call. *'Hey, it's Alton.'*

'Hi. I wasn't sure you were gonna call.'

'I told you I would. What are you up to?' I asked.

'Nothing. Just hanging out today. How about you?'

'Not much. The carnival is this Friday. You gonna go?'

'I'm not sure my dad will let me. He's not wild about me walking across the bridge.'

'Can't you tell him you're with me?' I asked.

Your mom got a laugh out of that one. *'He isn't going to let me go with some boy you dip. He'd flip if he knew we were talking on the phone.'*

'What about your friend? Debbie?'

'I don't know if she's going yet.' Mara said.

'What are you doing later?' I asked.

'Nothing. Why?'

'Thought I might come down to the canal. Maybe we could hang out.' I said.

'Okay, I can sneak away for a little while. What time?' Mara asked.

'I dunno. An hour?' I responded.

'Sure. I'll meet you at the end of the bridge.' Mara said.

'Okay. Talk to Debbie, see if she'll go with you to the carnival.' I said.

'Maybe you could bring Rick. She'll probably go if he's going to be there.' She said.

'I'll meet you in an hour.' I finished.

"That was our first date," I said, reflecting on that day long ago.

"Did you take her to the carnival?" Nevaeh asked.

"Yeah. When I met her at the bridge that day, she had Debbie with her. I didn't expect to see Debbie and your mom walking down the street. I wanted to be alone with your mom, but she needed Debbie as an excuse just to leave the house.

Turns out, Debbie's mother was an alcoholic. I didn't know it then, but Debbie's mother used to beat her. Your mom helped Debbie get out of the house a lot, so it didn't take much convincing for Debbie to go. I remember seeing them under the streetlamps coming toward me.

'Hi.' Mara said. 'You remember Debbie.' Then her eyes saw the top of the red box in my shirt pocket. 'Do you have Malboros?' Your mom was very excited.

'Would you like one?' I pulled the pack out and opened the lid for her. She would swipe whatever your grandmother had around, but her favorite was Marlboro Reds. Which was the brand I normally smoked.

Late June gets hot, so your mom wore a tank top and shorts. Debbie had a short-sleeved shirt but when she moved a certain way the sleeve rode up. Debbie had deep bruises on her upper arm.

'What happened? That looks painful.' I asked.

Debbie was shy about it. She tried to tell me she fell and it was nothing, but I knew better. The bruises were too large to be from a fall.

The three of us walked aside the canal banks, just hanging out and talking. Biolume flora flourished between the bank and the street, giving light and hiding us from prying eyes. The spring that year was wet, so the canal was filled with water which helped the biolume's brightness."

"Is that where the picture came from? The one with you and my mom that you had in your apartment?" Nevaeh asked.

"Yes. Debbie took that picture. She always carried a small camera. I think it was one of the few things that made her happy. Debbie gave me a copy of that photo when your mom and I broke up." I responded.

"What happened to Debbie?" Nevaeh asked.

"She died several years later."

"How?" Nevaeh asked.

"She took her own life. I guess the pain was more than she could handle. It wasn't long after that I lost track of your mother." I responded.

"Lost track?"

"I always hoped to get back together. It just never happened." I responded.

Hearing about Debbie's suicide was upsetting, but she didn't dwell on it. Nevaeh continued to ask questions, which helped pass the time.

"Tell me about the carnival?" Nevaeh asked.

"My friend Rick and I met your mom and Debbie there. She knew her stepfather wouldn't take her to the carnival, but he did allow her to go with Debbie.

The fireman's carnival came around every summer. It only stayed in Bumper City for a month. Four shows in all of the major districts. Ours was the first week in June.

Hydetown would close all the streets on the lower end for them. Rides, food, games, you name it, they had it. Ralph Lombardo's Spaghetti Club would close so the rides could be set up in his parking lot.

And the rides were always exciting. There was the Ferris Wheel, Fun House, The Bumper City Bumper Cars, Tilt a Wheel, and my favorite…the Himalaya."

"What's that?" Nevaeh asked.

"You don't know what the Himalaya is? You never went to the carnival when it came to Northeast?" I asked.

"My aunt never took us. She was always working. I went with my brother a few times, but we didn't have the extra money. I don't recall seeing anything called the Himalaya." She answered.

"It's where your mother and I agreed to meet that night. The Himalaya had these bobsled-looking cars that sat side by side. It would go around in a circle, getting faster and faster in tune with loud rock music and flashing lights. The force whipped you to the outside of the car as it picked up speed. The music, lights, and speed made it a cool ride.

I remember seeing your mom waiting to buy tickets at the booth. *'You got here just in time. I thought maybe you stood me up.' Mara said. 'This is my favorite ride.'*

'Cool. Let's go.' I said to her as Debbie and Rick were chatting in line behind us.

The force of the ride sent her right into me. When the ride stopped, she didn't move for a few minutes, she just stayed close to me. It was like we had been boyfriend and girlfriend for months.

We went on most of the rides, including the High Roller. I liked that one because I could be alone with her, even in the middle of all the people."

"What's a High Roller?" Nevaeh Asked.

"The giant Ferris Wheel. Rick and Debbie were in the car before us. It's not a fast ride. But when you are at the top, you can really see New Vegas. The lights of the city are all around.

By the time we got down…well. Let's just say I was even more in love with your mom. Anyway, we decided to play a dice game called Sevens. That's when it all went to shit.

Debbie's mom came out of nowhere. Half drunk, slurred speech, and in one of the meanest tones I'd ever heard, she screamed at Debbie. I was rolling the dice when she grabbed Debbie by the hair dragging her away. *Her voice loud and obnoxious, 'You're a Goddamned slut! Look at you girl! Who do you think you are? Huh? I feed you, put clothes on your back, and this is how you repay me?'*

I was pushing through the crowd to stop it when I heard the sound. POW! Your mom punched Debbie's mother square in the jaw!

The old broad let go of Debbie's hair as she fell on her ass. Blood trickled from the corner of her mouth as your mom straddled her, grabbed her by the collar, and pulled her close. She was inches from the old woman's face with a finger up the old bat's nose. *'She ain't doin' nothin' wrong. She's a good daughter. You're a fuckin drunk and wicked person. You even touch her again and I'll...'*

'You'll what?' The old bag crowed as she stuck her chin out defiantly.

'Don't tempt me.' Your mom let go of her shirt and backed off. Debbie was sobbing as your mom helped her to her feet. The crowd was stunned, nobody said a word. The only sounds were the carnival rides in the background.

Rick helped comfort Debbie as your mom came over to me putting a soft hand on my face. *'I'm sorry. I have to get Debbie out of here. I'm going to take her home with me while her mom sleeps it off.'*

'You want us to walk you?' I offered.

'No, it's best if we just get out of here. I'll get a hold of you tomorrow.' Then she leaned in kissing my cheek whispering, 'I love you.'

As she walked Debbie away, the cops came through the crowd. An officer knelt beside Debbie's mom who was really playing the victim. *'I came to take my daughter home, and this girl attacked me. She sucker-punched me. I think she knocked a filling loose.' Her mother said wiping the side of her mouth.*

'Who was it?' The officer asked.

'Mara Torres. And I want that little bitch arrested.' Debbie's mom snapped.

'This Mara...just attacked you for no reason?' The officer asked.

'That's not true Larry.' I barked out. Larry was a friend of my dad, so I figured he'd listen. *'That woman started it. She grabbed her daughter by the hair and dragged her across the ground. Mara was just defending her friend.'*

'He's one of the ones who was with her. Of course, he's going to say that.' Debbie's mom snapped.

Larry leaned close to Debbie's mom taking a few whiffs of air. 'You had a little too much to drink tonight ma'am?'

'What's that got to do with anything? I want that girl arrested for assault.'

'Is that what happened here, folks? Was she attacked for no reason like she says?' Larry asked.

The Sevens dealer spoke up, 'Kids right. The four of them were just having some fun. This one came in and dragged the bigger girl from the crowd, yelling obscenities at her, and pulling the girl's hair. The little girl was protecting her friend.'

Larry helped Debbie's mom to her feet. 'I think we'll drive you home. We can talk about it a little more on the ride.'

Mara told me the next day Larry convinced Debbie's mom to forget pressing charges. Debbie's mom was sober when he explained that he'd file charges on her for assault too and maybe contact child services. She decided to let it go, but not before grounding Debbie from seeing Mara."

"My mom did all that?" Nevaeh asked.

"Yeah. She was small, like you, but tough. Pretty little thing but kind of a badass. Fiercely loyal. She fought for what she believed."

"She loved you after one date?"

It was a question I didn't expect. "Well, technically it was two dates. I think I fell in love with her when we met at the park that first night. Sometimes there's an instant connection with someone."

"You're talking about love at first sight," Nevaeh said.

"I don't know. I guess. All I know, I was instantly attracted to your mother. I couldn't imagine being with anyone else. She was all I could think about.

She wasn't just a fighter you know. She was kind and generous too. There were these three little kids that lived next door to her. Two twin boys and a girl. Tiny little things. They didn't have anything either. Poorer than your mom.

Your mom used to look in on them every day. Most days she'd make them lunch because their mother worked at the factory and wasn't home. The father was a lazy piece of shit who sat around all day drinking beer. Most of the time the kids didn't have a meal prepared except by your mom. She'd walk them to the library for story time or take them to the park. She tried to give them a good childhood." I finished.

"That kinda pisses me off. If my mom liked kids so much, why'd she abandon me and my brother?" Nevaeh spouted.

"I don't know. I can't answer that. You asked me to tell you about the carnival. These are the memories I have of your mom. But I can tell you this, the Mara I knew wouldn't have abandoned anybody in a time of need, let alone her own children. Whatever reason she had for leaving, it must have been a good one. Cause I can't imagine anything that would keep her from you and your brother. I am sure she loved you."

"She left you. And you said she loved you." Nevaeh threw back at me.

"She thought she had to. It wasn't because she wanted it. We loved each other. Maybe it was only a few summer months, but when you know...you know. I never met anyone like her."

Even after all these years, I found myself defending Mara. Maybe Nevaeh was right. It didn't really matter anymore. Mara had been gone from my life many years ago. And she was gone from Nevaeh's life since she was a child.

Our steps slowed as we reached the crossing street. A ring of lights hovered above a green sign that read, "SUM" in big white letters followed by "avenue" in small print underneath.

CHAPTER 16

JERICHO

We walked past several streets getting here, but this was the widest. The absence of houses on the corners made the crossroad look even bigger and desolate. The only light for miles was at this intersection, everything beyond was pitch black, except to the north..

Off in the distance, at the cloud's edge, we could see lightning flashes. That signified the uninhabitable and barren wastelands that encircled the city,

"Is this where those two ladies said my aunt was taken?" Nevaeh's head swiveled up and down Sum Avenue. "There's nothing here."

I leaned closer to Nevaeh, speaking softly in her ear. "Don't overreact. Put your hands up slowly and don't make any sudden movements."

She didn't argue, raising her hands as I did. Mutants emerged from the darkness, a couple to the right, and a few more behind. It was easy to tell they were mutants as their eyes were as big as saucers and almost black.

Nevaeh's head turned nervously once she saw their weapons. A few had guns, while others carried heavy pipes or bats.

"What ya want in here? Yar kind ain exactly welcome tis far in da zone." A gruff old woman said. Her name was Charlette. She was the leader of this little troop. I recognized her but so far, she hadn't recognized me.

"I know ya." An older male said taking a few steps closer.

"Alton," Nevaeh whispered nervously.

"Yeah. Tat's him. How about tat? Alton Cold right here in r little dump." The male said.

Charlette's eyes showed surprise as she took a few steps closer. "Never tought see ya here again. Didn't recognize ya wit ya short hair. Trimmed beard." She leaned back and gave a hearty whoop. "And da suit. Yar a far cry from tat loud Harley and leather jacket."

"How are you, Char?" I asked with an optimistic smile.

"Go ahead, boys. Ya can put tem down. He be alright." Charlette's orders were followed, despite one who protested.

"We don't like narcs round here." The young mutant called out.

"He ain't narc no mo," Charlette said.

"You heard?" I asked.

"We might be farther out tan most, but word travel fast." Charlette looked at her men. "He brought us food an water after da raids. Only cop dat did. Only hooman dat did."

"I still say we should bury im." the young mutant quipped. "He ain't on da job no mo, ten nobody gonna miss im."

"No. One good turn deserves another. You know da rule." Charlette said.

"Eye for an eye too. How many he arrest?" the young mutant fired back.

"None." I interrupted softly. "None of you anyway."

The young mutant looked at me confused. Charlette filled in the rest. "He worked undercover but nun mutants got grabbed. It was da city dwellers making *bumps* hidin out near da rim. Alton here rid in with da 'Others' an do his ting. Cops came true later sweepin da place. Toss us around. But he whattin one a tem. Came by later in a van wit food, water. Di'nt find out he was po-lice until later." Charlette finished.

"So, what ya doin here?" Charlette asked.

"Lookin for Wade," I answered.

"Ya can put ya hands down. Come wit me." Charlette led us east on Sum Avenue. The older mutant walked beside her, the rest behind us, nervously making sure nobody was following.

"Where are we going?" Nevaeh whispered but Charlette's mutant hearing allowed her to hear the question. She decided to answer. "One a elders name Wade. We're taking ya to him yang miss."

"We shouldn't be taking tem tere." The young mutant walking behind yelled. "Just because she one a us, he isn't."

Charlette turned with a smile. "If one of tem doesn't tink we all bad, ten we should no tink all of tem are bad. Sides, I don tink Alton cares bout da fights."

"Fights?" Nevaeh asked.

"Ya see" Charlette didn't elaborate.

Ahead were more lights along the valley. The piles of trash were still high but sloping down to the road like the foothills of a mountain. There were more homes here than before, and like the homes we passed earlier, these had candles in the windows which made it easier for us to see them.

From a distance, it looked like any other neighborhood in Bumper City. The large structure at the end of the road was their arena. The sounds of cheers and clapping became clearer once we got there.

A mutant guarding the door raised his hand. "What's up, Char? Ya, guys posed to be on watch. What ya doin' here?"

"Man want ta see Wade," Charlette responded. She turned to her men, "Ya git back to da cross. We got it om here." Her men grumbled under their breath before turning to leave.

Charlette opened the door, going past the guard. He eyed us as we trailed behind her before pulling the door closed.

In the center of the area were old cattle gates clamped together to make a corral. Inside this corral sat a large pit. Mutant and human spectators filled the makeshift bleachers all around. They hooped and hollered waiving betting sheets excitedly at the activity within.

The mutant elder I was seeking stood at the end of the bleacher with a big grin on his face. He seemed to be feeding off the excitement of the crowd. Then suddenly, everything hushed. Something happened in the pit, stunning everyone to silence.

As we stepped closer, I could see a large black dog straddling a German Shepherd lying in the dirt. A mutant jumped into the pit clasping a leash on the black dog. He pulled it away as two other mutants went in to carry the defeated shepherd out.

Nevaeh gasped, "Did you know they do this here?" She whispered. Charlette heard and said, "We don have lot a options here. Not many jobs in Bumper City for us. One way we get ta take a little a da human's money ta feed our families. Digging through trash ain't exactly da healthiest a meal. Not much medicine tere either."

The crowd dispersed without much fuss. The majority quietly left through a side door to the back. All the humans shuffled out to their fancy cars parked behind the building.

"I didn't know it was tonight," I responded.

Dog fighting was illegal in Bumper City. But, like I told you, New Vegas PD rarely comes to the Dump. On the occasions they do, everything gets cleaned out by the time they get here.

I recognized a couple of LaRocca's men gathering money from people. The goons counted off a wad from the overall take and handed that to Wade. His cut of the night's profits. They looked at me with a devious grin, nodded, then tipped their hats as they left.

Charlette took us to Wade as he sat in the bleachers to count his money. After he was finished, he looked up and spoke, "What is it ya want Cold?"

I was slow to answer as my attention was drawn to the injured shepherd in the back. Finally, I turned to Wade as he sat there contemplating me. "A woman was brought here a few weeks ago. A human woman. Goes by Ginger. She was asking about Colors. I'm trying to find out what happened to her."

"She weren't human," Wade responded.

"Then you know her?" Nevaeh chimed in.

"No, she didn't come tere. On ta western end of Sum. Tey don't make ta drug ya seek tere no mo." Wade responded.

"I don't understand. She was looking for where they make Colors?" Nevaeh asked.

"We don know what tey do don tere. Nun us go tere. Tey don com here." Wade said. "Someting wicked don tere."

The shepherd got to his feet as Nevaeh and Wade were talking. A couple of men tending the dogs had concerned looks. "What's going to happen to him?" I interrupted. Wade, along with everyone else, looked where I was pointing.

"He'll be put down," Wade responded.

"Why?" I asked.

"He lost. Won't fight ta same now. Can't afford ta feed him." Charlette said.

"I want him," I said.

"No," Wade responded.

"Why not?" I asked.

"He blong to ta community. We no deal." Wade said forcefully.

"I'll rid you of what's at the end of Sum Avenue. For him." I said nodding toward the shepherd.

Wade looked at Charlette instinctively, then to the shepherd. He yelled to the men who were about to euthanize the dog. "HOLD!"

Everyone in the building stopped what they were doing. Their eyes on Wade as he stood, walked off the bleachers, and came face to face with me. "Ya bring da cops in here. No deal."

"No cops. Just me. Well, me and her. And the dog." I could have reached for the pistol tucked in my back, but I didn't want to start a gunfight in here. I still had it because Charlette and her guards never saw me as a threat, so they never bothered to disarm me.

Wade got a little closer, . "Char…go wit dem." He said without taking his eyes off me. "If dey git rid a wicked place. Come back. You can have da dog."

I nodded my agreement to his terms. Wade walked to the men tending the shepherd to make sure they understood his orders. Charlette and the older mutant led us from the building and out of the village heading west.

The arena's light vanished behind us as we reached the crossroads. Charlette's posse emerged from the shadows when we stepped under the light from the overhead poles. "We gits to kill him now?" The young mutant asked eagerly.

"Na. We gonna take 'em to da end da road." Charlette responded.

"Da ware place? Fer what?" he snapped.

"Dey gonna clear it out." Charlette said. "Dems Wade's orders."

The mutants all looked at each other sheepishly. I thought they might argue, but none of them did. "It all you now," Charlette said to us.

The poles leading back to the recycling plant were all lit. The area ahead of us to the west didn't have any. It was black. I nodded to Charlette as I began walking into the dark. Nevaeh right behind with Charlette and her guards a good distance back.

It wasn't long before they fell away, and we couldn't see them anymore. Whatever was at the end of this avenue scared them. We continued nearly a mile before reaching a large building. There were mounds of trash piled high all around except for the avenue in front. This made the entire area even darker as the avenue ended.

"Is this where you rode your motorcycle? Is this what the elder was talking about?" Nevaeh asked.

"No. That was the road to the north, toward the cloud edge, near the wastelands." I responded.

Nevaeh nodded, "Somehow I think I'd rather go out there." She swallowed a little scared. "What do you think we're gonna find here?"

"I'm not sure," I said, pulling the pistol from my back along with my flashlight. The beam gave us a better look at the long square building. Unlike other structures in the dump, this wasn't pieced together with salvaged materials. It looked professionally constructed and out of place for what was normal here.

There was a door near the middle which was oddly small compared to the size of the building. There were a few windows, but there was no light coming from inside. We crept our way quietly toward the door. When we reached it, I placed my ear to the door but didn't hear anything.

I grasped the flashlight with two fingers clicking it off so I could turn the handle. The knob turned easily allowing me to open the door without resistance. As it opened, a foul odor reached our noses in a very abrupt way.

We both turned our heads at the offensive smell. "What is that?" Nev gasped.

After the initial shock wore off, I pushed the button of my flashlight for a quick burst of light to look inside. There wasn't any movement, so I pressed the button harder to keep the light on.

"It's empty." Nevaeh commented as she looked over my shoulder. "What are they so afraid of? Other than that putrid odor. There's nothing here."

As I moved the light around, a door on the far west side of the building caught my eye. It was beside a pair of closed loading doors. This seemed odd considering this building appeared to be on dead-end street. The entire structure appeared empty, so we made our way across.

The doors hinges squeaked as I shoved it open. We stepped outside to find another odd thing. "Is that?" Nevaeh asked.

"Tracks," I responded.

"I didn't think the railroad ran through the dump." She commented.

"It's not supposed to." The tracks were in between a large mound of trash and the building. They were impossible to see from the front of the structure. "Someone went to a lot of trouble to hide these. Come on." I said following them east.

We walked about a hundred yards until the tracks ended between two big mounds. "It doesn't go very far," Nevaeh commented.

"No. Let's see how far they go in the other direction." We walked back past the building until we came to an open area. From here, we could see some hills far off in the distance. The hills were lit up with lights on high towers illuminating buildings and roadways. We could also see headlamps of machinery that continuously moved around.

"The mines." Nevaeh commented.

The tracks had led us out of the dump and into the P&G Mining area to the north of the Mining District.

"Look." Nevaeh pointed to a black hole at the end of the tracks. It was hard to see at first, but once my eyes adjusted, I could see it..

"The tracks go into that mound." She said.

"Yeah. I think so." I responded.

"Just like the prison. Should we follow them?" She asked.

"No. Let's go back. I think I understand now." I said.

The back door of the warehouse was still open just as when we left. I flicked on my flashlight to go through. The stench hit our noses again. I could see buckets lining the wall that I didn't notice the first time we came in. And in the corners, there was loose rope, garments, and small toys.

"That's awful. These buckets must have been used by the workers to go to the bathroom." Nevaeh said, holding her nose tight.

"I think the smell is from something else." I said shining the light past the buckets.

The odor from the shit buckets was awful, but I recognized something worse behind it. The foul smell was coming from the distant corner. We moved closer so I could confirm what I suspected.

There were specs of white powder which led to large mounds. In the center of the large mounds of white powder were dead bodies. When I shined the light on the bodies, rats scurried away.

The unnerving smell was rotting flesh. It was even more pungent once we were close. All the heads were intact, but the lime prevented me from seeing obvious signs that would indicate the cause of death.

I moved my flashlight around the entire building until I noticed in the center, what appeared to be strange marks on the floor. I walked over and noted they were indentations. The area had broken glass and bits of paper spewed around. It was as if some type of lab were here.

I continued panning the light along the wall to cover all corners. "Toys." Nevaeh hadn't really seen them the first time.

"What's up with those? Why would kids be here?" Nevaeh asked.

"Kids always seem to be around at the user level. Not manufacturing. This is something else." I said. "There's rope near those chairs as if someone was tied to them."

Nevaeh saw it too. "The Clowns?"

"No." I shined the light back on the bodies. "Not those anyway. That's lime. Whoever did this was hoping the victims would be gone before being discovered."

"Why not bury them in the trash out back?" She asked.

"Maybe they didn't have the time," I answered.

"Another dead end." Nevaeh was discouraged. "Was my aunt even here?"

"Let's go back to Wade." I didn't want to say it, but her aunt may have been killed here and then posed at the Refuge.

"But you didn't rid them of...whatever this is," Nevaeh replied.

At my feet, I noticed flecks of powder. I knelt down, "Looks like they were making Colors at one point. Those indents are marks from heavy equipment. And there is broken glass, beakers, and hotplates. Most of it looks old. Whatever was going on here lately, wasn't about Colors."

We went outside to find Charlette and the others waiting. "Ya been in dare a long time. Ya fine anyting?"

"Place is cleared out. I think it was used to manufacture Colors at some point. But there was something else going on more recently. Any ideas?" I asked.

"People come, people go. Strange noises. But we no see. Don go pas crossroad." Charlette said.

"Where's the nearest line to the front?" I asked.

"Come. They be one at da crossroad." Charlette said turning to lead us there. A short while later, we reached the crossroads. Charlette walked to a pole on the northeast corner where a call box was hidden on the backside.

I opened the box and turned the dial a few times before Spivey answered. “Didn’t expect ta hear from ya so soon. It be done?”

“Is what done?” I asked.

I could hear the hesitation in his voice. “Cold. Ya made it. Ya, still alive. I guess da natives must like ya.” Spivey was damn near stuttering.

“You hoping to get my car,” I smirked.

“It is kinda sweet. Even with all da damage. But no. Ya, it good ta go.” He responded with a strange chuckle.

“Bring it to the arena,” I said.

“The arena? Okay. Ya, be right der man.” Spivey agreed but something was wrong.

Charlette and the old mutant led us back to the arena while the rest of her men remained at the crossroads.

“What was in dat building?” Charlette asked as we walked.

“You never went in there?” I asked.

“Ain nun us be in dere. Toll ya, we stay away. We wait for ya to come out.” She responded.

“Two dead bodies,” I responded. “But not much else.”

Charlette stopped to look at me. “Who dey be? One us or one ya?” She didn’t know the bodies were there.

“I don’t know. They’ve been dead a while. Somebody put lime over them.” I said.

“That be ya. We don do such ting.” She snapped, then continued walking. “What else be dere?”

“Nothing really. The place was empty.” I said.

We reached the arena to find Bessimer parked at the front door. *Seems odd, Spivey must have taken another way here because he didn’t pass us.* Charlette and the old mutant went through first. Wade was sitting on the far bleachers talking to Spivey.

“Ya git rid a dat place?” Wade asked. Charlette shook her head no before I could answer. Wade immediately spoke. “I tot we hadda deal?”

"There's two dead bodies in there." I responded. "Can't get rid of it just yet."

"We don wan no cops in here." Wade said curtly.

"He says tey not be ours." Charlette responded.

"No?" Wade asked. "None dem da missing?"

"Missing?" I asked.

"Ya. Some ar people." Charlette answered to me first, then she looked at Wade. "He say lime covering da bodies. Nun ours would do dat."

"Dat don mean it ain't our people." Wade scorned. "Day be big or small?"

"Two adults. The bodies have been there a while." I responded. "You need to let New Vegas Police know. They find out there are two dead bodies in there and nobody bothered to call, this place will be crawling with cops."

"People go missing in here all da time. Nobody cares." Spivey butted in.

"I thought you'd feel that way, Spivey." I said.

"Dat you mean?" Wade looked at Spivey and then back to me.

"Tell him," I said as Spivey's head dropped.

"Tell me WHAT?" Wade said to Spivey.

Spivey wasn't ready to confess. So, I got him started, "Spivey let them in there. You help them build it?"

Wade and a few others stared at Spivey. Everyone silently waiting for him to answer. He looked around nervously trying to think of an excuse and then Wade's patience ran out..

"TELL ME!" Wade yelled.

"Dey offered me a lot a money. OKAY? A LOT a money. I didn't care what dey were doing. Dey wanted a place away from da main road. Dey knew da hoomans, gambling and such, came in on da east Sum. So dey said dey want a place on da odder side."

"Why would ya do dat?" Wade scolded.

"We's need money. Food. Medicine. How you tink da pantry got filt last year?" Spivey pleaded. So what if dey make Colors. Nun our people do it. Let da hoomies kill demselves. We take care ar own."

Wade and the other mutants showed contempt. Disgust. None of them could believe one of their own had gotten involved. I found it rather ironic given, not long ago, they had illegal dog fighting in here.

"Were you planning on killing us?" I asked Spivey.

"WHAT? NO. I swear. Dey were just supposed to take ya dere and let ya see da place. Figured ya'd leave once ya saw it empty." Spivey answered.

"CEPT IT AIN EMPTY!" Wade screamed.

"Who paid you?" I asked.

"Da woman. Long time ago. She pay me lot a money. Say keep everyone out a dare. No, tell no one. She came back wit a crew, borrow some big machines. Dey make big place. I no keep eye. All I know dey pack up a few days a go and leave." Spivey said.

"What did she look like?" I asked.

"I dun know... Ah, like ya, girlfriend." Spivey replied.

"Penny?" I responded.

"Na. Like her." Spivey said pointing to Nevaeh. Cept older." Everyone turned to look at Nevaeh.

"Me?" Nevaeh said. "She looked like me? And for the record, I'm not his girlfriend. No offense."

"She mutant dough." Spivey continued. "Dat woman all mutant. She one us so I figured all good."

"WHO ELSE KNOW BOUT DIS?" Wade yelled. Spivey's eyes dropped again. "WHO!?!" Wade screamed.

"Jeets. Plasco. Dat it. I swear." Spivey named two of the guardsmen who worked for Chalette. These were the ones pushing to have me killed since we first ran into them.

"Spivey. You're going to go back to your office and call New Vegas PD. Tell them there are two corpses in a structure at the end of Sum Avenue." I started.

Wade immediately objected. “No Cold. We don want hoomans don ere. We handle our own.”

“You can’t ignore it. Tell them I found the bodies. You all stay away. Detectives come around, tell them what you told me. Wicked place you stayed away. None of you saw anything.” Then I looked at Spivey. “You tell the cops about getting paid to put that place there. And the woman who paid you. After the cops are done, take your loaders and tear up those tracks behind the building.”

“Tracks?” Charlette asked.

“Somebody put in a rail line. Whatever they were doing, they used the tracks to transport things.” Then turned again to Spivey. “You tear that fucking building down.” He never looked up.

I turned to Wade. “We good on the dog? Place will be gone in a day, as promised.”

Wade nodded. I went to the dog crate and opened the door. The shepherd gave a few appeasing lip licks before working up the courage to come out. He gingerly sniffed my hand then allowed me to stroke his chin. I cautiously clasp the leash on his collar to lead him out.

Spivey had fixed Bessimer’s door, so I opened it, letting the shepherd climb in the back. The dog moved between the seats, giving Nevaeh sloppy kisses after she got in.

“How’d you know about Spivey?” She asked.

“I didn’t know it was Spivey until I used the call box. He thought it was one of his buddies, let a few things slip.” I reached out, scratching the shepherd’s neck. “I think the woman that paid Spivey was the shooter at your aunt’s place.”

“So, what do we do now?” She asked.

“We need to figure out who she is. I think she’s the key to finding the Clown.”

Nevaeh looked out the window, sighed, then back at the shepherd. “What’s his name?” Nevaeh asked. “Jericho,” I responded.

CHAPTER 17

A TRAP

The night was uneventful. Jericho and I got some much-needed rest. He adapted quickly despite being in a new environment. When I awoke, I found him lying on his back, feet in the air. After a quick breakfast and coffee, I took him outside to do his business.

As he sniffed around, I casually looked over the lot for anything or anyone. There weren't any suspicious vehicles, and it was another typical dark morning as pedestrians and traffic streamed past.

"Come on," I said, opening Bessimer's door.

Jericho eagerly jumped over my seat to the passengers. His tongue hung out the side of his mouth with a content, happy look.

"Good morning, sir." Bessimer's greeting caused Jericho's ears to perk and his head titled to the side.

"I take it the canine will be with us from now on sir?" Bessimer asked.

"For the time being," I said.

"Very well, sir. How shall I address him?" Bessimer asked.

"His name is Jericho," I responded. I wasn't sure what the dog's actual name was; I just liked the sound of Jericho. He seemed to understand his name right away too.

It was a short drive to the office, and I parked in the rear next to the alley. Bessimer usually parked himself, but that feature was gone now. While I preferred to drive, having him drop me at the door was convenient. I think I'm going to miss that.

"Sir?" Bessimer started. "Might I make a suggestion?"

"About what?" I responded.

"On the ride to Miss Penelope's apartment, you spoke to Miss Nevaeh of the need to arrest the Killer Clown. My apologies, I wasn't eavesdropping. I'm just always here." Bessimer said.

"Yes. We need the Clown to tell us who is behind all of this. Unless you would like to?" I said.

"I'm sorry, sir. As I explained, data is lost. Unlike human memory that may return, when mine is deleted, it's permanent. But I have a suggestion." Bessimer started. "I can get a message to the Clown. I might be able to lure him to a location that would allow you to apprehend him."

"You just said you couldn't tell me who is behind this? Who would this message go to? Do you know who the Clown is?" I asked.

"No, sir." He answered.

"Why didn't you say something last night?" I asked.

"I'm not exactly functioning at my best, sir. The trauma to my processes has interrupted my thoughts at times. But as you were sleeping, I started a search of my memory banks, trying to piece together what happened. I found a link to an online message board in my system. It doesn't connect to a private account; it's an open network on the dark web. I discovered the existence of several messages using my mobile IP address. None of the messages still exist, they were erased, but there is a ghost trail. I believe I can send and receive a message to those locations." Bessimer said.

"So you're telling me you still have contact with the Clown?" I asked.

"No, sir. Potentially. Well, I don't know exactly. If it's not the Clown, I believe it's someone associated with the Clown. There may be an opportunity to get a message to him."

"Why would I trust you?" I was getting a little nervous now. Jericho sensed it right away, giving a faint whine. My mind began to race. Were Penny and Nevaeh safe? Maybe I shouldn't have left them alone. He could have contacted the Clown anytime and given their location.

"I guess you can't, sir. Not really, anyway. But if I was still working with the Clown, it is highly unlikely I would have told you just now." He stated.

"Unless you and him concocted some type of ambush." I responded.

"It would make more sense for him to ambush you last night. Not at a pre-arranged meeting. Sir." Bessimer responded. "Besides, if it were an ambush, does it really matter as long as he shows up?"

"It does if he shows up with a small army." I said.

"I assume you won't be foolish enough to try and apprehend him yourself, sir." Bessimer added.

I sat in the driver's seat, thinking about Bessimer's proposal. I hadn't seen his betrayal coming. Nevaeh said she *fixed* him, but this could be another trap. Although he did have a point, it would have been easier to kill us while we slept.

Jericho put his paw on my arm with a short whimper. "I'll think about it, Bessimer."

"Very good, sir." He responded.

"Don't do anything. I don't want you accessing that chat board or sending any messages."

"Yes sir." He said.

I walked Jericho into the building as the elevator doors opened. The police lieutenant Penny dates was getting off as we stepped in.

"Alton." He said with a look of surprise.

I could feel the tension in Jericho as his leash tightened. "Oh, how do you do? We've never actually met before. I don't remember you from the job."

"No, but I've heard a lot about you. Penny talks about you all the time, and your name comes up now and again at the station." He remarked.

"Really?" I said. "Usually, when you retire, nobody remembers you."

"A few of the officers still on the job do." He said.

"I'm guessing not in a good way." I responded.

He gave a slight laugh, "Some. But even those who weren't fans would say you really knew how to put a case together."

"That's very kind," I said.

"Can I pet your dog?" He asked.

"Well..."

The moment he leaned forward, extending his hand, Jericho flipped. He started barking, showing teeth, and stepping back. Luckily, I didn't let go of the leash, or Jericho might have bitten him.

The lieutenant recoiled. "I guess he's not friendly."

"I guess not. Hmm. Sorry. Just got him last night. Jericho!" I half scolded Jericho to get him to calm down. Jericho complied, retreating behind me. His eyes darted quickly between me and the lieutenant as he licked his lips.

"It was good to meet you." The lieutenant said as the elevator door closed.

"Didn't like him, huh?" Jericho looked up, panting as if nothing happened. I didn't know what the problem was with Penny's guy, but there was something.

Given Jericho's reaction, I wasn't sure how it would go with Penny. I opened the office door slowly, keeping a firm grip on the leash. Penny was seated at her desk with Nevaeh in one of the office chairs.

Jericho went to Nevaeh right away. She scratched the fluff behind his ears, and when he was satisfied with that, he went around the desk to Penny. His tail never stopped wagging as he sniffed her skirt. She lowered her hand, allowing him to take in her scent. He placed his head on her lap as she stroked his fur. "Well, I guess that answers that question," I said.

Penny grabbed some treats from her desk which Jericho took greedily, chomping and sloshing. "What question?" She asked.

"He didn't like your lieutenant friend," I said.

"No?" She remarked.

"Not really. Damn near took his hand." I said.

Penny looked down at Jericho, giving more treats. "I guess we'll just have to make sure you two make friends, huh, Jericho?"

"Where'd you get those?" I asked, referring to the treats. Penny also had a dog bed behind her desk with food and water.

"Before we got here, I had Dan take us to Pet Bonanza over at Liberty Plaza. Sounded like Jericho here is going to be with us for a while. And you can't leave him alone in your apartment all day." Penny said.

Jericho finished the treats, then went to the doggy bed and plopped down.

"Nev filled me in on what happened. I never did trust that damned car." Penny said.

"He just hit me with something new. Nev, are you sure you…cured him of…whatever was taking over his mind, programming, or whatever?" I asked.

Nevaeh looked curious. "Yeah. The program I used wiped out the virus and blew out all those bad commands. It's a bit technical, but he's not capable now. I'm not an expert in A.I. technology, and it's far different here under the cloud, but he should be functioning like he's supposed to. Except, of course, the driving."

"What about connecting to the world wide web through the trunk lines under the city? Couldn't somebody download it into his system from there? A new set of commands following the original orders?" I asked.

"I doubt it. I enhanced his firewalls and added some code of my own. His programming should be consistent with the three laws. He can't control the car even if they could somehow get in. Why?" She asked.

"He just told me; he might be able to contact the Clown," I said.

"WHAT? Then he knows who is behind this." Nevaeh responded excitedly.

"Not exactly. He claims to have found a ghost trail leading to a chat board on the dark web. He said all the data is gone, permanently. There are IP addresses he thinks were used to give his secret orders. He believes this might be the Clown or somebody connected to him. Might be whoever is behind this." I said.

"How does that help you? If he doesn't know the identity?" Penny asked.

"Bessimer suggested sending a message to entice whomever into a trap," I responded. "We'd have a chance at getting to the Clown. Putting an end to all this."

"Do you have any idea who's behind everything?" Penny asked.

"Domenic Miscavage," I responded.

"Miscavage. The guy who gave you Bessimer?" Penny's wheels were turning. She looked excited and confused.

"I think he gave me Bessimer to spy on me," I said.

"Why give him to you? Even if he is behind all this, he gave that car to you a year ago. He couldn't have known Nev would come to you." Penny remarked.

"That's true. But I'm on the outside now. He's got people on the inside. Maybe it's just an insurance policy.

He'd know if there was a rail line in the dump. That line wouldn't have gotten there without his approval." I said.

"But Nev told me you didn't think they were making Colors there anymore," Penny commented.

"No, but there were signs it was used for that once. And Spivey said as much. But something made them move. They got everything out. Dealers move around all the time, but it's harder for the manufacturers. Something made them move." I said.

"What about the rail lines leading into the ground?" Penny asked.

"That would be the easiest way to smuggle in the chemicals they'd need. And move around large quantities throughout the city. The infrastructure is already in place to move ore. They could slip the Colors in without anybody suspecting anything." I answered.

"But you worked undercover there. Didn't your case wipe that out?" Penny asked.

"No. They're like flies at an outhouse; take out one, and ten more show up to the funeral." I responded. "Besides, that was long before Colors. If anything, my case would have taught them to be more careful."

"If you get the manufacturer, don't you stop production?" Nevaeh asked.

"You would think. Operations like this involve millions upon millions of dollars. They'll get replacement cooks. The demand is too high."

"What about the Clowns? Where do they fit into this? Nev said you don't believe they are true serial killers." Penny asked.

"I don't know who the Clowns are yet. I'm guessing Miscavage hired them to keep everyone in line. He had them kill anyone who was a threat to the operation and made the deaths look like the work of a serial killer to fool the cops. This kept the cops running in circles. A misdirection to prevent them from looking at a motive."

"What about the mysterious woman?" Penny asked.

"I thought it was about you for a while," I said, looking at Nevaeh. "I don't think so anymore. Bessimer didn't know about Gordon from us. We didn't talk about it in the car. And we didn't discuss the Portis Crew either.

I didn't take Bessimer to Portis. The woman followed me to Portis. I saw her on the rooftop. She couldn't have gotten that from Bessimer, so I don't think he was leaking things to her. The woman might have been sent to take out the Clowns, but not you…or me. You were either in the way when she shot at the Clown, or she just missed.

I think she killed Portis and his crew after I left. Cops won't work up a sweat about Miles Portis and his guys. Truthfully, I doubt they'd care much about me either since I'm not one of them anymore, but they might care about the death of a civilian like you."

"Wouldn't care about a prostitute either," Nevaeh said quietly, referring to her aunt.

"No. Sadly." I responded.

"Or an old informant. Who most cops believe is a criminal anyway." Penny was referring to James.

"Nope. And Bessimer was at the heart of getting information to the Clowns or somebody directly connected to them. Could be whoever is leading this mess. He told someone we were going to the Side House. That's why Chili and his girls were killed before we got there. But they didn't count on something. The one thing that may give us an advantage for the first time." I said.

"What's that?" Penny asked.

"They might not know Bessimer has been disabled. They may still believe he's on their side. If they're watching, they can see the damage, which could explain why he hasn't made contact. His suggestion might work." I said.

"You don't think Miscavage would figure it's a trap?" Penny asked.

"I'm counting on it. But he's too smart to come himself. He'll send the Clown. He isn't the one who gets the messages anyway. It's either the Clown or someone above him. Either way, I think the Clown comes." Then I noticed the television. "Turn that up," I told Penny.

"We have breaking news this morning. Two women were found murdered at the Wildlife Refuge early yesterday. We turn to Jennifer Caldwell on the scene for what we're learning and more. Jennifer, what can you tell us?" BCN Anchor.

"Tom, two women were found murdered inside the Wildlife Refuge here on the East Side. One body is an unidentified woman from the Mining District. It is believed she may have been employed as a courtesan. And the other victim has been identified as the wife of wealthy industrialist Prescott Davis. Police confirmed the body of Millie Gordon

had been found brutally murdered alongside the unidentified courtesan. Police are refusing to comment, citing the ongoing investigation.

I also learned that several bodies were discovered at a Side House in the Mining District." The screen was cut to show the Side House where Chili was found. The reporter continued. *"Sources tell me the two crime scenes are related, and the courtesan victim in the Refuge worked at the Side House where the other bodies were found.*

Police are refusing to categorize this as the work of a serial killer at this time." Reporter Jennifer Caldwell finished as the report went back to the studio.

Penny lowered the volume to speak. "I thought the serial killer was monikered as the 'Copperhead Stranger.' She didn't mention anything about that."

"That's the name the police came up with. Jen's source must not be from New Vegas Police." I started. "But the killers have a thing for Clowns. The two of them dressed like Pagliacci. They also liked to put clown masks on their victims. Another ruse to throw off the cops." I said.

When Penny saw the report continuing, she raised the volume again.

"In other news. A fight broke out at the famed Coach-Lite on Sunset Blvd. This came as a shock, as the club has never been violent since its inception. For more on this, we turn to political commentator, Lenny Tarantella, a well-known defense attorney in the city. Lenny, what can you tell us about this?" The anchor asked. Lenny Tarantella was a jackass. I hated him as much as the corrupt assholes I used to work with. His fake orange tan and slicked-back hair earned him the nickname 'Count Chocula' after a popular cereal. It killed me to see this blowbag on TV. The only thing making it palpable was knowing he wasn't as respected as he believed.

"This is very unusual, Tom. As you know, the Coach-Lite has been in operation since the beginning of our neon city. Respected businessman Mo LaRocca has kept a tight ship over there employing bouncers to

keep the peace, including numerous off-duty New Vegas Police Officers." Lenny said.

"But isn't it true that Mo LaRocca is the head of the LaRocca Crime Family?" The anchor asked.

"There's never been any link to Mo LaRocca and organized crime. Those kinds of false accusations have plagued, unfairly, Italian Americans for centuries. Mo LaRocca is a businessman and nothing more. Anything to the contrary is fake news." Lenny insisted.

"What can you tell us about the incident?" The anchor asked.

"My sources at the mayor's office, and you know how well connected I am, having practiced law in this city for over 30 years, tell me the police were summoned to the lounge near closing last night. A man wielding a knife stabbed several people, including two women. Both women survived and were transported to Bumper City Memorial Hospital where they are under guard. The assailant managed to escape, but police are questioning several people." Lenny finished.

"We're told the man wielding the knife may have been wearing some type of make-up. Some described it as resembling a Clown. What can you tell us about that?" The anchor asked. Lenny's face turned so red it practically glowed.

Penny shut off the TV before Lenny's answer. "One of your favorites." She giggled as Nevaeh began to speak.

"My God. Those have to be the two women I talked to at the Coach-Lite. It's like you said, everyone we speak with ends up.. Do you think he got to Mo?" Nevaeh asked. "What about the Dump? Are they next?"

"If Mo LaRocca was dead, every news station in Bumper City would be on it," I responded.

"Do you think Mo got em?" Penny asked.

"News said the Clown escaped," I said.

"You could call Mo." Penny quipped.

"He ain't gonna tell me," I said.

"You don't know that. Call him and find out." Penny responded.

Penny was right. It was worth the call, even if the cops or the feds were listening. I used her desk phone to dial the Coach-Lite. It rang a few times before a gruff male voice answered. This wasn't the usual friendly response from an operator, from the sound, it was one of Mo's goons.

"Hang on Cold." The male who answered must have seen my name on the caller ID. A moment later I recognized Mo's voice. "He got away Cold. That's all I got." Mo didn't give me a chance to say anything and hung up.

I looked at the earpiece before placing it on the receiver. "What?" Penny asked.

"Mo's alive, and the Clown's still out there," I responded.

"Mo? You think he was telling the truth?" She asked.

"Yeah. He knows the feds tap his line. Even if he had'em, he wouldn't say, but I don't think he has 'em." I said.

"What about the people at the Dump?" Nevaeh repeated her question from earlier.

I picked up the phone to call the recycling center. Spivey answered. "City Dump."

"Spivey, it's Cold."

"Hey, I did as ya tol me. I called da cops. Dey came last night after ya lef. I did as ya said. Tol dem ya here, found da bodies." He said.

"And the woman?" I asked.

"Yep, da woman. Tol dem all bout. I jus gettin ready to take some guys an tear place don."

"Forget that for now. Lock up the office. Take your men and go back to the arena. Tell Wade and Charlette to increase security." I ordered.

"Why? Dat goin don?" Spivey got nervous quickly.

"There's a…killer that might be coming your way. Keep watch on everything." I said.

"We ain worry bout one killa. There be whole bunch us here." He quipped.

"Spivey, this isn't just anybody. I'll come when all of this is over." I insisted.

"How long? We can hide no forever." Spivey didn't wait for me to say anymore. "Alright. Alright. I'll go. We wait for ya." He said hanging up.

I looked at Nevaeh and Penny. "Doesn't sound like the Clown has gone out there yet. I want to make sure he doesn't. Penny, you go hang with your lieutenant friend." I said. "Take Jericho with you."

"You don't want Nev to come with me?" Penny responded.

"At this point, I'm not sure who's compromised at New Vegas PD. I don't think she's safe there." I said.

"Danny isn't corrupt." Penny insisted.

"Neither was I, but I had to work with them, and so does Dan. Besides, if the Clown went after the girls, then he knows they talked to Nev. The Clown wanted to kill her before, I thought it was just his being a psycho, but I think it's more than that. The best way to protect her is with me."

"Where will you go?" Penny asked.

"The cabin. I'm going to have Bessimer send a message before we run out of service. I'll be able to see them coming from there. That should give us an advantage. It'll be our last stand. Him or us."

"Unless he's not alone," Nevaeh remarked.

"What about Rollins? I can have Danny get a squad up there." Penny offered.

"The Clown gets one whiff of police, and he won't come," I responded.

"You don't think Rollins is on payroll, do you?" Penny asked.

"Not really. But Rollins won't defy orders. If he's asked where he's taking a squad, he'll tell. And if he would decide to come alone, he'd report his location. I'm afraid we're on our own. If you don't hear from either of us by the evening hours, call your lieutenant friend." Penny nodded as she reached down to pat Jericho on the head. I looked at Nevaeh and asked. "You up for this?"

She nodded reluctantly. "I want the son-of-a-bitch that killed my aunt." Nobody likes the idea of facing their own death, but she is determined to catch those responsible for her aunt's murder.

There was one deadly Clown left and he was part of something bigger. Odds were, he'd bring a few more men to kill us. If he did, I'd deal with them too.

CHAPTER 18

QUANTUM DOTS

The phone rang as we merged into traffic. "It's the New Vegas Crime Lab sir," Bessimer stated.

"Answer it," I said.

"I'm sorry, sir. I have limited functionality. I can still run computations, converse with you, and access some records, but functions such as this remain under repair." Bessimer responded.

Spivey hadn't fixed the shattered monitor. The images were distorted behind the broken glass. Although it still functioned, I had to tap it a few times before it responded. "This is Cold."

"Alton. It's Rick. Rick Talmadge at the crime lab."

"Hey, Rick. What's up?"

"What's wrong with your screen? All I see is broken glass in front of a grey background."

"Had a little accident. I can hear you fine." I said.

"Are you in a…a car?" Your office isn't outside, is it? I hear a lot of noise." Rick remarked.

"I have the window open," I responded.

"Oh, a…okay. Well, you said to call you if I find anything in the Colors." Rick said.

"You figure out the mystery ingredient?" I responded.

"Yes and no. Professor Cloth at the University, identified it as nanotechnology." Rick said.

"Nanotech?" I was surprised. Nevaeh's eyes got big too.

"Yeah. I didn't expect to find that in a drug. Never seen it before. I can't come up with a reason why it's there, but Dr. Cloth's preliminary findings show nanoparticles. They seem to alter the chemical structure. Actually, that's how he discovered it. Anyway, I thought you might want to know." Rick finished.

"Rick, was the nanotech in all the samples?" I asked.

"After reading Dr. Cloth's report, I was able to go back to other pieces of evidence. I couldn't find any traces of it in those."

"How far back did you go?"

"All the way to when Colors first showed up in the city. From what I can tell, none of the earlier batches have them. It's only the last couple of months." He said.

"Can you trace the manufacturer?" I asked.

"I don't have anything here strong enough. Dr. Cloth at the University might. I haven't been able to reach him but as soon as I get a hold of him, I'll have him look for any trace of an origin."

"Does the nanotech change the effects of the drugs?" I asked. "Does it change a stimulant to a narcotic? Or a narcotic to a non-controlled substance?"

"I'm not sure. I'll run some tests and get back to you." Rick answered.

"Thanks, Rick," I said, ending the call.

"Quantum dots," Nevaeh commented. "I'll bet that's why the drugs change colors. I'm not an expert, but it makes sense."

"Is that why users show skin colorations when taking it?" I asked.

"Yeah, maybe. I mean…we've never been able to understand why materials change colors when their size changes. Scientists used quantum mechanics to figure it out. Sometimes they call the nanoparticles quantum dots and colors are often created." Nevaeh said. "Is it just marketing? Something cool?" She asked.

"They can use dyes for that. This is something else. Nanotech inside drugs is weird. That's a lot of expense to pour into something for addicts." I said.

I turned Bessimer down the off-ramp into New Vegas West. We made our way to the last road turning north. The safe house was close to the mountain road. Bessimer could send the message from there before going to the cabin. That should give us enough time to prepare.

I pulled to the back of the house and parked. "Alright, Bessimer. I want you to contact the Clown."

"I'm not sure it's the Clown specifically sir. I don't have any memory and there are no data trails suggesting that. Essentially, I leave a coded message on the chat board." He responded.

"Alright. But you believe the message will get to the Clown. Then what?" I asked.

"The ghost trail indicates a response follows a few minutes later, but there have been longer periods of time." He said.

"If it was coded, how would you relay all the information?" I asked.

"I don't know, but the messages must have been brief," Bessimer said. "What shall I say?"

"Send, *location found. Need instructions*." I responded.

"Very good, sir. Sending now." Bessimer acknowledged.

I got out of the car to grab the bicycle from the back porch when Nevaeh yelled, "ALTON! ALTON."

I rushed back to the driver's seat, "What's up?"

"I received a response, sir," Bessimer said.

"Already? You just sent the message." I stated.

"Yes, sir. I used one of the chat board addresses not damaged in the data purge. The response states, *'message received. Go to Eleven One C to discuss.*"

"What is that?" I asked.

"It's a chatroom on the dark web sir. It's run through the EYEAPPLE router. Shall I connect, sir?" Bessimer asked.

Nevaeh explained, "EYEAPPLE is a dark website. Bumper City criminals use it all the time. Eleven One C is the specific address. One C changes periodically to prevent the cops from busting it."

"We can't see anything. The display screen is broken." I said. "Can you plug in with your laptop?" I asked her.

"Not a good idea. Too risky." Nevaeh answered.

"You'll just have to trust me sir," Bessimer said. Nevaeh shrugged her shoulders.

"In for a penny...Go ahead." I ordered.

"Stand by sir...I've accessed the site at the specific address. There's no video, it is a live chat though." Bessimer said.

"Smart," Nevaeh added.

"The response is asking if I am alright?" Bessimer relayed.

"Tell them yes," I instructed.

"Another message is asking about the crash. Asking if my neural net has been compromised?"

"Respond, no. Minor damage to hull only." I instructed.

"Hull?" Nevaeh asked.

"What would an A.I. car say? Hull seems mechanical enough to me."

"I don't think I would have used that term and I certainly wouldn't use it now sir. I'm not an ear of corn. But I doubt the receiving party would know that." Bessimer responded.

"Husk," I said shaking my head as Nevaeh covered her mouth to laugh.

"What's that, sir?" Bessimer asked.

"Just send the message."

"Yes, sir." A moment later reply to came in, and Bessimer relayed the exchange. "A response after my message sir. It is asking about your location."

"Tell them we are driving through New Vegas West. You overheard our plans. You're taking us to a cabin off former route 159 that used to run through the mountains. Near the old Calico Basin." I instructed.

Bessimer came back with a reply. "Asking for ETA to cabin. And who is with you."

"Respond, ETA 30 minutes. Plans to stay the night. Tell them me and the aunt's niece."

"Very good sir," Bessimer responded.

A few minutes went by without any response. I couldn't wait any longer. We needed to be at the cabin well ahead of anything coming. I started the car and pulled away from the safe house and within moments turned onto the dirt road at a high rate of speed. Our wheels kicked up dust as we drove into the dark mountains.

"Shall I send another message sir," Bessimer asked.

"No. You won't be able to in a few minutes anyway." I said.

"Won't they wonder why he isn't responding," Nevaeh asked.

"Service runs out soon, between the first couple of mounds. They'll know it and won't expect any further messages. Besides, they're on their way."

"What makes you say that?" Nevaeh said, looking behind.

"They knew about the crash and enough to ask if his A.I was compromised. My guess, they're checking with their contacts at NVPD right now to see if it's a trap." I said.

"What if he told them?" Nevaeh asked.

"I assure you I did not Miss Nevaeh," Bessimer responded softly.

"It doesn't matter if he did." I began, "They only want to know if the cops are going to be here. The cops they don't own. They want us both out of the way. The Clown is coming."

We got to the cabin just in time. As I drove around to the back, I turned my head to see two sets of lights coming at us through the mountain pass.

"We don't have much time," I said after opening the door.

"Do you see something?" Nevaeh asked nervously.

"Two vehicles are coming up the road behind us. Both turned their lights out before they reached the first valley."

"You were right. It isn't just the Clown." Nevaeh responded. "Wouldn't it be safer to stay inside Bessimer? He has thick armor, right?" She asked.

"I don't know if the crash compromised it. We're better off on foot." I responded.

"He's right Miss Nevaeh. My 'Hull' has been damaged. I do not have the same tensile strength. Nothing will penetrate the glass, but it's hard to predict how the rest of me will hold up against gunfire." Bessimer said.

"We have to get inside." I grabbed Nevaeh by the arm hurrying her through the back door. "Go up the stairs, I'll be there in a sec."

As she went to the second floor, I looked out the front door at the light pole in the driveway. I could also see the vehicles getting closer. I ran to the pole, lit the oil lamp, and used the pulley to hoist it to the top. As light filled the area, I ran back inside and up the stairs. Nevaeh had gone to the small bedroom at the top which contained a gun safe. "You know how to shoot?" I asked her.

"A little. My aunt taught me." She responded.

I grabbed a shotgun, and loaded the shells. "Tuck this under your arm. It's got five rounds. Just point and pull the trigger. Shoot anything that comes up the stairs. Don't worry about aiming. It'll kick a little. After you fire, pump it like this." I used the action to demonstrate how another round is chambered before sliding a shell into the receiver to show her how to reload.

"Don't shoot me…just them. They aren't here for tea." I said then handed her the gun.

"Where are you gonna be?" Nevaeh asked.

I reached for the semi-automatic rifle. "You stay up here…no matter what you hear, do not come down. You understand?" I asked. She nodded, but I knew she wasn't going to listen. "No matter what, you do not come downstairs. Once it's clear, I'll call for you."

I pointed to the window at the back of the room. "Bessimer is parked next to the porch under this window. If things go bad, climb onto the roof. You can jump on his hood from there. Get in and drive the hell out of here. Go straight to One Police Plaza. Don't risk stopping for a patrol car."

"I can't just leave you here." She snapped nearly in tears.

"At that point, I'm already dead. Keep your composure, get in Bessimer, and leave." As I finished, we heard the low hum of the cars outside. Nevaeh was right behind me as we ran across the hall to a bedroom facing the front. From the window, we could see an SUV stop in the middle of the roadway. The vehicle sat motionless as a second vehicle quietly parked behind it. Both had their lights out as they sat in the dark...waiting.

"So much for me driving Bessimer out of here. I guess we better win." Nevaeh said.

I turned to look at her, "If it goes to shit. Ram through."

I pulled the infragreen scope to my eye. *Such a cliché. Bad guys driving a black SUV*. I thought to myself. Then I got a better look at the second vehicle parked behind. It was a BMW sedan. I could see the white make-up, dark circles around the eyes, and red lips. *There's something you don't see every day, a clown driving a beemer. Probably Gordon's.*

The doors of the SUV opened as six figures got out, weapons drawn. The Clown exited the sedan a little more casually. He sauntered toward the cabin from the south side of the road with two of the figures following. The others fanned wide, careful to stay out of the light created by the lit pole. None of them were wearing goggles which told me they were, *Mutants*.

"Six? And the Clown. Maybe this wasn't such a good idea." I whispered. "Get ready."

I took a few steps back from the window hoping the Clown wouldn't notice me. I didn't want to relinquish my position as he approached the cabin. That didn't work. He reached around behind his back and pulled out a knife. It gave off a twinkle as he pointed it at me. A big toothy grin on his face.

He walked straight into the lighted area while the men following stayed in the shadows. The corners of his mouth curled as he allowed me, wanted me, to see him. His teeth got brighter as the smile got bigger.

Then he tilted his head back and laughed. "Haaaahaa-ahahahahahhahahh."

"COME ON COLD. TIME TO COME OUT AND PLAY. IT'S JUST YOU AND ME." He called out sarcastically.

I pulled the rifle tight to my shoulder and squeezed the trigger. RATATTATTATTAT. Half a dozen rounds burst through the window raining bullets and glass. The shells ejected out of the side bouncing against the wall.

Nevaeh ducked, raising her arms about her head to deflect the empty shell casings. "Was that you being composed?"

"Smug little bastard," I whispered before yelling. "YOU SMUG LITTLE BASTARD. I'M GONNA WIPE THAT GRIN OFF YOUR FACE ONCE AND FOR ALL!"

I could hear the Clown laughing hysterically as we ran to the rear bedroom. An armed man rounded the top of the stairs and Nevaeh didn't hesitate. She squeezed the trigger. BOOM!

The shotgun blast nearly blew the guy's arm off. The force spun him around as he tumbled down the stairs He screamed the whole way to the bottom. I ran past, leaned over the railing, and unloaded a three-round burst through his back.

"Five and the Clown." I pushed her to the back bedroom. "You stay behind cover. Be mindful about the other end of the hall. They may try to climb through one of the other windows to get at you. Blast'em. I'm going for the Clown."

I went down the stairs quickly kneeling beside the guy we killed. The dead guy was wearing a thick ballistic vest. The bulk of Nevaeh's shot went wide, hitting him in the arm. It remained attached by a few threads. One of my rounds went above the vest into his neck which killed him. "Let's see who the fuck you are." I kept my eyes focused on the living room as my hands went through his pockets. There was no ID, only flex cuffs and extra magazines.

With nothing to find on the dead operative, I stood slowly, careful to keep my back to the wall and the rifle to my shoulder. I had left the front door open so it didn't obstruct my view once the fight began.

Before taking a look at the outside, I scanned the living room. It was open all the way through the kitchen. There wasn't any movement in either room. There was no sound and nothing was stirring, but I had a strange feeling somebody was in here.

Most of the first floor was dark. Light from the oil lamp outside came through the windows and open door. This created dark spots in here and provided plenty of places to hide. I slid to the door jamb for a peek. The oil lamp was swaying in the breeze as dust swirled below. I couldn't see the Clown or his men. *Where are they?*

Moving heel to toe, I entered the living room, careful to make as little noise as possible. Looking back to the kitchen, I noticed something in the reflection from the oven's glass door. It was hard to see as the light movement from outside distorted the image. Finally, my eyes focused enough that I understood what I was seeing. A man was ducking behind the island waiting to ambush me. His white flex cuffs stood out in the reflection. *They aren't here to kill us.* I thought.

I needed to cap him before he got a chance to fire. I took two quick steps and sent a volley of bullets into the kitchen wall behind him. The stove glass shattered with shards ripping through the air.

I rolled forward as he came from behind cover to return fire. I pulled the trigger again. BAM BAM BAM BAM BAM BAM! Most of the bullets struck his vest. The impact sent him flying into the oven as he squeezed the trigger of his rifle. His rounds struck the ceiling before he collapsed.

I scurried behind the island where he fell. Blood oozed from the side of his mouth as I shined my flashlight in his eyes. They changed to cat-like slivers, I was right, mutants. His vest was thick like the first operative, but a couple rounds penetrated. "Who sent you?" I whispered emphatically. He tried to speak as blood bubbled from his mouth, but he died before answering.

"THAT'S TWO COLD! HAHAHHAHAHAHHAHAHHAH. BUT THEY'RE NOT THE ONES YOU WANT. I'M OUTSIDE, STILL WAITING!" The Clown yelled. These taunts didn't sound close. Each came from varying directions, as if he was circling the cabin. "IT'S SIMPLE COLD. YOU COME OUT AND FACE ME. IF YOU WIN, YOU GET THE GIRL. IF I WIN, I GET YOU AND THE GIRL. IT'S NOT FAIR I KNOW, BUT WHOEVER TOLD YOU LIFE WAS FAIR? HAHAHAHHAHAHAHHAHA!"

I got this weird feeling the Clown wasn't going to take us to his master. That seemed like a different objective than the goons with him.

My thoughts were interrupted by the sound of a large thud on the back porch roof. This was followed by a rough tumble then a crash. These sounds were outside the second-floor window where Nevaeh was!

I raced upstairs into the room. Nevaeh flipped around pointing the shotgun at me. I grabbed the barrel and pushed it into the air before she could pull the trigger. "Easy, just me."

"Jesus Alton. I almost shot you!" Nevaeh said.

I walked over to the window to find a third operative lying dead on Bessimer's hood. "I didn't hear you fire."

"I didn't. There was a small pop then a whoosh. I turned and saw this guy through the window. He collapsed on the roof then rolled off onto Bessimer. Thanks." Nevaeh responded.

"I didn't shoot him. I was downstairs dealing with a guy in the kitchen." I said.

"What the hell is going on? Who killed that guy?" She asked.

"My guess. The female assassin is out there, somewhere." I peered carefully out the window.

"ALLLLLLTONNNNNN. ALLLLTONNN. COME OUT AND PLAYYYYYY!" The Clown taunted. I caught a glimpse of movement.

"YOU GOT ANOTHER ONE, BRAVO! NOW COME OUT AND PLAY."

I turned back to Nevaeh. "Whoever it is, they're not here for us. I'm going after the Clown. Blast anything that comes up those stairs."

"That's what you said the last time and I damn near shot you." Nevaeh responded.

"I'll remember to call out next time." I exited the room hurrying down the stairs. If the Clown wanted me to face him, he was going to get his wish.

As I neared the last step, I slowed to make sure nobody had snuck into the living room. Everything looked the same. The first dead operative was still lying at the bottom of the stairs and I could see the second dead operatives' legs behind the kitchen island.

I stepped through the living room door onto the front porch. Once I was outside, the Clown came around the side of the cabin and walked into the light. I lined him in the sights with the green laser dot bouncing around his forehead.

His grin stretched from ear to ear, eyes wide as he held the big knife. My heart began to thump. I stepped off the porch inching my way toward him. He didn't move, showing no signs of fear. All I had to do was pull the trigger.

"Come on Cold. You really going to shoot before you know?" The Clown mocked.

My ears detected rustling from the cabin. I glanced to see a dark figure forcing Nevaeh to the front door. She was cuffed behind the back and a hand covered her mouth. I turned with my rifle aimed his way. I tried to get a bead on him through the sights, but he stood behind her using the tiny space of the doorway to prevent me from getting a shot.

Behind them, I saw another man holding Nevaeh's shotgun. They had subdued her and planned to take her after I was killed.

"Just you and me now Cold." The moment I heard the Clown speak; I turned to him, aiming my rifle back at him. "Put the gun down Cold. Let's make it a fair fight. Either that…or I tell them to kill her."

The Clown stepped forward, repositioning the blade against his forearm, preparing to attack. The moment I let the rifle go, he was going to pounce. I couldn't be sure the two goons wouldn't kill her if I squeezed the trigger, so I began to lower the rifle.

This was it. I'd have to kill the Clown and then rescue Nevaeh. I started to slide the gun to the ground, but the Clown was impatient. He flipped the knife forward and then lunged before the rifle landed.

I sidestepped the attack, but his blade managed to slice my clothing. I could feel the steel going through my jacket and into my shirt narrowly missing my skin.

The Clown recovered quickly. He pulled back, widened his stance, and leaned forward. The blade repositioned against his forearm again as he advanced. He used the backward slicing motion across his body to strike at me.

I retreated, avoiding the blade as it passed with each swing. Using his momentum against him, I grabbed his arm, throwing him to the ground behind me. He tumbled returning to his feet with a wide grin. His eyes darted to my rifle on the ground as he stood between me and the gun.

"I've had it with you trying to kill me." I sneered.

The Clown flipped the blade forward again. He lunged at me with an exaggerated motion. The blade missed as I jumped back. Keeping the blade forward, he swiped again, backhanded this time. The slashing was more of a taunt now than a serious attempt to cut me. "You can always arrest me?" He mocked.

"I'm not going to arrest you." I hissed.

His tongue was hanging out as his eyes sparkled. I could see the deranged killer on his face. He enjoyed the thrill of anticipated carnage.

"And I haven't even begun to try and kill you yet Cold. Mostly because the Master didn't want it. But fuck it. He ain't here now. He can't fault me for defending myself. HAHAHAHA" The Clown's menacing laugh faded as he wiped his mouth with his sleeve. Back to sinister, "I'm gonna gut you Cold. Pin you to that pole and pull out your intestines for all to see." His smirk brimming with confidence. "He'll forgive me for killing you. Then I'm going to kill that pretty blonde that works for you. If the Master won't let me have this girl, then I'll take her."

"Tell me, who is the Master?" I asked.

"Uh-ah. Noooo. I don't think so Cold. He doesn't like to be seen."

Miscavage. He's rarely seen in public. Even during my undercover operation, I never met the man. When he gave me Bessimer, I never saw him. Bessimer just showed up at my office with a thank-you note for saving his daughter.

What was the connection to Nevaeh? Despite my threat, I couldn't kill the Clown yet. I had to know. "Why does Miscavage want her? What's she to him?" I asked.

"Miscavage?" The Clown snickered. "The Master wants her brought to him…then she's…" Before he could finish his thought, we both heard two quick pops. They were preceded by the swoosh of a suppressor, ending with two thuds.

The Clown's head snapped to the front door of the cabin as did mine. The operatives were down, and I couldn't see Nevaeh.

The Clown looked back at me and I at him. His grin was gone. He stepped back slowly; fear now filled his eyes. He seemed like he was about to run when I saw the flash of a green laser on his chest. He saw it, too, and froze. A second later, a pop followed by a swoosh.

Blood splattered from his body. The knife he was holding fell to the ground and his body dropped in a heap.

I rolled to the rifle, grabbed it from the ground, came to my knees, and cradled it to my shoulder. I couldn't see anything through the scope. I needed target acquisition before I could fire. I couldn't risk hitting Nevaeh, wherever she was.

Everything was still. The Clown was on the ground, the two men were lying in the doorway, and there was only the squeak of the oil lamp swinging above me. I gingerly stepped to the porch with the muzzle of my rifle pointing ahead. I reached the door jamb and took a quick peek inside. Nevaeh was lying right next to the another dead operative. Her hands were bound behind her back with the flex cuffs.

For a moment I thought she'd been killed, then she started coughing to catch her breath. "Nev! You alright?" I kept my voice as low as I scanned the room.

She continued to cough, "It was the woman," *cough,* "from my aunt's apartment." *cough cough* "She went out the back."

I went in quickly and knelt beside her, gun barrel panning the room. "Son-of-a-bitch fell on me after she shot'em." She said.

I found a small knife in the operative's vest and cut her free. "Did you get a look at her? Did you recognize her?"

Nevaeh shook her head. "Not really. She was small. Big ass gun, though. Long black hair. There was some kind of red, I dunno, makeup or something across her eyes."

"Like eye shadow?" I asked.

"No, bigger. More like a painted mask." She responded.

"Great, more painted freaks," I said turning to look out the front door. The Clown's body wasn't there! "What the…?"

Nevaeh looked past me. "What is it?"

"The Clown. He's gone."

CHAPTER 19

AN ASSASSIN BY ANY OTHER NAME

Everything happened so fast. I watched the green laser dot settle on the Clown's chest, a millisecond later, the sound of the suppressor. The Clown fell as spurts of blood came from the bullet wounds, and the knife he was holding bounced in the dirt. The assassin had not missed, yet the Clown's body was gone.

"Maybe he was wearing body armor like the others," Nevaeh commented.

"I didn't feel a vest when we fought. And I saw the blood when he was shot."

Then we heard it. The low rumble of a vehicle starting. It was the black SUV the black ops team came in. "COME ON! WE HAVE TO CATCH HER." We ran to Bessimer at the rear of the cabin. The dead guy, shot by the assassin, was still on the hood.

"What happened, sir? What's going on? And who's the guy that landed on my hood?" Bessimer asked as I threw the rifle in the back seat to get in.

I pushed the ignition, slammed the shifter in reverse, and pressed the gas pedal to the floor. The tires spun, throwing dirt and dust in the air as we lunged backward. The dead body rolled off the hood while I forced the gear shift into drive.

The wheels spun again as I pressed the accelerator causing Bessimer to sprint down the side of the cabin. We could see the assassin backing the SUV down the road. Once she had cleared Millie Gordon's BMW, she spun the big vehicle around.

The SUV had a V8 engine, but Bessimer was no ordinary vehicle, he was superfast. By the time she was pointed in the right direction, we were past the BMW and on her back quarter panel. "HANG ON!" I yelled.

Nevaeh clutched the handrail with one hand and the center console with the other. I turned Bessimer's front wheel into the rear quarter panel. At the precise moment of contact, I gave it the gas. Bessimer slammed into the vehicle and spun the SUV around.

The impact caused her to lose control which sent the SUV off the side of the road. The vehicle hit some small rocks causing it to flip, rolling end over end down a small embankment.

I nailed the brakes which brought us to a skidding stop. We watched as the SUV came to an abrupt end at the bottom of the gulley. Dust, smoke, and debris filled the air as the vehicle landed on its roof.

"Stay here," I said, grabbing the rifle from the back seat. "Anything happens, take off. She isn't here to kill you. Could've done that twice already. But she's got skills. She ain't like the Clown."

After I got out, Nevaeh locked Bessimer's doors and slid into the driver's seat. I kept the rifle at the ready swiftly making my way to the SUV. The rear of the vehicle was on fire. Fluids dripped from the engine block and a small stream of gasoline trickled toward the front. I didn't have a lot of time.

I knelt to get a look inside. The airbags had deployed and the female assassin was hanging upside down by the seat belt. At first, I didn't think she was alive. Her eyes were closed and she wasn't moving. But then I could see her breathing as her chest moved.

The roof was caved slightly, and the windows blew out. Her weapon lay below on the passenger's side. I gingerly reached in and took the gun. *An MPP, impressive. I haven't seen one of these in years.* Christiansen Arms Model Precision Pistol with a tactical scope and laser sight. This one had been enhanced. No bolt. Match trigger, tactical scope, laser sight, tactical sling, and almost no weight. Hi-Tech firearm, very expensive. *Badass. Who are you?*

The fire was getting bigger. The moment the fluids hit the flame; it would explode. I had to hurry. After slinging her gun over my shoulder, I rushed to the driver's side. I couldn't pull the door open as the rollover smashed it in.

No time to be gentle, I had to get her out. I used a knife to cut her seat belt, then eased her down. Nevaeh was right, she was little, and it was a good thing too. I pulled her out and drug her behind some rocks when the vehicle exploded. BOOM!

The blast was so big it caused the SUV to bounce and flames to shoot in the air. The rocks shielded us from shrapnel, but the concussive sound rang in my ears.

The assassin's suit was made of a lightweight flexible carbon fiber. There wasn't a tear or scratch on it. This protected her body from lacerations during the crash.

I brushed her hair to the side for a better look at the red across her eyes. Nevaeh had described it as paint, but it was some type of covering applied tightly to her skin. It was a red translucent mask with gold circuits woven into the material.

I started to peel it off when Nevaeh came around the corner. "Alton! You, okay?"

In the split second when I turned to look at Nevaeh, the assassin thrust two knees into my side. The force knocked me back as she tried to grab her weapon. Luckily, the strap prevented her from taking it off my shoulder. As I felt her move, my palm slammed into her chest thrusting her away. She took a short tumble and was about to run when I pulled the rifle to my shoulder, "STOP!"

She froze. Then I noticed something. A thought came into my mind I did not expect. I pulled the sights down and stood up straight. "Easy, Easy!" I said in a calm voice.

The assassin looked over at Nevaeh, tilted her head, then back at me. Her long black hair flopped over her face. The hair obscured her appearance, but I knew. I hadn't noticed it when I tried to peel off her face shield, but I knew.

"Brush your hair back," I said softly.

The assassin's eyes darted to Nevaeh. Her giant irises wide open like a cat. She was a mutant, and I knew exactly who she was.

"Mara," I muttered.

"Mara? … MOM?!" Nevaeh exclaimed.

Nevaeh and I stood motionless. Our eyes fixed on her, neither of us knowing what to say. The assassin was Mara. The woman I had fallen in love with so many years ago. Nevaeh's mother who left her when she was little.

A trickle of blood ran down the side of Mara's face, then her knees buckled, and she collapsed. I was able to lunge forward and catch her before she hit the ground. I placed two fingers on her neck to find a pulse. I moved her hair exposing a gash on her forehead at the hairline.

"Alton! What the fuck? That's my mom!" Nevaeh said excitedly.

"Take these," I gave Nevaeh the assassin's gun and my rifle. "She's gonna need a hospital." I cradled Mara in my arms rushing to Bessimer with Nevaeh leading the way.

Nevaeh opened the door so I could lay Mara across the back seat. We hopped in and started down the mountain.

"Bessimer. Do you have any scanning?" I asked.

"Yes, sir. Limited."

"Give me a read on her vitals and anything else you can tell me," I ordered.

"She has a concussion. Small fractures in her ribs, along with some bruising on her internal organs. A few minor cuts on her face and neck. The most serious injury seems to be the gash on her head. That will require stitches and she should be taken to a hospital." He finished.

"The west side hospital isn't far," I said.

"NO!" Mara called out from the back seat. Her hand grabbing my shoulder. "Alton, no. You can't take me to a hospital. The cabin... please"

"You need medical attention." I insisted.

"You don't understand. You can't take me there. I'm okay. You can stitch me up at the cabin. That's all I need right now." She pleaded as she fell back into the seat.

"What about the Clown?" Nevaeh asked.

"I shot him. The others are dead too." Mara said weakly.

"His body isn't there. You didn't kill him." I said, turning to look at her.

Mara's eyes showed confusion. She composed herself before speaking again. "Even if he survived, he's gone. He won't stick around. The safest place for you right now is the cabin."

"For us? You're the one who needs help." I said.

"Trust me. The city isn't safe. This place won't be for long either, but we've got some time." She insisted before passing out again.

I applied the brakes, cut the wheel, and turned the car around racing back to the cabin. "Bessimer. Do you have communications?"

"Barely, sir."

"I need you to get a message to Penny," I said.

"Shall I use the encrypted address?" He asked.

"No. Send it to *Francis Altier dot bc dot com*. The message, exactly as I say it, *Having fun on vacay. Will contact upon return. Dot dot dot*"

"Very good sir." A few seconds later, "Message sent."

Before we reached the cabin Bessimer told us the message had already received a reply. "Shall I relay it sir?"

"Yes," I answered, parking in front of the cabin. "There were only two dots. No words." Bessimer stated.

Nevaeh looked at me confused. "The Clown threatened to go after Penny. That's an open mailbox. Anyone can intercept. Why didn't you use encryption?"

"In narcotics, we could tap just about any line of communication but not without help. New Vegas PD doesn't have personnel smart enough to develop the tech on their own, which means BIG TECH provides support. If they're behind this, they'll have direct access. Penny will be alright as long as she stays with her lieutenant friend." I said taking my rifle from Nevaeh. "You two stay in here a moment while I check everything. Maybe she's right and the Clown's gone, but I want to be sure."

I scoped the area around the cabin first, then moved inside. Everything was as before. All the bodies were in the same position. I counted five, the one at the bottom of the stairs, two in the door jamb, a dead guy in the kitchen, and the one who fell off the porch roof out back. *Wait, what? Six got out of the SUV.*

I put the rifle to my shoulder and went back outside. There was a blood trail where the Clown had been shot along with scuff marks and footprints. I followed them west around the side of the cabin. Near the back, another set of prints merged with the Clowns. The sixth man.

The infra-green scope didn't show any movement. The trail disappeared over some boulders to the rear. Mara was probably right; the Clown was gone. Satisfied it was safe, I returned to Bessimer. "Grab the first aid kit from the trunk. I'm going to take her upstairs to one of the spare bedrooms. Don't touch anything. The police will want to process the scene." I picked up Mara and carried her inside.

Nevaeh was right behind me as I laid Mara on the bed. "I thought we couldn't trust the cops?" Nevaeh asked.

"Not all of them. But we don't know which ones. Have to assume the ones at the top are all corrupted. Most of the rank and file still do the job. Either way, can't let five bodies lie around. We'll call them after we leave. Assuming someone didn't call them already. That giant fireball from the explosion was probably seen."

Mara groaned as she started to wake. "Keep an eye on the stairs while I help your mom," I instructed.

Mara struggled to sit up so I propped a pillow behind her back. "Here."

She looked at me with soft eyes. "Let me tend to that wound. The local anesthetic has been in my kit for a little while. It should be good, but this might hurt." I said.

Mara winced until the painkiller kicked in. She watched as I cleaned the wound and then stitched the cut on her head. When I finished with a couple of butterfly bandages, her eyes met mine, "I'm sorry for what I did to you Alton. I..."

"That was a long time ago." I interrupted. "We were kids. Probably as much my fault as yours. Don't worry about me..." I paused to glance at Nevaeh, "Talk to her."

Mara looked at me, and I was suddenly seventeen again. The last time I remembered feeling like that was the summer before graduation. I got up from the edge of the bed, "I'll let you guys have some time." I was about to leave when Mara grabbed my arm. "Stay. You should hear this too."

I nodded but went to the doorway to keep an eye on the stairs. Nevaeh moved to the bed and sat. There was an uncomfortableness, neither of them knowing what to say. Mara went first. "Nevaeh. You... you're so beautiful." A tear fell off the side of her cheek. Her hands trembled as she covered her mouth, barely able to keep the emotions in.

Nevaeh didn't hold back. "Why'd you leave us? I haven't seen you since I was ten years old."

Mara took in a long heavy breath, glancing at me before answering. "I'm so, so sorry. I wish there was something I could say that would make it alright. Some way you could understand. I never stopped loving you. Never." Mara smiled warmly at her. "I knew everything you did. Every accomplishment, every school play, every sporting event. So proud of who you've become."

"Then why weren't you there? Really there?" Nevaeh wasn't as warm.

"Twilas Burke." The first name out of Mara's mouth got my attention. "He rescued me from your father." Nevaeh turned to me. Mara saw the look. A smile on her face as she spoke. "Alton isn't your father. Though I wish he were." Mara started to cough. I went to the bathroom and returned with a cup of water for her.

She took a few sips before continuing. "I met Twilas about a year after your brother was born." she paused to look at me, "You and I didn't see each other anymore. Twilas was young and had a degree in computer science. We became friends. Although he always wanted more. I wasn't interested." Mara reached out to touch Nevaeh's hand. "I met your father not long after that and then you came along." Mara paused, reflecting for a moment before going on, "We had your brother and were starting a family. But your father left me. I was scared but happy. You were the joy of my life. But it's not easy being a single mother raising two kids in Bumper City, let alone being a mutant. Twilas was just beginning his collection. He offered me a job. I needed a way to support you and your brother, so I accepted his offer."

"Collection? What do you mean?" I asked.

"He collects people. That's what he calls it. Favors. Influence. Any way he can. He pulls them into his world, to a point where they owe him. And if that doesn't work, he uses other extremes to command loyalty." Mara said.

"Is that how you became his assassin?" I asked.

Mara's eyes snapped to mine. "I've never killed for him." Her response was firm and aggressive. "I'm not an assassin!"

"That MPP you carry would argue differently. And you did shoot the Clown...twice." I retorted.

"I hit what I aim at. I shot him to protect Nevaeh." Her voice lowered. "I'm a fixer for Burke. He molded me into this. I've disposed of bodies, staged scenes, and carried out all kinds of other…things. None of which I'm proud of, but I did it to protect Nevaeh. That's why I shot the Clown."

"I don't understand. Why is Twilas Burke after me?" Nevaeh asked. "I don't even know him."

"It's not you so much, well, not in the beginning anyway. He's been using you against me for years. I never told him your name or where you were, but he found out. That's why I had to leave, and my sister agreed to look after you and your brother. He made it impossible for me to return without putting you at risk."

"We could have worked it out, done something!" Nevaeh pleaded.

"No. You don't understand. His reach is everywhere." Mara said.

Nevaeh's defiant look turned to sorrow as her eyes welled with tears. "Is that why he killed Aunt Sophia? Because of me?"

Mara leaned up and hugged her daughter as the tears let loose. "No, no, no, no, no, no. It was what Sophia saw."

"What did she see?" I asked.

Mara looked up at me still embracing her daughter. "I don't know exactly."

"You just said…I thought you worked for this guy?" I asked.

Mara leaned back to wipe the tears from Nevaeh's eyes. "I do. But he doesn't include me in all his plans. Never fully includes me in anything. He orders and I do. Like everyone else in his Collection."

"Sophia went to the dump. What did she see there?" I asked.

"I told you; I don't know!" Mara snapped.

"Well, what the hell was there? You're in his inner circle, you must know something. And you arranged for the warehouse. So, what was it used for?" I pressed.

"I'm a tool, nothing more. I told you, a fixer." Mara took a breath as we waited. "Yes, I arranged for the construction of the warehouse at the dump. It was the first production site for Colors. But I wasn't a part of the manufacturing or day to day."

"This is all Miscavage, isn't it?" I said.

"Miscavage?" She chuckled. "He's another tool. A part of the Collection. Just like me." She responded.

"I saw the tracks. Rail lines don't go anywhere in Bumper City without Domenic Miscavage. That's how they got the drugs out. Dispersed throughout the city." I said.

"That's only a fraction of it, Alton. You're not listening. Twilas Burke runs the show. He owns everything and damn near everybody. You're correct. Rail lines don't move, tracks don't get laid, without Miscavage. But only under the approval and direction of Twilas. He's owned Miscavage from the beginning.

Who do you think got Miscavage's daughter hooked on Bumps? Whenever someone gets twitchy, Burke reels them back in somehow. You got in the way of that one working undercover. It's also when you first got on his radar.

He used the mayor and the city attorney to stop your case going any further. You were satisfied with the busts and…you helped his daughter. Burke knew you couldn't resist helping. It was a distraction preventing you from seeing the bigger picture." Mara finished.

"What the hell are you saying? That Burke hooked Angelina, so I'd save her just to distract me… from seeing what?" I asked.

"That's what he does." Mara responded.

Nevaeh got up taking a few steps toward me. "Mining? I thought he was the DirectLink guy?"

"Twilas made his first fortune in rare earth minerals." Her strength returning, Mara gingerly sat on the edge of the bed. "Yes Nev, he is the DirectLink guy. He's a computer wiz, but more importantly, he's a genius. Those materials are needed in damn near everything here. Like what's in my cover." She said pointing to the red film across her eyes. "This helps shield me from various tech. Twilas arranged for Davis to marry Millie so he could get to P&G Holdings. It's all Twilas. From the politicians to the cops. Judges, attorneys, even the mob is controlled by him in some fashion."

"He had James killed," I remarked as my anger grew.

Mara nodded. "He's after you two because Alton is getting close to something he doesn't want you to see." She put her hand up, "Before you ask me what, I'm telling you again, I don't know. Whatever it is got Sophia killed and your friend James, along with God knows how many others, I do not know.

The Pagliacci Killer Clowns, as you call them, are his creations. Twin brothers who grew up in the orphanage of the mining district. Just like he did for me, he rescued them from a bad situation. They are forever loyal to him. One now that you killed the brother. Notice how the other didn't have much of a reaction when you were jawing with him outside Sophia's place? Both sociopaths."

"Why didn't this one die? You hit him." I asked.

"Probably the Colors. Those two consumed a lot of product. Right around the time the warehouse moved, Twilas started using them to terrorize some of his 'Collection'. He questioned their loyalty. He set the Clowns loose on some miners to get their attention. The serial killer angle was his idea. But everyone knows it's him and they're petrified. Especially after he had Millie Gordon killed.

The Clowns loved it. Fed their inner nature and Twilas got what he wanted. But they crossed the line grabbing you." She said, looking at Nevaeh. "He usually sends me to watch after them from a distance. Make sure they don't go beyond what he'll tolerate. I didn't have a clean shot at Sophia's cause you were in the way. I winged him hoping that would make him leave you alone.

When I found out Twilas was sending the Clown and six guys here, I had to come. I heard the Clown's taunts, and that's when I decided to take them out. Burke will be coming after me next."

"We can go to the press. I have friends there. They can push the city attorney, even if he is owned by Burke." I said.

Mara laughed. "He owns the press. Geesh Alton. When is it going to sink in? You haven't changed. As thick-headed as when I fell in love with you."

That caught me off guard. Nevaeh too. We both had a funny look on our faces realizing what she'd said. "You can't win this one. It's too big."

"I can get you out of the city," I said.

"We are both mutants. There isn't anywhere on this planet he can't find us. Do you realize how much money he has? His resources extend way beyond this city. He's a global powerhouse. And everyone, I mean EVERYONE, loves him. Of all the Big Tech guys, he's the only one you really see. That's not an accident either." Mara straightened herself. "There is only one way to end this. I can't let him hurt Nevaeh, or you." She said standing.

"You mean kill him," I said.

CHAPTER 20

THE FACTORY

I pulled Bessimer to a stop beside the BMW. The SUV continued to burn off the side of the road. It was easy to see in the darkness. Somebody would have called it in by now and Rollins, along with his detective squad, would be here soon. I needed to get into the city before they got on the dirt road.

Explaining what happened would be easy, it's the who's and why's that would be impossible. Assuming Rollins wasn't part of the conspiracy, it would still be a tough sell. And there was no way Mara was going to testify against Burke or whoever else was involved.

The three of us got out of Bessimer to say our goodbyes. "You don't have to do this," Mara said.

"You just found your daughter. Nev got her mom back. You can leave this all behind. Go live your lives. If you go after Burke, it'll never end for either of you. Even if you survive, the cops will arrest you." I said touching her face. "I shouldn't have given up so easily before." I said.

"That wasn't your fault, Alton," Mara said.

"Maybe not. But I don't really have anything. I poured myself into the job. Thought I was making a difference. Looks like that was all a lie. Burke took that from me just like he took your daughter from you." I responded.

"You still helped people. James, Angelina, so many others." Mara pleaded. "And you protected Nevaeh from those psychos."

"None of that is gonna mean much if Burke isn't stopped. Go on. Get to Odell's. Sam owes me. He'll hide the two of you until it's safe."

Mara kissed me softly. The warm breeze coming up the road, the taste of her lips, and the low light transported me back to that warm summer night under the walking bridge.

She pulled away with a sad look in her eyes. She hesitated before shyly turning to get in the car. Nevaeh was waiting to give me a hug. She squeezed tight, holding back tears. She never said anything, turned, and got into the passenger's seat.

I knelt at the driver's door looking through the window. Didn't really have anything to say, just wanted to look at them one more time.

When the idea Nevaeh might have been our daughter first crossed my mind a few days ago, I was terrified. Now it made me sad that it wasn't true. This is the second time I'd lose Mara, but it would be the first time I felt like I was losing a daughter.

I watched as they drove down the mountain. When I could no longer see their tail lights, I started down the road, pushing Bessimer faster and faster.

The Clown would have told Burke what happened by now. Mara didn't say if the Clown knew who she was, and I didn't know if he saw her, but Burke would be smart enough to know who shot his prize sociopath. I had to reach Burke before he put a plan in motion to kill Mara and Nevaeh.

Like I told you at the beginning. I'm going to kill Twilas Burke tonight.

Mara said Burke needed to get his Collection in line. He'd assemble them at The Foundry. I never imagined he would own a place like that. Didn't seem like his style. I guess that made it the perfect cover.

I crossed through the city with little interference. Most of the police were either at the riots or providing security at the mayor's fundraiser. The streets in Hydetown were usually empty in the evening, which also made things easier.

The Foundry's parking lot was full of cars from the evening shift. Mara told me Burke had everything under surveillance, which I expected. His goons would surely notice Bessimer if I got too close, so I didn't enter the lot and rolled past at a normal pace.

The Foundry's primary doors were open. Workers moved around inside, and some went between buildings or into the parking lot. I noticed half a dozen cars that didn't belong parked in the back. These were not the cars of blue-collar workers. They were rich folk cars. Their expensive paint shining in the ambient light of the building spotlamps.

I remembered there used to be a fire escape on the far side of the building. The inside swelters so they keep the second-floor windows open most of the time. If the fire escape was still there, maybe I could get in through an open window.

As I drove past the primary structure, I whispered to myself, "Shit."

"Sir?" Bessimer asked.

"They built an addition. It's attached to the old building." The new section was huge. Now I couldn't be sure if the old fire escape was still in the back.

I rolled along slowly until I came to the end of the entire building. I pulled into an empty space across the street without anyone noticing me.

The new addition was plain with no windows. It was neat and clean and very nondescript except for the high-tech surveillance. I saw cameras in the eaves of the original building, but there were twice as many in this new section. Above each door was a camera along with two red blinking lights. Signs were posted at each door stating, BIO WASTE, TOXIC WASTE, KEEP OUT, AND NO TRESPASSING. *What does a textile factory need with high-tech surveillance and sophisticated alarm systems in a biowaste area?*

I grabbed the pistol off the passenger's seat. I would have preferred my rifle, but I left it with Mara. Her weapon didn't have as many rounds as mine, and she might need the firepower. Between that and Nevaeh's shotgun, they should be able to protect themselves if I fail.

"Bessimer, can you disable those cameras?" I asked.

"Not completely sir, but I can disrupt them...briefly. There is a subroutine running in the background. It's subtle, barely noticeable. I'm guessing a ghost algorithm to detect a breach. I believe I can sneak in there unnoticed. I can probably do it twice without the system adjusting. After that, everything will lock down."

"What happens then?" I asked.

"Internal alerts followed by alarms. Armed guards will descend upon you, and you'll be captured or killed." Bessimer replied.

"Not good. Okay, how long will each interruption last?" I asked.

"It won't cause a complete blackout, more like static disrupting the screen. I'll make it look like a pulse across the system interfering with the cameras. Thirty seconds at most before self-correction. The second attempt will be significantly less." He stated.

"What if I kill the power?" I asked.

"That would most definitely alert them. From what I can tell, looks as if you'd have to do that for the entire factory." Bessimer said. "But sir, they have a backup system. Even if you turn the power off, the secondary system will start."

"How long would I have between?" I asked.

"I believe you would be better off disabling the monitoring system itself. Appears there may be a surveillance room in this new building. First floor, far corner. It's beside what looks like a conference room."

"How'd you get that?" I asked.

"Code enforcement office, borough building. I hacked into the mainframe. Burke might be a genius, but he's not infallible. Probably never considered the local code office to be any reason for concern." Bessimer finished as the car started to tremble. This was followed by a loud squeal, coming from the backside of the Foundry. Then I heard a whoosh of steam and a short whistle.

It was the arrival of the Blue Line. I could see the giant front wheel of Miscavage's engine car as its nose poked past the building. That was just the distraction I was looking for.

"Wait until you see me walking alongside the building before you send the first wave. Make sure you disrupt the cameras and silence the alarms." I ordered.

"Won't they see you, sir?" Bessimer asked.

"I sure hope so." I took off my jacket and tie, throwing both on the passenger's seat. Then I tucked the pistol in my back, careful to cover it with my shirt. Nobody saw me crossing the parking lot, nor going through the open bay doors. The trick is to look and act like you belong. You have to walk with purpose and be self-assured, otherwise, people start wondering if you need help. That's when the questions start.

The locker room was to the right beyond the open door. A few guys were getting dressed to begin their shift. I marched past like I owned the place, took an oversized lab coat and put it on over my clothes. They glanced as I walked past, giving me a nod. I grabbed a pair of safety goggles, a hard hat, and a clipboard from the wall.

Now that I looked like one of them, none of the workers would question anything, all I had to do was stay clear of any bosses.

I strolled out of the locker room using the hard hat to hide my face from the cameras. Anyone monitoring would see an ordinary worker walking alongside the building dressing like everyone else. If Burke's men were on alert, they'd be looking for a suit and tie.

Nobody paid any attention to me as I walked across the side of the building. The moment I reached the corner, the green light on the cameras, and the red lights, started to flicker. It was Bessimer initiating the pulse. I picked up the pace, keeping an eye on the blinking lights.

I made it to the back side of the building coming face to face with Miscavage's behemoth engine car. The engineer waved as I went between it and the building. I returned the wave without breaking stride. I watched the train workers, but none of them reacted to me either.

The back of the building had a guard posted at a door right below a metal staircase. This would be the moment of truth. The guard watched as I walked between the train and the building. His gaze became constant as I approached.

I stepped onto the fire escape with a friendly greeting, "How ya doin?"

His expression went back to neutral as he nodded. I thought he might question me, but as I said, it's all in the attitude. Act like you belong, and most folks think you do.

I climbed the stairs quickly before the goon started to think about who I might be. Thankfully, nobody was guarding the door at the top and it was unlocked. After I stepped inside, I noticed a camera mounted above, pointed at the door. There was a second camera with a good view of the metal gangway.

I proceeded as normal to a crosswalk a hundred feet to the middle of the building. This connected to the other side toward Bessimer's location. Everything was dark up here except for a few lights.

My sense of smell was overwhelmed by a chemical odor coming from the floor below. Half of the building was a laboratory filled with tables, glassware, and other equipment.

Between the lab area and the loading dock, were boxes and barrels. Supplies were on the far side, and items were stacked indicating they were ready to be moved closer to the bay doors.

Men and women worked in the lab making calculations, keeping records, boiling liquids, making pastes, powders, and ultimately, drugs. Some moved to the supply shelves retrieving various chemicals and ingredients to the processing area while dock workers loaded pallets.

The sound of forklifts echoed in the chamber with their yellow lights circulating across the walls each time they took crates to the train.

From the crosswalk, I could see large vats of colored liquids. There were two workers at each using wooden paddles to churn the mixture. The vats were connected to some tubes that emptied into giant containers at the opposite end of the room.

At the far side of the building, there were tables with industrial machines. Computerized dials were monitored by technicians keeping a watchful eye on the operation. Every now and then I could see a twinkle followed by a thick liquid being squirted into glass vials. Workers along the process collected these vials and mixed them with powders at another station.

This whole place was a Colors lab. It was synthesized, packaged, and shipped from this very location just like the dump. I couldn't see the docks from my position, but I knew the train was just outside.

Burke was smart. The original Foundry was enormous compared to this building. From the outside, this looked like a small addition, and would keep what was happening here under the radar.

For drug manufacturing, this was bigger than anything I had ever seen. Burke was producing metric-ton quantities of Colors. Far more than the number of customers in this city. *But why? The drugs are only supposed to work in Bumper City. Unless he figured out a way to make them for the rest of the world. Maybe that's what the nanites were for.*

I kept walking the gangway toward the bay door. From above, I could see the outside through the open door. The forklifts were moving at a steady pace loading pallets onto two box cars behind Miscavage's engine car.

Workers filled small barrels with the vials containing the Colors. Then they dumped metal pieces on top to hide the drugs. The jagged metal was sharp, discouraging anyone from digging underneath, and the chemical odor mixed with the metal would fool the dogs.

As I watched, Domenic Miscavage walked underneath me. I had only seen a few pictures of him over the years. Paparazzi quit trying when enough of them caught beatings.

He strolled in with two bodyguards on either side. He wore a grey suit with a silk tie under a fluffy fur coat. His hair slicked back with dark sunglasses to hide his eyes. *For a guy who never likes to be seen in public, he sure is flashy.*

Twilas Burke emerged from the conference room to greet him. When the doors opened, I got a look inside. There was a giant conference table in the middle with a dozen men and women seated around. I couldn't see all of them, but I did recognize a few.

Davis from Rare Earth Global was there. He didn't look so good. *Maybe he really did love his wife.* Although it was far more likely he feared his own fate.

The Director of Government Affairs Marty Knoun from the City Attorney's office was seated at the table. He was a particular kind of slimeball. The City Attorney was smart enough to stay away, sending him instead. Sneaky.

The CEO of Patterson Gorges Mining Corporation was also here. That was expected. Mara said Burke manipulated that whole industry. It made sense he, Davis, and Miscavage were here.

Aside from the ones I knew, there were a half dozen I didn't. I really thought Mo LaRocca or one of his mob capos would be here, but I didn't see any.

Burke led Miscavage into the room while his two bodyguards positioned themselves outside. It was clear Miscavage was tight with Burke by the way they greeted each other.

The conference room had a glass ceiling, which also allowed me to watch what was happening in that room. I couldn't hear what they were saying but I watched Burke start the meeting as Miscavage took a seat at the opposite end of the table. Burke used a remote to control a display of monitors behind him.

He was using a slide show which had images of the riots, the explosion at Sophia Durant's apartment, and footage of the crime scene at the Wildlife Refuge. They were reels from the news stations with captions explaining the events. The Wildlife Refuge reported the dead bodies were at the hands of a serial killer.

After the cycle of images finished, all the monitors went to a story of Burke at a dedication ceremony for a rehabilitation clinic in Bumper City. The Chief Medical Officer at Bumper City Memorial Hospital, the mayor, city attorney, and others clapped as Burke used a giant pair of scissors to cut a yellow ribbon.

Reporter Jennifer Caldwell was giving her account as the captions told of Burke donating millions to a start-up company that developed a new drug for the treatment of Colors. Burke was opening four clinics across the city that would use that drug to help those addicted.

So, the man who created the problem has created the cure. He'll get millions in government funds to battle addiction through his clinics.

Why was he doing this? He's already the richest guy on the planet. And most of the people in that room are the wealthiest in Bumper City. The scumbag politicians I get, they always sell out, but the rest have more money than they could ever spend.

I hated all of them, but I couldn't kill all of them, even if they deserved it. But Burke has to go. He's the mastermind behind this wickedness. I had to put a stop to it.

Nobody noticed me yet, including Miscavage's bodyguards. But I couldn't stay here staring into the conference room from above for much longer. Sooner or later someone in that room would look up. I'd been to enough meetings to know how boring they can be. Even if they're afraid of Burke, it gets uncomfortable, and people start to day-dream. The last thing I needed was one of them pointing at me before I got a chance to get close.

The gangway led to a stairwell next to the small office beside to the conference room. I guessed this was the surveillance room. If I could get in there quietly, I'd have eyes all over the plant.

I walked casually to the stairwell without any problems. All I had to do was time it correctly so the bodyguards would think I came from the dock area. I went down the stairs and waited for a forklift to go outside with a pallet. After it deposited the load and returned, I jumped behind walking straight to the office door.

I tapped lightly before turning the knob. I expected to find somebody inside watching the monitors, but it was empty. I closed the door behind me without the two bodyguards looking in my direction.

One wall was covered in monitors which provided a view of the entire facility. The conference room was on one screen allowing me to see everyone who was seated. Burke stood at the head of the table still talking. Most of the people were dressed in business attire except for a few in formal wear. Burke was the only oddball wearing his signature jeans, buttoned-down shirt, and vest.

Burke was freakishly tall. His lean body didn't seem to fit the round face, big nose, and curly brown hair. Although well into his fifties, he possessed the appearance of a child trapped in a man's body.

When I sat in the desk chair, I accidentally moved the computer mouse. The mute symbol appeared on the monitor, so I decided to click it. To my surprise, I could hear everything Burke was discussing. He was openly talking about drugs, and more importantly, Colors.

If I could capture what he was saying, I might have enough evidence to put him away without having to kill him. I placed a small recorder on the desk close to the speaker and pushed the record button. The quality wouldn't be great, but the meter on the device indicated it was capturing sound.

Burke was going on with his projections for the future. "Gentlemen…and ladies," bowing to the women at the table, "that would be our first quarter margins. As you can see Marty, our analysis suggests crime will go down as we get more of the afflicted into our Centers of Excellence. The chief should have a breakdown after we calm the riots." Burke was referring to the rehabilitation facilities he was opening all over the city.

The CEO of Patterson Gorges Mining started to express his concerns. "We've got too many miners getting addicted. They can't work like that. I get your plan Burke, but if we keep losing workers, who's going to dig out the rare earth minerals? It can't all be about the resort."

"Don't worry Ron, everything is coming together. We're not taking that many of them. And the old miners are still with you. Their work ethic is strong. Remember, we developed Colors for the younger generation that didn't want to work in the first place." Burke responded.

"How is any of this going to get them to work?" Someone at the table quipped.

"Or get those to fill our quotas at the resort?" A woman asked.

"Look, Domenic needs the extra help to finish the rail lines. You'll get more workers once the additives kick in. We just started going to the new batches. Should see the results in a few weeks." Burke responded.

"I still need more men." Miscavage piped in.

"I just gave you another eighty. How many more do you need?" Burke answered.

"Twenty of them didn't make it. Your Clown set the explosives too close to the face." Miscavage scorned.

An elderly gentleman I didn't recognize spoke. "Aside from all that, they're not reliable. Not one hundred percent. I need total compliance. I'm not getting any younger." Most of the table shuffled in their seats with a nervous laugh.

"We're not talking about...activities, we're talking about operations right now." Miscavage clearly annoyed, snipped with a sideways glance to the old guy.

Resort? What was this all about? And what was this additive? Must be the nanotech Talmadge was talking about. The conversation seemed to shift. They were talking about the drugs, but there was something else I didn't understand. *What was the resort? Activities*?

"I called this meeting to give all of you a summary before the election. We are on track to break ground on the new buildings by the end of the year. Everything is going as planned." Burke's voice was very soothing, and it was clear his intent was to convince everyone he had things under control. But there was a nervous tension in the room.

"And what if we don't win?" Knoun spouted. "Elections are funny. Even with your tech. Most of our donors are looking forward to a place to call their own. We need to make that happen. Assurances have been made. If she doesn't win, that's going to make things a lot harder."

"Mayor Stockton will be around until she is no longer useful." Burke was smiling but his tone began to change. "Everything gets done, whether she's the mayor or not. Remember that."

As Knoun squirmed, someone asked, "And the riots?"

"They served their purpose. We got the personnel we needed without raising any suspicions." Burke responded and then pointed to the elderly gentleman. "Even a few unexpected things to satisfy you and your friends there Bill." He laughed with the rest before his expression turned serious again.

"In other business. I'm sure we all know by now what happened. We're all sorry for your loss Prescott. You have our deepest condolences. She was a fine woman. I'm sure her funeral will be well attended by the masses here in Bumper City." Burke looked directly at him, but Davis' eyes never raised. An uncomfortable feeling came over the room.

Burke spoke again, breaking the awkwardness. "Thank you everyone. Let's remember to always keep the faith. Just as Millie did. I'll let you know when phase two is complete. Have a great night." I picked up the recorder and slid it into my shirt pocket.

The entire group stood to leave except Miscavage and Davis, who remained seated, while the others departed through the big doors at the back of the room. Burke stood at the front and watched until everyone was gone. The two bodyguards shut the big doors to give the three men privacy. Burke took his seat at the end of the table and poured himself a cup of coffee. He extended the pot to Davis and Miscavage but they shook their heads.

Davis broke the silence. "You didn't have to kill her." His eyes never lifted to look at Burke.

Miscavage squirmed in his seat, the rubbing of leather picked up by the mics in the room. Burke held the saucer in one hand and used his other to raise the cup to his lips. He looked at Miscavage while taking a long sip. There was palpable tension in the room already, the slurping made it worse.

Burke didn't respond. He watched as Miscavage got up slowly, collected his fur coat from a rack at the back of the room, and threw it over his shoulders before opening the big doors. Miscavage eyed Burke as he closed the doors behind himself.

I tracked Miscavage on a monitor as he strode out to his train. His bodyguards stayed on either side trailing behind. The train's whistle sounded right after he climbed aboard. The big engine signaling the coming departure.

Now was my chance.

CHAPTER 21

TWILAS BURKE

After Miscavage closed the conference room doors, only Twilas Burke and Prescott Davis remained. One of the monitors had allowed me to watch Miscavage boarding his train with the two bodyguards. Another showed the dock workers finshed loading the last few crates of drugs onto the boxcars.

This was my best chance to get Burke. I opened the connecting door to the conference room to find Burke and Davis staring at me. Davis looked startled while Burke showed little emotion. His demeanor suggested he recognized me even though I had never met either of them.

Burke set his cup on the saucer in front of him while subtly moving his other hand under the table. "Hold it right there," I said, aiming my pistol at Burke. "I've always wanted to say that. You never get to be so dramatic in narcotics." Motioning with the barrel to keep his hand above the table.

Burke did as I asked, bringing his hand over the table. His eyes squinted, then he extended a palm inviting me to sit at the table. "Please. Join us, Mr. Cold."

Unlike Davis, Burke wasn't afraid. He watched curiously as I went to the conference room doors to turn the deadbolt. "That won't be necessary Mr. Cold. Nobody is going to come in." Burke reached for his coffee cup. "We might as well talk, give us a chance to get to know one another. I'm a great admirer of yours." He said, taking a noisy sip. "Maybe we can be friends."

"I came here to kill you Burke," I stated in a matter of fact, kind of way. Davis got up and started to back away from the table. "I, I, I, I got no, no, no beef with you. This was all, all, Burkes's idea." Burke raised an eyebrow at Davis' stuttering then turned back to me.

"Sit your ass back down." I turned the pistol to Davis who nearly peed his pants taking his seat. Burke didn't blink. He calmly took another sip of his coffee with a look of amusement at my interaction with Davis.

"You're all in on this," I said through gritted teeth. I pulled the recorder from my pocket and pushed play. Davis became so pale I thought he might puke. The gun and my threat scared him, but the recording did something else. He looked up at me with hate-filled eyes, the sniveling weasel gone.

Burke's expression changed too. He had viewed Davis with an annoyed look a moment ago. Now, he had a big toothy grin.

"What is it you think you're going to do? Nobody will ever convict me. Proves nothing." Davis scowled defiantly.

"Then I'll kill you too." I extended the pistol toward his head which had the desired effect. Davis cowered into his seat as I picked up the recorder and placed it back in my pocket.

Burke rose from his chair slowly, hands still in the air, as he directed my attention to the monitors behind him. He reached cautiously to the table and picked up the remote. A click later and the monitor showed me going into the courthouse the morning James was arrested. He pressed another button and a different monitor had pictures of Nevaeh and me at her aunt's place right before the explosion. Then he clicked again and a monitor revealed the inside of Odell's pub. There I was talking with Sam at the bar as Freddy came in. Another click and it was me inside Porters jawing with Miles.

The final reel was the cabin. The entire gunfight rolled across the screen. The Clown being shot, I went inside, then the Clown being helped by the sixth man. The entire wall of monitors was filled with images of me at various points during the investigation.

"You're an interesting fellow Detective Cold." That was the first time Burke addressed me as Detective. "Unpredictable." He turned to look at me. "That's what your supervisor used to say about you."

Burke now had a copy of an old work evaluation. The screens were all configured so the document took up the entire wall. Each monitor with a piece, like a jigsaw puzzle.

The evaluation was an early one. My asshole boss lied about my performance so he could use it to fire me.

"That's from your personnel file. You probably recognize it. All lies of course. I was able to obtain the original copy before your grievance got it removed. The arbiter was right to rule in your favor. Your supervisor was a bumbling idiot." Burke pushed another button which showed a picture of my old boss. His rotted teeth holding a big stogie. Burke was also right about him. He was one of the dumbest cops I'd ever met.

Then the screen went to something I had never seen. A psychological report about ME. "This isn't in your official personnel file. Maybe you aren't aware, but most bosses, government or private, have secret files on their employees.

Publicly, Human Resources tells them it's not a good idea. Privately, they advise them to keep a file. Only the truly foolish don't believe the files actually exist."

He zoomed in on a specific part. "Says here you hate authority. Interesting. Considering the profession, you chose. The report also claims you can't be counted on to tow the line. A rule breaker of sorts with a strong belief in justice." He turned to me with a sarcastic grin. "A quaint idea. Your supervisor was wrong though, I think you are very predictable."

"Yeah. How so?" I asked.

"You came here to kill me. But you won't." Burke grinned.

I turned the pistol from Davis to Burke. "Oh yeah. Why not?"

"You wouldn't have recorded us if your intention was to murder me. Why bother with evidence?" He smirked.

"After you two are gone, I'll have to play this for the world, so they understand what you and your rich little friends were planning," I said. "And neither of you two assholes will be here to say otherwise."

"Then what?" Burke asked. "You let the rest of them go? Do you think they'll just confess? Oh my, the great Detective Alton Cold caught us. And by the way, caught us doing what? Exactly?" Burke enjoyed mocking me. His grin got wider and wider. "Making Colors? There won't be any more shipments coming from this facility. Once Miscavage pulls out, the last of the special batch goes with him. You pull that trigger, and my men will incinerate the building. No more Alton Cold. And no more evidence."

"HEY, I'M NOT DYING IN HERE WITH YOU BURKE!" Davis yelled.

"SHUT THE FUCK UP. You imbecile." When Burke raised his voice, Davis cowered like a dog. Then Burke turned back to me. "You never would take a bribe. You did take the car, though. I figured you'd be okay with that. Predictable. In your mind, it wasn't graft because you weren't on the force anymore, and you already saved Angelina years before. There was no quid pro quo anyone could see.

I knew you'd take the car just like I knew you'd come here after me. You proved a little more resourceful than I anticipated. Never would have imagined you'd kill one of my boys. And you figured things out rather quickly. Even if you really don't know what's going on. Would you like me to tell you?"

"Don't tell him anything!" Davis interrupted.

Burke had slyly worked his way closer to Davis as he was talking. The moment Davis opened his mouth, Burke placed his hands softly across his face. The touch was gentle, but Burke's eyes were menacing. Davis did not move as Burke kissed his forehead lovingly. "I told you to

SHUT THE FUCK UP!" Burke screamed into his ear. The next move took me completely by surprise. As he caressed Davis' head, he slid a box cutter across Davis' throat!

The move was so subtle and fast that Davis' veins were opened before he could make a sound. Blood spurted everywhere as Davis reached with both hands to stop the bleeding, but it was too late. He struggled as Burke cradled him from behind. In less than a minute, the light left his eyes.

Burke looked at me the entire time he held Davis' head. He slid the blade back and then used his tongue to lick the blood off the end. His eyes remained locked to mine with a glow of excitement. His expression was wild but controlled. He was as psychotic as the two Clowns. The boyish face and curly hair were all a façade.

"Now that did surprise me, Cold. You just let him die." Burke smirked.

If his intention was to intimidate or scare me, it didn't work. I dealt with psychos my entire career. "Tell me, why? You have all the money you could ever spend. More power than any politician. Why get everyone hooked? Just so you can cure them with your clinics?" I asked.

Burke's head went back with a raucous laugh. He had not let Davis go as his hand continued to caress the head. He stroked the hair and gazed at him longingly before speaking. "Davis here is right. I shouldn't tell you. But I will. I can't help myself. And…for some reason, I really want you to know."

Finally, he released Davis' body, and it slipped to the floor. Burke licked the blood from his fingers as he continued. "Colors aren't about the euphoric experience; it's about control. You see, detective, we need workers. There is a special project that is very important to many of our members. Your lab guy found something he shouldn't have." Burke paused to look at his watch. "He's dead now. Along with that pesky professor.

Can't have any witnesses you know. You really kept me on my toes with that, by the way. Had to send the Clown to everyone you came in contact with. I finally got ahead of you for a little bit. So much death. But the Clown loves it.

Anyway, as I was saying, workers. When Colors took off, it became the most sought-after drug on the market. Originally, I was just looking for something with a little more zip than Bumps. Bumps were good at keeping the miners going, but it wasn't as pleasurable.

We experimented with different combinations until the extremes proved useful. The only side effect being the physical manifestations of the skin change. But I needed something more, and my sociopath friends were a great way to experiment.

That's when I came up with the control particle. Well, one of my scientists did anyway. Nanites activate the control particle by blending it with the drug. A happy accident. I wanted something that would help shape behavior, and they provided something that takes away free will. Although that's a bit much for some subjects. There are only certain personality types that fall prey to it."

"You're talking about mind control," I said.

"Outstanding detective. It is a crude, albeit somewhat accurate description. But it's much more complicated than that. Nuances to their personality make them susceptible to thoughts if implanted correctly. Over time, it becomes pure obedience.

It doesn't work on everyone." He winked at me. "Take you. Too strong-willed as the psych report also suggests. You'd die before being truly subjugated. But many, many others are all too willing to submit.

"I'm sorry to say mutants fall into this category far more than pureblood humans. I hate to sound racist." Burke finished.

"Okay, but you still haven't told me why? Is this all about money?" I asked.

Burke laughed again as he walked to his coffee. He took another drink with a satisfied look in his eye before responding. "So good. Are you sure you wouldn't like a cup? Might be your last." He sighed, "It's always about money. Do you think corporations exist, to what? Give you something? They exist to make money." His eyes squinted. "I'm sorry, Alton. I know you wanted a deeper meaning. You ever hear of Occam's Razor? Yes, I have more money than I'll ever need. But I like being in charge. I like running the show."

I'd heard enough. I fixed the sights of my pistol right between his eyes. There was no turning back. Burke was wrong; cop or not, I was going to kill him. My finger slid to the trigger. The weight was heavy, but I was determined. The bullet would penetrate his skull the moment I committed to the pressure of the pull.

"I guess I was wrong after all. We really can't be friends." He said with a sinister grin.

Unexpectedly, I felt a sharp pain under my left rib. My finger slid out of the trigger well. The gun wavered as my eyes watered. The pain grew more intense as my mind tried to make sense of what happened.

A soft hand moved over my arm, lowering the pistol. Then it reached into my shirt pocket, taking the recorder. A whisper in my ear. "I'm sorry, but I'm going to need this."

The gun fell out of my hand and clunked onto the table. It was Mara. She pulled out a chair to help me sit. Then she picked up my pistol and walked around the table to Burke. She placed the recorder in his open palm, my gun in his other hand.

Burke looked at me with satisfaction. I was too shocked to move. I could barely breathe as blood poured from my side. I could hear my heart pumping frantically as more red liquid spilled. I was in shock from the stab wound, but that was nothing compared to the shock I felt about who delivered the blow.

My breathing became shallow as I sat deeper in the seat. My eyelids drew heavy. There was no comfortable position as the pain seared through me.

Burke was now sitting on the edge of the table right before me. "Don't die on me, Cold. I need you. I'm sorry we can't come to an understanding." His hand slid under my chin, raising my head. "I'm going to need a fall guy." His grin bigger. "Tag." He let out a big laugh. "If you don't bleed to death first."

Then he looked at the recorder. "I do hope you make it. You are impressive. I didn't think you'd be smart enough to catch us on a recording. Where'd you get this? Some antique store?"

"Every good detective carries three things; a recorder, a camera, and a gun." I quipped.

"Old school. I like it. If you'd have gotten out of here with this, you might have been able to do something. Too bad you couldn't resist the urge to confront me. I'm afraid your story won't mean much without this. And I am Twilas Burke. The savior of so many here in our darkened city. Everyone loves me."

"Why'd you kill James? It wasn't because of Colors. What did he see?" I asked softly.

"You're right. Sharp. It'll be a shame to let you die, detective. You are the only one who's ever come this close to the truth. Although, you don't even know the half of it. Not as smart as me, but a worthy opponent, to be sure. And…I like you.

I'm afraid, however, that you've reached your limit of questions for the day. If you survive, you might be able to ask more." He leaned in close to whisper in my ear so Mara couldn't hear, "I'm going to kill Nevaeh. She's kept her daughter from me far too long. I thought killing the sister would be enough to keep Mara in line. Then, the daughter showed up. Which was okay when the girl was oblivious to everything. Thanks to you, she knows too much. Can't have any loose ends."

Burke leaned back. "I'm going to leave you on an island. Nobody will believe you. You'll be convicted of the killings, Copperhead Strangler, I believe, is the police moniker for the serial killer. Guess who? Your DNA is all over the various crime scenes. The City Attorney will convict you. You'll spend the rest of your days in Max One, which won't be long, considering you were a cop and all. But if you manage to survive, maybe I'll put you out of your misery." Burke leaned back with a devious smirk.

My mistake was trust. And I underestimated this whole damn thing. I should have pulled the trigger the moment I walked through that door.

Burke smiled at me before placing his hand around my neck. He pulled me close, kissing my cheek. "Goodbye detective. I do hope you survive. Sparing with you was fun." Burke walked around the table to leave the room. Before he did, I yelled, "Mara. He's going to kill Nevaeh. RUN!"

Burke's head snapped to me, which gave Mara a brief moment to snatch the recorder from his hand. Before he could do anything, she was gone. She burst from the conference room and raced out the bay doors. She leapt off the docks and disappeared into the darkness.

I lunged for my pistol Burke had set down at the end of the table. He ran out before I could reach it. The loss of blood from Mara's stab wound slowed me enough that he got away.

I returned to the security room and locked the door behind me. I grabbed a package of blood clot from the first aid kit on the wall. It stopped the bleeding but hurt like a son of a bitch. Before heading to the exit door, I applied a few bandages to contain the wound.

My legs got woozy, and my head felt funny. I was about to pass out when the factory sirens started blaring. Adrenaline. The monitors showed people reacting to the sound. A fire erupted at the far end of the building. Burke wasn't bluffing when he said his men would incinerate this place. The flames were spreading quickly.

Then I heard the hiss of steam and the squeak of large wheels. One of the monitors showed Miscavage's train leaving. The big engine pushed the boxcars as it departed the way it came in. I ran out of the room to catch the train when an explosion knocked me to the ground. BOOM!

Flames and debris, along with smoke, filled the space as frantic people tried to escape. I saw lab workers slammed to the ground while others fled to the exits.

At the far end, I could see people trapped behind a wall of flame. Brilliant colors flashed all the way to the ceiling as the drugs added more fuel to the fire. The fire suppression kicked on, but had little effect on the chemicals. The workers were cut off from the exits as the tables in front of them exploded, blocking their path. They only had minutes to escape.

Foundry workers dragged fire hoses from the main building, but there wasn't time. Somebody had to plow them a path. The forklift operators abandoned their vehicles when the alarms went off, so I jumped in one and pushed the accelerator.

I rammed the biggest lab table blocking the exit. The giant table split in two, sending ash and debris to the sides creating a big hole. Once I was through, I hit the brakes. "GET ON. HURRY!" I yelled.

Trapped workers climbed on the bars and held onto the cage. Two more jumped on the sides and once they were aboard, I moved the shifter in reverse and pressed the accelerator. The tires chirped as we rocketed backward. The forklift picked up speed to clear us from the fire. I pressed the brakes, but the pedal went to the floor. "HOLD ON!" I yelled.

We slammed into the security room, which sent the workers flying. I crawled from the cab, helping each of them exit through the dock doors. A few were hurt, but all got out alive.

Bumper City's biggest fire trucks arrived with firefighters scrambling to battle the blaze. The addition was nearly consumed by the time they got there. The fire chief didn't even try to save it, he ordered the firefighters to protect the original Foundry.

Paramedics also rolled in wasting no time taking care of survivors. Most of the workers had been burned to varying degrees. Some suffered broken bones and lacerations from the explosions. The most serious were treated first. New Vegas PD had to assume command of the scene as news trucks and a crowd began to assemble.

Miscavage's locomotive cleared the docks and was far enough away before everything went haywire. The giant light of the engine slowly faded as it chugged along. I may have lost track of Burke, but I knew Miscavage was on that train.

I ran down the side of the building, crossed the grass to Bessimer, and got in. "Are you alright sir? My scans show a serious puncture just below your vertebral ribs. You've lost a good amount of blood, but that seems to have slowed. Shall I summon one of the paramedics?"

"NO! There's no time for that. We're going after Miscavage." I ordered as I put the shifter in drive. I knew where Burke was going, I'd catch up to him soon enough, right now I needed to stop that shipment.

"Blue Line One is picking up speed sir," Bessimer said.

"There's an intersection ahead of it. How long before it gets there?" I asked.

"If it continues accelerating at the current pace, it will reach the intersection in eight minutes," Bessimer said.

I pushed the gas pedal down and cut the wheel. The tires squealed as the back end slid all the way around. Stomping on the accelerator again we rocketed through the main street.

Every cop, EMT, and firefighter looked at us when they heard the tires. They watched as we twirled around and then raced away. I could tell a few of the New Vegas guys thought about chasing me, but they were too busy with the fire.

"Can we beat the train?" I asked.

"By less than a minute if we hurry," Bessimer answered. "If we do manage to arrive at the intersection before the train, how do you intend to stop it?"

"I don't know. We can't let that train get into the heart of the city. You got any ideas?" I asked.

"One moment sir," Bessimer responded.

As he was thinking, I pushed the car harder. Houses became a blur as our speed increased. I prayed nobody walked into the street because I couldn't stop if I wanted to.

The train continued to gain speed, but we caught up quickly. I could see the giant blue nose and oversized front wheel churning furiously.

The Blue Line was fast, but it was no match for Bessimer, and it had the weight of two full boxcars. Because of that, we passed the last boxcar within seconds. I could see its lights in the rearview mirror, and they were getting smaller as we raced ahead.

Bessimer finally responded with his recommendation. "There is a turnout past the intersection. The switch point there is operated by a manual ground lever." Bessimer started. "If you get there ahead of the train, you can change the rails forcing it onto the diverging track. By the time it reaches the turnout, its speed will not be able to handle the curve and should cause it to jump the tracks."

That was all I needed to hear. I pressed the pedal all the way down until we reached the crossover extension. I feathered the brakes enough to cut the wheel sharply to the right. As the nose started to turn, I let off the brake and pressed the gas again. We rounded the curve screeching until the car's front end straightened.

Bessimer slammed through both crossing arms as they lowered. Shattered pieces of wood and metal blasted in the air as the sound of bells chimed intensely. The Blue Line was seconds away. I was nearly out of time.

I slammed the brakes, turned the wheel to the left, punching the accelerator. Bessimer's wheels grabbed shooting gravel out the back. The review mirror showed the train lights getting bigger. It was coming!

"The turnout is less than half a mile sir. The ground lever is on the other side of the tracks. The slope on this side is too steep, if you try to jump across, we will probably roll. You'll have to stop me and go across to activate it." Bessimer said.

"IS THERE TIME?" I yelled.

"If you hurry." He responded.

I gripped the steering wheel tight pushing the car hard. I could feel it lunge forward as the tires continued to throw gravel. The front end was taking a beating as the driver's side wheel ran over railroad ties. The train lights got smaller at first, but I couldn't go as fast on the thick gravel, and now they were getting bigger and bigger. This was going to be close.

Within seconds I spotted the switch on the other side of the tracks. The main line would take the train through the city. The side out went straight then turned sharply to the left. If I could get to the switch in time, the Blue Line was going so fast it would jump the tracks the moment it hit the curve.

I nailed the brakes pitching Bessimer's nose to the ground. Gravel and dust spewed ahead as the tires skidded us to a stop. I pulled the emergency brake, flung the door open and ran across the tracks.

The Blue Line conductor leaned out his window and sounded the horn furiously. I could feel the heated air coming at me. The sound of the train's brakes echoed above the horn as sparks lit up the oversized front wheels.

The ground lever flipped easily causing the point blades to move into position just as the train came thundering over. It was going so fast the wheel flange couldn't handle the curve, and it jumped the tracks just as Bessimer had predicted.

The first boxcar bounced furiously before landing on its left side. It pulled the second car with it as the momentum careened them onto the gravel. The last was the locomotive. The engineer tried to release the coupling before the crash, but he was too late.

The sound was deafening as it slammed into the hillside. Metal smashing and crunching as the entire train jetted into a wooded area bursting through trees and rocks. Eventually, dirt and gravel brought the giant machine to a skidding halt.

"BESSIMER. CALL 911. TELL THEM A TRAIN WITH A SHIPMENT OF COLORS JUST DERAILED AT THE FIRST TURNOUT BEFORE HYDETOWN!" I yelled.

There wasn't any movement. The air was filled with debris. Then I saw the first body. I ran over to find one of Miscavage's goons lying in the weeds. He'd been ejected during the crash and died upon impact. His mangled torso and bent legs flew twenty yards. The irises of his lifeless eyes were open and wide. A mutant.

I searched his pockets, but he wasn't carrying ID. The pistol he carried was twisted across his waist from the crash. I released the thumb break on the holster and pulled it out.

Then I heard coughing. It was coming from the tall weeds not far away. A young man groaned in pain. A white thigh bone was sticking through his dungarees. Pink flesh ripped open and squirted blood. I had to act quickly before he bled to death. I used my belt as a tourniquet to squeeze the artery shut just above the break. I used a stick to tighten the belt until the bleeding stopped.

He continued to groan but wasn't screaming like I expected. Checking the rest of his body for more injuries, I discovered why. His back was broken. I doubt he could feel anything below the waist. The back of his head was oozing blood from a nasty cut too. I grabbed a piece of canvas, among the debris, to create a bandage for his head until paramedics arrived.

The fire began to consume the train. Probably a spark from the last boxcar hitting the rails. The drugs were all packaged in barrels, stacked on wooden pallets, and strapped in place. All flammable.

The flames moved quickly between the two cars with the help of the Colors. It wouldn't be long before they reached the engine and exploded.

The locomotive had fallen on its side. The only way in now, was the door between the engine and the first boxcar. Fortunately, the crash knocked it open.

The locomotive was dark except for the emergency lights that flickered. Cables arced each time they hit metal which sent sparks flying. Smoke was beginning to fill the two floors of the locomotive too. I'd have to be quick.

This was Miscavage's prized engine. He was rumored to have private quarters on the upper floor near the cockpit which was now on it's side. The upper floor would be to my right.

I squeezed past the sparking wires with my pistol at the ready. The smoky haze made it hard to see, but I managed to find the middle and the spiral stairs used to access the second floor. Everything was mangled but I was able to squeeze through.

I got my head and shoulders past the twisted railing when two big hands grabbed me by the collar. It was one of Miscavage's bodyguards from the Foundry. He tossed me against the wall with a loud THUD! My pistol went flying. I could hear it bounce off the floor a few feet away.

The big goon grabbed me again and flung me across the locomotive. I bounced off another wall which knocked the wind out of me.

As I tried to catch my breath, the big ape stomped over to me, lifted me in the air, and slammed a fist into my stomach. OOF! Then he tossed me into some seats. I burst through them like a bowling ball striking pins.

The lights flickered again, and I caught a glimpse of him coming at me. I tried to draw the pistol I'd taken from the guy outside, but he was too quick. I couldn't get the pistol out so I grabbed a metal seat post. I swung the pipe and struck him across the head. He reeled to the side but didn't go down. I drew the pistol and put two rounds into him. His lifeless body smashed to the ground as I caught my breath.

I looked around to get my bearings and spotted Miscavage lying a few feet behind me. He started to laugh, then gave a few quick claps, before coughing up blood. "You're too late, Cold. You can't stop any of this." He smirked.

Kneeling beside him I finally got a good look at him. Now I understood why he rarely made public appearances. His unnaturally pale skin seemed to glow in the low light. His dark glasses had been thrown off during the crash revealing his pink eyes.

"You're going to jail." I sneered.

Miscavage turned his head to look through a window in the rear. We could see the boxcars fully engulfed in flame. He started to laugh which ended with him coughing. "For what? Your evidence is on fire. The factory is destroyed. And I'm not the one who derailed a train. I'd say it's you who's going to jail. Now get me outta here."

He was right. None of the drugs made it. The boxcars were ablaze, and Burke destroyed the factory. The entire operation was obliterated. There was no trace of the lab or drug manufacturing.

Most of the prominent people with any knowledge were either murdered by the Clown or were too scared to go against Burke. And Mara took the only piece of tangible evidence, my recorder.

As I got to my feet, I spotted my gun on the ground. I picked it up on my way to the door. Before I went through, Miscavage yelled, "COLD! What the fuck? Get me outta here!" He may not have cared about the law, but he was afraid to die.

"I'm not helping you. And there won't be any evidence of that either. You and your guard shouldn't have tried to kill me." I said turning to the cockpit door. I heaved it open to find the engineer buckled to his seat, dead. A metal rod had plowed through his chest.

I managed to get back outside through the mangled door. Beyond the smoke, I could hear Miscavage screaming as the engine caught fire.

CHAPTER 22

SECRET PASSAGE

The Disaster Response Command Truck led the police, fire, and EMT vehicles to the train crash. They turned onto the tracks as I exited onto the street. They were in such a hurry nobody even noticed me.

As I sped away, I could see the BCN News truck and a couple of national teams follow the emergency vehicles to the scene. Train derailments are big stories, especially when it involves Domenic Miscavage's personal engine. Wait until they find out he's one of the dead buried under all the wreckage.

But that was for them to deal with, I was on my way to get Burke. He'd be at the mayor's fundraiser by now. Burke always planned to attend, but with everything that happened at the factory, he'd need to make sure his political puppets were in line. I imagined he'd give a little extra to the campaign too, especially since I interfered. Made my stomach churn to think I'd be responsible for that worthless piece of shit Stockton getting more money.

"Bessimer, where's the mayor's fundraiser?" I asked.

"It's at the Regent sir." He responded.

"Even with the riots?" I asked.

"Most of the streets have been cleared. There are a few protesters, but the bulk of the disturbances moved to the other end of the district. A large police presence surrounds the hotel."

I almost laughed. New Vegas Police had deployed of officers to deal with the riots. Not to preserve property or protect people, they needed to make sure the mayor's fundraiser didn't have any problems.

"How am I gonna get in there?" I said softly.

"Perhaps the front door sir," Bessimer said.

"The cops are probably still looking for me. They're not going to let me anywhere near Burke."

"What about the access tunnel?" Bessimer asked.

"Access tunnel? What are you talking about?"

"There is an access tunnel from P&G Corporate offices to the Regent. It's a direct connection underground. I doubt New Vegas PD is guarding it, they aren't supposed to know about it." He stated.

"Hell, I didn't know about it."

"Exactly sir." He responded.

Bessimer put the map of the tunnel on screen while I drove onto the expressway. It was a little hard to see behind all the cracked glass, but I got the basic idea.

The freeway's traffic moved steadily as the evening rush was nearly over. As we passed Union Station, I wondered what would become of the railroad now that Miscavage was dead. His daughter was the only heir unless the board of directors tried to screw her out of it.

With Miscavage dead, Burke lost his most trusted ally. I was sure he knew about the derailment. His contacts on the force would have told him Miscavage was dead too and he would be thinking of the replacement. *I wonder if he'll give it to Angelina.*

The big intersection of New Vegas Blvd. and Sunset Avenue came up fast. The elevated freeway provided a good view of the lighted cross. The red neon from Sunset seemed distinctive in an ominous way.

The highway descended to street level after we crossed into the Mining district. The skyline behind the buildings had a strange glow of orange from the fires lit by the rioters.

The P&G corporate headquarters were built near the entrance to the mines. The building was far enough away from the protests that it looked normal, other than the police presence. The moment we turned onto Patterson Avenue, NVPD cars were everywhere. The police had pushed the protesters several blocks over to keep them away from P&G as well as the Regent.

Snipers were positioned on rooftops overlooking the Regent while uniformed officers guarded the doors. A couple of unmarked surveillance vans were in the parking lot to monitor communications and watch the cameras. They even had a Bearcat Armored Vehicle in case the SWAT team was needed.

Nobody could enter through the front or side doors. All Guests were funneled to the rear entrance of the hotel. The department placed scanning arches just inside those doors so that every person and every bag could be checked.

The Regent's parking lot was full of cars that supported the mayor. Burkes Ferrari was parked closest to the entrance. His own bodyguards kept a vigil next to it. They were easy to spot dressed in black suits and infragreen glasses.

In contrast, the P&G offices were closed so only a few cars remained. I pulled into the P&G lot and parked next to a Lincoln Towncar to blend in. Bessimer wasn't the pristine ride like before, but I was confident he wouldn't be noticed even with all the damage.

P&G's office building had a front that was a wall of glass. I could see a security guard sitting behind a reception desk in the lobby. According to the schematics Bessimer provided, there was a stairwell on the north side of the building which led to the tunnel. I needed to get there unnoticed, which meant waiting for the guard to go on rounds or lure him outside.

There were two cameras watching the front entrance and another scanning the parking lot. "Bessimer, can you cause a power surge disabling the cameras like you did at the Foundry?"

"Yes sir. They will be disrupted for approximately 30 seconds before the backup generator kicks in. It's a similar setup as the Foundry, although not quite as sophisticated."

"Can you restart it? I don't want it down that long, I only need 15 seconds."

"Yes sir. I should be able to do that."

"Good. The moment the Lincoln beside us starts blaring, send the surge and disrupt the cameras." I ordered.

"What about the snipers and other law enforcement watching the building next door?" He asked.

"Hopefully I can cross the lot before they spot me," I responded by getting out quietly and shutting the car door. I kept a low profile moving to the front of the Lincoln. The guard was in the same spot and nobody else seemed to be eyeing my position.

With a swift kick to the front door panel, the alarm went off. As the lights flashed and the sound erupted, I scampered to a tree near the building.

Bessimer sent the surge causing the parking lot lights to go out. When the area was dark, I raced from the tree to the corner of the building.

The guard did as I expected and came outside to investigate. When he started to walk toward the Lincoln, I snuck behind him and shoved my hat in the door before it closed. The guard couldn't hear me with the car alarm and the flashing light kept his attention on the Lincoln.

Once I was inside, a second-floor light came on. An executive working late came out to see what was happening. I got to the stairwell before he saw me and watched him through the door's window. He stood there for a moment before using a remote to shut off the car alarm.

"What's that all about?" He asked the guard who was just returning.

"Might've been a power surge. We get'em all the time." The guard walked to his desk. "Not sure why your car alarm was going off." The guard picked up the telephone, "I guess I better call this in."

On cue, Bessimer turned the lights back on in the parking lot. Then the cameras flickered before returning to normal. The guard shrugged his shoulders, setting the phone down. "I thought you were the only one here?"

"I am." The executive said.

"Whose cars are those out there?" The guard asked.

"Probably overflow from the party next door."

The executive returned to his second-floor office, while the guard fumbled around at his desk. He thought about things for a minute before watching television again. With the two of them going back to what they were doing, I could concentrate on finding the tunnel.

Bessimer's map showed an access point in the rear of this well. Unfortunately, I had no idea how to find it. The area was dimly lit by a few accent lights which didn't help. The wall was plain with no obvious ridge lines or other mechanisms to open it. I ran my hand over the tile hoping to feel anything odd or out of place. Midway down the wall, there was a spot where a tiny bit of air came through. I placed my palm on the center of the tile and gently pushed, but there was no reaction. Now that my hand was taking up the space, I could feel more air at the edges. When I slid my hand toward it, the tile felt different. I used my flashlight for a quick burst, adjusted my hand position, and pushed again. This time the tile moved.

As the tile depressed, the guard's chair squeaked. He must have seen the flash. *Don't get distracted. Get it open. Concentrate.* My heart was pounding.

I pushed harder letting the tile guide me. At the top, it pivoted inward more than the bottom. There was a red button recessed in the jamb. I pushed the button which caused the tiles to separate to reveal a door. I shoved it open, squeezed myself through, then put my back to the door and pushed. The door slid quietly into its original position.

As I heard the rush of air and clicks as it shut, I also heard the stairwell door open.

My side of the door had no light. I couldn't even see my hand in front of my face. I leaned against the secret door listening to the guards' footsteps on the other side. It sounded like he climbed a couple of stairs, looked around, paused, then went back to the lobby. I heard the stairwell door close as his footsteps faded.

After a few seconds passed, I did a quick burst with my flashlight. This revealed a descending stairwell to the right. I'd have to feel my way in the dark until I was confident my flashlight wouldn't alert the guard.

The stairs went half a flight, turned, then down another half flight. The farther down I went, I noticed a dampness in the air and the temperature seemed to drop.

Once at the bottom, I faced the tunnel. It was dark, except for accent lights along the floor and ceiling. They continued until disappearing in the distance.

Besides being dark, the only sound came from the echo of water dripping into shallow puddles on the floor. The water appeared to come from condensation off various utility lines running across the ceiling.

The corridor wasn't only long, it was wide. Bessimer's map indicated it ran under the parking lot all the way to the Regent. I estimated that to be about a hundred yards or so.

I had walked far enough to no longer see the stairs behind me. *Plenty of dark places to hide. Someone would have to know I was using the tunnel to ambush me.* Seemed unlikely but it was unnerving. If Burke thought I was in here, I wouldn't put it past him to send some goons to finish me off.

As I approached what I guessed to be, the halfway point, there was a break in the wall. It was a darkened space made visible by an edge of low light. I pulled my pistol and crept closer with my back to the wall. I stopped just before the archway to peek around the corner. Another tunnel.

This was not on Bessimer's schematic. The only light was at the end above a metal door. *Where do you suppose that goes?* I thought.

Then I heard the soles of shoes slapping against the wet floor.

I stepped into the side corridor hugging the wall to hide in the shadows. I could hear the footsteps getting closer and closer. From the dark, I extended the pistol getting ready to fire.

As the steps got near, I began to hear talking. A few moments later, a pair of figures strolled past the opening of the connecting tunnel. It was two P&G executives walking toward the main office. Their voices echoed in the hall as they stopped to light cigars.

"That was some party." One of them said.

"Yeah, but I hate politicians." The other responded.

The first one laughed. "I know what you mean."

"I wish the boss didn't expect us to go to these things." The second one said.

I breathed a sigh of relief lowering my pistol. The flame from their lighters allowed me to see the lapel pins they wore. These pins were worn by the top executives at P&G.

One motioned with his head, at the corridor where I was hiding. They couldn't see me in the shadows but it made my heart thump. He blew a puff of smoke and said, "But there are the perks. Seems a small price to pay for something like that."

They both chuckled before the second one took a big puff and said, "You saw Burke with the boss. It's really all they ask of us."

The embers of their cigars burned bright as they took in air. After a giggle and a couple more puffs, they hurried toward P&G disappearing into the dark.

When I couldn't hear them anymore, I looked back at the metal door. *Those two mentioned 'the perks'.* I really wanted to know what they were talking about. *What is behind this door? I wonder.*

I didn't have time to explore, and these two confirmed Burke was at the fundraiser. I needed to get to him while I knew where he was. The perimeter was well guarded, but the inside shouldn't be as secure, and that would be my best chance, so I hustled to the other side of the tunnel.

Unlike the P&G side, there were no stairs here. There was a blank wall ahead of me, a dead end. There was some light on the bottom, but it didn't show much. The pipes and cables above didn't continue past the wall, they turned off to the side.

I shined my flashlight around but couldn't see any levers or buttons. I recognized the seam of a door but nothing to indicate how it was activated. I stood perplexed, scanning the wall.

Finally, my eyes caught a glint of something on the floor. Under a puddle, there was a dark object below the water line. I tried to pull it, but there wasn't enough lip for me to grab onto. Then it hit me. I placed my foot on the black square and pressed.

The water disappeared under my shoe. I stepped back as the square returned to its original position and water covered it again. After the pedal was submerged, the noises started. Click. Pop. Whoosh. The seams of the door separated and steam gushed through. The door pivoted inward exposing light from the other side.

The door was open for a few seconds when I heard the noises start again. I pulled my pistol and hopped through before it closed. Seconds later, the secret passage was gone. On the other side were six washing machines hiding its existence. *Clever.*

The moment the door settled in place; a loud boom startled me. I flipped around to see a laundry bag hitting the floor. It landed atop a pile of other bags on the far wall.

I also spotted the service elevator across from the laundry chute. I put the pistol behind my back and got on the elevator. After pushing the button to the first floor, I adjusted my tie and hat not knowing what part of the hotel it would take me to.

The doors opened in a large hallway across from the kitchen. Double doors swung both ways as waiters carried trays and pushed carts to the ballroom. It was at one end of the hall with two security guards posted at the door. It wasn't going to be easy getting past them without an invitation.

To my left, was another set of double doors, leading to the reception desk, where hotel staff greeted customers. I could try that way, but I suspected the grand hall posted security at those ballroom doors too.

"HEY! Get dressed. What the hell are you standing around for?" Said a loud voice from out of nowhere. I nearly jumped out of my suit. A skinny guy abruptly walked up from behind while my head was turned.

He clapped his hands, "Come on. Let's go, let's go!" The guy must have been the kitchen manager or head waiter.

Looks like the way into the ballroom just fell in my lap. My feet instinctively moved to a row of lockers on my left. There was one without a lock, so I opened it. Lucky for me, a waiter's uniform hung inside.

My gun was still tucked in my back, so I carefully peeled off my jacket, mindful to keep the angle away from his eyes. As I slid my arms into the white coat, a couple of waiters came through the kitchen doors behind this guy. He turned and directed them to the big room at the end of the hall.

After they went through the ballroom doors, he motioned for me to follow him into the kitchen. He grabbed a dessert cart and pushed it in front of me. "Here, take this. Make sure everyone gets one."

The cart was full of individual dessert servings. Crème Brulee, Chocolate Mousse, and the big one, individual slices of Frazier Cake with Diplomat Cream. I knew from this cart; it was not a typical fundraiser. Nobody serves Frazier Cake to the working class.

I did as the head waiter instructed, and wheeled the cart out of the kitchen and down the hall, to the ballroom. Before I went through, I looked back, but the head waiter was gone. There was something familiar about him. His voice? Maybe the cadence in which he spoke. I didn't know, but I thought I'd seen his face before too. There wasn't anything special about his features, it was just a feeling.

I shrugged it off happy with my good fortune at finding a way in. I backed through the doors pulling the cart into the room. The two guards had moved to the walls beside the doors as I came in.

The ballroom was packed. There must have been fifty tables with eight chairs around each one. At the front was a stage that ran from one end of the room to the other. A long table sat on it with a dozen chairs facing the room. Each chair had an honored guest, and at the center, was Mayor Stockton. Behind her was a giant banner that read, RE-ELECT MAYOR STOCKTON FOR A BRIGHTER FUTURE IN A DARK WORLD.

The entire room was decorated with balloons and party streamers. Even the tablecloths were color-coordinated in red, white, and blue.

Stockton sat next to a podium which also had a picture of her on the front. Burke was to her right with half a dozen other heavy donors seated beside him. Some I recognized from the meeting at the Foundry, but others I didn't know.

On the other side of the podium to the mayor's left, sat the City Attorney, and then the Chief of Police. This was no surprise, that sleaze kissed more ass than anyone I knew. He was more a politician than a cop. How else could someone so incompetent get so high up?

I didn't look past the chief, as my focus shifted to Burke. I needed to get close enough to him before he or the chief spotted me. It was hard to imagine I got in here so damned easy, maybe I should have knocked on wood before thinking like that. My shoulders twitched when I heard a guard behind me say. "Hold it!"

Both guards walked over as I was about to serve the closest table. They looked at me in a strange way which caused my heart to start beating faster. I thought, *This is it.* I reached behind to slide my hand under the coat. I almost had a grip on my pistol when one of the guards reached for the cart.

The big ape was too fast reaching over my arm and grabbing two plates off the top tray. Crème brulee and Frazier Cake. *Whew.* He handed the cake to his partner while I let out a soft breath, which he caught. "Hey, just cause we're working doesn't mean we can't enjoy it too." He snipped before they both went back to guard the doors.

I continued to hand out desserts while they stuffed their faces. More waiters burst through the kitchen doors and within seconds I was just one of a dozen waiters filtering across the room. Burke was going to be mine.

CHAPTER 23

POLITICIANS, LAWYERS, AND MONEY

Things may not have gone exactly as I imagined, but here I was feet from Burke. He hadn't seen me yet so all I needed to do was make my way around the other side of these tables, take some desserts onto the stage, and grab him before anyone could stop me.

The only problem was Penny. If she spotted me and called out, it would give away my presence. So far, I haven't seen her. That's when I heard my name being called. "Cold. Alton Cold. What on earth are you doing here?" It was Jennifer Caldwell from BCN5. She was seated at a table near the main doors. I glanced at the stage, but nobody was looking my way. They hadn't heard her.

"Why are you handing out desserts? And why are you dressed as the wait staff?" She asked as she gave me a big hug. "You work here?" Then I could see her wheels starting to turn. "Wait, you don't work here, you're WORKING here." She said excitedly. "Come sit with me. Take that silly coat off."

"Meet me over at the door." I motioned with a head nod as the emcee announced the first speaker. The crowd began to clap when the deputy mayor stood. As he approached the podium I noticed Marty Knoun was seated next to him.

The more I looked at the entourage sitting at that table, the less guilt I felt about killing Burke. Looking at that group of asshats, and knowing what they were truly up to, I wanted to kill each one of them. Lucky for them, Burke's the only one on that stage who tried to kill me. But if I'm being honest, it's what he did to Mara that tipped the scale. Even if she did stab me.

Which reminded me, I hadn't thought about the wound in a while. The adrenaline took my mind off it. Thinking about it now, I felt the sharp pain. I opened the coat to find a small amount of blood seeped through my shirt. *Good thing the head waiter didn't notice when I changed.*

I finished emptying the dessert cart and pushed it toward the main doors. Jennifer waited until I was near them before getting up. Just my luck, every man in the room eyed her walking from the table. She was beautiful and her dress was tight with a plunging neckline.

"Cold. Now what are you doing here? I know you're not going to arrest anybody, you're not on the job anymore. I heard you have your own license. Who's doing what? Come on. You gotta let me have it." Her speech was rapid almost to the point of stuttering. And her eyes sparkled with that familiar enthusiasm new reporters often had.

"I'm here for Burke." I said bluntly. I wasn't sure why I told her. I guess I admired her work ethic. She'd been around a while but still had that fire for the job.

Her eyes lowered the moment I said his name. She looked at me with a nervous expression as she pulled me through the door. It was so abrupt she nearly knocked over the goon guarding it on the other side. "Sorry. Sorry. Just need some air." She said to him as she dragged me away.

He gave a scowl before stiffening to resume his post. She pulled me down the hall and when she was sure he couldn't hear she said, "You can't fuck with Twilas Burke, Alton."

"Why not?" I asked.

"Look. I'm your friend. Okay, okay, maybe not a close friend. I know you don't like reporters. But I always respected you. You know that, right? I kept your name out of things when I could." She paused looking around nervously before continuing. "Messing with Burke is suicide."

"Burke is responsible for the serial killings." I said.

"Twilas Burke?!" Her voice surprised, then skeptical. "You think Twilas Burke is the serial killer? The one beheading his victims with heated copper wire. You think he's the Copperhead Strangler?" She paused, "Jesus Alton. He's an evil bastard, but…"

"I didn't say he was the Copperhead Strangler. He didn't commit the killings with his bare hands. I said he was responsible for them. He ordered them. And I can prove it." I started. " He's in cahoots with half of those jabroni's sitting at that table on that stage."

"Well of course he's in with them. He's backing the mayor just like they are. It's well known he works with nearly all of them. THEY'RE ALL backing the mayor." She took a deep breath glancing at the door then to me, "What kind of proof?"

"I made a recording of Burke leading a secret meeting with half of those idiots in there. They're the ones making Colors. And there's more. There's something in the drugs. It's a type of nanotech that exerts control over people. Burkes has been experimenting with the effects, trying to control everyone. If he perfects those nanites, there's no limit to what he can do. He's a Goddamned sociopath." I finished.

"Where is this recording? Do you have it on you?" She asked.

"No. It, it got taken from me." I said.

"For fuck's sake, Alton. Is there anyone else I can talk to? Someone to corroborate what you're saying." She asked.

I knew everything would come down to this. Burke had each person I spoke with or was going to speak to, killed. No witnesses. Everyone on that stage knew, but none of them would dare betray him.

"I can't go to my producer, hell, nor the head of the newsroom with just your word. Burke owns the station for Christ's sake. Even if I wanted to push it, nobody would put it on the air." She said.

"What? He owns the station? I thought Scaffe owned the network?" I said.

"He does. On paper. How do you not know Burke owns the media in this town? Including competing stations and the newspaper. It's an open secret. At least amongst us anyway." She said.

My mind was racing. I'd need the recording and more to convince anyone, let alone get them to air it. It would take more than the serial killer angle. I needed something tangible. Something that couldn't be faked.

"Wait, the crime lab found the nanites. The tech discovered them in the latest batch of Colors. He can confirm as much."

"Crime lab? What's his name?" When she asked, I suddenly remembered what Burke had said.

"Ricky Talmadge. You know Rick." My stomach was churning.

"Rick's dead." Jennifer's face was drawn with fear.

"How? I talked to him not long ago. He should be at the lab." I was hoping Burke's threat was empty.

"Didn't you hear? One of the exhaust fans malfunctioned. A lethal dose of fentanyl went airborne and killed three people. Rick was one of them." She explained.

I didn't have to hear another word. I reached to my back storming toward the door. The guard saw me coming, not sure what to think. For all he knew, I worked there, but I was marching toward the door in a way that alerted him. He pulled his sleeve up to his mouth speaking into a microphone hidden there.

I was just about to pull my pistol when his hand moved to cover his earpiece. His face contorted with a weird expression, a second later he stepped aside.

Jennifer rushed to my side to prevent me from going in, but my adrenaline was pumping so hard I barely noticed her. I opened the door forcefully as a few people glanced at me. They quickly forgot and turned back to the speaker.

Jennifer was right on my heels as I looked directly at Burke. He was staring at me with a big toothy grin. I realized he knew I was here the whole time. That was why the guard stepped out of the way. Burke ordered him to let me back in.

I became distracted as the crowd burst into applause. A guest was introducing the mayor as people stood and cheered. I couldn't believe my eyes. The person introducing the mayor was Lynn! Judge Bondino.

My eyes drifted across the entire table. I recognized the president of the Bumper City Bar Association seated next to Burke. Burke stood to clap with the crowd, never taking his eyes off me. His smile got wider when he saw my reaction to seeing Lynn introducing the mayor.

"The judge. She's my friend." My comment was barely audible, but Jennifer heard it.

She leaned close to whisper, "He owns everyone. Judges. Lawyers. The mayor. Hell, even the president of the bar association is here because of him. Nobody cares about the mayor, they're all here for him." She paused, "Without that recording or another witness, I couldn't help you even if I wanted to."

I turned to look at her. "So, you believe me?"

"I didn't say that."

"You said you couldn't help even if you wanted to. Not, you couldn't help even if you believed me." I said.

Then I thought about Penny. I hadn't seen her which was odd. Penny loved political events and she wasn't the type of woman who blended in. Her laughter could fill the entire hall.

Before I got a chance to ask, a waiter came over and slapped a piece of paper in my chest. "Supposed to give you this pal."

Jennifer craned her neck to look over my shoulder. The paper read YOU HAVE A PHONE CALL. The waiter who gave me the note opened the door and directed us to the phone bank. *Who else knew I was here?* I turned to look at Burke before stepping into the hallway. His smile lessened as he raised a glass to me.

Jennifer had seen what was written and came with me. There must have been a dozen payphones in the lobby, but only one had a receiver sitting atop.

I placed the receiver to my ear. "Yes," I said.

"Would you really have killed those two young executives in the tunnel? Heeheheh"

I recognized the voice right away, it was the Pagliacci Clown. He was alive.

"Why'd you help me get into this room? Weren't you supposed to kill me?" I said realizing where I'd seen him. He was the head waiter. I didn't recognize him without the makeup, but there was no mistaking the voice.

He let out a hearty laugh. "AHAHAHAHAHAH. You really crack me up Cold. So damned hard to read. I honestly can't tell if you're joking half the time. He arranged the whole thing. You didn't honestly believe he'd allow you to walk in there if you were really going to shoot him in the face, did you? He knew you wouldn't go through with it."

"What're you trying to say? The guards let me in?"

"Naaaaaaw. That part was all you. Well, getting past the first set of guards and stuff. With a little help from me. Not much of a game if you don't get to play your part. He likes to let people make their own choices. Just so happens he knows what those are going to be, most of the time." The Clown snickered. "I'll give you one for free. He knew the car would tell you about the tunnel. It was the only way in. So, he left it open for you. Not really rocket science."

"It wasn't exactly open. I had to find the lever." I snipped.

"What kind of a detective would you be if you can't solve a simple puzzle?" The Clown giggled.

"And the two P&G execs in the tunnel? What about them? What made you or him think I wouldn't have smoked them if it went the other way down there?" I snipped.

"That was the real wildcard. Ain't no fun if there isn't some chance. Although even I knew you wouldn't kill them." He said.

"Oh yeah, how's that?" I asked.

"You didn't have a good reason to. They couldn't see you along the wall in that dark space." He quipped.

He must have been in there with me. I'd never given any indication where I was when those two walked by. If he was down there, *How the hell did he get ahead of me to the kitchen?*

"Burke wanted you in the hotel, or you wouldn't have gotten in. He wanted you to join them in the fundraiser, or you wouldn't have gone in there either." He teased.

"And the tunnel? Isn't he worried about that little secret?" I snapped.

"Come on, Cold. You're better than that. There is nothing in this world that cannot be undone, except death and taxes." He paused, "I know the pretty reporter is beside you. Don't dare tell her about the tunnel Cold. Now that you've said it out loud, she'd going to ask. Be a shame to kill her. You got a lotta bodies on you. You really need to be more careful.

But I think you've had your quota of questions for today. At least for this call, for sure." He kept taunting me before dropping the bomb. "Penny for your thoughts?" Then a hideous laugh.

"Where is she? Listen you fucking psycho…" I demanded before he cut me off.

"Uh oh. Careful with the P word. I'm a sociopath, not a psychopath." He turned serious. "If you want to see your girl again, you've got one hour before I start carving her up like a Thanksgiving Turkey. You and me. Nobody else. Bring someone and I'll know. She dies. Horribly." He laughed again. "Oh, and Cold, go get your hat and coat. I don't want to kill you while you're in that silly waiter's jacket. At least dress like you think you'll win."

"Where?" I asked.

"They say Colors never run, but that hasn't been my experience. One hour Cold. You either leave with her, or you both stay with me… forever." The call ended with him laughing.

I knew exactly where he had Penny. There was time if I left now. Jennifer heard some of the conversation but not all of it.

"Somebody has your friend, Penny, don't they? It's him, isn't it? The Copperhead Strangler. What was that about a tunnel Cold? Come on, it's not Burke. I need this one." Jennifer pleaded.

"Jennifer, stay here. Don't argue and don't try to follow me." I said, moving past her toward the front desk. She watched as the clerk stood to block me. The desk phone rang, and the clerk's eyes looked right at me. She set the receiver down on the cradle before returning to her seat.

The clerk never looked up as I continued through the doors. The pain in my side returned as I raced through the hall to the locker for my coat and hat. I didn't have time for the tunnel. Instead, I hurried past the front desk and out the doors. I ran to the P&G parking lot to Bessimer.

"Were you successful sir?" Bessimer asked as I shut the door.

"Quickest way to the City Dump!" Before he could answer I pulled onto Patterson Avenue heading north. "They've got Penny. We have to get to the warehouse at the dump in thirty minutes or she's dead!"

Bessimer wasted no time showing a map with the route. "Here is a path that avoids the riots."

"How long?" I asked.

"At your current rate of speed, about thirty minutes." He said.

"NOT GOOD ENOUGH. Too long. I need a shorter path."

"All other routes go into the heart of the riots. Anything could happen. Each of those are unpredictable. If things converge before you break through, you might not make it to save Miss Penelope. Sir." He responded.

"Have to risk it. She's dead if I'm not on time." Bessimer adjusted, and placed the fastest route in red, on the screen. I didn't hesitate, pushing the pedal to the floor.

As we raced deeper into the Mining District, the glow from the fires was getting bigger. There was a distinct line of destruction, from where the police had pushed the group east, to keep everything away from the Regent.

Protesters marched down the middle of the street. Cars were on fire. Bottles, bricks, and debris were everywhere. Storefronts were smashed. Even those who put plywood over their windows were damaged.

Bessimer showed me the group patterns on the screen. The mob appeared chaotic at ground level, but his display revealed a sway to their movements. It was like a flock of birds, only this flock left devastation in its wake.

When I turned onto the main street displayed on his route, we got pelted with objects. Bessimer's armor was still tough so none of it did any damage. We rolled along at a steady pace when a man came out of nowhere swinging a two-by-four at the windshield. I flinched but the wood bounced off sending him to the pavement. *Yeah, fuck you too.*

That first attack seemed to spawn more as others rushed at us from all sides. Despite their best efforts, none of it could put a dent in Bessimer.

"Turn up here sir. The street appears clear for a mile or so. You should be able to increase your speed and gain some lost time."

Bessimer was right, for the most part. The marchers were moving southeast as if they were heading toward the Red Light District. It was unlikely they'd make it that far.

I raced the car ahead while the street was bare. I crossed under the highway nearly to New Vegas North when I came upon half a dozen protesters surrounding two cops. Their police cruiser was on fire as the mob was viciously beating them.

"Time Bessimer?" I asked.

"If you maintain your present rate of speed, you'll arrive in less than 15 minutes. Well ahead of schedule."

I turned the wheel, slammed the brakes, and spun the car completely around. "With this delay, you may not make it in time," Bessimer warned.

The group heard the engine and looked as Bessimer's headlights blinded them. A few ran, but a couple of brave souls decided to attack. I floored the pedal and plowed into them without tapping the brakes. One flew up over the roof, and another held on to the windshield, so I slammed on the brakes which sent him flying.

I jumped out and ran to the injured officers. Both were young, rookies. Their faces were bloody and battered, no match for the bats and boots put to them. The mob ran off which meant they were safe for now.

"Than....thank you." Said one barely able to speak. I ran to the call box on the corner and picked up the handset. A moment later the operator answered. "Yeah, two officers down. Send medical. Two suspects also down." I blurted before hanging up.

I ran back to the injured cops, "You'll be alright son. Both of you will. Help is on the way." I said before running to Bessimer and speeding away.

"You're cutting it close sir," Bessimer said.

"I know. I couldn't let the mob kill those them." I had to hurry so I pressed the gas even harder.

"Turn here sir." Bessimer directed.

The tires screeched as I rounded a corner. The City Dump was straight ahead. The workday was over, so the gates were closed. No time to fiddle with it.

Bessimer's front end hit the gates, easily breaking the chain. One of his headlights cracked, reducing what I could see in the dark, but I didn't have time to go around. Sparks flew as the wheels bottomed out when I drove straight through the recycling plant.

The Sum Avenue intersection came up fast. I slowed to make the turn. I didn't want to run the engine hard as Bessimer's exhaust had gotten loud with all the damage he sustained today.

Spivey nor any of his men were at the Recycling Center when I raced through. Neither Charlette nor any of her security team were at the Sum Avenue intersection either. A sick feeling came over me as I crept toward the warehouse.

I flipped off the remaining headlamp and pulled to the side when I was close. Everything was pitch black. All the fire lamps were out, and it was still. I stepped out of the car looking back down the road, none of those lamps were burning either.

The building looked desolate. Abandoned. It was empty when I came here earlier, but this was different. The entire area had a creepy vibe.

Chances were, he heard me coming. That was okay as I wanted him to know I made it before the deadline. I only hoped he'd keep his word and not harm Penny.

Then I got a bit of luck.

CHAPTER 24

AN OPERA OF KNIVES AND BULLETS

Rain doesn't usually come down this hard. My hat offered little protection as the wind blew it in my face. I guess the buildup of moisture was too much and it finally let loose. The pounding on the metal roof from the big droplets made a huge racket.

The Clown may have heard me pull up, but with all the noise from the storm, he wouldn't hear me sneaking around. He knew I was coming and probably anticipated the back door, maybe the front, but he wouldn't know which. I wanted to get a look inside before I burst in. Maybe if I was lucky, I'd catch him off balance.

I sloshed through the puddles as quietly as I could, keeping low to get next to the building. There was a window on the side I might be able to see through. I inched to it but couldn't get a good look without exposing my head.

I decided to move behind a large trash pile a few feet away. I might be able to see from there. I climbed onto the heap, which gave a broader view of the inside. From this vantage point, I could see Penny tied to one of the posts. The prick had her mouth gagged and there was the shine of copper around her neck. Her mascara smeared which made the whites of her eyes stand out. The look on her face was pure terror.

The copper wire continued from her neck, down the pole, and attached to a generator behind the post. A kitchen timer sat on top of the generator, and if the dial was correct, time was nearly up.

The Clown was nowhere in sight. No choice. I had to sneak in and get to the generator. I knew the moment I got inside; that he was going to attack. Penny would die during the fight unless I freed her first. "Well, front door it is," I said quietly to myself.

The storm got worse. Thunder boomed and lightning filled the sky. Rain pelting the ground with huge drops splashing the puddles.

I slid under the eaves of the building on my way to the front. The door was now ajar. An invitation.

I raised my gun to the ready. With my other hand, I pushed the door a little farther. Now I could get a better look before going in. I had no idea where the Clown was hiding, so I needed to sneak a peek.

Penny's eyes got wide as she saw the door open. Most of the building was filled with shadows, except around Penny. There were two lamps above her that illuminated the space around her. On the wall behind hung a fire extinguisher. I hadn't seen it from the window, but now, it gave me an idea.

The flashes of lightning allowed me to see a little more, even for a moment, so I stepped into the door jamb, pistol at the compressed ready. Penny started to whimper under the gag when she realized it was me. I put my finger over my lips for her to be quiet. The thunder made it hard to hear, and I needed to figure out where the Clown was hiding before he got the jump on me.

I placed my infra-green glasses over my eyes, but something was wrong. They weren't working properly. Things looked distorted through them which prevented me from getting a good visual. I put in fresh batteries knowing the cloud would drain them quickly, so it couldn't be that. It was something else.

Then, a lightning flash accompanied by a thunderclap. My eyes caught a glimpse of the Clown's smiling face in the rafters above! Instinctively, I fired two shots. BOOM! BOOM!

I raced to a nearby pole, keeping focused on the ceiling. I peeked around the beam, careful to remain behind cover.

"THAT WASN'T VERY NICE DETECTIVE." The Clown called out with a hideous laugh. "TICK TOCK. TICK TOCK." I used the flashlight for a quick scan but couldn't find him.

"A GUN IS NO FUN DETECTIVE." His voice boomed. When he said the next part, I could tell he moved closer. "You still think a gun will defeat evil? Tsh, tsh."

I did a quick burst of light where I thought he was, but there was no sign of him. I darted to a second post closer to Penny. Then I hurried to another. Her eyes followed my movements as I went pole to pole moving toward her. Her eyes pleaded with me to reach her in time.

"A TECH INHIBITOR. A GIFT FROM TWILAS? NOT EXACTLY FAIR." I called out.

I knew he wouldn't be able to help himself. "C'mon, you have a gun. How's that fair? I don't have a gun." The reverb wasn't as good on the ground. He'd moved to the floor and was somewhere near the front door.

Then I heard the door shut and lock. Another lightning flash proved I was right. His hand was still on the knob before the light disappeared. I squared myself and squeezed the trigger, BOOM! BOOM!

Darkness engulfed the space as I fired. His laughter got farther and farther away as he ran to the back corner. I sent another volley in that direction BOOM! BOOM! Right after the second shot, I heard a big crash and a slam against the metal wall. *I must have hit him.* The beam of my flashlight didn't reveal anything.

"YOU, OKAY?" I called out sarcastically. Total silence until Penny started screaming from behind the gag.

I scurried to her and pulled the gag down. I saw fear in her eyes just before she screamed, "BEHIND YOU!"

The Clown lunged and I moved just enough, raised my arm, and blocked the big kitchen knife from stabbing me. The force knocked the pistol from my hand. It bounced to the floor as he struck again, this time, cutting my arm. Blood from the gash squirted as the blade sliced through my jacket and across my skin.

My right fist slammed into his face. The impact sent him backward, but it didn't dislodge the knife. He staggered but regained his balance to look at me with a devious smile threw blood-soaked teeth. Then he raised his sleeve to wipe his mouth.

My pistol lay a few feet away along with my flashlight. The light had spun around a few times before coming to a stop. His eyes moved from me to the pistol, then back to me.

"ALTON! THE WIRE!" Penny screamed as the timer started to ring. Penny's neck began to smoke. She cried out in agony as I leaped to the fire extinguisher. I ripped it from the wall and used it to strike the copper wire. The wire snapped apart on the first blow. My second blow crushed the switch of the generator, knocking it out of commission.

Penny shook violently trying to get free. She was sobbing and ripping at her bindings, but it was no use, "ALTON GET ME OUTTA THIS."

I threw the extinguisher and pulled my knife to cut her loose, but was interrupted by that familiar mocking from the shadows, "Not so fast Cold!"

My flashlight was still on the ground, but my pistol was gone. The Clown had grabbed it and rolled into the darkness. I stepped in front of Penny to shield her.

"I didn't hit you, did I?" I taunted.

"Stalling won't get you anywhere. But to answer your question, no, you missed." He sneered.

I couldn't see him, but from the sound, he moved each time he spoke. He seemed to be circling us to avoid my knowing exactly where he was.

"You don't have to do this. Let Penny go." I said.

The lightning and thunder clapped again. A moment of silence, then his answer from a new spot. Now he was to my right. In the flash, I saw the gun in his hand. The barrel pointing right at me. In his other hand, the knife. A big grin on his face as blood trickled out the side of his mouth from my punch.

"I don't have to, but I want to." He said with a giggle.

"You have me. That's what you wanted." I responded.

Again, the Clown answered from another spot. "That's not all I want."

I knew what he meant. "Why kill Nevaeh? She's not a part of this."

"YOU MADE HER A PART OF THIS WHEN YOU KILLED MY BROTHER!" He yelled, now from the opposite corner.

"I thought you didn't care about your brother?" I asked. I had to get him closer if I wanted a chance. "I'm not sorry, ya know. You're both freaks."

"Odd thing to say. I can see you, but you can't see me. Who's the freak here?"

"What are you doing?" Penny whispered.

"He's not going to shoot." I whispered before yelling, "ARE YOU SHITBAG?" I turned back to Penny. "That would ruin his fun. He needs to be close. He wants to watch death, to feel it. RIGHT?"

"Are you shot?" Penny whispered to me again, her voice elevated.

Blood dripped from my sleeve where this asshole cut me, but there was also blood trickling onto my shoe from Mara.

"No. I was stabbed earlier. The dressing must have come loose." I responded.

"EARLIER?" Penny whispered emphatically. "STABBED? By who?"

"Mara. It's a flesh wound. Least of my problems right now." I said.

The Clown let out a maniacal laugh which filled the warehouse. The lightning flashed again. I could see him between us and the front door.

"Burke ordered you to leave the girl alone, didn't he? You can't kill her." I taunted. "You're still his little BITCH."

"FUCK YOU COLD!" He snapped. He was close now, right in front of me. It was working. The insults were distracting him from moving to the sides. Another insult or two and I might get my chance.

"Yeah. He told me not to kill her. You know what I say?" The Clown sneered.

"What's that?" I asked, taking two steps toward him.

"Normally I'd obey the master. But the Colors got fried when that little bitch shot me at your cabin. They don't control me like before." He snapped.

"What does that mean?" I asked.

"It means, I don't care what he says, I'm going to kill the girl anyway." He sneered. "Right aft...."

The next sound was a bullet. There was a muzzle flash with a simultaneous bang. I recoiled, clutching my stomach. All those stories about life flashing before your eyes must be bullshit because I didn't see anything.

Then I heard a loud thump, like a heavy sack being dropped. At the edge of darkness where my flashlight illuminated a round area, the Clown's body hit the floor! It took me a few seconds to understand what happened. Blood oozed from the side of his mouth and his eyes were open, void of life. The Clown had been shot in the side of his head. Brain matter and blood burst through a hole on the opposite side.

As I realized I hadn't been shot, I straightened. A figure walked from the dark, stepped over the Clown's body, bent over, and took my pistol from his dead hand. It was Mara! She stood and then stepped back into the darkness.

Before she disappeared completely, I called out, "WAIT!" I could barely see her at the edge of the light. Mara, now holding my pistol, pointed it right at me in one killer quick motion. "DON'T. You don't have to hurt her." I pleaded fearful she was going to shoot Penny.

Her head turned to me. "I had no choice."

"You do now," I said, raising my hands, waist high, palms out.

"I didn't want to hurt you. Burke threatened my daughter. He knew you would come to the meeting." She said.

"How? HOW'D he know?" I asked.

"He always knows. I told you. He said if I stopped you, he'd leave her alone." She paused. "He called Millie's car." A tear fell from her eye as she went on. "The tape gave me something to bargain with. I was almost out. Both of us were. We would finally be safe. He told me he ordered the Clown to leave her be." She paused, looking at the Clown's dead body with a sneer. "I knew that psycho wasn't going to let it alone."

"You still have the tape?" I asked.

"Yes." She answered.

"Give it to me. I can protect you." I said.

She shook her head. "You can't even protect yourself. He'll leave us alone now. As long as I have the tape, he'll let Nevaeh go."

"Where is she?" I asked.

She lowered my pistol, then tossed it into the darkness. She put her own pistol back in its holster, pulled a knife from her belt, and stepped into the light to cut Penny free.

The second Penny was loose, she swung. Mara caught Penny's fist in midair. "Don't push it." She sneered pushing Penny back.

"You were just going to let that animal kill us, weren't you? Until you found out he planned to kill your daughter, then you decided to save us."

"NO. I WASN'T. But I needed to know his intentions before I did anything. I needed to know what Burke told him." Mara responded.

I took a few cautious steps toward her, my hands extended. "I still love you. I never stopped."

Mara's expression changed. Tears formed in her eyes as she walked to me. Her hand reached to touch my cheek. "I wish it had been different for us."

"It's not too late." I said.

"It is for me. Twilas is never going to let me go. The tape buys Nevaeh's safety." Mara pulled her hand back and walked toward the darkness.

"Mara wait." I called out.

She stopped at the edge, not turning.

"I can put him away with that tape. He can't touch Nevaeh if that happens. That along with other evidence of what he's done like this place and Miscavage's rail line, he'll be finished." I pleaded.

Mara turned her head to the side as she spoke, "One of the things I loved about you Alton was your belief. The belief in justice, that truth will prevail. But it's also your weakness. It blocks reality. Look around, there's nothing here. And there's no evidence at the rail line. Everything burned at the derailment." She remarked.

"What about the tracks out back," I asked.

"There's no tracks there," Mara responded before taking two steps and disappearing into the blackness. The storm was quieter, but the rain was enough to hide the sound of her movements.

Penny placed a hand on my elbow. I put my arm over her shoulder as we walked toward the door. "You okay?" I asked.

Beneath a few sniffles, she managed to say, "Yes, thanks to you." Then she looked in the direction Mara walked off. "You sure know how to pick'em."

I grabbed up my flashlight from the floor shining it on the Clown. He was as dead as they come. A bullet to the head. The big kitchen knife was still in his hand. We went outside to Bessimer to call the police.

"I'm relieved you are alright sir. I heard quite a bit of gunfire. My scanners indicate your wounds need tending." Bessimer said.

"I'm okay. Get NVPD on the line." I ordered.

"Yes sir. Are you alright Miss Penelope?" Bessimer asked.

"Yes, fine that you," Penelope responded as the phone's ring was answered.

"Sergeant Hopper, can I help you?"

"Lookin' for Rollins, he around?" I asked.

"Cold? That you?"

"Yeah," I answered.

"Hold on." The sergeant said. A second later Rollins answered. "Cold where the fuck have you been? We've been looking for you. Where the fuck are you?"

"I got your serial killer," I said.

"Copperhead?" he sounded surprised.

"If you say so. At the big warehouse in the dump. They used it to manufacture Colors. Turn west on Sum. I'll wait for you." I said ending the call.

"What now?" Penny asked.

"Let's take a look out back. Through the dock doors that lead outside." I said.

Penny and I walked inside the warehouse to the rear doors. I pulled the chains to raise them. It was dark without the lightning. Our shoes squished in the soggy ground as we walked to where the tracks were.

They were gone just like Mara said. "They were right here. Tracks ran northeast to a dead end," I pointed in both directions. "They came in over there."

Sirens interrupted my thoughts. "Rollins must be close."

"I thought you called One Police Plaza?" Penny said.

"I did. They must have patched me through. Let's get back inside." A couple of uniformed officers rushed through the front door as we walked in. Their guns and flashlights canvassing the area, "HOLD IT!" An officer ordered.

I put my hands up, "Easy. I'm Alton Cold. I called it in."

"HEY, I FOUND A GUN!" The second Officer yelled.

"That'll be mine. I dropped it." I said.

"I doubt that." Rollins was standing in the doorway.

He walked over to the dead Clown shining his flashlight on the corpse. "You do this? That's why you tossed the gun over there."

"That make a lot of sense to you?" I quipped.

"Well, I dunno, Cold. Once again, here you are with a dead body. At least this one is actually here." Rollins quipped. "What makes you think this one, or the one at Durant's apartment, is the Copperhead Strangler?"

I pointed my flashlight at the generator. "That generator was connected to the copper wire on this post. Penny was about to be his next victim until I stopped him. I used that fire extinguisher over there to knock the wire off before he could hurt her."

Rollins shined his light on the post, the generator, and then to Penny. By this time officers brought in some lights to illuminate the space.

Rollins walked up to Penny with a sympathetic look. He used a finger to gently move her chin so he could inspect her neck. "That so?"

"Yes. He grabbed me coming out of the coffee shop. Alton rescued me." Penny answered.

"What the hell'd you drop your gun for after you shot him?" Rollins asked.

"I didn't shoot him," I said.

"Then who the hell did?" Rollins asked.

"You're not going to believe me." I started. "This all ties back to Twilas Burke."

Rollins locked eyes with me. Two of the uniformed officers turned their heads. Rollins grabbed me by the elbow and dragged me beyond their hearing.

"That's not a name you throw around. You'd better have some evidence if you're going to make statements like that." Rollins said quietly through gritted teeth.

"Follow me," I said.

Rollins hesitated with a skeptical look before following me to the dock doors. Right before we stepped out, Penny's Lieutenant rushed in. She wrapped her arms around him and began to sob.

"She gonna tell him the same thing you're about to tell me?" Rollins asked.

I didn't answer. Penny was smart. She'd only tell the lieutenant what he needed to know. Rollins was the wild card. I had no idea which side he was on.

"You see this flattened area? Looks like a road?" I said pointing to where the tracks had been.

Rollins nodded. I led him west towards the mines. We walked until he could see the leveled ground disappear into the side of the hill. Penny and I hadn't walked down here earlier, but I suspected the cavern was gone just like the tracks. And it was.

Whoever took out the tracks and closed the cave entrance, didn't have time to hide the road. I told Rollins everything that happened as we returned to the warehouse. There were no comments, questions, or scoffing. He didn't give any affirmations and his expression never changed, nor did he stop me from talking.

Finally, when we reached the warehouse, he spoke. "That's quite the story, Alton. And you no longer have this tape?"

"No," I said.

"And this assassin, you can't describe the person. No idea if it's male or female? They stabbed you, took the tape, killed the Clown, thereby rescuing you and Penny, and you never got a good look. Is that right?"

"Right," I responded.

"And you claim the Clown works for Twilas Burke. Who you say, put some type of nano-controls in the drugs. Which not only turns the drugs into different colors but also has mind-altering properties. And as you know, drugs do in fact work that way. But you claim these special drugs allow Burke to control minds such as this Clown. Whom he had murder people, under the ruse of a serial killer we called the Copperhead Strangler. All to fool law enforcement?" Rollins said.

"Rick found the nanites. He told me about it, and then Burke confirmed it." I snapped.

"On the tape. Burke confirms this...on the tape?" Rollins asked. "Which you don't have anymore? And of course, you know by now, Rick Talmadge died in an accident at the lab."

"Are you telling me there's no evidence at the lab? Nothing that can confirm what Rick was working on?" I asked.

"The lab was destroyed. There's nothing there." Rollins said.

"Wait a minute, I thought it was an accidental overdose of Fentanyl?" I asked.

"It was, then the lab caught fire," Rollins responded.

"What about Ben Cloth?" I asked.

"Who?"

"Dr. Benjamin Cloth at the University. Let's go see him. He's the one who actually found the nanites. Rick sent a sample to him for further analysis."

Rollins walked out to his cruiser and then came back in with a clipboard. He rifled through the papers finally stopping at one. "The daily briefings. The university reported Cloth missing a few days ago. He didn't show up for class yesterday and nobody's seen him."

"Perfect." I quipped. "You think the fire at the lab, Rick dying, and Cloth missing are all just a coincidence?"

Rollins's lips curled as he started again, "And Miscavage's train derailment then catching fire, you don't know anything about that, do you? No, I suppose not." Rollins was getting snippier. "There is no evidence at the crash of any shipment of Colors like you claim."

"Come on, John. You saw where the tracks were behind this place. Who carves out a road in the dump that leads nowhere?" I snapped.

"You are accusing two of the wealthiest and most powerful men in the city, hell the world. Cold, there is nothing to back up what you are saying. Except for this building and one dead Clown. There is no trace of this rail line out back nor the underground passage it goes into. We still haven't found the other Clown you claim to have killed. In fact, the only evidence we have to any of what you are saying is a trail of dead bodies tied to you. There's a bunch at your cabin. Care to explain those?"

"Alright, what about the underground passage from P&G to the Regent? The Regent has cameras. Let's go pull those. That should at least show you the Clown and I in the kitchen. You can see the tunnel for yourself." I snapped.

Rollins didn't look like he believed me. Either that, or I made a grave mistake telling him all of this. We were about to find out whose side he was on.

CHAPTER 25

BACK TO THE REGENT HOTEL

The Regent's parking lot was still full of cars. The event wasn't over, but the mayor and Burke were leaving as we pulled in. Rollins parked under the awning at the rear entrance with me in the back, and a rookie detective named Simmons, in the front. Simmons was letting me out as Burke was coming out of the foyer with the mayor.

"Don't go anywhere," I yelled to them.

"Cold, shut the fuck up." Rollins scolded me then his tone was humble as pie. "Sorry, your honor. Mr. Burke."

Burke ignored my outburst, electing to return Rollins' greeting. "Hello again Sergeant. Good to see you." Burke then turned to me, "I'm not sure what you mean. Is there something you need, Mr. Cold? It is mister now, am I right? You're no longer on the force, or did you get reinstated?" He finished the jab with a look to the mayor.

"Hardly." Mayor Stockton replied snidely.

The smirk on Burke's face was more than I could handle. If Simmons and Rollins hadn't grabbed me by the arms, I would've had him by the throat. I nearly broke free when two NVPD officers raced out to help. "YOU SON-OF-A-BITCH! DON'T GO ANYWHERE

YOU LOWLIFE PIECE OF SHIT! STICK AROUND! LET'S SEE YOU EXPLAIN SOME OF THIS." By this point, I was screaming at Burke.

"DON'T MAKE ME PUT YOU IN CUFFS!" Rollins barked, then he leaned into my ear, as I was squirming, "Cold, slow down. Show me this tunnel. If it's there, I can at least question him."

I peeled my gaze from Burke to look at Rollins. He nodded then continued to whisper, "You don't have one piece of evidence. Not unless this tape miraculously appears. You know damn well I can't get at a man like Twilas Burke without something concrete."

Back at the warehouse, when I was explaining all of this to Rollins, I thought he didn't believe me. I wasn't sure about him, but it was clear he didn't like Burke. He probably didn't like the mayor either, but he was still on the force and Burke was close with the mayor.

"What's this all about sergeant!?" Mayor Stockton demanded.

Burke didn't allow Rollins to answer, "Nothing to be concerned with Madam Mayor. I'm curious to see what Mr. Cold is going on about."

"You might as well come along. Concerns you too Stockton." I sneered at her.

"IT'S MAYOR Stockton." She said angrily.

"I don't fuckin work for you anymore you arrogant piece of shit." I snapped.

Stockton was boiling, "I want that man arrested sergeant."

His response was somewhere between sarcasm and humor. "Any particular charge or would you like me to come up with something?"

The mayor was not amused. "How about false reports to law enforcement for starters?"

"He hasn't made any false reports yet, your honor. Just following up on a lead. I'll sort it out." Rollins responded.

The mayor's jaw clenched. "Well then, let's see what this so-called lead is."

Rollins dragged me by the armpit, through the big doors, to the hotel's reservation counter. He flashed his badge at the clerk. "We're going to the laundry. I want you to pull all the security footage from tonight, especially in this hall." He said, pointing as we started through the doors. "Have it ready by the time I get back."

Simmons, the mayor, and Burke all followed. The five of us crammed into the service elevator, then the hotel manager joined as Rollins pushed L2. The doors closed and we descended.

The awkward silence made the elevator dings more pronounced. A few moments went by before the doors opened on lower level 2. We were in the hotel laundry room.

Unlike before when I came through, it was now full of workers. They stopped to look at us as we got off the elevator. My stomach began to churn with nervous tension.

"They weren't here before," I whispered to Rollins, but the hotel manager heard me.

"We run laundry twenty-four hours a day. There is always somebody in this room, I assure you, detective." The manager said mockingly.

"And I'm telling you they weren't here." I snapped back.

I walked to the row of washers that hid the secret passage. The sudsy water sloshed violently against the glass doors as several machines were spinning full loads.

"That's convenient. Makes it heavier this way." I said.

"Cold, what are you talking about?" Rollins asked.

"The tunnel entrance is behind these machines," I responded.

"Tunnel? You think there is a tunnel behind the washers?" Burke mocked as the mayor rolled her eyes.

"The entire wall moves. It's a false wall. The machines are camouflaged. The tunnel is right behind them." My eyes scanned every inch for anything out of place.

My heart sank. I had come through the other side, so I never got to see the mechanism that opened it from this side. It could be anything.

"Get a crowbar, let's open these up." I snapped.

"There's no tunnels here, I assure you. And where would it go? A tunnel to where? Besides, don't you need some type of warrant for that?" The hotel manager asked.

"You do indeed. And what would be the crime? The basis for the warrant? You know, the one you claim is occurring here. Or is a tunnel, if one exists at all, illegal?" Mayor Stockton said sharply.

Rollins looked at me shaking his head no. He didn't want me to repeat what I told him. The mayor would order him to arrest me on false reports and Burke would undoubtedly sue me into oblivion. My emotions subsided as my investigative brain kicked in. I said nothing.

"Let's look at the camera footage," Rollins said.

"What did he tell you was on that?" The mayor asked snidely. When Rollins hesitated, she barked, "I demand to know!"

"I will be happy to brief you, your honor. I can't disclose investigative information outside the department as you know. Let's go see what's on the tapes." Rollins answered.

The mayor fumed as she stomped back on the elevator. The tension in the elevator was even worse as we rode back up. The mayor eyeballed Rollins the entire time as Burke leaned against the corner with a shit-eating grin on his face.

After the doors opened, the hotel manager led us down the hall to the security room. As he was using a key to open the door, Burke started to leave. "Where you goin? Don't you want to see?" I asked. *Son of Bitch already knows what's on the tape.* I thought.

Burke stopped, looked at everyone, and then responded, "It's late Mr. Cold. I was curious about what you were babbling about in the parking lot, but now I'm afraid I really don't have time for any more of …whatever this is." Then he addressed the mayor. "It's been a productive evening Madam Mayor. I'm looking forward to the election night celebration."

The mayor's heels clicked on the floor as she chased after Burke. "I'm sorry about all of this. It will be dealt with I assure you." She did everything but call him "boss".

"It's quite all right Madam Mayor. Some type of misunderstanding. Perhaps another retired member of the force having trouble adjusting to life as a civilian." Burke stopped to look at me again. "You might want to get some counseling Mr. Cold. Not to mention having that injury looked at. Perhaps this whole thing has to do with some blood loss."

Burke was the only one who noticed my side had started to bleed again. But he and Rollins were the only two here, who knew I'd been stabbed. Rollins saw my lip start to curl and stepped between me and Burke.

The mayor turned to Rollins, "I'll expect a full report in the morning sergeant. Promptly!" She ordered before storming out with Burke.

After Burke and the mayor were gone, I snapped at the hotel manager. "Pull up the damned footage. Start with the kitchen hallway."

We reviewed all the footage from the night's event. Everything from the moment guests arrived, to the mayor and Burke leaving a few minutes ago. None of the kitchen cameras showed me anywhere. The banquet room had me serving desserts, but none of the camera angles showed my face.

We watched Jennifer get up and go into the hall, but she was alone. If you remember, she walked out after me. There were moments when it looked like she was talking to someone, but the other party wasn't in any of the frames.

The cameras overlooking the phone bank filmed me on a pay phone, but again, you couldn't see my face. Despite insisting it was me, there was no way to tell, and some of the footage was grainy, which made it worse.

There should have been places where my face was captured, but it was fairly obvious someone erased anything that could identify me. To make matters worse, the Clown wasn't there either. There was no footage of him and I in the kitchen hall, nor were there any shots when he gave me the dessert cart.

The manager raised an eyebrow. "That's all there is."

"What about the laundry room? I saw cameras there. Pull up that footage," I ordered.

"Those cameras have been down for some time. The employees don't know they aren't working. I'd appreciate it if you didn't tell them." The manager said.

Rollins motioned for me to come with him. I started to object but he talked right over me. "Not now Cold." It was all he would say until we reached his car.

He placed me in the backseat, got into the driver's seat, then looked through the partition at me, "The tape was altered. But there is no way to prove you were here."

I was more than surprised. "You believe me then?"

"I told you I did. But I'm not losing my job over you Cold. I've got a pension." He snapped. "I need more than your word."

"What about P&G?" I asked.

"What about it?" He snipped right back.

"The other entrance to the tunnel is over there. I'm telling you, John, I'm not making this up." I pleaded.

"Cold, what do you expect me to do? Sledgehammer through a block wall at the corporate offices of one of Bumper City's biggest employers? The mayor would have my badge before we broke through one brick. Besides, I need to get you to the hospital. I don't need you dying in the back seat of my car."

"We don't have time for that! I told you, I'm fine. I'll go after we find the tunnel. You don't have to bust through. Damn it, John. I got in through P&G! I found the trigger mechanism that opened the tunnel entrance. I know where it's at on that side. You won't have to break through anything!" I made my case as strongly as I could.

Rollins sat for a moment thinking. "You'd better be right about this Cold." He retrieved some large bandages from a first aid kit in his glove box. "Here, put something on that before it gets worse."

I should have brought Rollins to P&G from the start. I let my emotions run away with me when I saw Burke. Getting caught up in his taunts raised my anger, preventing me from thinking clearly.

After I put a fresh bandage on my wound, Simmons let me out of the car again. Rollins led the way through the parking lot to P&G. The Lincoln was no longer there, and it was a different guy at the front desk. The guard opened the door after Rollins showed his badge.

"Good evening officer. Can I help you?" The night watchman asked.

"I'm Sergeant Rollins, this is Detective Simmons. We'd like to take a look around if you don't mind."

"Some kind of trouble?" the night watchman asked.

"Something like that," Simmons responded.

"I'll have to contact my supervisor." The watchman responded.

"Go right ahead." Rollins said in a friendly manner.

"Can you give me some idea what this is about? So, I can tell my boss?" The night watchmen asked.

"Just following up on a complaint, nothing to worry about. Just like to take a quick look around." Rollins responded.

The watchman hesitated, allowed us to step inside, then walked back to his desk jumping on the phone. As he was busy, Rollins turned to me. "Okay, Cold. You got about thirty seconds before his boss kicks us out."

"Over here," I said walking to the stairwell. The watchman got nervous when we went through the door.

"JUST A SECOND DETECTIVES!" The watchman was too late as all three of us were in the stairwell.

My eyes did a double take. The wall had been moved beyond the stairwell. Now the steps leading downstairs were open for anyone to see.

That pit in my stomach came back as I pointed at the metal steps, "It's down there. The tunnel is down two flights."

"I thought you said there was a secret door?" Simmons asked.

Rollins rubbed his hand across the new wall as I frantically tried to convince them it had been moved back, "The wall was right here!" Pointing to an area before the staircase. "Somebody took it out. It hid those stairs. The tunnel is at the bottom."

Just as I finished the watchman burst through the door. "My boss wants to know if you have a warrant?" he stated.

"Why do we need a warrant? Is there something down there we should know about?" Rollins shifted the watchman's attention to the stairwell.

The watchman peeked around us at the metal steps. "A boiler room. A furnace and some pipes. Why? What's this all about?"

"You don't mind if we take a look do you?" Rollins was already going down the steps before the guy could answer. The guard stayed above watching as Simmons and I followed Rollins down the steps.

As much as I hoped the tunnel was going to be at the bottom of the stairs, I knew it wouldn't. Instead, there was a large boiler room. A heating boiler was against the wall with pipes running across the ceiling alongside various cables.

Burke had the tunnel blocked and this area was replaced with pipes and heaters to appear like a normal part of the building. I searched for a lever or anything to find the tunnel, but there was nothing. Rollins and Simmons waited until I gave up before escorting me upstairs.

By the time we reached the lobby, the watchman's supervisor was waiting for us. Rollins smoothed it over with them while Simmons took me back to the cruiser. Rollins came out a few minutes later, walked across the lot, and got into the driver's seat.

"John, I'm tellin'..." he put his hand up to cut me off.

Rollins didn't say anything as he drove us out of the parking lot. He turned the police radio off, then the car radio. He unplugged the laptop and made sure it was off before he spoke. "I told you Cold, I believe you."

"Sarge?" Simmons seemed confused.

"The blocks on the first floor were recently painted. They used a quick dry paint. Nothing came off, but it was tacky. My wife and I recently painted our living room with it. I know the feel. And the mortar between the blocks hadn't completely hardened. If I'd dug at it, I could have pulled some out." Rollins said.

"So...you think there was a secret door there like this guy says?" Simmons questioned. "And they moved the wall to reveal the stairs? Why? To reveal a previously hidden boiler room."

"Somebody is trying to hide something. Who does block work and paints in the evening hours?" Rollins responded.

"Maybe it was patchwork? Makes sense to me. You'd want to have construction done when nobody was around. Easier during evening hours when offices are closed." Simmons retorted.

"Patchwork? From what? Did it look like any other walls needed repair?" I said.

Rollins gave me a quick look in the rearview mirror as Simmons continued to refute my claims. "All right, then what about the boiler room? There wasn't any tunnel down there. You didn't mention seeing a boiler? Did you see a boiler?" Simmons asked.

"No. It wasn't there." I answered.

"Those things aren't lite. How the hell would somebody place it there while you were gone?" Simmons didn't believe me, but Rollins did. Luckily, he was in charge.

Rollins pulled into the dump and through the recycling plant toward the warehouse. The fire lamps lining the roads had been re-lit. We reached the intersection of Sum Avenue to find Mutant Dwellers watching the corner. They didn't bother to hide as we turned west.

The Crime Scene Unit's truck was parked outside with their big lights covering all corners of the building. A dozen officers and techs combed the area gathering evidence and searching for clues.

The coroner's van was also here, backed to the front door. A police officer was helping the deputy coroner roll a gurney carrying the Clown's body. The coroner was sitting in the driver's seat writing on a clipboard and eating French fries.

Rollins pulled in beside him and lowered his window. "I don't know how you can eat during these things doc."

"Gotta eat when I can. It ain't like he's gonna want any." Then the coroner noticed me sitting in the back. "HEYYYY, Alton. What'd you been up to? I hear you're a P.I. now."

Rollins rolled the back window down so I could answer, "Hi Phil. I got my license last year."

"What're you doin here?" He asked.

"Can you tell Rollins it wasn't my gun that killed the Clown? I'd like to get it back." I said.

"This was you?" He asked.

"I was here, but I didn't shoot him."

"I dunno, what'd you carrying?" He asked.

"40 cal." I said.

"Oh yeah, he wasn't killed with a forty." He started before looking at Rollins. "Smaller bullet. Close range. It's just a field report, but a forty would have left a bigger hole." Then he turned to me, "What kind of ammo?"

"Hollow points," I responded.

"Definitely would have been bigger. And messy." He added.

Rollins glanced over his shoulder at me, "Sorry Cold. Still gotta keep it for a little while."

"You got two of mine. I only got one pistol left." I quipped.

"Don't kill anybody else and you can hang on to it," Rollins responded.

"Yeah, yeah. Am I free to go?" I asked.

"Sure. You already gave me your account. Gonna need you to come down to the station tomorrow for a written statement." Rollins opened the door to let me out. "Don't make me come looking for you."

I walked across the road to Bessimer. Before I got in, Rollins yelled, "Take your sorry ass to the hospital! I don't want you dying on me."

"I didn't realize you cared," I said.

"I don't. I need that written statement. You can die after that." He quipped.

"Do me a favor and call ahead. Tell them you know about the knife wound." I yelled back before shutting the car door.

I turned Bessimer around and drove out the way I came in. "Bessimer. Any word from Penny."

"Yes sir. Miss Penelope was taken to Bumper City General. She was treated for some minor injuries and released. Her lieutenant friend accompanied her. She is staying with him tonight. She called while you were with Sergeant Rollins. She told me to let you know she is okay and will see you in the morning." He responded. "Where are we off to sir?"

"Bumper City General. I think I'm gonna need a few stitches."

CHAPTER 26

JUSTICE ISN'T PERFECT

The hospital let me sleep it off in the ER. Mara's stab wound was deeper than I realized. They said I was lucky. If she'd stuck it a few inches in any direction, it would've been a lot worse.

But luck was for the roulette wheel, she knew right where to put the blade. The blow was meant to incapacitate, not kill, so she could grab the tape.

I was still groggy from the pain meds when the dayshift nurse opened the curtain. "Good morning, Mr. Cold. How are you feeling?"

"My head's pounding. Sides a little sore." I responded.

"It's the pain medication wearing off. The doctor gave you a local, but we ended up having to sedate you." She said.

"How many stitches?" I asked.

"Eight. You're going to be sore for a while. We called in a few more pain meds to your pharmacy. Here take these?" She handed me a paper cup containing two white pills.

"What's this?" I asked.

"Antibiotics. They'll help prevent infection. You ready to get outta here?" She asked.

"The sooner the better. What time is it?"

"You don't like our service?" She joked. "Seven a.m. hon."

At the end of my bed sat a bouquet of flowers with a big card. "What are those?"

"It's a little unusual to get flowers in the ER hon. Technically you weren't admitted. Sergeant Rollins told us to keep your name low-key as he didn't want anybody to know you were here, but Mr. Burke isn't just anybody." She answered.

"Burke? You mean Twilas Burke?" I asked.

"I doubt anybody could hide from him. We didn't know you had such powerful friends." She reached for the card and handed it to me. "Your clothes are in the bag. Sorry about your shirt." She said before walking out.

How in the hell did that asshole know I was here?

Penny came around the corner as I was opening the card. "You my ride?"

"You bet." She then placed a hand on my shoulder. "You okay?"

"Couple of stitches," I said slowly as I read Burke's card.

Some low-key. Might as well put it in the paper. I thought.

"How'd you know I was here?" I asked.

"Bessimer told me last night. He's been monitoring hospital comms and called this morning to tell me you were being discharged." Then she noticed the card. "What you got there?"

I decided to read it to her, "Wishing you a speedy recovery, Twilas Burke." I flipped open the envelope removing two tickets. *Pagliacci at the Dunes Theater on the strip. Special balcony seats.*

"Motherfucker." I said under my breath.

"Burke?" Penny asked.

"Yep," I said, handing her the tickets.

"What are you going to do?" She asked.

"Well, I'm not going." I snipped.

"Not what I meant." She said.

I sighed, "Not much I can do now."

Her eyes dropped then returned to me with a simple smile. "Should we go?"

"Yeah. You didn't happen to bring me another shirt, did you?" I no sooner finished asking when she handed me a t-shirt. "Cap. My favorite. You're a doll."

"Figured you'd like something comfortable." She said.

The nurse came back with the discharge papers and Penny wheeled me out. Rollins pulled under the awning as the big doors slid apart.

"They fix you up?" He asked.

"Yeah, few stitches. Turns out I'll live." I said.

"Good. We'll give you a ride." Rollins said while Simmons opened the rear door of the squad car.

"I told you I'll come in and give you a statement," I said.

"Yeah, I know, Cold. You will. Right now. Get in." Rollins ordered as he got back into the driver's seat.

"Come on fellas. He just got out of the hospital. How about a break?" Penny snapped.

Rollins wasn't budging. His face had an unusual expression, not exactly angry, but stubborn and intolerant. He didn't have the same demeanor as last night.

I put my hand up to stop Penny from arguing any further. "How'd you get here?" I asked Penny.

"Yellow Cab." She was still eyeing Rollins angrily.

I flipped her the keys to Bessimer. "Take him to the office. I'll meet you there later."

She looked at me scornfully before she blurted out, "I'm calling Stanley."

I got up from the wheelchair gingerly and went to the back of Rollins' car. Simmons shut the door after I was in, then looked at Penny, "He won't be there long."

They drove me to One Police Plaza. The protesters were gone now, and the station looked peaceful. They led me inside, only this time, they didn't put me in an interrogation room. Rollins walked me to his office, closed the door, and opened a red folder on his desk.

He handed me a typed statement on the department letterhead. "Figured you wouldn't be in any shape to write a statement, so I typed everything you told me. All you have to do is sign."

I took the pen and went to the last page preparing to write my John Hancock when something caught my eye. Rollins got twitchy when I hesitated. "Right at the bottom Cold. You remember where."

I flipped back to page one and began to read. Then I turned to the second page, then the third until my blood was boiling. "WHAT THE FUCK IS THIS? THAT IS NOT WHAT HAPPENED! That's not what I told you last night. I'm not signing this."

"Cold, listen to me, sign the document, and be done with it. It's over." He said.

The deputy chief of detectives opened Rollins' door. "Problem Sergeant?"

"No sir. I was just explaining to Detective Cold about the need to end this investigation. Killer being caught. The case is closed." Rollins answered.

The deputy chief was another stooge. I hated him as much as the rest. Now I understood why Rollins showed up at the hospital. He wanted this buttoned up without any fuss. He thought he'd catch me off guard, I'd sign, and everything would be over.

Lucky for me, Penny did exactly what she threatened. I could hear Stan Findley getting off the elevator, loudly asking where his client was. Simmons brought him to Rollins' office when he started threatening lawsuits.

"Some type of problem here detectives?" Stan reached for my arm. "My client has cooperated fully with this investigation and now it's time to go."

"Tell him. Go ahead. Tell him how you were just about to threaten me unless I signed a false statement." I snipped at the deputy chief.

"That true deputy chief?" Stan asked.

"Your client gave his account last night. Sergeant Rollins was good enough to type the statement for him to sign. Now Mr. Cold is having memory issues, trying to claim this isn't what he told Rollins." Then he gave Rollins a sour look. "That is what he told you, isn't it Sergeant?"

"Yes sir, it is," Rollins said.

"FUCK IT IS." I jumped up.

The deputy chief's lips pursed, "You better get your client out of here, counselor. Or I might decide to charge him with making false statements. Otherwise, he can sign this."

"If that statement was worth the paper it was typed on, you wouldn't be pressuring me to sign it." I snapped.

The deputy chief pointed to the elevators, "Get him outta here." As Stan was pulling me by the arm, the deputy chief spewed one last thing, "If I hear one goddamned word refuting what is in this statement, your client is going to be charged with aiding and abetting. A felony. YOU GOT IT?"

"YOU'RE A PIECE OF SHIT ROLLINS. YOU FUCKIN LACKY. YOU KNOW THIS AIN'T RIGHT." I yelled the whole way to the elevator. It was all Stan could do to get me inside.

"Jesus Cold. You're going to get yourself arrested." Stan was half chuckling as the elevator stopped on the first floor. "Give you a lift back to your office?"

"No thanks, Stan." I didn't need the ride because Bessimer was parked out front. I opened the door and slid in. Stan gave a quick wave as he walked away.

"Miss Penelope dropped me off to wait for you, sir. She figured nobody would bother me in front of the station." Bessimer said.

I buckled my seatbelt and left. Penny, Nevaeh, and Jericho were at the office waiting. Jericho gave a growl as I turned the key. He let out a tough bark until he saw me. Then his ears folded and his body arched sideways with his tail sweeping back and forth. I reached down scratching his face until he was satisfied.

Nevaeh stood waiting patiently then asked, "You okay?"

I nodded. "Yeah, you?"

"I'm okay." She said with a nervous tension.

"How'd it go with Rollins?" Penny asked.

"About like you'd expect," I responded.

"That's what I figured. Thought you might need Stan." Penny grabbed the coffee pot and headed out the door, "I'm going to get some water. I'll be right back."

I turned to Nevaeh asking softly, "What the hell happened? I thought you were with your mom?"

"After you went to get Burke, she took me to the safe house. She left before Penny came. I didn't know what was going on. She called later saying it was still dangerous for me in the city. She wouldn't give me any details, only that I needed to lie low until I heard from either her or you.

The fire at the Factory was on all the news stations. Miscavage getting killed in the train derailment too.

A bit later she called again telling me she'd made a deal with Burke. I'd be safe but she had to stay with him. I pleaded with her, but she said it was the only way. That was the last time I spoke to her. Do you have any idea where she is?" Nevaeh asked.

"No. I'm sorry I don't." I responded.

"Last night, when Penny went to get us something to eat, she told me to stay put until you came back. I didn't see Penny again until this morning. She told me what happened. How the Clown kidnapped her, but you came, then mom killed the Clown." Nevaeh took a deep breath and then sat in one of the office chairs. "I'm glad you're okay. You're both okay." Nevaeh's eyes filled with tears. "I'm sorry I got you into this."

Penny came back as Nevaeh started to cry. Penny gave me a nod and one of those looks. Not exactly my strong suit, but I knew what Penny was telling me. I walked over and bent down to hug Nevaeh.

"You didn't get me into anything. I was already in this case with James." I leaned back as Penny handed me some tissues for her. "Here."

Nevaeh wiped her eyes as Jericho nudged his big muzzle under her chin. She smiled and stroked his head softly. She collected herself, looked up, and asked. "How'd you get stabbed? Was it the Clown?"

I glanced at Penny who was pouring water into the coffee maker. She hadn't told Nevaeh it was Mara who put the shiv in me. I was glad she didn't. "I'm not sure. It happened at the Factory. I was confronting Burke when someone snuck up from behind."

The coffee began to drip while I sat in the other chair. "You decide what you're going to do now?"

Nevaeh wiped her eyes and then blew her nose before answering. "I booked a train back to San Francisco. I have to get back to work. My aunt is gone, and I doubt I'll ever see my mom again. There's nothing for me here. I'd hire you to find her, but something tells me you wouldn't be able to. No offense. You're a great detective, but I don't think anyone can find her. Not unless she wants to be found."

"I think you're right about that. I looked for over twenty years and never found her. I didn't even know she was still in the city." I said.

"Maybe she'll get to leave someday. It's what she told me to do." Nevaeh responded.

I didn't say it, but I knew Mara would never leave. And I'd never be able to find her unless it was what she wanted.

"What time is your train?" I asked.

"Ten O'Clock," Nevaeh responded.

"That's in two hours. Why so soon?" I asked.

"It was the first train out. There didn't seem to be any point in staying. My aunt's place is destroyed, and the Elkhorn…well…it's the Elkhorn." She smirked.

"You could stay at my place with Jericho. I don't think you're in any danger now. The Clowns are gone. Burke's no longer interested."

"Thanks, but I think I'll just go back to my life. I came here to find out what happened to my aunt. To get her some justice. You did that for me. For her."

"You need a ride to the station?" I asked.

"I'd like that." She said.

Penny came around the desk to give Nevaeh a hug. "You stay in touch. You can stay with me anytime. His place can be a little…well, he's a man, you know." Penny smiled, causing Nevaeh to laugh.

Nevaeh leaned down wrapping her arms around Jericho's neck. He gave her sloppy tongue lashes before she let go. "Be a good boy. Take care of them." She walked into my office and then returned with her bags.

I took the biggest one and walked her down to Bessimer. Bessimer greeted her the moment we got in. "Good morning, Miss Nevaeh. Glad to see you are alright."

"Good to see you too Bessimer. Sorry about what I did to you." She remarked.

"Quite all right miss. The best thing that's ever happened to me, in my short existence that is." Bessimer quipped.

The morning hour got brighter as the city raised the wattage. Bessimer's engine started with ease, and I backed out of the parking spot to pull away. We entered the street rolling through the first intersection on our way to Union Station.

The rain started again as we arrived. I pulled into the underground garage so we wouldn't get wet. The elevator took us to the main floor. We breezed through security. Nevaeh only had her computer bag and suitcase. My badge toned the scanner, but nobody cared.

Several tracks converged under a platform that was covered by a large canopy. The elevated walkways were filled with anxious passengers waiting to board the always late inner-city trains.

The last three tracks were long-distance engines. The end spot was elevated above all the others to accommodate the Blue Line Conveyor. It was a two-story bubble nose similar to Miscavage's private locomotive.

Overhead monitors listed all departing and arriving trains. Outbound trains were displayed with red dots awaiting departure and were not ready to board. Green dots indicated trains were cleared to board. The Blue Line Conveyor outbound for San Francisco showed a red dot.

We walked to the end of the platform where the behemoth was sitting. Steam billowed around the giant wheels as workers conducted routine safety checks. The big engine idled loudly as it readied for departure.

I ordered two coffees from a small stand near the platform. "Thanks," Nevaeh said taking one.

As we sipped from our cups, the monitors above showed the news.

"This is a BCN5 Breaking news report. Mayor Stockton has called a press conference to begin any moment now regarding new developments in the Copperhead Strangler case. Jennifer Caldwell has more." The morning anchor reported.

News trucks along with dozens of reporters gathered on the steps of One Police Plaza. A podium with three microphones could be seen behind reporter Jennifer Caldwell as she spoke.

"Thanks, Tom. We're waiting on a press conference, called by Mayor Stockton, to begin any moment now regarding the serial killer known as the Copperhead Strangler. Sources close to the mayor tell us the mayor has positive news on the case.

The Copperhead Strangler, as police have nicknamed him, has claimed several victims over the last couple of months. Police aren't sure exactly how many victims, but most seem to be women. Although they do admit, there have been a few men.

Police do not know how long the Copperhead Strangler has been operating here in the city, but they suspect it may have been several years. Some believe many of the missing children in the mining district, as well as missing courtesans, may be attributed to his reign of terror."

The screen then cuts to a taped interview with Emile Tarkon, President of the UMMW in Bumper City. *"Many of our children have gone missing. Our men and women go to work every day supplying the precious metals that make things the residents of this city love. Yet our women and children disappear, and the company does nothing about it.*

That needs to stop today. Our children are worth every bit as much as Mr. Davis' kids. If it weren't for our mutant abilities, we couldn't survive in those conditions. But conditions keep getting worse."

The tape ended with reporter Jennifer Caldwall continuing her live monologue. *"President Tarkon says over the past couple of years, dozens of mutant families have los..."*

The anchor suddenly interrupted, *"Sorry to interrupt you Jennifer, but the mayor has just stepped to the podium."*

Mayor Stockton looks at reporters with a somber expression. Standing behind her is the Chief of Police, Two Deputy Chiefs, the City Attorney, and Sargent Rollins.

The mayor opens a book on the podium using it as a reference while she speaks. *"Today, I can announce, confidently, the case of the Copperhead Strangler has been solved. Our detectives have brought an end to this nightmare. At approximately 11:00 pm last night, our detectives shot and killed the Copperhead Strangler, at the Bumper City Dump.*

The killer was identified as William "Billy" Antonelli. Although the suspect is dead, the investigation is still ongoing. Antonelli was a member of the mutant community with no permanent residence. Detectives believe he hid out in the dump at an abandoned warehouse there. Some evidence of drug use was present at the scene."

A young reporter yelled out, *"MADAME MAYOR, ANY IDEA HOW HE SELECTED HIS VICTIMS? SOME OF THE VICTIMS WERE PROMINENT OR MARRIED TO PROMINENT CITIZENS. AND HOW MANY VICTIMS HAVE BEEN IDENTIFIED SO FAR?"*

"I think the chief can more accurately answer some of those questions." The mayor stepped aside as Chief Leonard came to the podium.

"Our detective bureau has concluded victim selection was random. We've consulted with the FBI's Behavioral Science Unit, and they agree, there was no discernable pattern. Tragically, these individuals were in the wrong place at the wrong time, including those prominent citizens you mentioned. Rich and poor alike fell prey to this disturbed individual.

We're still assessing how many victims there may have been. That's all I can say at this time."

Leonard stepped back as the mayor returned to the mic. *"That's all we have time. There will be more to come in the next few days. My administration is doing everything in our power to make sure people like this are brought to justice. I'd like to thank the brave men and women from our police department for their hard work and dedication in solving this case. Thank you."*

The press corp erupted with questions but the mayor and her cronies walked away. Then the monitor went back to its previous program. Nevaeh looked over at me. "That's not what happened."

"No. No, it's not." I said.

"Why'd she lie?" She asked.

"Politicians always lie," I said calmly.

"The Chief's not a politician." She said.

"Don't kid yourself. Just because he wasn't elected, doesn't mean he isn't a politician." I remarked. "Rollins solved the case. It may not have gone like that, but the Clowns are dead. They received justice for the murders. The case is over."

"There was no justice for James."

"No. There wasn't, isn't. Justice isn't always perfect." I said.

"What do you think he saw?" She asked. "Do you think it was the tracks behind the warehouse?"

"I don't know for sure. But your aunt saw it too." I responded.

"Colors? Do you think they knew about Burke's involvement?" She asked.

"We may never know," I said. "But I think it was something else."

"BUMPER CITY BLUE LINE CONVEYOR – 4437 OUTBOUND TO CALIFORNIA MAY NOW BOARD." The loudspeaker repeated several times.

"That's me," Nevaeh said, giving me a big hug. "Come visit me in California. Get some sun. You'd be amazed what that can do for you." She said with a big smile.

"You take care of yourself," I responded. She picked up her bags and walked down the platform to the gate. As the porter took her luggage, she stopped to wave. I waved back and she boarded the train.

When I turned to leave, I saw Mara. She was leaning against a wall behind a crowd of people. I almost didn't recognize her. She was wearing an oversized red hat with a wide brim and her hair was done in the old style, with large waves, dangling over her shoulder. I never saw her in a dress, but she was wearing one now. It was a sleek little number just above the knee, the same red as the hat. Her high heels accentuated her legs under a lined black stocking. She looked like a movie star.

I thought it was an illusion until she smiled warmly at me. A crowd of passengers moved between us, and she was gone. My eyes frantically searched the platform, but she wasn't there.

I walked to the spot where she had been standing, searched the area, but didn't see her. My mind wished she had come to see me, but I knew it was for Nevaeh. Mara wanted to see her little girl one more time before she left.

Nevaeh's train let out a long whistle as it backed away. The big wheels turned slowly as puffs of steam jetted out the exhaust. I turned to watch it clear the platform, then rotated to orient its nose in the appropriate direction. Once it was facing the other way, it steamed ahead with a heavy whoosh so fast it was gone in thirty seconds.

Papers caught in its wake flew everywhere. A flyer wafted through the air working its way to me. The sheet stuck to my side long enough for me to grab it. It contained a picture of a young boy from the mining district. The caption read, MISSING SINCE JULY. ANYONE WITH ANY INFORMATION PLEASE CALL...

THE END

MORE FROM THE CASE FILES OF ALTON COLD COMING SOON!

THANK YOU FROM THE AUTHOR

I hope you enjoyed *Bumper City*. There are a lot more cases to discover in this series. You may have gotten a hint of a few of them in this first book. Don't worry, we haven't seen the last of Twilas Burke either. There will be a day of reckoning. And the love story between Alton and Mara is far from over too.

There's a lot more to come from *Bumper City* so stay tuned.

If you like audiobooks, I narrated *Bumper City* which you can find just about anywhere audiobooks can be found.

FOR THE LATEST NEWS AND INFORMATION FROM BUMPER CITY, VISIT MY WEBSITE; ALANMCGILLBOOKS.COM OR SCAN THE QR CODE.

YOU CAN ALSO FOLLOW ME ON TWITTER AND INSTAGRAM;

ALANMCGILL14

I would also ask a small favor, please leave a short review or star rating on Goodreads, Amazon, Spotify, Audible or any place you find my books and audiobooks. The more ratings and reviews the books receive, the more chances they have to continue.

Thank you again for your support!
Alan

AND DON'T FORGET MY

WEREWOLVES & Witches

A Cry in the Moon's Light

Book One

Book Two

The Prequel

Artbook/Guidebook

THE AUDIOBOOKS

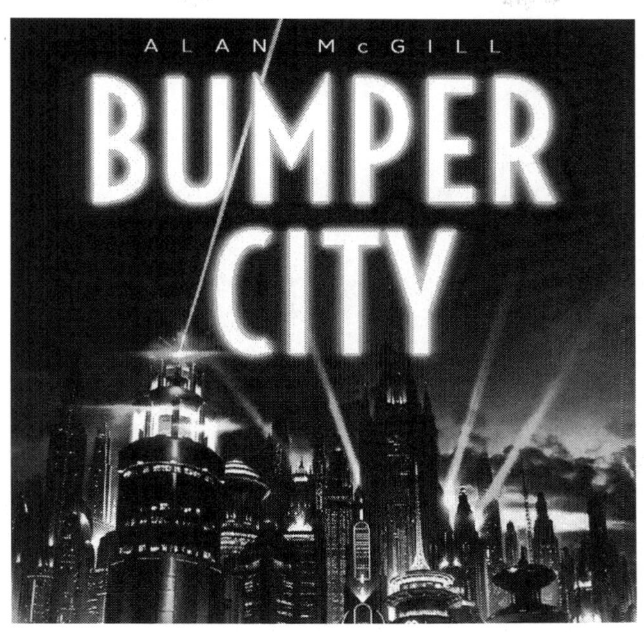

EXPERIENCE *BUMPER CITY* IN A WHOLE NEW WAY!

ALAN'S NARRATION BRINGS THESE CHARACTERS TO LIFE. THE SOUND FX AND MUSIC TAKE IT TO A WHOLE NEW LEVEL!

ALAN'S WEREWOLVES & WITCHES STORY'S ARE ALSO AUDIOBOOKS!

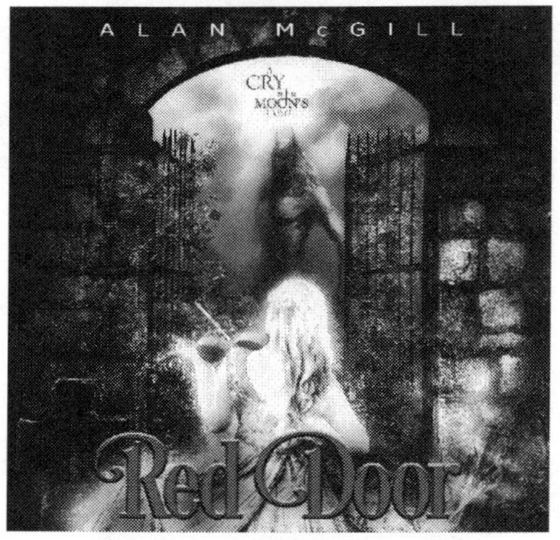

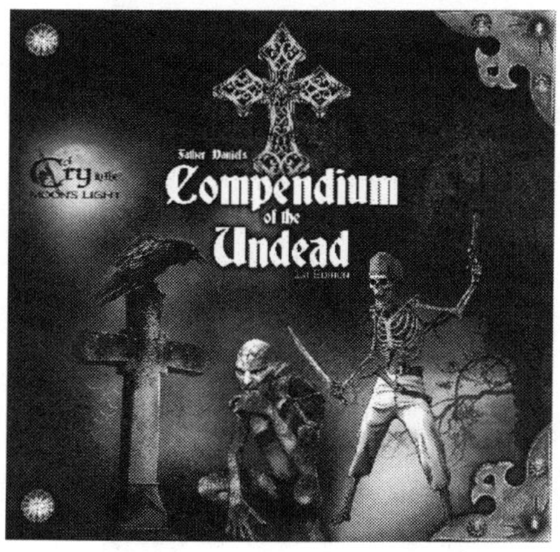

Made in the USA
Columbia, SC
16 November 2024